I0604910

THE HAUNTING OF ABERDEEN MANOR

C.K. SMITH

WELCOME TO
ABERDEEN
MANOR

BOOK 1 OF
THE ABERDEEN HAUNTINGS

C.K. SMITH

OTHER WORKS BY C.K. SMITH

POETRY BOOKS
(BY DINA EZZEDDINE)

COFFEE SEASON
DANCE IN THE RAIN
SEASONS IN BLOOM
LOVE LETTERS FROM JAPAN
BLOOM: A COLLECTION OF
SELF-LOVE POEMS

ABERDEEN MANOR SERIES
(BY C.K. SMITH)

THE HAUNTING OF ABERDEEN MANOR
(AVIALABLE NOW)
RETURN TO ABERDEEN MANOR
(MAY 2025)
THE END OF ABERDEEN MANOR
(SETPTEMBER 2025)

ROMANCING THE CEO
(BY C.K. SMITH)

ROMANCING THE CEO (SPICY OFFICE ROMANCE)
(JUNE 2025)

THE CEO AND HIS ROSE (SPICY OFFICE ROMANCE)
(NOVEMBER 2025)

THE CEO'S SON (THE FORBIDDEN
ROMANCE)
(DECEMBER 2025)

CHAPTERS

1	Road Trip	1
2	Old Trenton Bar	15
3	Trenton	36
4	End of the Road	59
5	Aberdeen Manor	74
6	Ghosts	97
7	Grave Keeper	108
8	Games	129
9	Uncle Joe	150
10	Phone Call	165
11	Eric Stephenson Part 1	181

CHAPTERS

12   Eric Stephenson Part   2   197

13   Gwen   217

14   Tara   234

15   Contact   256

16   Justin Shawn Smith   282

17   Luke   300

18   Escape   314

19   Aftermath   329

20   End Game   343

21   One Year Later   360

     Return to Aberdeen
     About Author

ROAD TRIP

I STOOD BY THE WINDOW, watching the rain beat against the glass, each drop splashing like tiny warnings—warnings of something to come, something I did not anticipate. The sky was a dull, relentless gray, absorbing any hint of sunlight. My suitcase sat by the door, half-packed, like it was as hesitant as I was. Something about this trip felt off— wrong, even. It wasn't just the cold October air that seeped into my bones, it was the way every instinct screamed at me to stay home.

My name is Maeve Adams, I'm 22, and today, I was planning to leave my home here in Florida to travel twelve hours by car to my old family home. It had been abandoned for over thirty years but remained in our family. My great uncle owned it for ten years until his disappearance. Earlier, Gwen's voice crackled over the phone, brimming with excitement. "Come on, Maeve, don't back out now! We've been planning this for weeks. It's just a fun Halloween trip. You love this stuff."

And she was right—I did love it. Ghost stories, haunted places, the thrill of the unknown. But ever since Luke mentioned Aberdeen Manor, I couldn't shake the feeling that we were stirring something we shouldn't. The estate wasn't just another decaying mansion with a haunted reputation.

It had secrets.

The more I thought about it, the more the pit in my stomach grew.

Gwen, my 21-year-old college roommate, was a blonde with blue eyes, a sharp tongue, and a body sculpted by plastic surgery. Use your imagination. She and her boyfriend Luke had just returned from visiting her family in Minnesota. They were staying at a hotel nearby, ready to head to Aberdeen Manor—my family's home. I picked up my phone and hesitated. I wanted to call them, cancel the trip, and say that something just didn't feel right. But I could already hear their voices in my head—Ethan's laughter, Gwen's teasing.

None of them would understand. Not Ethan, my half-brother, who was in another on-again-off-again phase with Tara, and certainly not Gwen, who would guilt-trip me into going, no matter what.

Then there was Tara, she's 22: a tall, thin brunette with striking green eyes—a real bombshell. Loud, obnoxious, and undeniably high-maintenance, Tara clearly would have preferred if I stayed home, leaving her with Ethan all to herself.

None of them would understand my hesitation.

They never did.

I rubbed my eyes, trying to push away the images that had been haunting me all week. Shadows shifting in the corners of my vision, whispers that seemed to come from nowhere, and flashes of a dark figure standing just out of sight.

Dreams that felt so real that I woke up gasping, drenched in sweat. I'd see the manor—tall, foreboding, like it was alive—and then I'd see us there, trapped, trying to escape something we couldn't see but could feel. I didn't know how to explain any of it, and maybe that's why I hadn't tried.

"Come on, Maeve," I whispered to myself. "It's just nerves. It's all in your head." Nerves. That's what I'd been telling myself for days. But it wasn't just nerves. Ever since Ethan called, saying he'd found our great-uncle's key to the manor and convinced Mom to let us spend four days there, the nightmares had gotten worse. I nearly panicked after that phone call. How was I supposed to tell Ethan about the nightmares?

The last time I shared a dream with him, he laughed and told me to lay off the caffeine. This wasn't a caffeine buzz. These nightmares felt like premonitions—sharp-edged warnings that something bad was going to happen. And it was going to happen at the manor.

I tried to stay calm. I told myself not to panic, to keep cool. But no amount of reasoning could stop the dread pooling in my chest. Ethan, Tara, Gwen, and Luke were on their way to pick me up. Any moment now, they'd be outside, honking and calling my name.

But deep down, I wasn't convinced.

...

It was exactly 8:45 p.m. when Ethan picked me up. We took two cars: me and Ethan in one, Tara, Gwen, and Luke in the other. Apparently, Ethan and Tara were off again, and he preferred to ride with me rather than deal with her. The car ride was supposed to be the fun part—a road trip through the countryside with the windows down, music blasting, and laughter filling the air as we left the city behind. Instead, it was quiet. Tense. I kept tilting the rearview mirror to glance at Luke's car behind us, and each time, Ethan reached over to tilt it back.

"So, it's been a year," he said, breaking the silence.

"Sorry, I've been busy," I managed to reply, my voice even but clipped.

Ethan glanced at me briefly, then tilted the mirror again, this time to look at Luke's car himself.

I had left Nebraska right after high school when I turned 18. I couldn't get out of that town fast enough. The breakup with my ex had been the final push. He ended things so suddenly, so completely, that I didn't want to face the memories—or anyone else. Florida seemed as far away as I could go while still staying practical. A fresh start. A new university. A chance to leave everything behind.

Ethan glanced at me briefly before tilting the mirror again. "Busy enough that you can't even call your own brother?" he pushed.

Ethan was my half-brother—his dad had married my mom—but we used to be close. At least we were, until the night he bailed on me and left me stranded in a bar.

"Come on, May. You're still not mad about the bar thing, are you? That was three years ago. Let it go. They caught the guy..." he trailed off, clearly hoping I'd let bygones be bygones.

I bit my lip, suppressing the frustration that still simmered beneath the surface. That night had been burned into my memory. It was supposed to mark the start of an epic road trip. We had agreed to meet at a gas station off Highway 40, south of Trenton. I'd taken a bus to get there. But Ethan never showed. Instead, I ended up at a bar, trying to use the phone to call him. What followed was an altercation with some guy who assaulted me. I fought back, hit him hard, and the cops caught him three miles down the road. It wasn't an experience I could just "let go," no matter how many times Ethan brushed it off.

"How did you convince Mom to let us use the mansion? I mean, it's been abandoned since great-Uncle's disappearance three-four years ago. The cops quarantined it off and called it a homicide, and they never found his body. The case went cold," I reminded him. Ethan chuckled, signaling left as we left Florida and merged onto Highway 40, heading south toward Trenton and the manor.

I glanced at him, studying his profile. It had been a year since we last spoke, and three years since I'd actually seen him in person. He still looked like the same old jerk I remembered—tall, with his familiar tousled brown hair, the same green eyes I had, and that ever-present stubble on his chin. But there was something different about him now, too. He looked stronger, more muscular, like he'd been spending hours at the gym. I couldn't help but chuckle at the thought of Ethan working out.

Holy biceps, Ethan. His arms looked like they were about to rip right through his shirt. I bit my lip, stifling a laugh, trying not to make it obvious that I was noticing. It was so unlike him. Instead, I turned my head toward the window, feigning disinterest.

For a moment, I let myself drift back to when we were kids. Ethan hadn't always been the infuriating person he'd become. Back then—before life got complicated and we started drifting apart—he was my partner in crime. I thought about the summers we spent at our grandparents' cottage by the lake. He'd shove me into the water, laughing as I splashed and screamed, only to dive in after me seconds later.

One summer, when I was about eight and he was ten, we decided to sneak into the woods behind the cottage, even though we'd been warned a million times to stay out. Naturally, we got lost. I panicked, convinced we'd never make it back, but Ethan stayed calm. He took my hand, reassuring me that we'd be fine. And after what felt like hours of wandering, he led us back to the cottage like it was no big deal.

I remembered feeling safe with him then, like he could fix anything.

But that was a long time ago.

Those carefree days had faded into distant memories, replaced by a growing distance between us. The Ethan sitting beside me now wasn't the same boy who used to protect me. He was someone I barely recognized—someone who had left me behind too many times.

I sighed quietly and turned my gaze back to the window, letting the memory slip away. The warmth of those childhood moments faded, replaced by the growing tension between us.

"Easy! I told Mom I wanted to spend more time with you and make up for that road trip... you know, the one I didn't ditch you on. I had a flat tire!" His tone was casual, but the defensiveness crept in, as if he hadn't already used that excuse a million times.

I rolled my eyes, unwilling to rehash the argument. "Right. Sure."

I doubted Mom was thrilled about the idea of us driving twelve hours to an abandoned family mansion. But Ethan had a knack for twisting things to get what he wanted. I tilted the mirror again, catching a glimpse of Luke's car behind us. Ethan and Luke had brought a CB radio for the trip—just in case we got separated or lost.

Luke's voice crackled through the CB. "Yo, the ladies are complaining they're hungry. Ethan, is there a place to stop and eat along the way?"

Ethan grabbed the receiver. "Yeah, there's a bar on south 40 just off Trenton," he replied, glancing at me as he said it. I knew exactly which bar he was talking about. It was the only one along the route to the manor, and I really didn't want to stop there.

"I'm not going to that bar!" I said firmly.

Ethan glanced at me, his jaw tightening for a moment before he sighed. Without a word, he signaled toward the right shoulder and slowed to a stop. Luke honked as he passed us, pulling over ahead.

"What's up, Ethan? Something wrong?" Luke's voice crackled through the CB.

Ethan picked up the receiver again. "No, Luke. Just need a breather. We'll be on our way again soon."

Through the windshield, I saw Tara and Gwen stepping out of the car. Tara lit a cigarette while Gwen stretched her legs and started chatting with her. Luke stayed by the car, puffing on his own cigarette.

Ethan turned to me, his expression softening. "Look, May, I'm sorry, okay? I don't know how many times I can apologize. Something happened to the car before I even reached Trenton—it was like a force caused me to swerve, and my tire blew."

I stared at him, not buying it for a second. He'd used this same excuse before. Some "force" caused him to swerve off the road and blow a tire? Right. Ethan swore he'd seen a man in a black fedora and a long trench coat standing in the middle of the road, forcing him to veer into the ditch.

"Okay, Ethan, was that all you wanted to say?" I asked, my tone surprisingly calm, even though my stomach was still in knots and my nerves hadn't settled.

"Maeve…" Ethan began, but I held up my hand, cutting him off.

"Let it go, Ethan. Can we just get back on the road now?" I snapped, my voice sharper than I intended.

Ethan let out a long breath and turned the ignition. Luke, seeing us start to move, called out to Tara and Gwen, who quickly got back into their car. Once we were back on the road, Luke pulled in behind us, and the caravan continued in tense silence. Ethan's focus was locked on the road, his hands gripping the wheel a little too tightly. His usual calm demeanor was starting to crack, and I could feel the tension radiating off him. I debated telling him about my dreams—nightmares, really. Ethan had always believed in my premonitions, no matter how strange they seemed. He never made me feel like I was losing my grip on reality.

But I wasn't sure if now was the right time to bring it up.

Maybe I should wait until we passed the sign for Trenton—or at least until we got past the bar.

"Ethan…" I started, thinking I could ease the mood, maybe break the tension between us. He was wound tight, maybe even more than I was. This drive had to be dredging up bad memories for him, too. After all, it was on this very stretch of highway, just three miles from the bar, where he'd had his accident.

"Ethan!" I said again, louder this time, trying to get his attention. He was so focused on the road that he didn't seem to hear me until we reached a fork in the highway. One sign pointed south toward Trenton: the other veered north to an unfamiliar road. A place we'd never explored.

He slowed the car and came to a stop, right in the middle of the fork.

"Ethan, why'd you stop? I'm right behind you, bro! I could've plowed into you," Luke's voice crackled over the CB radio.

Ethan grabbed the receiver quickly, his voice rushed as he tried to cover up his hesitation. "Sorry, I forgot which way I was going," he said, his tone strained, as though he was trying to avoid explaining why he'd really stopped.

Luke didn't reply, but the silence on the other end of the radio felt heavy.

"Ethan, we're supposed to go south, remember?" I said gently, placing a hand on his arm. He let out a deep breath, glancing at me with an expression caught between embarrassment and fear.

"We go south," he repeated softly, signaling as he shifted the gear.

Luke's car followed close behind us as Ethan drove forward—slowly, almost cautiously, as if the road ahead carried more weight than the car itself. I didn't need to ask why. Two miles down this stretch was where the accident had happened. I kept my hand against his on the wheel, a silent effort to calm his nerves. His fingers brushed mine briefly in acknowledgment, a quiet thank-you.

"Maeve… this is where it happened," he said, his voice low and strained as we approached the bend in the road. The car had slowed to barely 20 km/h, each meter forward tightening the tension in the air.

"Pull over. I'll drive," I said firmly. "You're not up to it."

He hesitated, his grip tightening on the wheel before he finally exhaled and brought the car to a full stop in the middle of the road. The sky had darkened quickly, the last streaks of daylight fading into dusk. Luke's car pulled up beside us, and he rolled down his window, frustration evident on his face. "Ethan, come on, what's your problem?" he called out. Gwen sat beside him, throwing her hands in the air as if to echo his question.

Ethan rolled down his window, forcing a chuckle in an attempt to diffuse the tension. "Sorry, May wants to drive. We're just switching," he said casually, carefully avoiding the real reason he'd stopped.

Luke raised an eyebrow, skeptical but unwilling to push further. He knew Ethan well enough to sense something was off, but not enough to understand why. Despite being his best friend since high school, Ethan had never told Luke about the figure he'd claimed to see in the middle of the road that night. Luke knew about the accident—knew how bad it had been—and shared Ethan's unease about driving this stretch of highway at night. But the details of that night, the shadowy figure Ethan swore was standing in the road, were something Ethan had kept to himself.

As I stepped out of the car to switch seats, I glanced at Ethan. His face was pale, his eyes darting nervously toward the shadows, as if he expected something—or someone—to emerge. For a moment, I hesitated, debating whether to say anything. Instead, I slid into the driver's seat, feeling the tension lingering in the air like a tangible force. Ethan was trying to keep it together, but it was clear—he was terrified.

And so was I.

"Try to keep up," I called to Luke, buckling my seatbelt and pulling it tightly across my chest. Ethan did the same, his movements deliberate and shaky. He ran a hand through his hair and let out a deep, unsteady breath. I shifted the gear into drive, and we rolled forward. Luke's headlights flickered as he pulled in behind us.

"Just ahead... before the bend. That's where it happened," Ethan said quietly, nodding toward the dark stretch of highway in front of us. His voice was tight, the unease in it sharp enough to make my pulse quicken.

I focused on the road, gripping the wheel harder than I needed to. Not a single car passed us, the highway eerily empty. It struck me as odd, especially with the bar nearby. But here we were, alone on this desolate road on Halloween night. It felt wrong, like some unseen force had cleared the path for us—like this stretch of highway existed solely for what was about to happen.

"I've got this," I told Ethan, trying to keep my voice steady. My heart, however, was pounding against my ribs.

Ethan exhaled again, his hand gripping the handle above the door so tightly his knuckles turned white. As we neared the stretch of road that haunted us both, a strange shift seemed to ripple through the air. The heaviness was impossible to ignore, like a silent, oppressive presence pressing down on the car. It felt as if a forcefield had opened just long enough to let us through, then closed silently behind us.

The temperature inside the car dropped. My fingers tingled with the cold, but the dashboard showed no change in the heater's output. It was like the chill wasn't coming from outside—it was something else.

Ethan shifted in his seat, his unease palpable. His hand didn't leave the handle. Then, without warning, something darted across the road ahead.

"Shit!" I slammed on the brakes, my heart racing as the car

jerked to a stop. My eyes scanned the road, but there was nothing there. The asphalt stretched out, silent and empty, under the dull glow of the headlights.

"Did you see that?" I whispered, my voice trembling.

Ethan's face had gone ghostly pale, his eyes wide as he stared at the road. "Yeah," he murmured, barely audible. "I saw it. It's happening again, Maeve."

His words hung in the air like a weight, pulling us deeper into silence. I eased the car forward, every nerve in my body screaming for me to turn around. But I knew Ethan wouldn't agree. And deep down, despite the fear clawing at me, I couldn't shake the feeling that the manor was waiting for us.

Waiting for me.

"WHAT THE HELL WAS THAT? Ethan, Maeve, did you see that?" Gwen's panicked voice crackled over the CB. Ethan quickly grabbed the receiver, his hands trembling slightly. We were both stopped dead in the middle of the highway, the weight of what we'd just seen hanging heavy in the air.

"Yeah, we saw it," Ethan replied, his voice tight and shaky. I could hear the strain, the barely-contained fear, in his words.

Luke was the first to get out of the car, slamming his door shut with more force than necessary. Tara and Gwen followed quickly, their eyes wide and scanning the shadows like prey sensing a predator. I adjusted the mirror to watch them approach, my pulse still pounding.

"Great," I muttered under my breath, unbuckling my seatbelt. Ethan and I stepped out of the car, the cool night air immediately biting against my skin. As we gathered between the cars, Gwen's gaze never wavered from the dense forest pressing in on either side of the road. The trees loomed like sentinels, their gnarled branches twisting toward us as if they were alive.

"Was that a man? I mean... what *was* it?" Tara asked, her voice quivering. Her usual bravado was nowhere to be found. Ethan moved toward her, wrapping her in a reassuring hug.

"No one panic," he said, trying to sound steady, though his voice betrayed him. "I'm sure it was just an animal. No way it was a person."

Even as he said it, I caught the flicker of doubt in his eyes.

Luke wasn't buying it. His gaze stayed locked on the trees, his body tense, radiating unease.

"Yeah, Ethan's right. It's fine!" Luke said, his tone overly casual, as if he was trying to convince himself as much as us. "Let's just get back in the cars and get to the house. I don't want to be out here any longer than we have to."

Tara and Gwen exchanged uneasy glances before heading back to their car. I gave Ethan a slight nod and followed, but the weight of the unspoken fear between us was suffocating. As I opened my door, I paused, catching Luke speaking to Ethan in a low, urgent tone just out of the girls' earshot.

"Tell me right now, Ethan—what the hell was that? I know you saw it. I can see it in your eyes, man. You're scared, and that's not normal. You've seen that figure—or whatever it was—before, haven't you?"

Ethan turned his back to the cars, his voice dropping to a whisper.

"Remember the accident on this road three years ago?" he said, the words slow and deliberate. "It happened because I swear, I saw a man standing in the middle of the road. I swerved to avoid hitting him, flipped the car, and blew the tire. It was like something didn't want me to reach Maeve that night."

Luke ran a hand through his hair, exhaling sharply. His jaw clenched as his eyes flicked nervously toward the woods, then back to Ethan.

"Damn, Ethan. And you couldn't have told me this three years ago? We wouldn't have planned this trip," Luke muttered, his voice low but tinged with frustration.

Ethan stepped closer, lowering his voice even further. "Do *not* tell Gwen or Tara. Let's just get to the manor, alright? I want to get off this godforsaken stretch of road."

Luke nodded reluctantly, his expression tight with concern, and without another word, they both headed back to their cars. Ethan climbed into the passenger seat, his face pale as he shut the door with a heavy thud. I stayed frozen for a moment, my hand gripping the door handle as a chill ran down my spine.

Whatever we'd just seen wasn't finished with us.

I couldn't shake the feeling that it was only the beginning.

"Go, May. Let's just get to the bar, grab something to eat, and head straight to the house. I don't want to linger on this road any longer. The bar is two miles out—just go!" Ethan's voice was sharp, almost pleading, his usual calm replaced with a raw edge of agitation. It was clear he wanted nothing more than to put as much distance as possible between us and whatever it was we'd just seen.

I shifted the car into drive and clicked my seatbelt into place, my heart pounding as I pressed down on the gas. The car inched forward, the tires crunching against the pavement like the only sound in the world. My eyes darted from one side of the highway to the other, scanning every shadow, every flicker of movement, as if that... thing might reappear at any moment.

What the hell was that?

It had moved too fast, faster than anything human, yet its shape had seemed like that of a man—or was my mind just twisting the memory? I replayed the scene in my head, trying to slow it down, to make sense of it. The way it moved—it wasn't right. My skin prickled with unease, the hair on the back of my neck standing on end as I wrestled with the thought. Whatever it was, it wasn't natural. It wasn't *normal.*

Ethan grabbed the CB, breaking the tense silence. His voice was tight and deliberate. "Luke, the bar is two miles from here. We'll get in, grab some food, and take it to go. I don't want to stay on this road any longer than we have to."

Luke's response came quickly, his voice clipped but steady. "Agreed. The girls are scared. Let's just get some food and get the hell out of here. How far is the house from the bar?"

"Another nine hours south," Ethan replied, the strain in his voice unmistakable. "We'll hit an old, abandoned road—that's where we turn. It'll take us straight to the manor."

"Sounds good," Luke replied. The CB crackled for a moment before falling silent again.

As the car picked up speed on the deserted highway, Ethan shifted in his seat, running a hand through his hair. I kept my focus on the road, but the weight of his earlier words settled heavily in my chest.

Nine more hours.

Nine hours of driving through endless, isolated roads in the middle of nowhere, with nothing but the night pressing in around us and the memory of that figure burned into my mind.

My grip on the wheel tightened, my knuckles turning white as I tried to keep my breathing steady. I wanted to believe Ethan—that it was just an animal, something explainable. But deep down, I knew better. I could feel it. Something wasn't right.

The darkness outside seemed to grow heavier, as if it were alive, pressing against the car, watching us, waiting. The two miles to the bar stretched endlessly, each second feeling like an eternity. Every sound—the wind rustling through the trees, the faint creak of the tires—was amplified in the oppressive silence.

Even as I told myself we were safe, that my mind was just playing tricks on me, the gnawing sense of dread refused to loosen its grip.

OLD TRENTON BAR

THE BAR WAS EXACTLY two miles south of Trenton—the town where we were headed. The long stretch of road leading there would eventually take us to Trenton, and nine hours beyond that lay my family's old home. As I pulled into the bar's parking lot, the flickering neon sign overhead cast an eerie red glow over the cracked asphalt. The gas station sat just next to it, its single pump standing like a relic from another era. Luke followed close behind, and we both stopped to refuel.

Ethan and Luke got out of their cars first, the crunch of gravel under their boots breaking the silence. Ethan leaned against the pump, his movements tense. "Get in, get food, and get out," he called over to me, his voice clipped, still edged with anxiety from the road. I stepped out of the car but didn't move right away. Instead, I lingered by the open door, my eyes drifting toward the bar's entrance. As I stood there, memories of the last time I was here came flooding back, unbidden and sharp.

The bus had dropped me off right here—this exact spot. I'd waited outside for what felt like half an hour for Ethan, but his phone had been dead, and I couldn't get a signal. Desperate, I'd gone into the bar to use their phone.

It was packed that night. Mostly men, their laughter loud and coarse, drowning out the clink of glasses and the crackle of an old jukebox in the corner. I was probably the only woman there, aside from the three overworked waitresses weaving between tables. From the moment I stepped inside, I felt the weight of their stares—hungry, assessing.

The bartender, a gruff man in his forties, barely glanced up as I asked to use the phone. He jabbed a thumb toward a corner near the washrooms where an ancient payphone hung on the wall.

I'd barely picked up the receiver when I felt *him*.

His presence pressed against me like a cold shadow. His slurred voice was the first warning. "Hey, sweetheart, you lost, precious?"

My heart quickened, but I forced myself to stay calm. Slowly, I turned to face him, doing my best to keep my voice steady. "I'm waiting for my brother," I said, my tone firm, projecting confidence I didn't feel. "He should be here any minute."

I wanted him to believe me—that I wasn't alone, that I wasn't vulnerable.

But he didn't care.

His grin widened, his steps slow and deliberate as he closed the gap between us. The stench of stale alcohol on his breath made my stomach churn. "Nah, sweet thing. Tonight, you can have some fun with me..."

Before I could react, his hand was on me, rough and invasive. Panic surged through me like a bolt of electricity.

"Get your hands off me!" I shouted, my voice trembling with fear and anger.

The bartender heard me and rushed over, his heavy boots pounding against the wooden floor. He grabbed the man and yanked him off me, but instead of retreating, the drunk spun around and swung. His fist collided with the bartender's jaw, the sickening sound of the impact echoing across the bar.

I remember the fear that gripped me then, how my heart pounded in my chest as he turned back to me, his eyes wild and predatory. Before he could lay another hand on me, I swung with everything I had, my hand connecting hard with his face. The slap echoed through the bar, cutting through the noise like a gunshot.

"Get the hell out of my bar," the bartender growled, stepping between us. His voice was low and full of menace, enough to make the drunk man stagger back a few steps.

The man swayed unsteadily toward the door, rubbing his reddened cheek, but not before turning to leer at me one last time. His lips twisted into a cruel smile, and he puckered them mockingly, making obscene kissing noises.

"Don't go far, sweetheart," he sneered before stumbling out into the night.

I stood there, shaking, tears streaming down my face as the adrenaline ebbed and fear surged in its place. My hands felt cold and clammy, my knees weak. A waitress hurried over to me, her eyes full of concern. She put a comforting arm around my shoulder, whispering, "It's okay now. He's gone."

They called the police, and I remember sitting in the back of the bar, clutching a cup of water in trembling hands, waiting for them to arrive. When they did, I gave my statement in a shaky voice, my words halting as I relived every awful moment. Afterward, they offered to drive me back to the main road, where I caught another bus home.

That night lingered with me, flashing in my mind like a terrible reel I couldn't stop. The fear, the helplessness, and that man's sick smile haunted me for months. I was pulled out of the memory by the sound of Ethan's voice. He was calling my name, sharp and urgent, and it took me a second to realize he'd been trying to get my attention.

"Maeve, I'm here this time," Ethan said softly as he walked over to me. His voice had lost its earlier edge, replaced with a gentler tone meant to reassure. "Do you really think I'd let anything happen to you again? Not on my watch."

He meant well, but the tension in my chest refused to ease. Gwen and Tara approached, zipping up their jackets against the bite of the night air.

"Maeve, let's get something to eat. I'm *dying* of hunger, girl," Tara said with a laugh, her attempt to lighten the mood falling flat.

I glanced toward the bar again, my unease growing. It hadn't changed. The same rusted exterior, the same grimy windows, the same aura of unwelcome that clung to it like a second skin. The memories of that night pulsed in my mind, vivid and unrelenting. Every instinct screamed at me to turn around and leave, but I knew we couldn't. We had to keep moving, and the bar was just a stop along the way.

I forced a smile at Tara, nodding as I tried to push the dread aside. "I'll be quick," I told Ethan, giving his hand a quick squeeze before letting go.

He returned a faint, reassuring smile, but the concern in his eyes lingered as I turned and followed Gwen and Tara toward the bar.

"This place looks so old and rusted," Gwen said, wrinkling her nose in disgust as she grabbed the screen door. The door groaned in protest, its hinges stiff with age, and we stepped inside.

The bar wasn't as crowded as it had been that night, but it still carried the same oppressive atmosphere. The usual crowd of men lingered at the tables, their voices low and rough. Two waitresses moved through the room, weaving around chairs as they carried trays. Behind the counter stood the bartender—the same man from before.

"Hey, I remember you!" he called out, his round face lighting up as his gaze landed on me. I froze for a moment, scanning the room before forcing a smile and stepping toward the bar. He wasn't particularly old, maybe in his late forties, with a bald head, solid build, and a face that was hard to forget.

"Oh, hi," I said, my voice steady but clipped. I could feel the weight of his attention as I slid onto one of the barstools, trying to suppress the unease curling in my stomach.

Meanwhile, Tara and Gwen had wandered over to a waitress near the cash register, ordering enough food to feed a small army. They were oblivious to the tension threading through the air, their laughter ringing faintly behind me. Gwen glanced back briefly, her expression neutral, then turned her attention back to the menu board.

"You doing okay, darling?" the bartender asked, setting down the glass he'd been wiping. His voice was friendly, but there was a note of genuine concern. "You left in a hurry last time. Cops were all over this joint after you left."

I managed a faint smile, playing at nonchalance. "Yeah, I'm fine," I said, my fingers brushing against the bar's worn surface.

But the truth was, I wasn't. Not entirely.

"Yeah, I made it home safely," I replied, my voice steadier than I felt.

The bartender shook his head, his expression darkening. Setting the glass down with deliberate care, he leaned in, his voice dropping to a near whisper. "They caught Jake three miles south of here," he said, and my stomach tightened at the sound of that name. "He was so drunk, just wandering along the road toward Trenton. But when the cops found him…" He paused, his words hanging heavy in the air. "He was nothing more than a corpse."

I leaned forward, my pulse quickening. "What do you mean?"

I asked cautiously, my curiosity tangled with a creeping dread. "Like… dead from alcohol poisoning or something?"

The bartender glanced around, his gaze flicking to Gwen and Tara to make sure they weren't paying attention. When he nodded, it wasn't in affirmation—it was more like acknowledgment of something too heavy to carry alone. "No," he murmured, his voice barely audible. "Not just dead. It was like something had drained the life out of him. He was just… bones. A corpse. There's no way it could've happened so fast. He'd only been gone ten minutes after the cops got here."

My breath caught in my throat, my fingers gripping the edge of the counter for balance. *Jake*—the man who had assaulted me—reduced to nothing but bones? My mind reeled, the room tilting as I tried to process what he was saying. How could that even be possible? The memory of that night hit me like a punch, vivid and unrelenting. I saw Jake's face, his leering grin, and felt again the rough grip of his hands. The terror I'd buried surged back to the surface, raw and all-consuming. I remembered how powerless I'd felt—until I fought back. But now, the thought that something, some unseen force, might have done this to him was equally terrifying.

The bartender's voice pulled me back to the present. "The cops couldn't explain it," he said, shaking his head grimly. "One minute, he was just a drunk causing trouble. The next… it was like the life had been sucked right out of him. They said it was the strangest damn thing they'd ever seen."

I swallowed hard, my mind racing as the bartender's words settled like stones in my chest. Was this just a bizarre coincidence? Or was there something darker—something sinister—at work?

The figure we'd seen earlier on the road flashed in my mind. The way it moved, unnaturally fast, like it wasn't bound by the rules of this world. Could it be connected to what had happened to *Jake*?

The bartender leaned back slightly, his eyes scanning my face with quiet concern. "You alright, darling?" he asked, his voice gentle but weighted with unspoken worry.

I nodded, though my heart was pounding in my chest. "Yeah, I'm fine," I lied, forcing a weak smile. But the truth was far from it. The creeping dread that had wrapped itself around me wouldn't loosen its grip. Something about this place, about this stretch of road, felt inherently wrong. It was as if the darkness here wasn't just an absence of light—it was alive, waiting, watching, ready for us to make a mistake.

Tara approached, blissfully unaware of the gravity of the conversation. "Maeve, let's get going," she said brightly, holding up two large bags of food with a triumphant grin. "We've got enough to feed an army!"

I forced another smile, though it felt hollow. The bartender's words about Jake still echoed in my mind, sending an icy chill through my veins.

"We paid for the gas; let's head back out on the road," Gwen said, her tone light as she swayed playfully and placed her hands on my shoulders, giving me a little shake. I exhaled deeply, trying to release some of the tension coiling inside me, but the weight of the bartender's earlier warning clung stubbornly.

"Yeah, girl," Tara chimed in loudly. "We've got nine hours to Trenton and then one more hour to the mansion." Her words, cheerful as they were, seemed to draw the bartender's attention. He set down the glass he had been wiping, his expression shifting to something far more serious.

"You're not thinking about driving out to Trenton at this time of night, are you?" he asked, his voice low, almost a warning. His gaze landed on me, and the concern in his tone made me instinctively move closer to the counter. There was something behind his words, something unsaid but heavy with meaning.

Before I could ask him why, Ethan and Luke walked into the bar.

Ethan moved behind me, his hands settling gently on my shoulders. Luke, laughing, grabbed the bags of food from Gwen and headed toward the parking lot. Tara followed them, joining in their laughter, but their voices barely registered in my mind. My focus stayed locked on the bartender, on the weight of the moment, and on the unease that gripped me.

"This is my brother, Ethan," I said, stepping aside as Ethan extended his hand. The bartender shook it firmly, his concern etched into his face.

"I couldn't help but overhear your conversation," the bartender said, his attention now fixed on Ethan. "But Trenton Road is off-limits at this time of night." His tone carried a sense of urgency, almost as though he were pleading with us not to go.

Ethan raised an eyebrow, his arm pulling me closer as he studied the man. "Is there something we should know about?" he asked, his voice light, but I could hear the curiosity creeping in.

The bartender's eyes flicked to mine, his expression almost haunted. "Let's just say… there've been many deaths along that road," he said quietly, the words hanging in the air like a curse.

My stomach knotted as his gaze lingered on me, and in that moment, Jake's corpse flashed in my mind like a silent, chilling warning. Whatever the bartender meant by "deaths," I knew it wasn't just the usual dangers of a rural highway. It was something more. Something darker.

Ethan chuckled, loosening his hold on me as he tapped the counter. "Well, you don't have to worry about us. We're only here for a few days. Tell you what—if we don't show up at your bar in four days… send out the cavalry," he joked, flashing the bartender a grin.

But the bartender didn't laugh. His face darkened, his gaze drifting to the clock that hung over the hallway near the bathrooms. For a moment, the only sound was the faint hum of the fluorescent lights. When he finally spoke, his voice carried a weight that made my chest tighten.

"Four days? I'll hold you to that," he said, his tone deadly serious. "I mean it, son. All of you better come back here in four days."

It wasn't just a casual remark—it felt like a plea. His words were laced with something unspoken, a warning he couldn't or wouldn't fully explain. The bartender knew something about that road, something more than he was letting on. I could see it in his eyes, and it chilled me to the bone.

This was the first time we'd be heading to our family home since my uncle's disappearance. And now, as the bartender's words echoed in my mind, I realized something unsettling. Three years ago, we'd never even made it to Trenton. That night, when Ethan had his accident, it was as if something had deliberately turned us back. Ethan had been rushed to the hospital, and I'd returned home without ever reaching Trenton.

I had tried to bury that memory, to dismiss it as a freak accident, but now it resurfaced, gnawing at me with a renewed intensity. The weight of it all pressed down on me, sharp and unrelenting.

Ethan seemed calm as he thanked the bartender and grabbed my hand, pulling me toward the door. But my heart was pounding, the flashes of that night replaying in my mind. I had almost lost Ethan—twice—and the fear of it had never fully left me. After his recovery, my doctor had put me on medication for the severe anxiety attacks that had started haunting me. Even now, they weren't fully under control.

As we stepped outside, the night greeted us with a chill that felt heavier than the temperature could explain. I glanced down the long stretch of road that lay ahead. It seemed darker now, impossibly so, as if the shadows had grown deeper, swallowing the horizon whole.

A familiar wave of anxiety began to build, tightening in my chest. My breath quickened, my vision narrowing. I knew this feeling—it wasn't just unease. This was the onset of a full-blown attack. My thoughts spiraled, the edges of reality blurring as dizziness crept in.

I stopped abruptly, gripping Ethan's hand like it was the only thing keeping me tethered to the world. Slowly, deliberately, I forced myself to take deep breaths, willing the panic to subside. But this wasn't just anxiety about the road ahead. This was deeper, instinctive, primal.

My body knew, even if my mind refused to accept it: something was waiting for us out there.

Ethan looked down at me, noticing my sudden hesitation. "You okay?" he asked, his voice softer now, the playful edge gone and replaced by concern.

I nodded quickly, though my throat felt like it was closing up. "Yeah… I'll be fine," I lied, trying to suppress the growing weight in my chest. The road ahead stretched out endlessly, a black void that felt alive. It wasn't just darkness—it felt like it was watching us, waiting for its moment.

"That guy has some serious problems," Ethan muttered as we reached the car, his words almost lost in the haze of my spiraling thoughts. I reached for the driver-side door handle, my fingers trembling, but before I could grasp it, a sudden wave of anxiety crashed over me, drowning me in its intensity.

My heart raced violently, and my vision blurred as the edges of the world seemed to tilt. My knees buckled under me, and I gasped for air, my breaths shallow and panicked.

"Maeve! Hey, hey, calm down," Ethan's voice was sharp, urgent, as he rushed around the car to catch me before I hit the ground. His arms wrapped tightly around me, holding me steady as my body trembled uncontrollably.

"MAY!" Gwen's shout echoed across the parking lot as she and Tara sprinted toward us, their faces pale with alarm.

"Get her anxiety medication!" Ethan barked, gesturing wildly toward the car. His voice was laced with panic, but his grip on me was steady, grounding. Tara and Gwen darted to the backseat, rummaging through my belongings with frantic hands as I slumped against Ethan's chest, my head resting against him. His heartbeat was steady, strong—a fragile anchor in the chaos.

"Maeve, deep breaths, come on," Luke knelt beside me, his hands moving in soothing circles on my legs. His voice was calm, but I could hear the strain behind it.

The bartender, who had been watching from the doorway, stepped outside, his boots crunching against the gravel as he approached cautiously. "Hey, darling, are you alright? Do you need an ambulance?" he asked, his voice gentle but firm. A waitress followed close behind, holding a can of ginger ale in her hands.

I gratefully accepted it, my hands shaking as Ethan popped the tab and held it to my lips. The cool, fizzy liquid slid down my throat, soothing the dryness left by the panic attack.

Behind us, I could hear Gwen and Tara bickering, their frantic voices cutting through the haze.

"It literally says *anxiety medication* right on the bottle!" Gwen shouted at Tara, her voice rising in exasperation as they rifled through the bag.

"Then give it to me!" Tara snapped back, their argument a blur in the background of my muddled thoughts. I wanted to speak, to tell them where it was, but the words stuck in my throat, swallowed by the panic still clinging to me like a shadow.

"No need for an ambulance," Ethan said, pressing his forehead gently against mine. His voice was low but trembling, his nerves barely masked. "She's fine. She'll be fine."

Luke, growing increasingly impatient, snapped at Tara. "Did you find it? Tara, come on!" His tone was sharp, teetering on the edge of desperation.

Finally, Tara emerged from the backseat with the bottle of medication in her hand, the cap already unscrewed. She hurried over, holding it out as if it were a lifeline. Ethan took the bottle, shook out a pill, and pressed it gently to my lips.

"Maeve, it's okay. I'm right here," he said softly, his voice steady despite the tension thick in the air. I swallowed the pill, the bitter taste lingering as I forced it down. Slowly, I felt the crushing weight of the panic start to lift, but the fear remained, coiling in the pit of my stomach like a living thing.

Ethan stayed close, his arms wrapped protectively around me as the trembling in my legs began to subside. My friends surrounded me, their worried faces blurring as I tried to focus on my breathing, willing myself to calm down.

"I told you, darling," the bartender said, his tone tinged with disapproval as he snapped the cloth in his hand against his leg. "These roads aren't for you." Without waiting for a response, he turned back toward the bar, the waitress trailing behind him with a sympathetic glance before they disappeared inside.

Luke placed a gentle hand on my back, his concern etched in every movement. "You sure you're okay, Maeve? We don't have to do this. If you want to head back, just say the word."

Ethan pulled me upright, his arms still wrapped around me. I leaned into Ethan, letting the steady rhythm of his breathing soothe me. His arms tightened around me, and he whispered something soft, though I couldn't make out the words. My mind was still reeling, the echoes of the panic attack fading but the fear refusing to let go. It lingered, like a shadow, whispering that something was waiting for us further down the road.

"We'll keep going," I murmured, my face pressed against Ethan's chest. The words didn't feel like my own, but they tumbled out anyway. Ethan nodded, his hold loosening slightly. Luke glanced at me, reading my expression, before turning to Tara and Gwen.

"We're going to keep going," he said, his voice steady but cautious. Tara stepped closer, resting a hand gently on my shoulder.

"Alright," she said softly, her concern evident. She lingered for a moment, then turned and followed Gwen back to the car.

"May, hey…" Ethan pulled back just enough to look into my eyes, his brow furrowed with worry. "Are you sure you want to do this? This was a stupid idea. We don't have to spend Halloween at the mansion." He brushed a hand against my cheek, his tenderness catching me off guard and making my chest tighten.

"No, no, I'm okay! I *want* to go," I said quickly, forcing the lie out before I could second-guess myself. The internal scream of fear still echoed, but I buried it deep. Ethan studied my face for a moment, his eyes searching mine, then gave a small, playful tap to my chin.

"Alright," he said, a faint smile breaking through his worry. "I'll drive this time, and you can sleep."

I nodded, grateful for the excuse to retreat. Moving to the passenger side, I climbed into the car and turned on the heater, the warmth doing little to chase away the cold gnawing at my insides. I buckled my seatbelt as Ethan pulled onto the highway, Luke's headlights casting long beams across the empty road behind us.

I closed my eyes, trying to find some semblance of peace, but the unease remained, a constant presence. Letting out a shaky breath, I sighed heavily, my chest tightening with the weight of everything I hadn't said.

"Is there something you're not telling me, May?" Ethan asked, breaking the silence. His voice was calm but probing, cutting through the darkness like a blade. I hesitated, the truth clawing at the back of my throat. I wanted to tell him about the nightmares, the vivid premonitions that had haunted me for weeks. But I wasn't ready to share that yet. I couldn't.

So, I did what I always did. I lied.

"Remember when you met Luke? He was so drunk at that high school year-end party," I said, hoping to distract Ethan from probing any further.

Ethan let out a loud laugh, slapping the steering wheel. The tension in the car lightened as he let himself fall into the memory.

"Damn, that jackass was so drunk he literally bumped into me at the party," Ethan said, shaking his head. "I was about to ask Tara out when Luke stumbled into me and knocked me into the pool. We both fell in, and next thing I know, we're swinging punches at each other in the water."

His laughter filled the car, and I couldn't help but grin at the ridiculousness of it.

"We got kicked out of Gwen's family home," Ethan continued, "and ended up walking eight blocks to a McDonald's, soaking wet."

I laughed with him. "Yeah, and I still don't understand why you two stayed friends after that."

Ethan's grin widened. "He's good for me. Got me out of my shell. You know, I used to carry so much anger toward my dad for remarrying after my mom passed. I guess I took it out on everyone and everything. But Luke? He didn't care. He didn't care about my anger. He just… pulled me along and made me loosen up."

The memory became more vivid in my mind. I could see it all again—the chaos of that night. Luke, tipsy and already unsteady on his feet, crashing straight into Ethan and sending them both tumbling into the pool. The fight that followed was pure chaos, water splashing everywhere as they wrestled like overgrown kids.

At first, Ethan had been furious, his frustration bubbling over as he shouted and swung at Luke. But then something shifted. I remembered watching the anger drain from him, replaced by something lighter. By the time they clambered out of the pool, dripping wet and out of breath, they were laughing at the absurdity of it all.

And then Gwen stormed over, her face red with fury. "Get out of here! You've ruined my family's house!" she had screamed, pointing to the gate like a furious drill sergeant.

That's how Ethan and Luke ended up walking through the quiet streets, drenched and laughing as they made their way to the nearest McDonald's. I had followed a few paces behind, worried they might kill each other before the night was over.

But instead, they bonded—over soggy clothes and late-night burgers. By the time we sat down at a sticky table under the fluorescent lights, they were joking about who'd thrown the worst punch. What should have been a fight that ended in bitterness somehow became the start of their friendship.

"That walk to McDonald's…" Ethan said, his voice softer now, pulling me back to the present. "That's where it all changed. We weren't fighting anymore. We were laughing. I guess I needed that." He smiled faintly, the warmth of the memory softening his features.

"Yeah," I said, resting my head against the window, watching the road stretch endlessly ahead of us. "Luke's been a good influence in ways I never expected."

The thought hung in the air, heavy with the weight of everything Ethan had carried over the years. The death of his mother, the anger he harbored toward his dad's remarriage—it was like a storm that had raged inside him for so long, slowly losing its intensity, thanks in part to Luke's friendship. Luke had a way of pulling Ethan out of the darkness, lightening the load he carried. But even with that, there were things we didn't talk about—things that lingered, unspoken. That party had been a turning point for Ethan, but I couldn't shake the feeling that this trip, this mansion, was stirring something much deeper.

For a while, the car was silent except for the low hum of the engine. The road ahead was quiet, the occasional shadow from a tree flickering across the headlights. I tried to close my eyes again, hoping for even a moment of rest, but the memory of the mansion and the vivid dreams I'd been having made it impossible to fully relax. Every time I closed my eyes, I saw flashes of the manor: tall, menacing, and alive in ways it shouldn't be.

"Maeve," Ethan finally said, his voice breaking the silence after two hours of driving. My gaze was fixed on the road ahead, my nerves still on edge. I felt like I was on constant alert, waiting for something to lunge out of the darkness.

"What?" I replied, sharper than I intended.

Ethan hesitated, his hands tightening slightly on the steering wheel. "Whatever happened to Mike? Has he ever contacted you again?"

The mention of Mike sent a jolt through me, though I tried to keep my expression neutral. Mike. His name alone stirred something raw and unresolved in me. He had been my boyfriend for five years. We were supposed to get married—or at least, that's what he'd told Gwen.

Mike and I had met in my junior year of high school. We were the picture-perfect couple, or so everyone thought. I was the petite brunette with long hair, big green eyes, and a baby face. He was the tall, charismatic jock on the varsity team—the guy everyone admired. His hair was golden blonde, always styled effortlessly, and his brown eyes seemed to draw people in. His face, chiseled and flawless, made him look like something out of a Greek myth.

But Mike's charm wasn't enough for Ethan. My brother had been a senior when we started dating, and he'd taken his role as the overprotective brother to extremes. He didn't trust Mike, not one bit. I could still vividly remember the day after school when Ethan confronted him. They had nearly come to blows right there in the parking lot. Ethan had accused Mike of being a player, someone who wasn't good enough for me. Mike had laughed it off at first, but Ethan's anger boiled over, and the two of them started swinging.

I'd had to physically get between them, shouting at Ethan to stop. "Ethan, I'm dating him! You can't just fight every guy who talks to me!" I had yelled, furious and embarrassed. Ethan hadn't spoken to me for days after that.

And now, years later, here he was, bringing Mike's name up again. It was like he couldn't let it go, even after all this time.

It wasn't until years later, on our fifth anniversary, that everything fell apart. Gwen, Tara, and I were at McDonald's for lunch when Gwen casually dropped the bombshell: Mike had been telling Luke he was planning to propose to me. I pretended not to know anything, but inside, I was thrilled. Like any girl, I started imagining the moment—how he'd ask, what I'd say. I could practically feel the ring on my finger, glowing with excitement as I pictured him asking my stepfather and Ethan for my hand in marriage.

But then came *that* night. The night that shattered it all. Mike never showed up at my house with his big proposal. Instead, Luke caught him cruising around in his Camaro, the top down, a car full of cheerleaders packed inside—and one of them wasn't just a passenger. She was his girlfriend.

Luke, ever loyal to me because of his bond with Ethan, confronted Mike at a party later that night. He didn't tell Ethan—he knew Ethan would've gone nuclear—but Luke handled it his own way. He roughed Mike up, made it crystal clear that he was to end things with me, and warned him to stay far away. Luke wanted to protect me from the truth, to give Mike the chance to break things off cleanly, on his own terms.

Two days later, Mike called me. His voice was cold, distant, as though the five years we had spent together meant nothing. "We're done," he said, and then he hung up. Just like that. No explanation, no closure—just silence. I don't think I'd ever cried so much in my life.

When I told Ethan about the breakup, he was livid. From that moment, Mike was on his radar, though I kept the full story to myself. Ethan never found out about the cheerleaders or Luke stepping in to protect me. If he had… well, things might have gone very differently for Mike.

Later, I heard Mike had transferred to another university far out of state with that cheerleader. That's when I knew—he'd been cheating on me all along.

I tilted my head toward Ethan, unsure how to answer his question. "No, I haven't spoken to Mike since… well, you know," I said softly.

Ethan nodded, his jaw tightening as relief washed over his

face. "Good," he muttered, the word carrying a finality that signaled the end of the conversation.

But as silence settled over the car, my mind drifted back to those days. I could still see Ethan's face after I told him about the breakup, his fury barely contained. He'd been ready to hunt Mike down, to make him pay for what he'd done.

I sighed, leaning back in my seat and closing my eyes, thankful that part of my life was behind me. And yet, the sting of betrayal lingered, like a wound that never fully healed. Even after all these years, it still ached in a way I couldn't quite ignore.

...

"What the hell… is that?" Ethan muttered, breaking the heavy silence. He slowed the car to a complete stop, his grip tightening on the steering wheel. Behind us, Luke followed suit, his headlights casting long, distorted shadows in the fog that had suddenly materialized in our path.

"A fog?" I asked, my voice trembling slightly. This wasn't normal fog—it was too dense, too sudden, like a wall of mist had been dropped deliberately in front of us. The clock on the dashboard read 11:00 p.m., and the night was suffocatingly dark. No moon, no stars—just the oppressive blackness of the road and the thick haze stretching endlessly ahead. A chill crawled up my spine as we sat stranded on the empty stretch of highway, the car's engine humming quietly beneath the weight of the moment.

Luke stepped out of his car, his silhouette barely visible through the haze, and reached for the CB receiver. "Ethan, there's no way we can get through that fog," he said, his voice distorted slightly by static. Ethan grabbed the receiver, his jaw tense, his eyes fixed on the wall of mist ahead.

"There's another road to the right—it goes around Trenton. We passed the sign for it a few miles back. We could try taking that way. It'll add time, but at least the fog will be behind us… I think," Ethan said, his voice strained with uncertainty.

I glanced at him, unease gnawing at the edges of my mind. This fog wasn't natural. It felt wrong—like it had appeared deliberately to block our path. As if something—or someone—was waiting for us on the other side, determined to stop us from continuing.

"What if it stretches that way too?" Luke's voice crackled over the CB, tinged with apprehension. I tilted the rearview mirror and saw Tara and Gwen leaning forward in their seats, their faces pale as they stared at the mist, their expressions mirroring my own unease.

"We can't risk driving through it, Luke," Ethan said, his tone steady but firm. His knuckles were white against the steering wheel, his gaze locked on the unnatural fog as if it might move or shift at any moment. "We'll go around. It might extend further north, or it might not—but staying here isn't an option."

The radio went quiet for a moment before Luke's resigned voice came through, heavy with tension: "Alright. Let's just get this over with." His usual light-hearted demeanor was gone, replaced by something grim and serious. The weight of the situation pressed down on all of us, silent but undeniable. The fog loomed ahead, an impenetrable curtain of gray that felt alive, as though it was watching us. My chest tightened as my thoughts spiraled. What if this wasn't a natural phenomenon? What if this fog was something else—something sent to stop us from reaching Trenton? Or worse… from reaching the manor?

Ethan edged the car forward cautiously, the tires crunching over the gravel as we left the fog behind. The straight, familiar path we had originally planned was gone. In its place, a narrow, unmarked gravel road curved ahead, leading us straight through Trenton—a place we had meant to avoid at all costs. My chest tightened, the weight of dread pressing down as I gripped the seatbelt, my fingers digging into the fabric like it might anchor me somehow.

"Are we really doing this?" I whispered, more to myself than to Ethan. He didn't answer, his focus locked on the dark, winding road ahead, his jaw clenched tight.

The road seemed to stretch endlessly, each turn drawing us closer to the ghost town that had been abandoned for over thirty years. Every crackle of gravel under the tires felt louder, sharper, as though the silence was amplifying every sound. The closer we got, the heavier the air became. It was as though the town itself was alive, holding its breath, waiting for us to cross its threshold.

"No one lives there," I murmured, trying to reassure myself, but the words rang hollow in the frigid air. My mind raced with images of empty streets, boarded-up windows, and houses left to rot—a town frozen in time.

"No one's been in Trenton for decades," Ethan said, echoing my thoughts. His voice was low and tense. "But instead of avoiding it, we're heading straight into the heart of it."

A shiver ran down my spine. The idea of passing through Trenton felt wrong, like we were walking into a trap we couldn't see. I had heard the stories—everyone had. Tales of people who ventured into the town and never came out, of strange lights and sounds that didn't belong to the living. Those stories had always felt distant, like folklore meant to keep kids from exploring. But now, as the road pulled us closer, those stories felt like warnings we should've heeded.

The landscape around us began to shift. The trees lining the road grew twisted and gnarled, their bare branches stretching out like skeletal fingers, reaching for the car. The fog thinned as we approached the edge of Trenton, but the suffocating sense of unease it had brought lingered, clinging to my skin like a second layer.

"We're almost there," Ethan said, breaking the silence,

though his voice lacked any semblance of comfort. The headlights cut through the darkness, illuminating the faint outline of the first buildings in the distance. Trenton loomed ahead, its abandoned streets waiting silently, as though the town had been expecting us all along.

TRENTON

RENTON—THE GHOST TOWN. We had finally arrived. Ethan drove slowly along the gravel road that sliced through the heart of the abandoned town. To our left and right, empty homes loomed in eerie silence, their windows shattered, their doors barely clinging to rusted hinges. The air was heavy with a suffocating stillness, broken only by the crunch of gravel beneath the tires. Scattered remnants of another time surrounded us—an old gas station with its pumps rusted and useless, a convenience store ransacked long ago, its walls scarred with faded graffiti that read like forgotten whispers of a dead town.

I glanced over at Ethan, his face rigid with tension, his knuckles white as they gripped the steering wheel. The dim glow of the dashboard lights reflected off his pale skin.

"Okay, just a mile through here, and we'll hopefully be back on the main road and around the fog… I hope," he muttered, though his voice didn't carry much confidence.

"And if it isn't?" I asked, my voice trembling. The weight of my unease pressed down on me, thick and inescapable. "What if this fog doesn't end? Maybe…" I hesitated, the words catching in my throat. "Maybe it's trying to stop us, Ethan. Maybe it's warning us not to go to the mansion."

My chest tightened as the urge to tell him about the premonitions clawed at me—the nightmares that had been haunting me for weeks, the flashes of foreboding that felt more real every day. But before I could speak, a sudden flash in the rearview mirror caught my attention. Luke's car swerved violently, its headlights swinging wildly as if it had hit something unseen.

"Ethan, stop!" I shouted, pointing at the mirror. Ethan slammed on the brakes, the car jerking to a halt as he gripped the wheel tightly.

"Luke?" Ethan called into the CB, his voice sharp with urgency.

"ETHAN, DID YOU SEE THAT?" Luke's voice exploded through the CB, trembling with panic. In the background, Tara and Gwen were shouting, their voices high-pitched and frantic.

Something had happened. Something was wrong.

I spun around in my seat, my heart pounding, but the darkness outside revealed nothing. No movement. No figure. No explanation for what could have caused Luke's car to lurch like that. My breath hitched.

"What are they seeing?" I whispered, fear creeping in and rooting itself deep.

Without hesitation, Ethan unbuckled his seatbelt and flung the door open. The sound of it echoed into the quiet night as he stepped out, leaving the door slightly ajar behind him. He sprinted toward Luke's car, his silhouette swallowed by the dim glow of the headlights

"Ethan!" I yelled, fumbling with my seatbelt, ready to follow. But before I could move, the driver's door slammed shut with a deafening finality.

The locks engaged with a harsh *click*.

"What?" I gasped, my voice shaky with disbelief. I reached for the door handle, yanking at it with all my strength, but it wouldn't budge. Panic surged as I leaned over, trying the driver's side door. Locked. Every door in the car was sealed shut, trapping me inside.

Outside, I could see Ethan and Luke. They were shouting—arguing—but their voices were muffled, unreachable, like they were speaking from another world. My fingers clawed at the handle, desperation flooding through me as I pulled again and again, but the car didn't yield.

"What's happening?" I whispered, the question lingering in the cold, suffocating silence.

I started kicking at the door, panic overtaking me as my breath came in short, sharp gasps. Something—or someone—had locked me inside. My heart thundered in my chest, every instinct screaming that I wasn't alone.

And then I saw *him*.

Standing directly in front of the car was a man—or something that looked like a man. My breath hitched, freezing me in place as my eyes locked on his figure. He wore a dark, classic British-style fedora, the brim low enough to obscure his face, and a long black trench coat that draped down to his feet. He didn't move. He just stood there, impossibly still, staring directly at me.

But I couldn't see his face.

A scream tore from my throat, my body trembling with pure terror. It was him.

The figure I'd seen in my nightmares—night after night, lurking in the shadows of my mind. And now, he was here. Real. Standing in front of me.

Ethan must have heard me, because he and Luke both

stopped mid-argument, their heads snapping toward the car. Their confusion turned to horror as they saw him—the fedora-wearing figure standing like a phantom in the mist.

"HEY! HEY! GET AWAY FROM HER!" Ethan shouted, his voice cracking with raw desperation. He and Luke broke into a sprint, rushing toward the car.

But before they could reach me, the figure moved.

Not forward—backward. One deliberate step into the fog. And then he vanished.

The thick mist swallowed him whole, as if he had never been there.

I was still trapped in the car, my hands clawing at the door handles as tears streamed down my face. My screams echoed in the suffocating silence, the air inside the car heavy and oppressive. My chest tightened, every breath a struggle, as if the figure had taken all the oxygen with him—leaving behind nothing but suffocating dread.

Suddenly, Gwen and Tara appeared beside the car, their faces pale and stricken with fear. They yanked at the door handle, and miraculously, it unlocked with a soft *click*. The door swung open, and I spilled out onto the gravel, collapsing to my knees.

My body shook uncontrollably, and I leaned forward as my stomach lurched. Hot bile rose in my throat, and I vomited onto the cold ground, my hands trembling against the rough gravel. The world around me spun, the image of that figure still burned into my mind.

Ethan dropped to his knees beside me, his hands gripping my shoulders. "Maeve! Maeve, look at me!" he demanded, his voice panicked. I could hear Luke shouting something in the background, but it was muffled, distant—like it was coming from underwater.

I couldn't answer. My body refused to respond, the fear still coursing through my veins like ice.

"What the hell was that? Who *was* that?" Tara's voice trembled, her panic evident in her wide, frantic eyes. Ethan stood and stepped toward her, his attempt to calm her undermined by the visible tension etched across his face.

"I don't know, Tara. Just... breathe," he muttered, his eyes flicking toward the shadows, scanning for any sign of movement.

Gwen and Luke stood by the car, locked in a hushed but heated argument. Their words were sharp, tense, but the details were lost to me as chaos pressed in from all sides. My heartbeat thundered in my ears, drowning everything out. I couldn't focus. I couldn't breathe.

The pressure inside me built like a storm, unbearable and unrelenting. My chest tightened, and I gasped, clenching my fists as panic clawed its way to the surface. Not here. Not now.

"*NO!* STOP FIGHTING... ARGUING!" I screamed, my voice cracking and raw as it tore through the heavy night air.

The others froze, startled into silence by my outburst.

Ethan was at my side in an instant, kneeling beside me and pulling me into his arms, his grip steady but trembling. It was the same gesture he always used when things became too much, grounding me in the chaos.

"We're leaving," Luke's panicked voice cut through the stillness. He stood by Ethan's car, his fists clenched tightly at his sides, his breaths ragged. "We can't stay here. Whoever—or *whatever*—that man was... I almost hit him. This place is wrong."

"We're turning around," Ethan said firmly, still holding me but now addressing the group. "We'll get back to the main road, head to the bar, and go home. End of discussion."

I jerked out of his arms, anger surging to the surface as fear burned beneath it—raw, sharp, inescapable. "*No!*" I snapped, frustration lacing my words. "Have you *seen* the fog? It's not going away—it's *thickening!* Even if we make it to the bar, what makes you think we'll get any further?"

My gaze flicked toward the swirling fog behind us, curling like living tendrils, creeping closer with each second. The thinning haze that had blanketed Trenton was closing in, sealing us inside. There was no way out.

"I need air," I muttered, my voice barely audible. No one tried to stop me as I turned and walked toward a cluster of old houses. The structures loomed in the darkness, their shattered windows like hollow eyes watching me. Their decayed, skeletal shapes cast long, eerie shadows in the dim light.

Ethan's gaze followed me as I stepped into the overgrown yard of one of the homes. The grass was high and wild, brushing against my legs as the stillness of the place seeped into my skin. A chill crept through my body, and I rubbed my arms, trying to shake it off.

"Damn it! I blew a tire," Luke cursed from behind. The sound of the trunk popping open followed, his voice cutting through the quiet like a knife. I glanced back briefly, watching as Ethan and Luke worked to replace the tire, their movements quick and methodical, clinging to any semblance of control in the unfolding nightmare.

Tara and Gwen leaned against Ethan's car, their hands trembling as they lit cigarettes. The flickering glow of the lighter painted their pale faces in fleeting orange light. They smoked in silence, their eyes tracking me warily, as if afraid I might vanish into the fog.

I tilted my head back, staring at the endless, starless black sky. The weight of the emptiness pressed down on me, heavy and suffocating. My breath came out in shaky clouds of mist, and I wrapped my arms tightly around myself, desperate to anchor myself to something real.

Who or what was that? I whispered to the void, the question slipping from my lips. The darkness swallowed it whole, offering no answers—only silence.

...

After Luke and Ethan managed to secure the new tire, Luke climbed into his car and rolled it forward a few feet to test it. Ethan gave a satisfied nod, picked up the flat tire, and tossed it into the open trunk before slamming it shut with a loud *thunk*.

"Maeve!" Ethan called, his voice firm and insistent. I didn't respond. I knew what he wanted—to regroup and figure out our next move—but I wasn't ready. Not yet.

Gwen knew Luke kept a map in the glove compartment, and she pulled it out, spreading it across the hood of the car. She, Tara, and Luke huddled together, their fingers tracing roads and alternate routes as they murmured anxiously.

"Maeve," Ethan called again, this time closer. His voice startled me from my trance-like focus on the house in front of me. Something about it wasn't right. My gaze was locked on the window—on the faint flutter of curtains that shouldn't have been moving.

"I was calling you," Ethan said, his sudden presence behind me making me flinch. His hands gripped my arms gently, pulling me back into the moment.

"I swear I saw something," I whispered, spinning around and swatting his arm in frustration. "Don't sneak up on me like that!" My nerves were frayed, and my voice trembled.

Ethan scanned my face, concern etched into his features. His hand brushed a strand of hair away from my face, his touch grounding me. "We're heading back to the main road," he said softly. "This trip is over. We'll figure something out—plan another trip. For now, we—"

"There's someone in that house," I cut him off, my voice hushed but firm. I pointed toward the window, my heart pounding. Ethan followed my gaze to the fluttering curtains, and his body stiffened as he saw it too. A shadow—indistinct but undeniably there—moved inside.

"Luke, get the bat from my car," Ethan barked, his tone sharp and urgent.

Luke looked up from the map, confused. "Why do you need

the bat?"

"Just get it!" Ethan snapped, already unlocking the car with his key fob. Luke didn't question him further, jogging to the trunk and pulling out the bat Ethan always kept for emergencies.

Tara and Gwen exchanged nervous glances, their cigarettes dangling from trembling fingers as they watched the scene unfold. Smoke curled around them like a ghostly warning.

As Luke handed the bat to Ethan, a sharp crash shattered the tense silence. Glass breaking. The sound came from inside the house, loud and jarring. My breath hitched, and my chest tightened.

Ethan's expression darkened. His grip on the bat tightened, and without a word, he and Luke began moving toward the house. Their steps were slow but purposeful, the bat heavy in Ethan's hands.

I stood frozen in the yard, fear rooting me in place as they ascended the rickety steps.

The door was barely hanging on its hinges, swaying slightly in the faint breeze. With a groan of wood protesting its movement, Ethan pushed it open.

Suddenly, a blur of motion erupted from inside. A man bolted through the house, heading straight for the back door.

"LUKE, BACK DOOR!" Ethan roared, his voice slicing through the tension like a whip.

Luke reacted instantly, sprinting past me and around the side of the house. I stood frozen, my breath caught in my throat, unable to move as I watched the scene unfold. From the corner of my eye, I saw Luke dive at the man, tackling him to the ground just as he reached the back door. The impact sent both of them crashing into the dirt, a sharp grunt escaping the man's lips.

"WHAT THE—MIKE?!" Luke's voice rang out, incredulous and tinged with disbelief, as he rolled off the man. "What the hell are you doing here in Trenton?!"

Ethan appeared in the doorway, bat gripped tightly in his hand, his face a storm of confusion and barely suppressed anger.

The weight of the bat in his hand seemed to mirror the tension in the air.

"My car broke down a mile away from here," Mike muttered, sitting up and brushing dirt off his clothes. His face was pale, his eyes bloodshot and wild with exhaustion. "I crashed in this house for a couple of nights. I've been stuck here for two days, man."

The words sounded rehearsed, but there was a desperate edge to his voice. By now, Tara, Gwen, and I had edged around the side of the house, hovering near the scene like spectators to some terrible play. From my angle, I could barely make out Mike's face, but I didn't need to see him to know something was wrong. The whole situation felt off, like a puzzle missing too many pieces to make sense.

"Stay there, Maeve," Ethan barked, his voice low and firm, his grip tightening on the bat. His tone held a warning, one I couldn't ignore. Tara and Gwen pulled me back slightly, their hands gripping my arms as if to ensure I wouldn't move. I could feel the tension radiating off Ethan as he stepped toward Mike, his shoulders squared, his posture guarded.

Luke hauled Mike to his feet, gripping his arm with a strength that made Mike wince. He dragged him back toward the house, shoving him into the dimly lit interior as Ethan followed, his jaw clenched, every muscle in his body coiled like a spring ready to snap.

Outside, we were left in tense, suffocating silence. I didn't know what was said inside until much later, when Ethan and Luke filled in the blanks. They had confronted Mike, cornering him in the dim light of the living room.

"Start talking," Luke demanded, his tone cold, his usual easy-going nature gone. "What the hell are you really doing in Trenton?"

Mike yanked his arm free, glaring at Luke. "I told you! I was driving through on my way to New Port. I live and work there," he said defensively, his voice rising with frustration. "The fog came out of nowhere. I blew two tires near the bend on the highway. I ditched the car behind some bushes and walked here. I've been holed up ever since, waiting for someone to pass by so I could hitch a ride."

He folded his arms tightly across his chest, his eyes darting between Ethan and Luke. But his defensive stance only made him look more suspicious. Ethan's knuckles whitened as his grip on the bat tightened further, his eyes narrowing as though he could see straight through Mike's words.

Something didn't add up. The way Mike spoke, the way his voice quivered ever so slightly despite his tough exterior—it had all felt wrong. And judging by the grim look on Ethan's face, Luke had noticed it too.

"That's all?" Ethan spat, his eyes narrowing as he lowered the bat slightly, though his grip remained ironclad. His body was taut, a coiled spring ready to snap.

"Yeah, why would I lie about that, man? I'm being honest," Mike said, his hands raised in a placating gesture, his voice strained. For a moment, Ethan seemed to ease his stance, but when Mike's gaze flicked toward the door at the sound of our voices outside, the tension snapped like a live wire.

"Maeve's with you? Is she doing okay?" Mike asked. The words were barely out of his mouth before Ethan lunged. In an instant, he had Mike pinned against the wall, the bat pressed hard against his chest, his face inches from Mike's.

"Stay away from Maeve," Ethan growled through clenched teeth, his voice low and seething. "Don't talk to her. Don't even look at her... after what you did..."

Mike's eyes widened in panic, his breaths coming in shallow gasps as he struggled against the pressure of the bat. Luke rushed forward, grabbing Ethan by the shoulders and pulling him back with force.

"Don't, Ethan," Luke warned, stepping between them, his arm outstretched to keep Ethan away.

Mike stumbled forward slightly, rubbing his chest as he tried to catch his breath. "What the hell is your problem, man?" he snapped, his voice hoarse. "I didn't have a choice, okay? I broke up with her. It's over. It's ancient history."

Ancient history or not, the room was thick with tension, every breath heavy and stifling. Ethan reluctantly stepped back, his jaw clenched so tightly I thought it might shatter.

By the time Ethan moved away, I had stepped into the room, Gwen and Tara trailing behind me. The sight of Mike hit me like a jolt to the chest. My breath caught, my voice shaky as I finally managed to speak.

"Mike?" I said, the word tasting bitter in my mouth. Anger and confusion swirled inside me, threatening to spill over.

Ethan's eyes immediately flicked to me, his hand brushing against my arm protectively. His touch was grounding but also stifling.

Mike met my gaze, his expression unreadable. "Maeve…" he began, his tone softer, but whatever words he was about to say were cut off when I raised my hand.

"What are you doing in Trenton?" I asked, keeping my voice steady despite the storm brewing inside me. The question was simple, but the weight behind it was anything but.

Mike shifted on his feet, glancing at Luke as though seeking an ally. "Look, can you just drop me off at the end of Trenton?" he said, his voice edging toward desperation. "I'll figure it out from there. I just need to get to New Port."

Ethan scoffed, the sound cutting through the room like a knife. "Outside. Now," Luke muttered, gripping Mike's arm and dragging him toward the back door.

Tara and Gwen followed, their voices rising in sharp disagreement, clearly opposed to whatever Mike had proposed.

I stood rooted to the spot, my thoughts racing, my emotions threatening to overwhelm me. Ethan's touch on my arm jolted me back, but I shook him off, my voice low but cutting. "Why is Mike here? What is he doing in this area?"

Ethan avoided my gaze, his jaw tightening as he exhaled sharply. "Don't worry about it, Maeve," he said, his tone strained but firm. "Let's just get back on the road, okay?"

His hand brushed against my cheek briefly—a gesture meant to reassure me—but it only left me more unsettled. Without waiting for my response, he turned and followed the others toward the back door, leaving me standing alone, my thoughts spinning.

Something didn't add up. Mike's presence here wasn't a coincidence, and Ethan knew more than he was letting on.

Outside, we gathered near the cars again. Ethan and Luke huddled behind Luke's car, their conversation growing increasingly heated. Though their voices were low, their tense movements gave away the argument's intensity. Ethan's hands sliced through the air, gesturing toward me, his anger evident in every motion. I couldn't hear the exact words, but the sharpness of Ethan's voice carried fragments through the still night.

"I'm not taking him with us—not after what he did to Maeve," Ethan snapped, loud enough for me to catch.

I crossed my arms, leaning against the car, my stomach twisting in knots. How had the night spiraled this far out of control? What had started as a road trip to the manor had morphed into something none of us had been prepared for. The weight of the moment pressed down on me, suffocating and unrelenting.

Mike stood apart from the others, his back to the decrepit house he'd been hiding in. Gwen and Tara hovered close by, their unease written across their faces. The silence was thick, stretching between us like a taut string waiting to snap.

"You doing okay, Maeve?" Mike's voice broke the quiet. It was calm, but it carried an emptiness that grated on my nerves. I turned my head away, biting my lip, refusing to respond. Talking to him was the last thing I wanted to do.

Before Mike could push further, Ethan's voice cut through, sharp and final. "You're coming with us. Keep your mouth shut, and we'll drop you off at the edge of Trenton. After that, you're gone."

I hadn't noticed Ethan and Luke walking back toward us until they were standing right there. Ethan's cold glare locked onto Mike as he shoved past him, his jaw tight with barely contained fury.

"He's got quite the temper," Mike muttered under his breath, glancing in my direction like he expected me to agree or soften. I kept my eyes fixed on the car, the bitterness rising in my throat.

Luke stepped forward, his voice firm and unyielding. "If you've got anything inside, grab it now. You're riding with them," he said, jerking his head toward Ethan's car.

Mike hesitated, his gaze flicking between me and Ethan, who was already gripping the steering wheel so tightly his knuckles were white. Without waiting for a response, I moved to the passenger side and opened the door, sliding in silently.

Mike turned reluctantly and trudged back toward the house, disappearing into the shadows. Luke stood rigid, arms crossed, his eyes never leaving the door. In the distance, Gwen and Tara's hushed argument spilled into the air, their words sharp and resentful. Gwen's loyalty to me clashed with Tara's long-standing hatred of Mike—a tension that mirrored my own emotions.

Inside the car, silence wrapped around Ethan and me like a suffocating blanket. Neither of us spoke, but the atmosphere buzzed with unspoken words and unresolved anger.

Through the windshield, I saw Mike emerge from the house, a small bag slung over his shoulder. Luke intercepted him, his towering frame blocking the path to the car. "Listen up," Luke said, his voice low and dangerous. "Maeve is like a sister to me. You so much as look at her wrong, and I'll make sure you can't walk for a month. You got that?"

Mike stiffened but didn't back down. He gave a tight nod, the tension between them palpable. Without a word, he reached for the back door of Ethan's car. The brief moment of defiance in his eyes faded, replaced by something closer to resignation as he pulled the door open and got inside. Luke stood there for a moment longer, watching him, his muscles coiled with tension. Only when Mike was securely inside did Luke step away, his jaw still clenched.

As Ethan started the engine, the car seemed to hum with the weight of everything unsaid. I stared straight ahead, my fingers gripping the edge of my seat, every nerve in my body on edge. Mike might have been riding with us now, but the distance between us—emotional and physical—felt insurmountable. This was far from over.

The fog clung to the landscape like a living thing, swirling in thick, dense waves as we crept along the gravel road, inching our way out of Trenton. Ethan gripped the steering wheel tightly, his eyes straining through the haze. It had taken nearly an hour to navigate through the ghost town, and now the night pressed in on us, stretching what was supposed to be a one-hour drive to the manor into an endless ordeal.

Ahead, the road split in two directions: right would take us back on the path we needed, away from the fog, while left led toward New Port.

"If you take a left here, there's a fork. I can get out there," Mike's voice broke the silence from the back seat. His tone was casual, but I could sense an urgency beneath it. I hadn't even realized how much time had passed since we'd entered Trenton—everything felt like a blur.

Ethan remained silent, completely ignoring Mike's suggestion, his jaw clenched as he stared straight ahead. The headlights from Luke's car glared in the rearview mirror, his vehicle trailing closely behind us.

"Okay, did you hear me, man?" Mike repeated, more insistent this time. "You can park here, and I'll take the left road."

Ethan's grip on the wheel tightened, and his silence only grew heavier. His focus stayed locked on the road as though Mike hadn't spoken at all. The weight of the moment pressed down on all of us like a suffocating force. I glanced at Ethan, my frustration building. Without thinking, I reached over and tapped his arm.

"Ethan," I said, my voice low but firm.

He glanced at me briefly, his eyes flickering with anger, concern, and something else—something I couldn't quite place. Then he exhaled sharply, his voice cutting through the silence. "Maeve," he said suddenly, his tone almost a plea. "Whatever happens next… just stay close to me. Don't wander off, don't argue—just stay where I can see you."

The intensity of his words startled me. I nodded slowly, my throat tight with unspoken questions. His protective tone wasn't new, but there was something deeper in it now, something that made my pulse quicken.

Mike grumbled from the back seat, leaning back with a resigned sigh. "Fine," he muttered, his voice filled with annoyance.

Ethan finally spoke, his voice cold and deliberate. "We're taking the right. The fog should clear up soon. I'll drop you off three miles up the road—there's a bus station two miles east from there."

Mike muttered something under his breath, but he didn't argue further. Ethan slowly accelerated, the car picking up speed as we finally left Trenton behind. The fog began to thin, but the tension inside the car only thickened.

I sat in silence, stealing glances at Ethan. His expression was unreadable, his features tense and closed off. There was no warmth in his eyes, no trace of the usual protectiveness that he wore like armor. Just a cold, flat stare as he focused on the road. Something wasn't right. I could feel it gnawing at the pit of my stomach. Ethan wasn't just trying to get Mike out of here. He wanted to keep him close—to maintain control over him.

Maybe it was to ensure Mike didn't disappear too quickly. Or maybe Ethan had something else in mind, something darker. I shifted uncomfortably in my seat, my thoughts racing. Whatever Ethan's intentions were, they weren't good.

Luke's voice crackled through the CB. "Ethan, you passed the split. It leads to the fork where Mike needs—"

Before he could finish, Ethan reached over and snapped the CB off.

"ETHAN!" I shouted, my frustration boiling over. He ignored me, pulling the car over onto the right shoulder. We were in an empty clearing, the kind of place that felt too quiet, like the world had stopped moving. Towering trees loomed around us, their twisted branches stretching into the night. The fog had thinned to a wispy haze, swirling like ghostly smoke at the edges of the headlights.

Luke, clearly worried, pulled in behind us. His headlights carved long, eerie shadows through the haze, adding to the tension thickening the air. Ethan's knuckles were white on the steering wheel. His voice was calm, but it vibrated with restrained fury. "Listen, jerk, we're heading to Aberdeen Manor—my parents' old place. Before we get to the road that leads to the mansion, I'll drop you off."

The sharpness in his tone sliced through the silence, heavy and dangerous. Mike didn't flinch. His face remained unreadable, like he had nothing left to lose. Leaning forward slightly, he smirked, his voice oozing with sarcasm. "Aberdeen Manor? Maeve told me about that place. What is it now, thirty years old? Sounds cozy."

Ethan's jaw tightened, his nostrils flaring as he stared straight ahead. "It's none of your business. You'll get out, and after that, I don't ever want to see your face again." His grip on the steering wheel tightened as if he were barely holding himself back.

Before Ethan could unleash more, I reached out and swatted his arm. "Stop it!" I whispered, my voice trembling. The tension between them was suffocating, a toxic pressure that was eating away at all of us. I just wanted it to end.

Ethan glanced at me, his expression softening for a fleeting moment before he shifted in his seat and exhaled sharply. He reached over and flicked the CB back on, the static filling the car. Luke's voice immediately broke through. "What the hell, Ethan? What are you doing?"

"We're fine, Luke. Heading back out," Ethan replied, his tone steady but laced with exhaustion.

Luke muttered something under his breath—probably a string of creative curses—but didn't push further. The CB fell silent again, and Ethan pulled back onto the road.

The drive stretched on, the hum of the engine the only sound. Outside, the night pressed in, cold and endless. I shivered, the chill creeping into the car despite the heat being on.

I reached into the back seat for my jacket, my hand brushing past Mike. He noticed and handed it to me without a word. His fingers grazed mine briefly, and I pulled back quickly, slipping the jacket on and hugging it close for warmth.

The tension in the car was thick, suffocating in its silence. My stomach growled, breaking the stillness, and I remembered the bag of food in the back seat. I grabbed it and rummaged through until I found a burger. Unwrapping it, I held it out to Ethan.

"Here. Eat," I said softly, trying to pierce through the wall of tension. Ethan took the burger without a word, his focus fixed on the road.

Hesitating for a moment, I glanced back at Mike. He sat there, silent and detached, staring out the window like he wasn't even part of this anymore. Against my better judgment, I held out a burger to him too. Mike's eyes flicked to me, surprised. For a second, I thought he'd refuse, but he took it, his voice quieter than I'd ever heard it. "Thanks."

The silence returned, but it wasn't as sharp. Uneasy, yes, but it wasn't the biting, suffocating quiet that had followed us out of Trenton.

As the miles stretched on and the road narrowed, the cold seemed to seep deeper into my bones. I pulled my jacket tighter around me, the thought of Aberdeen Manor looming larger in my mind. It was as if the house itself was waiting for us, its heavy presence reaching out through the dark, already pulling us into its grasp.

The drive ahead would take exactly nine and a half hours before we merged onto the road that led to the mansion. The silence in the car was oppressive, each of us lost in our own thoughts. After what felt like an eternity, Ethan pulled over to the side of the road for a quick bathroom break. The air had grown colder, biting through the fog that had thinned to reveal a starless sky. Ethan and Luke stepped out first, disappearing into the shadows beyond the car.

I stayed inside, the engine idling softly. Mike sat directly behind me, the tension between us almost unbearable. "May," he murmured, his voice low and hesitant. I stared out the window, refusing to acknowledge him, willing the moment to pass.

"It's been four years," he continued, his tone threaded with something that sounded like regret. My eyes locked on Tara and Gwen, who were partially hidden behind a tree. I kept pretending not to hear him.

"You're still as beautiful as you were in high school," Mike said, his words cutting through the silence, uninvited and unwelcome. I clenched my jaw, my grip tightening on the edge of my seat. The compliment sat heavy between us, like a thread pulling at wounds I had no intention of reopening.

Ethan reappeared, his steps deliberate, his face hard with unease. Without a word, I opened the door and stepped out into the frigid night air, desperate to escape the suffocating tension. Mike followed, his eyes on me. For a brief moment, we stood still, facing each other, caught in a silent standoff of unresolved memories and unspoken tension.

Ethan's gaze burned into Mike from behind, his posture rigid, his presence a warning. Mike finally looked away, his expression unreadable as he turned left and disappeared into the trees. I moved toward Tara and Gwen, each step heavier than the last as the unease clawed at my skin.

Tara and Gwen stood nearby, chatting in hushed voices. I

joined them, forcing myself to focus on the mundane task of brushing dirt from my hands after finishing my business. But then I saw him.

The air froze in my lungs.

The dark figure—the same one we'd seen before—stood just three feet away, partially obscured by the trees. His silhouette was unmistakable: the man in the fedora. He didn't move. He just stood there, his presence oppressive, his unseen eyes boring into me like they could peel away every layer of my being.

I stumbled back, gasping, the world narrowing to the outline of that trench coat and fedora. Tara and Gwen noticed my sudden stillness, their heads snapping toward me in alarm. The man moved—just barely—a slow, deliberate motion as his hand slid into his coat.

I didn't wait to see what he was reaching for.

The panic surged through me, wild and uncontrollable. I screamed, the sound ripping through the stillness of the night. My body collided with Tara and Gwen as I stumbled backward, my limbs trembling.

"MAEVE?!" Ethan's voice rang out, sharp with fear and urgency.

Tara and Gwen grabbed my arms, their faces pale and frozen in terror. We turned together and ran, our steps uneven and desperate, crashing toward the cars. Ethan, Luke, and even Mike sprinted to meet us, their expressions a mix of confusion and alarm.

"What happened? What's wrong?" Ethan grabbed my arms, his hands firm, his eyes frantic as they searched mine for answers.

I tried to speak, but the words caught in my throat, my chest tight with fear. Luke shook Gwen gently, his voice low and urgent as he tried to snap her out of her daze.

Finally, I managed to choke out the words, each syllable trembling. "He's here… the man in the fedora. We saw him."

The weight of my words settled over the group, the reality of the threat sinking in.

"Get in the cars," Luke barked, taking control. He pulled Tara and Gwen toward his car with swift, precise movements. Mike, his earlier arrogance stripped away, hurried back to Ethan's car without protest. I slid into the passenger seat, my hands shaking as I fumbled with the seatbelt. My breath came in shallow gasps, and the cold sweat clinging to my skin refused to fade.

Whatever waited for us at Aberdeen Manor felt closer now, like it was reaching out, pulling us into its grasp.

My heart was still pounding, the adrenaline from the encounter coursing through my veins. Ethan came around the car, his movements stiff and deliberate as he slid behind the wheel. For a moment, his eyes flicked toward me, questions lingering there, but he didn't say anything. The engine roared to life, and the car lurched forward, leaving the clearing—and that eerie figure—behind.

"Who, Maeve? What happened? What did you see?" Ethan's voice was tight, almost frantic, as he accelerated away from the spot we'd just left.

I swallowed hard, my throat dry, and forced the words out. "The man... the man in the fedora," I stammered, my voice shaking. Saying it aloud made it all feel too real, the weight of the encounter pressing down on me.

"Fedora?" Mike scoffed from the back seat, his tone dripping with skepticism. Still, there was a slight edge of unease there, betraying the bravado in his voice. Before I could respond, Ethan let out a long breath and started recounting the night's events— the fog, the strange encounters, the suffocating sense of being watched. His words were clipped, his tone measured, like he was trying to make sense of it himself as he spoke.

"Just get us off this road," I muttered, tapping my hands nervously on the dashboard, my eyes darting to the dark trees lining the road. Every shadow felt alive, every flicker of movement a potential threat.

"Maeve, calm down," Ethan said, his voice softer now, an attempt to soothe me. "We'll be through this in an hour, and then it's just open highway—no trees, nothing but road."

His words were meant to reassure, but they barely touched the fear gripping my chest. The image of the man in the trench coat loomed large in my mind, his silhouette burned into my memory.

"Seriously?" Mike's voice cut through the tension, his mocking tone grating on my nerves. "A man in a hat and trench coat? Come on, Maeve."

That was Mike. If he didn't see it with his own eyes, it didn't exist. Everything was a joke to him unless it directly impacted his life. His flippant attitude was infuriating, especially now, when everything was dangerously real. My hands trembled, and I clenched them into fists, pressing them against my thighs to steady myself.

"I don't care what you think, Mike," I snapped, turning in my seat to glare at him. "I know how you are. I know what kind of jerk you can be. Believe it or not, we all saw him."

My voice was firm, but it carried the unmistakable tremble of fear. I was trying to sound confident, but the tension in my body betrayed me. My hands shook, my chest tightened, and I could feel the energy of the moment vibrating through me. Ethan remained silent, but the way he gripped the wheel told me everything I needed to know—he was just as on edge. The car sped faster, the engine straining as he pushed it to nearly 100 km/h. The fog thinned, giving way to the dark expanse of open road, but the unease inside the car was as heavy as ever.

Mike let out a quiet chuckle, the sound cutting through the silence like nails on a chalkboard. "Okay, sure, Maeve. A mysterious man in a hat lurking in the middle of nowhere—sounds like something out of a bad horror movie."

I clenched my jaw, forcing myself to stay quiet. Fighting with

Mike wouldn't help; it never did. I stared out the window, willing the tension in my chest to dissipate, but it clung to me, thick and unrelenting.

Ethan glanced at me briefly, concern flickering in his eyes. "Just try to breathe, okay?" he said softly, his voice breaking through the storm of panic in my mind.

I nodded but didn't trust myself to speak. My heart pounded in my ears, drowning out the sound of the engine. The memory of the man—the way he had stood there, impossibly close, watching—refused to fade. We weren't imagining it. I wasn't imagining it. And no matter how far we drove, I couldn't shake the feeling that we hadn't left him behind.

As we finally emerged from the suffocating fog, the trees behind us faded into dark silhouettes, swallowed whole by the night. The air felt different—lighter, yes, but no less eerie. We had found the road we needed, a long, empty stretch of black asphalt that disappeared into the void ahead. No trees. No shadows lurking at the edges. Just road.

The absence of the fog should have been comforting, but it wasn't. The vast emptiness surrounding us felt just as menacing, as though we had traded one prison for another. The moonless sky above offered no solace, only amplifying the isolation. The car's headlights carved a narrow path through the darkness, illuminating nothing but the barren road. I should have felt relief. We were out of Trenton, out of the fog. But something gnawed at me—a deep, unsettling feeling that we weren't truly alone.

The hair on the back of my neck prickled, and I couldn't shake the sensation of being watched. The kind of watchfulness that made your skin crawl, like unseen eyes boring into your back, waiting for you to slip.

Ethan kept his eyes locked on the road, his grip on the steering wheel tight, his shoulders stiff with tension. He hadn't spoken since we left the fog behind, and the silence in the car was deafening. None of us dared to break it, as though speaking would shatter the fragile barrier keeping the darkness at bay.

Even Mike, who always had something smart to say, leaned back in his seat, unnervingly quiet. The sarcasm and casual arrogance he carried like a shield had vanished, leaving behind something I wasn't used to seeing in him: unease.

The road stretched endlessly before us, empty and still. And yet, I couldn't shake the feeling that something was still following us, lurking just beyond the reach of the headlights. The man in the fedora—the shadowy figure that had appeared in the fog—had vanished, but his presence hadn't. It clung to the edges of my thoughts like a dark whisper, impossible to ignore.

I glanced into the rearview mirror, half-expecting to see him standing on the road behind us, silhouetted against the faint glow of the moonless horizon. My breath caught as my eyes searched the darkness, my heart pounding with every second. But there was nothing. Just the fading outline of the trees dissolving into the black void behind us. Still, the unease didn't leave. Even if I couldn't see him, I could feel him—watching, waiting, biding his time.

We had escaped the fog.
But we hadn't escaped him.

END OF THE ROAD

WE HAD STOPPED FOR the second time on the side of the road. The emptiness around us was suffocating, the night darker and heavier than ever. If we made it to Aberdeen Manor, it would be just as dawn was breaking—or so we hoped. The clock read 2 a.m., and none of us had slept for more than a few stolen minutes.

Luke and Gwen had taken turns driving, while Tara slept most of the trip away in the backseat. The rest of us were running on fumes. Ethan hadn't slept at all, nor did he plan to. He didn't trust Mike being awake while I drove, and the tension between the two of them simmered just below the surface.

"I'll sleep at the house when we get there," Ethan had said for the third time, but I knew better. He was running on pure adrenaline, his protective instincts cranked up to full volume. I let him have his empty promises but ignored them all the same.

We stepped out of the cars, stretching and breathing in the cold night air. Exhaustion weighed heavy on me. I hadn't slept in two nights, haunted by the same inexplicable nightmares, and all I wanted was to reach the manor and collapse. The thought of that cold, ancient house being my only sanctuary was unsettling, but even that sounded better than the road.

I wandered a little away from everyone, needing space, each step carrying me farther into the open field. I felt Ethan's eyes burning into me with every inch of distance I put between us. His gaze never wavered, as though he expected something to happen the moment I wasn't under his watch.

I stopped in the middle of the field, staring up at the void above me. No moon. No stars. Just an endless blanket of darkness that seemed to stretch forever, as though the world had been swallowed whole.

By Luke's car, Tara and Gwen stood talking in low voices, their figures barely visible in the shadows. Meanwhile, Luke and Ethan were bent over the map, their conversation quiet but tense. Ethan was focused, but his eyes darted toward me every few seconds, his anxiety pressing against me like a physical weight.

Mike, who had been silent for too long, decided to insert himself into the conversation. His tone, uncharacteristically serious, cut through the quiet.

"If you're heading to Aberdeen, this road will take us another five hours before we hit the split to the manor," he said, leaning over the map. His finger traced a different path, stopping at a three-way fork. "But if we take the left in two miles, it'll bring us directly to the manor gates. Cuts the trip down by hours."

Ethan's head snapped toward him, his suspicion visible in every line of his face. "How do you know we'll end up at the gates on this road?" His voice was sharp, a low growl of mistrust.

Mike hesitated, glancing at me briefly before diverting his

gaze back to the map. "You might not like me, Ethan, but I was in a relationship with your sister. Remember Christmas, four years ago? Your great-aunt—married to your uncle, the one who disappeared—mentioned this road. She told your dad that investigators used it because it was faster and safer."

Ethan's expression tightened, his brow furrowing as though he was trying to recall the memory. The tension between them was thick, like the fog we'd just escaped, curling around us and making it hard to breathe.

That Christmas came back to me in hazy fragments. Our families had gathered—Luke's, Gwen's, and even Tara's parents. The house had been full of people, the air charged with unspoken grief. I remembered my great-aunt's voice as she spoke to our parents about the investigation, still ongoing, still searching for my uncle. Ethan had been there too, standing close by, overhearing everything just as Mike had.

The memory pressed against me like an old scar, one that hadn't quite healed.

"I was the only one who didn't hear that conversation," I muttered to myself, the memory faint but unsettling.

"We're not taking that road," Ethan said firmly, his voice low and edged with anger. His protectiveness over me was crashing head-on with his distrust of Mike, and it was clear he wasn't going to be swayed easily.

Mike's jaw tightened, his temper simmering just beneath the surface. "The cops said it was safer than the other route, Ethan. You remember what they told your mother when they broke the news about your uncle. The road to the manor is dangerous— wolves, coyotes, whatever the hell it is, those animals own that road."

Ethan's face darkened, his jaw clenching as old wounds threatened to resurface. I knew the mention of the police—the night they came to deliver the news—was like a punch to the gut. He'd been the one to open the door, to stand there in the hallway while they explained what had happened, their words leaving cracks in our family that had never fully healed.

"The road to your family's mansion is dangerous," the investigator had told our parents that night. "We don't know why, but it's not safe. Animals roam that area—possibly wolves. It's the most direct route to the manor, but it's risky."

"That's where they think your uncle disappeared," Mike added, his tone challenging, as if daring Ethan to deny it.

"Ethan, Mike's right," Luke chimed in, his voice calm but firm. "We can't take that risk, no matter how much time it saves. The left road is safer."

Ethan's glare shifted to Mike, his chest rising and falling with the weight of the decision. His eyes flicked between Luke and Mike, his mind clearly working through a battle of logic and emotion. I could see the struggle playing out in his tense posture, the way his hands balled into fists at his sides.

Finally, he nodded, though his reluctance was clear. His gaze landed on me, softening slightly as if he was seeking reassurance—or maybe silently reminding himself why he was choosing caution over stubbornness. I stood still, unmoving, watching from the edge of the group, unsure whether to step in or stay quiet.

The air between them was thick with tension, the unspoken distrust crackling like static in the cold night. Ethan's overwhelming need to protect me clashed with his instinct to ignore Mike entirely. Logic had won—for now—but it was obvious that it wouldn't take much to ignite the smoldering conflict between them.

...

The car remained eerily silent as we got back on the road, the tension thick enough to suffocate. Mike had finally dozed off in the back seat, his steady breathing the only sound breaking the stillness. I stayed wide awake, my eyes locked on the endless black road ahead. The emptiness surrounding us pressed in, heavy and oppressive. There was nothing out here—no trees, no lights—just darkness stretching endlessly in all directions.

"I'm sorry," Ethan said suddenly, his voice cutting through the silence.

I turned to him, surprised. He kept his eyes on the road, his grip on the steering wheel tight. "I know you have a past with Mike," he continued, his tone low but steady. "I just don't trust him right now. Everything he said about being stuck in that house… it doesn't sit right with me."

I reached over, resting a hand on his arm. "I get it," I said softly. "But right now, all I want is to get off this damn road, get to the mansion, sleep, and eat. That's it." I managed a weak smile, hoping to lighten the mood. "Maybe if the phone still works there, we can call Mom and Dad, let them know we're okay."

Ethan nodded, though the worry in his eyes didn't fade. None of our phones had worked since we left the bar. It was like we'd crossed into some isolated bubble, cut off from the rest of the world.

"If you want, Maeve…" Ethan's voice trailed off, hesitation thick in the air.

Before he could finish, I tapped his arm, playful this time, trying to break the tension. But he flinched, brushing my hand away with more force than I expected.

"Cut it out!" he muttered, sharper than usual. His eyes flicked toward me briefly, frustration breaking through his usual calm.

I blinked, startled, but before I could respond, he sighed, his shoulders sagging. "I was going to say… if you want Mike to stay at the manor, I'll allow it." His voice was softer now, almost resigned.

The words hung in the air, heavy and uncomfortable. The idea of Mike staying with us for four days hadn't even crossed my mind. The thought felt wrong—like inviting chaos into an already fragile situation. I turned my gaze to the window, staring into the endless night as my thoughts churned. Did I want Mike there? Could I handle being around him for that long, with all the unresolved history between us?

The car jerked suddenly as Ethan slammed on the brakes, throwing me forward against the seatbelt. My heart leapt into my throat as Luke's car screeched to a stop behind us, his horn blaring.

"Damn it," Ethan muttered, gripping the wheel tightly.

I snapped my eyes to the road ahead, searching for what had caused the sudden stop. Illuminated in the headlights was a pack of wolves, their eyes glowing like embers in the pale beams. Four, maybe five, stood in the middle of the road, perfectly still, their presence unnervingly calm.

Ethan honked the horn, the sound shattering the silence. The wolves didn't move. They didn't snarl or growl, didn't bare their teeth. They simply stood there, watching us, as if guarding the road.

"What the hell?" I whispered, my stomach twisting with unease.

At the head of the pack stood a tall, majestic female wolf with deep brown fur. Her eyes locked onto mine through the windshield, and for a moment, it felt like she was speaking to me—warning me. A shiver ran down my spine as I stared back, frozen by the intensity of her gaze.

"Wait," I said suddenly, placing a hand on Ethan's arm as he went to honk again. "Don't. I don't think they're dangerous."

Ethan shot me a skeptical glance. "Maeve, they're wolves. Of course, they're dangerous."

"No," I insisted, my voice trembling but firm. "They're not here to hurt us. It's like… they're trying to stop us from going further. Like they're warning us."

Ethan hesitated, his eyes flicking between me and the wolves. The tension in the car was thick, his disbelief clear in his furrowed brow.

"Seriously?" he said, his voice sharp with doubt. "They're

wild animals. They're probably hungry or planning to attack."

From the back seat, Mike leaned forward, his voice groggy but serious. "I don't know, man. I'm with Maeve on this one. Something about this feels… off."

The wolves didn't move, their eerie stillness sending a chill through the air. The road ahead seemed to stretch into an endless void, but in that moment, it felt like the wolves were the only thing standing between us and something far worse.

"You've been watching too many wilderness movies," I muttered under my breath, trying to mask the tension tightening in my chest. My eyes locked onto the female wolf, her piercing gaze never leaving mine. "Look at her. It's like she's trying to tell us something. I can feel it."

Ethan clenched his jaw, his expression a storm of uncertainty. He shifted the car back into drive and inched forward, the engine humming softly as he accelerated cautiously toward the wolves. They didn't move, standing their ground as if daring us to push through. The female leader remained unyielding, her regal stance illuminated by the headlights. Her fur shimmered in the pale light, and she seemed larger than life—almost supernatural.

Ethan hesitated, his knuckles tightening on the steering wheel. Rolling down the window slightly, he leaned out into the cold night air. "Come on, move! Please!" he called, his voice cutting through the eerie silence.

What happened next left us all stunned. The female wolf lowered her head, a slow, deliberate motion that felt almost… respectful. Then she let out a low, haunting howl that seemed to resonate through the stillness, sending shivers down my spine. In perfect unison, the pack began to part, moving to either side of the road as though they had been waiting for this moment.

Ethan exhaled slowly, his shoulders relaxing as he pressed the accelerator. The car crept forward, the wolves holding their positions as we passed. Luke followed closely behind, his headlights casting long shadows across the pack. I could hear the soft, mournful howls rising behind us, echoing faintly in the distance.

Turning my head, I watched as the wolves began running alongside the car, their forms gliding effortlessly through the fields like ghostly sentinels.

At least a dozen wolves surrounded us now, their movement fluid and graceful. They stayed with us, flanking the cars like an otherworldly escort. It didn't feel threatening—it felt purposeful. They weren't chasing us. They were guiding us.

For nearly a mile, the wolves ran silently beside us, their eyes glinting in the dim light. My pulse raced as I watched them, a strange mix of fear and awe flooding my senses. It was impossible to ignore the feeling that they knew something we didn't—that they were leading us somewhere. Or protecting us.

Then, just as suddenly as they had appeared, the pack began to slow. The female wolf came to an abrupt stop, her powerful frame illuminated by a sliver of moonlight that broke through the dense clouds. She lifted her head and let out one final, piercing howl—a sound that seemed to carry a warning, or perhaps a farewell. One by one, the rest of the pack stopped and dispersed, melting into the darkness of the fields around us.

Ethan's fingers dug into the steering wheel, his hands rigid with tension. "What the hell was that?" he muttered, his voice barely audible.

I couldn't answer. My breath was shallow, my heart pounding in my chest as my mind raced with questions. The wolves hadn't attacked us. They had cleared a path. They had run beside us like guardians. But why? What were they guiding us toward—or away from?

The car hummed softly as we continued down the road, the oppressive quiet settling in once again. The trees had thinned, the fields stretching endlessly on either side of us, but the weight of what had just happened lingered in the air. As the wolves' howls faded from earshot, they echoed in my mind—a haunting reminder that whatever lay ahead, we were far from alone.

...

By 4:00 a.m., the first slivers of sunlight began creeping over the horizon, painting the sky with soft streaks of orange and pink. Relief washed over me as the night's oppressive darkness began to retreat. Daylight felt like a shield—nothing sinister could hide in the daylight, right?

Ethan noticed my shoulders relax, a small smile tugging at the corners of his lips. He drummed his fingers on the steering wheel, clearly just as happy as I was to see the sunrise. No wolves, no shadows—just an endless stretch of open road ahead. We still had three hours before the highway split, where we'd decide our final route to Aberdeen Manor. For the first time in hours, the tension in the car had eased.

Then I saw Ethan's hand drifting toward the stereo.

"No!" I warned, swatting his hand away. "Don't even think about putting on that country crap."

He shot me a devilish grin, his hand darting right back toward the dial.

"I swear to God, Ethan, if you play that garbage—"

Before I could finish, the unmistakable twang of a country song filled the car. My eyes widened in horror as Ethan grinned ear to ear and started singing along with exaggerated gusto.

"I got a truck full of beer and a heart full of pain..."

"AUGH!" I groaned, throwing my head back dramatically. "Why? Why do you hate me?"

Ethan, not missing a beat, pointed at me with one hand while keeping the other on the wheel.

"This song speaks to me, Maeve. It's about my pain… dealing with you," he said with a mockingly solemn expression before belting out the next line even louder.

"She took the dog and left me the rain!"

Mike, now fully awake, burst out laughing. "Man, this is the best thing I've seen all night," he managed between gasps for air.

I glared at both of them, but the ridiculousness of it all chipped away at my annoyance. Despite myself, I felt a smile tug at my lips. The absurdity of it all—the off-key singing, Mike's uncontrollable laughter, and Ethan's ridiculous grin—was almost therapeutic. After everything we'd been through, maybe we needed this. A little stupid fun to break the tension.

"Fine!" I threw my hands up in surrender. "Sing your heart out, cowboy, but don't blame me if I rip that stereo out and drive this car off a cliff."

Ethan winked, cranking the volume up another notch. "Challenge accepted."

For twenty torturous minutes, he serenaded us with the worst rendition of country music imaginable, pausing only to take deep breaths and throw in even more exaggerated twang.

"She stole my heart and left me the pain…" Ethan sang, dragging out every syllable like it was a grand finale.

Mike was practically rolling in the back seat, and even I was struggling to keep a straight face. Then, mercifully, the radio signal began to fade, dissolving into static.

"Damn it," Ethan muttered, twisting the dial in search of a new station. "I wasn't finished with my masterpiece."

"Thank God for bad reception," I said, rolling my eyes.

But as he flipped through the frequencies, a faint, distorted voice crackled through the speakers. "Huh," I said, leaning forward. "What's that?"

Ethan paused, his hand hovering over the dial. We both strained to listen as the voice became clearer.

"Radio CB 18915, this is lieutenant Michaels broadcasting on channel 9, do you copy?" The voice was faint, distorted by static, but unmistakably real.

Ethan froze, his expression shifting from amused to alarmed in an instant. "That's not the stereo," he said, his voice low.

"That's the CB."

He reached for the receiver, glancing at me before pressing the button. "This is 18915," he replied, his tone steady but sharp with curiosity. "How'd you catch our signal? Who is this?"

Without another word, Ethan flicked on the turn signal and pulled over onto the shoulder. The sudden seriousness in his demeanor made my heart race. The sunlight streaming through the windows felt less comforting now, as if the humor from moments ago had been sucked out of the air.

I quickly turned off the radio, my focus locked on the CB. Mike leaned forward, his usual smugness gone, as we all listened intently. Whatever was happening, it wasn't just another random frequency. It felt like the night wasn't done with us yet.

"Is this Ethan Adams?" the voice on the CB asked. Ethan shot me a sharp look, his surprise mirroring my own.

"Maybe," he replied cautiously, his grip on the receiver tightening. "Who's asking?"

"I thought I mentioned that, boy—lieutenant Michaels from Nebraska. It took me hours to catch yer signal. Where are y'all headed?" The man's thick American drawl added an unsettling weight to his words. I glanced at Ethan, unease creeping into my chest. Who was this man? And how the hell did he know Ethan's name?

"We're, uh, south of Trenton, heading to our—" Ethan hesitated, his voice faltering. He clearly didn't trust the situation, and something in his tone warned me that he wasn't about to spill more than necessary.

"I know where ya are," Michaels interrupted, his voice steady but carrying a note of urgency. "Yer parents told me how to find ya and gave me a message to pass along."

Ethan's jaw clenched, his knuckles white around the receiver. "What message?"

A brief pause followed, the kind that seemed to stretch endlessly, thickening the air around us. When Michaels spoke again, his words were measured but devastating. "We found yer great uncle's body, son. Three hours ago. Floating in the Hobbs River... 10 miles from yer parents' home."

My stomach dropped. The world seemed to tilt. Ethan's face went ghostly pale, his wide eyes meeting mine. Neither of us spoke, the weight of the revelation crushing every other thought. Our uncle—missing for three-four years, presumed dead but never confirmed—had been found. And now, of all times, as we drove toward the very place he'd vanished, his body surfaced?

"What?" Ethan's voice cracked, barely audible. The disbelief in it mirrored the shock pounding through me.

Luke had been knocking on Ethan's window, his fist thumping repeatedly, but neither of us noticed. The lieutenant's words consumed every ounce of our focus. On my side of the car, Tara and Gwen tapped at the glass, their faces shadowed with concern. I waved them off, motioning for them to stop. They backed away, sensing something was seriously wrong.

"Yer parents want ya home now, son," Michaels continued, but his voice began to waver, and static crept into the transmission. "Turn around—head back—"

The last words dissolved into an eerie hiss as the connection broke.

"Lieutenant Michaels! Repeat that last part!" Ethan shouted, clicking the receiver repeatedly, his voice rising in panic. "What did you say?!"

Nothing. Just static.

"Damn it!" Ethan swore, slamming the receiver down onto the dashboard, his breath coming hard and fast. He pounded the wheel, his frustration palpable.

Meanwhile, hundreds of miles away, lieutenant Michaels cursed under his breath in his small Nebraska station. He stood with one foot out of his patrol car, surrounded by officers who were hanging on his every word. The gravity of the situation weighed on him like a lead blanket.

"Get to those kids!" he barked, his voice sharp and urgent.

"They need to know there's a goddamn serial killer on the loose in Trenton!"

The officers didn't hesitate. They scrambled toward their vehicles, engines roaring to life as sirens wailed through the early morning stillness. Michaels slammed his door shut and gripped the wheel tightly, his eyes hard with determination. They knew the drive would take at least a day, but Michaels wasn't going to stop until they reached us. Time wasn't on their side, and the danger was closer than anyone could have imagined.

In the car, Ethan slammed the CB receiver down, the coiled wire bouncing with each impact. He let out a long, ragged breath, his hands gripping the steering wheel as though it might anchor him to something solid. We sat in stunned silence, the weight of what we'd just heard pressing down on us like a storm cloud. Our great uncle's body—missing for years, the subject of endless searches and unanswered questions—had been found. But why now? Why, as we were headed toward the manor where he had vanished, had his body suddenly surfaced? And why had lieutenant Michaels sounded so damn urgent?

"We need to figure out what to do," I whispered, the words thin and hollow. It felt impossible to make sense of this. The disappearance of our uncle had always been shrouded in mystery, but now it felt as though we were being pulled toward something far darker, something we couldn't escape.

Ethan nodded, but his eyes remained distant, his thoughts trapped somewhere between shock and the need to take action. I could see the strain behind his expression—the way his jaw clenched tightly, the way his breathing came just a little too fast.

"Ethan!" I shouted, my voice sharper than intended. He flinched, snapping out of his daze just as Luke opened the driver's door and called his name.

"Maeve, what's going on? What happened?" Luke's voice was tight with concern.

I unbuckled my seatbelt and stepped out of the car, the cold morning air biting at my skin. Ethan followed, his movements stiff, his hands still trembling slightly as he ran them through his hair. Mike, climbed out of the back seat, his usual cocky demeanor replaced by something more subdued. We gathered near the car, the chill in the air cutting into us as we explained what had happened.

"Your uncle?" Luke's voice cracked with disbelief. "They found him?" His eyes widened, the shock evident on his face.

I nodded, the words sticking in my throat. "Lieutenant Michaels said they found him three hours ago. He's been trying to reach us ever since, but the fog must've interfered with the signal." My voice wavered as I spoke, the reality of the situation pressing harder with every word.

Ethan's tone was steadier, though the tension in it was undeniable. "He said the body was found in the Hobbs River, about 10 miles from our parents' house."

The gravity of it hung in the freezing air. Even as the first hints of sunlight began to warm the horizon, the chill had sunk deep into my bones. It wasn't just the cold—it was something darker, a sense of unease that refused to let go. I wrapped my arms around myself, trying to fight it off, but it wasn't working.

"So, what do you want to do?" Luke asked, breaking the silence. His voice was calm, but his gaze flicked between Ethan and me with a tension that betrayed his unease. "Head back home or keep going to the mansion?"

Ethan exhaled slowly, his breath visible in the cold air as he turned the question over in his mind. "We're three hours from the split that leads to the mansion," he said, his voice heavy with deliberation. "If we turn back, it's nine hours to get home."

The options sat heavy in the air, each one feeling more precarious than the other. None of us spoke, the decision looming over us like a shadow we couldn't outrun.

I rubbed my hands over my arms again, trying to ward off the chill, but the cold wasn't just from the air—it was from the heavy uncertainty hanging over us. Every breath felt sharp and shallow, the weight of our decision pressing harder with each passing second.

Mike noticed me shivering and reached for his jean jacket, pausing as if to offer it to me. But before he could, Ethan swiftly shrugged off his own jacket and draped it over my shoulders. The warmth of the fabric was immediate, but it was the look in his eyes that caught me off guard. Protective. Possessive, even. His gesture was swift and deliberate, cutting off Mike before he had the chance.

I stared at Ethan, my brow furrowing. The silent message in his actions wasn't lost on me—it was more than just keeping me warm. I didn't need to be shielded like this, not from Mike, not from anything. I shot him a stern look, one that said as much, but he only tightened his jaw and turned back toward the car.

Mike raised an eyebrow at the exchange, his expression unreadable. Slowly, he stuffed his jacket back into the car, the tension between the two of them practically vibrating in the frozen air. Their rivalry was like an unspoken storm, always brewing, always on the verge of spilling over.

We stood there, silence stretching out between us, the cold digging deeper into our skin. Even the early light creeping over the horizon did little to break the chill. The world around us felt frozen in time, as if it, too, was waiting for a decision.

Go back or move forward into the unknown.

ABERDEEN MANOR

AFTER AN HOUR of back-and-forth discussion, Ethan and Luke finally reached an agreement: we'd continue on to the mansion. There was a landline there, and once we arrived, we could call our parents and figure out our next steps. It wasn't the perfect plan—hell, it barely felt like a plan—but it was the best option we had. Our parents would want us safe, well-rested, and thinking clearly. The idea was simple: reach the mansion, call home, get some sleep, and maybe hit the road again after a few hours.

"Agreed," Luke said, nodding firmly as if trying to convince himself it was the right choice.

But despite the plan, an uneasy feeling twisted in my stomach, tightening with every mile we drove closer to the manor. It wasn't just the news about our uncle or the wolves earlier—it was something deeper, something I couldn't quite shake. The mansion, with all its history and dark secrets, felt like it was pulling us in, and not in a way that felt safe.

"I don't know, Ethan…" I said softly, barely audible over the hum of the engine. "I've got a really bad feeling about this. Maybe we should just turn back—head home."

Ethan's expression softened, but there was a shadow behind his eyes. He reached out, gently turning my face toward him by my chin. "Hey, May," he said, his voice low and soothing. "You heard the plan. We'll get there, use the phone to call home, and figure it out from there. I promise, okay?"

There was reassurance in his tone, but I could sense the cracks beneath it. It wasn't just me he was trying to comfort—he was holding himself together, too.

I gave him a small nod, though the tightness in my chest didn't ease. "Okay," I whispered, though the unease wouldn't let me go. I exhaled deeply, trying to push the anxiety down, but it clung to me. The mansion was only a couple of hours away, and no matter how much I tried to shake it, I couldn't ignore the feeling that something was waiting for us. Something we couldn't avoid.

As we settled back into the car, Ethan adjusted the seatbelt across his chest and restarted the engine. The road stretched out before us, long and empty, and it would take exactly three hours to reach the double highway. From there, we would take the left turn that Mike had suggested—the "safest" route to the mansion. The sun was fully up now, casting a strange light on the barren landscape, but it didn't ease the tension that hung thick between us. Mike ran a hand through his hair, leaning back into the seat, seemingly unfazed by the events of the morning.

I, however, was still cold, despite the sunlight. I pulled my arms tighter through Ethan's jacket, and he silently turned the heater on, glancing at the clock. It was only 5:00 a.m., but the day felt endless already.

After several moments of silence, Ethan spoke, his voice

calm but cautious. "May," he said, breaking me from my thoughts. "Open the glove compartment."

I frowned, confused by the sudden request. But I reached forward, clicking the latch open. What I saw made my stomach drop.

"You have a gun in my car? ETHAN!" I practically shouted, my voice cracking with disbelief and anger. My pulse raced as I stared at him, my hands frozen. "In *my* car?"

Ethan didn't even flinch. He leaned forward, calmly grabbing the gun from the glove compartment, his eyes fixed on the road. "For protection," he said flatly, as if it was the most logical thing in the world. "We're out in the middle of nowhere, May. I brought it because we might need it."

"ARE YOU INSANE?!" I shouted, my voice rising with every word. I couldn't believe what I was seeing—my brother, my overly cautious, paranoid brother, had brought a gun along like we were headed into some kind of war zone.

I knew Ethan too well. He'd spent hours online, scouring forums, obsessing over wilderness dangers, unsolved mysteries, and worst of all—the rumors surrounding our uncle's disappearance. Ever since that day, Ethan had changed. He was convinced a killer had kidnapped our uncle, maybe even murdered him. It had turned him cautious—borderline paranoid.

With practiced motions, Ethan clicked the clip from the gun, checking it like he'd done it a hundred times before. My instincts kicked in, and I reached for the steering wheel, keeping the car straight as he handled the weapon. The entire situation felt surreal, like we were teetering on the edge of something dangerous—something I wasn't ready for.

From the backseat, Mike let out a low chuckle, his tone thick with amusement. "Awesome. You brought a gun. Real genius move, Ethan," he muttered, dripping with sarcasm. His comment only poured fuel on the fire.

I whipped my head around to glare at Mike before snapping

back to Ethan. "This is for protection? Really? Or is this just you being paranoid again?" I demanded, frustration bubbling over. I knew the truth. Ethan wasn't just worried about wolves or coyotes. Those were the excuses he told himself. The rumors that circulated about our uncle's disappearance gnawed at him, burrowing deeper into his mind with every mile we drove.

Now, with the revelation that our uncle's body had been discovered, those whispers had evolved into something darker. This wasn't just a trip home—it was a confrontation with the fears Ethan had been trying to outrun for years. And that fear was boiling over, transforming into something that felt dangerously close to desperation.

Ethan didn't answer, but I watched him reach back into the glove compartment, pulling out a box of bullets. He opened it and began counting the rounds like he was preparing for something none of us wanted to face.

"ETHAN!" I shouted again, my voice cracking with frustration and disbelief.

"I told you, May," he replied, his tone cold and unyielding. "For protection. There's no way I'm going out to that mansion without it." His gaze flicked toward me, his eyes hard and unrelenting, daring me to challenge him.

The tension in the car was suffocating. He pushed the gun and the box of bullets back into the glove compartment and snapped it shut with a loud click. Taking the wheel from me, his hands were steady, calm, as if this were just another part of the trip.

But it wasn't. None of this was normal, and we all knew it.

My mind raced, the pit in my stomach tightening into a knot. This wasn't the brother I knew—this was someone else entirely. Someone consumed by paranoia and fear. And now, with a loaded gun in the car, the stakes felt higher than ever.

"You're insane and stupid—" I snapped, my voice rising as I hurled a tirade of insults at Ethan. "What the hell were you thinking? Bringing a gun to our family home like we're heading into a damn warzone?" The idea was so absurd, it made my head spin.

Ethan glanced at me briefly, his expression unreadable, then turned his attention back to the road. A faint smirk tugged at the corner of his mouth, as if he were amused by my outburst. He didn't say a word, just let me rant—ignoring my insults and my jabs about how his idiocy had to be some kind of male genetic defect.

The road stretched out ahead, and the tension in the car was suffocating. We were about an hour away from the two-way split that led to the manor. That split was going to force a decision: left or right.

Right would take us toward the front gates—a longer, more convoluted route requiring us to punch in a code to get through the first set of gates before we even reached the circular drive-way. Left, though? That was a different story. The left route was practically a shortcut, leading directly behind the gates and into the driveway, bypassing the first checkpoint entirely.

But something about that left road gnawed at me. How did Mike know so much about it? His explanation didn't sit right. He'd claimed to overhear details at my parents' Christmas party years ago, but that didn't feel like the whole truth.

The left road wasn't just any shortcut—it had been closed off nearly a decade ago. My uncle had blocked it to keep stray animals off the property, and a solid brick wall now surrounded the entire estate, including that hidden path. No one had used that road in years.

"Hey, Mike," I said, suspicion creeping into my voice. "That left road you're talking about—it leads straight onto a gravel road into the back driveway, doesn't it? How exactly did you know about that?"

Mike leaned forward, his smirk still in place. "I already told you," he said, his tone casual, almost too casual. "I overheard it at your parents' Christmas party. The officer mentioned it."

I nodded slightly, but my unease only deepened. My voice sharpened. "Only one problem with that, Mike. Our uncle blocked that road off ten years ago—before he disappeared. He built a brick wall to keep animals out. So, how do you explain that?"

Mike's smirk faltered, his confidence cracking for just a moment. Something flickered in his eyes—uncertainty, maybe? But he recovered quickly, his voice softer now, almost placating. "Look, May, the officers didn't mention anything about a wall. If the road's blocked, fine. Take the right route. No big deal."

Ethan's hands were locked onto the wheel, his fingers curling tightly around the leather. His gaze flicked toward the rearview mirror, locking on Mike. "Maeve's got a point," he said, his voice low, almost growling. "Why didn't you bring this up earlier if you knew so much about the place? Did you know, Mike? Or is there something you're not telling us?"

Mike's smirk returned, but it was colder now, more calculated. "I didn't know until Maeve brought it up," he said, leaning back in his seat with an air of indifference. "Seriously, take the other direction if you're so worried. What's the big deal?"

His calmness felt off—too deliberate. Like he was playing a game the rest of us weren't privy to.

The tension in the car thickened, suffocating. Ethan's eyes flicked from the road to Mike in the rearview mirror, his agitation growing with every passing second. The distrust was palpable, simmering between them and spreading to the rest of us like a slow-burning fire.

"If you're trying to trick us or pull some kind of stunt—" Ethan's voice sliced through the silence, sharp and brimming with anger. "I swear, Mike, I'll handle it my way... if you try to pull any shit." His tone was hard, each word deliberate, the threat unmistakable. The air felt like it could snap at any second.

Mike didn't back down. His reflection in the mirror was calm, but there was something dangerous about the way he carried himself—too composed, too ready for this confrontation. He met Ethan's eyes in the mirror, his voice steady but edged with defiance. "What, you don't trust me? After everything, Ethan?"

The car became a pressure cooker, the tension pressing down on all of us. Ethan gripped the wheel like a lifeline, his eyes locked on the road ahead, his body coiled with tension, ready to snap. His anger was building, threatening to spill over, and I could see the conflict raging in him.

Before he could say anything, I reached over and punched him hard in the shoulder.

"Maeve!" he barked, flinching as he rubbed his arm. The sharp movement startled him out of his rising fury.

"Cut it out," I snapped, glaring at him. "This isn't helping anyone!" My voice was sharp, frustrated, but I could feel my own fear fueling it.

Ethan muttered something under his breath, his irritation breaking just enough for the tension to simmer down. The heat of the argument had cooled for the moment, but it wasn't gone. The unspoken hostility still hung heavy in the air, crackling like a storm waiting to break.

I turned my attention to the window, trying to block out the suffocating silence that followed. The road stretched out endlessly before us, but it felt like we were trapped in a loop, circling back into the same cycle of distrust and uncertainty. My stomach churned with unease, the pit inside me growing deeper.

I could feel Ethan's anger still lingering, and Mike's defiance hadn't waned. This wasn't over—not by a long shot.

...

We had finally reached the divide in the highway that split into two paths, both leading to Aberdeen Manor. Signs on both sides read: "KEEP OUT! PRIVATE PROPERTY!"—a stark reminder that these roads led to a place that belonged to us and no one else. It was eerie how deserted they were, even though they had been constructed specifically for our family. No one traveled these roads anymore. Of the four-way split, only the straight road to New Port was used by the outside world. The other two paths, looping around our manor—one to the front, the other to the back—seemed abandoned, forgotten like the house itself. It felt deliberate, as if the entire estate had been designed to isolate us, cut off from everything and everyone.

"You can drop me off here," Mike said suddenly as Ethan pulled over onto the right shoulder. Luke followed closely behind, parking his car. A wave of relief swept over me as I stepped out into the crisp morning air, away from the suffocating tension inside the car. I needed space—anything to break the heavy atmosphere between Ethan and Mike.

"We made it," Luke said, stretching as he walked over to join us. Tara and Gwen quickly linked their arms with mine, dragging me off toward Luke's car. They both fumbled for their cigarettes, eager for a smoke break. While I didn't smoke, I stayed with them, grateful for the brief escape as they lit up and inhaled deeply. The faint smell of tobacco filled the air, but neither of them seemed to notice the tension brewing just a few feet away.

Back by Ethan's car, the situation was far from calm. Ethan and Mike had stayed inside. Luke knocked on the window, trying to grab their attention, but Ethan ignored him, his focus locked forward, his expression unreadable. Without a word, he motioned for Luke to get into the back seat. Mike reached for the door handle, but it was locked. The sound of it clicking made my stomach twist.

Luke slid into the back seat beside Mike, confusion clear on his face. Ethan promptly locked the doors again.

"Bro, what's up? Why'd we stop?" Luke asked, his tone laced with confusion. He glanced between Ethan and Mike, trying to gauge what was going on. The unease in the car was thick, almost suffocating.

Ethan turned slightly, his face hard, his voice calm but edged with restrained anger. "Look," he began, his words deliberate, "because I love my sister and care about her feelings—something you clearly didn't—I'll let you stay at the manor for one night. One night." He paused, letting the weight of his words settle before continuing. "After that, you're on your own. Find your own ride, or your own way out. I'm done with your bullshit, Mike." His tone was final, brooking no argument.

Luke raised an eyebrow, shooting Ethan a puzzled look, the silent question clear in his expression: *What the hell are you doing letting him anywhere near the manor?*

"Fine," Mike muttered after a tense pause, his voice cool, almost indifferent. He didn't bother defending himself. "Trust me, I'm not interested in May. You don't need to worry about that."

Mike turned to Luke, and in an instant, the air shifted again. The silent hostility between them was unmistakable, lingering just beneath the surface. Luke's jaw tightened, the threat he'd made to Mike still hanging in the air—a warning Mike hadn't forgotten. They both knew the score. Luke had been the one to tell Mike to end things with me, to walk away. And now, that shared history between them felt like another unspoken storm brewing in the car.

Luke glared at Mike, his expression smug but warning. "If you make her cry while you're here, I'll handle you myself," he said, his voice low and firm, the weight of their previous conversation clear.

Ethan's eyes flicked between them, confusion darkening his expression. He hadn't known about this—about the conversation that had taken place between Luke and Mike. Without a word, he clicked the locks open, breaking the heavy silence. Mike smirked, pushing the door open and stepping out, but not before throwing one last glance at Ethan.

"Trust me, I'm not going to do anything to Maeve," Mike added, his voice dripping with insincerity. Then he walked away, disappearing into the distance.

Ethan watched him go, his jaw tightening, his teeth clenched. "I don't trust him for a second," he muttered under his breath, more to himself than to Luke.

Luke stepped out of the car, running a hand through his hair as he sighed heavily. "Look, Ethan, I told Mike to break up with

Maeve," he admitted, his voice steady but laced with anger. "I caught that jerk driving around with a car full of cheerleaders— one of them he was dating behind her back. He was planning to come to your house, ask for Maeve's hand in marriage. Can you believe that? But instead, he decided to cheat on her. That's when I threatened him. Told him if he made her cry again, I'd break his legs."

Ethan's hands clamped around the steering wheel, the taut muscles in his forearms betraying the storm of anger simmering just beneath his controlled exterior. "I would've never given Mike my blessing," he growled, his voice shaking with restrained rage. "Even if he came begging for Maeve's hand, I'd have broken his legs myself."

Luke nodded slightly, understanding the depth of Ethan's fury. "That's why I told him to end things with her. I knew what kind of person he was. He didn't deserve her."

Ethan exhaled, forcing himself to release some of the tension coiled in his chest, then finally opened the driver's door. He and Luke walked over to where the rest of us stood near Luke's car, laughing and talking loudly to break the tension that hung thick in the air. But even as Ethan joined in, I could feel the weight of unspoken words lingering between him and Luke—the truth simmering just beneath the surface, waiting to unravel.

"Well, my ladies, we have beer and plenty of food courtesy of our mothers, in the trunk of my car! Shall we head to the manor and celebrate?" Luke announced, throwing his hands in the air like he was hosting a game show. He did a ridiculous jig around his car, clearly running on fumes but somehow still in high spirits. Despite everything, I couldn't help but laugh as he popped the trunk open with exaggerated flair.

I leaned forward, peeking inside to find coolers neatly packed with ice, drinks, beer, and enough food to feed a small village. "This is enough to feed an army!" I said with a grin, remembering Ethan's similarly overstocked supplies from earlier.

"My mother, the overachiever, packed my car full too," I

added, chuckling.

Ethan shook his head in mock dismay. "Maeve, she packed enough for a week... for five people. We're practically ready to survive an apocalypse." His tone was sarcastic, but the glimmer in his eye gave away his amusement.

I laughed, giving him a playful shove to the chest just as Mike made his way over, his presence immediately killing the light mood.

"So, are we heading to the manor before all this food spoils, or are we just going to loiter on the side of the road all day?" Mike asked, his tone clipped as he pointed out that it was already 7:00 a.m., and none of us had gotten any sleep.

I shot him a cold glare before pointedly turning my back on him. I wasn't about to let him drag me into an argument—not now. Without saying a word, I walked to Ethan's car and slid into the driver's seat, making it clear I was taking over. Humming quietly to myself, I adjusted the seat and started fiddling with the mirrors.

"Buzz kill!" Gwen called out from across the lot, her laughter cutting through the lingering tension. She let out a theatrical sigh before opening the passenger door of Luke's car and flopping inside.

As we gradually began piling back into our respective cars, I kept my focus on the dashboard, determined to block out the irritation Mike had stirred up. Ethan walked over to the driver's side, leaning casually against the window with that familiar mischievous smirk.

"Ahem!" Ethan cleared his throat, eyebrows raised in exaggerated authority.

I rolled down the window and shot him a mischievous grin. "My turn," I said, my tone challenging.

Without missing a beat, he reached for the door and, in one swift move, wrapped his arms around my waist, pulling me out of the car like I weighed nothing. "Nope, not a chance..." he laughed, effortlessly hoisting me up while I flailed helplessly, grabbing at the door frame for support.

"This is my carrrr!" I stammered between bursts of laughter, trying to wriggle free. My half-hearted attempts to push his arms away only made him laugh harder.

"Oh ho! Little Maeve wants to drive, huh? That's adorable," he teased, his tone dripping with mock pity. He raised his fists in a mock defensive stance, pretending to guard his precious driver's seat. "But sorry, this car is mine now."

Without thinking, I swung a punch at his arm with all my might. Big mistake. Pain shot through my knuckles as I yelped, immediately regretting my decision. "Ow! Why are you made of stone?" I groaned, shaking out my sore hand.

Ethan doubled over in laughter, tears forming in the corners of his eyes. "You good? Did you really just punch me?!" He was clearly having the time of his life at my expense. "Alright, alright! I'll make you a deal—no country music," he said, still chuckling.

I narrowed my eyes, pointing at him like I was issuing a decree. "If I hear even one twang, one single note, I'm ripping that stereo out with my bare hands!"

From their car, Luke, Gwen, and Tara were in hysterics, laughing so hard they could barely breathe. Luke leaned out of his window, honking the horn obnoxiously. "Hey! If you two toddlers are done throwing punches, can we get moving? Some of us have places to be!" he yelled, his grin wide and unapologetic.

Ethan flipped him the finger, grinning back without missing a beat. He finally slid into the driver's seat, still chuckling to himself. I stomped around to the passenger side, muttering under my breath about how unfair life was, but my grin betrayed me.

As soon as I buckled in, I side-eyed Ethan, daring him to even think about reaching for the stereo. He started the car with a smirk, the hum of the engine punctuating the brief silence.

"Do it. I dare you," I warned, my voice low and threatening.

Ethan laughed, his shoulders shaking. "Relax, Maeve. I'm not suicidal." But the way his hand hovered near the stereo knob told me he was tempted.

"Ethan," I growled, my voice dripping with menace.

"Alright, alright!" he said, laughing as he focused on the road. "You're no fun, you know that?"

"Just drive, clown," I muttered, but even I couldn't hide the smile tugging at my lips. For the first time in hours, the tension in the car had lightened, replaced by the warmth of shared laughter.

...

Aberdeen Manor, standing for over thirty years, has been in my family for generations—tracing back to my great-great-grandfather on my mother's side. It's always been a part of my life, tied to family stories and memories. Back then, the house was alive—thriving and beautiful. A massive three-level mansion, it boasted ten grand rooms, five luxurious bathrooms, and a curved staircase that spiraled gracefully from the center of the house up to the second floor. Shaped like a horseshoe, the staircase was the first thing you saw when you entered the wide, open foyer, like something pulled straight out of an old-world fairy tale.

The manor also had two spacious living rooms and a kitchen so large it seemed like it belonged in a professional chef's dream. And then there was the basement—creepy, dark, and filled with remnants of our family's past. It held secrets: old furniture, dusty photographs, and an atmosphere heavy with history, like every creak of the floorboards whispered something from the past.

Before I was born, my mother and my biological father visited the manor together—just once. She wanted to show him the grand house her side of the family had left her, to share its significance. But the day I was born was also the day he left us. I guess he didn't want me, or maybe that's how I rationalized it as a kid. He left my mother, and not long after, she met Ethan's dad—my stepfather, James Adams. They married two years later. Ethan was just a toddler when we met, and from that moment, Aberdeen Manor became part of our shared history.

Things changed when my great-uncle—my mother's half-brother—took over the manor. He bought it from my mom, determined to keep it in the family, to preserve its legacy when she no longer could. For ten years, he cared for it, keeping it pristine, his pride and joy. Then, without warning, he disappeared.

After his disappearance, Aberdeen Manor was abandoned. No one came back to it, no one maintained it, and over time, it decayed into a shadow of its former self. The once-stately exterior, with its bright white paint and proud windows, was now blackened, its walls covered in moss. The air around it seemed to hang heavy, its legacy shifting from family treasure to eerie local legend. People began to talk about it like it was cursed—an untouchable landmark of tragedy. No one dared to go near it.

I'm still surprised we're going now, after all these years. Maybe it's because they finally found my uncle's body, but deep down, part of me wonders if that's the real reason. Ethan is set on staying the night, adamant that we'll head back home tomorrow as our mother asked. But the idea of spending even one night in that place sends a chill down my spine. It feels like we're walking into something we're not prepared for, something that has been waiting for us.

"Wow," I whispered as Ethan pulled up to the gates of Aberdeen Manor. It still looked the same—just older, its decay more pronounced, like an old photograph slowly fading with time. But it was unmistakably the place I remembered from my childhood.

"Do we even have the code?" Mike asked from the back seat, his voice breaking the quiet. I ignored him, undoing my seatbelt and stepping out of the car. Ethan watched as I approached the old touch panel, hidden behind a tangle of overgrown ivy. My fingers hovered over the keypad, hesitating for a moment before

I entered the code—my birthdate. This code had been passed down in our family for generations. It wasn't just my birthdate—it was also the birthdate of my great-great-grandmother.

"Awesome," Gwen said, her voice cutting through the silence. She and Tara had already gotten out and were standing nearby, watching as the gates creaked open. The sound was loud and haunting, echoing in the still morning air. Ethan drove through slowly, Luke following behind in his car. I lingered by the gate, waiting for it to open fully before stepping in to close it behind us.

The circular driveway stretched out before us, leading to the once-imposing bronze statue at its center. It was a masterpiece, a symbol of family history. The statue of a woman holding an urn had stood for over a century, honoring my great-great-great-grandmother. In its prime, water had poured gracefully from the urn, but now the fountain was silent, the woman's figure coated in black dust and streaked with mold.

"That statue is still beautiful," Ethan said softly as he parked near it. His voice held a rare gentleness as he stepped out of the car and stared at it. The memory of my great-great-great-grandmother might not have been part of his bloodline, but our family—my family—had embraced him as one of their own.

My uncle had made sure of that. God, I missed him. He had been the kindest, most caring man I'd ever known. When my mom married James, Ethan's dad, my uncle had thrown a massive welcoming party just for Ethan. It was his way of making sure Ethan felt like he belonged with us, even when Ethan had been difficult, angry, and grieving the loss of his mother.

"Hey, bud," I remembered my uncle calling out to Ethan that day. "Let's fly!"

Ethan had stood stiffly in this very yard, arms crossed and his expression guarded. But my uncle had been undeterred. He'd scooped Ethan up like he weighed nothing, throwing him onto his shoulders.

"Hold on tight, captain, we're about to take off!" my uncle

had exclaimed with a grin.

Ethan had clung to him, at first skeptical, then laughing as my uncle sprinted around the yard, zooming him through the air like an airplane. It was the first time I had heard Ethan laugh—a real, carefree laugh—in years.

"I'm flying!" Ethan had shouted, his face lit up with joy.

"See? Told you I'd make you fly!" my uncle had replied, laughing along with him.

Now, years later, I glanced at Ethan as he touched the dusty statue, his fingers tracing the edges of the urn. His gaze swept over the yard, and I saw a faint, wistful smile tug at the corners of his lips. He was remembering too.

"Well, are we going in, or are we just going to stand here gawking at the scenery?" Tara's voice broke the moment, teasing as always.

I chuckled, shaking off the memories. "Alright, let's go."

I climbed the creaking steps to the porch and pulled the key from my pocket—the one Ethan had handed me earlier. Sliding it into the lock, I turned it slowly, and the door groaned as it swung open. The dim foyer stretched out before us, untouched but blanketed in a thick layer of black dust. The once-vibrant air of the manor was now heavy with the sharp, unsettling scent of sulfur.

Everything was still in place, as though time had stopped inside this house. Yet, it felt like the house itself had been holding its breath, waiting for us to return.

"Gorgeous," Gwen said, dropping her bag near the door. "It just needs a little cleaning, and we could make this place feel like home again."

Luke and Ethan were outside, unloading the coolers and bags of food from the cars. Meanwhile, Mike had wandered off, his curiosity pulling him toward the trees and overgrown brush surrounding the manor. He had disappeared from view, and none of us felt compelled to go looking for him.

Inside, the rest of us busied ourselves settling in, carrying our supplies into the foyer. As I wandered into the left living room, nostalgia hit me like a wave. It was just as I remembered—frozen in time, untouched but layered in dust. The old fireplace still bore remnants of soot, evidence of the warmth and life that once filled this space. I ran my hand along the mantel, brushing away years of neglect as memories of winters spent here flickered through my mind like embers from a long-dead fire.

Across the room, I noticed Ethan hunched over the rotary phone, its faded beige plastic a relic from another era. Somehow, the phone still worked, its line alive despite the passage of time. To my surprise, even the electricity and water were still running. My uncle and mother must have continued paying for the utilities, keeping the manor breathing despite its abandonment.

Ethan's voice pulled me back to the present. He was dialing, the soft clicks of the rotary wheel filling the quiet room. As the connection went through, his expression changed, his body tensing as my mother's voice came through the receiver.

"Ethan, oh, thank God, you made it to the manor!" she said, her tone warm but fraught with frantic energy.

"Everything okay?" Ethan asked, gripping the phone tightly. The long cord trailed behind him as he paced the living room, his eyes scanning the dusty furniture and fading wallpaper. There was something about the way he carried himself—protective, yet restless—that made me uneasy.

"No... they found your uncle's body three hours ago," my mother choked out, her voice cracking. I could tell she had been crying. Ethan's shoulders stiffened, his grip on the phone tightening. He had always hated seeing her upset. To him, she was never just a "stepmom"—she was his mom in every way that mattered.

"Mom, what's wrong? Your voice is worrying me," he said, his voice soft but strained, trying to steady the growing tension in the room. I inched closer to him, drawn by the worry etched on his face.

Across the hall, I could hear Luke, Tara, and Gwen laughing as they worked in the kitchen. The sound of their voices felt jarring against the weight of the conversation happening here, their lightheartedness only emphasizing the heaviness that hung between Ethan and me.

"No, my boy," my mother continued, her voice breaking. "Lieutenant Michaels is coming your way..." Static cut through her words, distorting her message.

Ethan frowned, pressing the receiver tighter to his ear. "Mom, I can barely hear you—why is officer Michaels coming here?" His tone grew sharper, worry clear in his words.

Her response was swallowed by more static, her voice fragmenting. "...I just... Please, Ethan... be careful..."

"Mom, I can't understand you—it must be the phone. It's old," Ethan said, his voice tinged with frustration. Suddenly, the line went silent, a soft click followed by dead air.

"Huh. Strange," Ethan muttered, staring at the receiver in his hand. After a moment, he carefully placed it back on its cradle, his brow furrowed in thought.

"Everything okay?" I asked, my concern rising. "Is Mom alright? Does she want us to come home?"

Ethan's expression softened slightly as he looked at me, though the tension lingered in his eyes. He ran a hand through his hair, his movements deliberate as he processed the call. "She's... fine," he said, though his tone betrayed a hint of doubt. "She just said Michaels is on his way, but the rest of her message was too garbled to make out. The phone cut out before I could get anything else."

I bit my lip, glancing at the old rotary phone. "Maybe we should try calling her back?"

Meanwhile, back at my mother's house, panic had set in. She paced the living room, her hands wringing nervously, her voice trembling as she turned to my stepfather.

"James, we have to call officer Michaels—we have to let him

know the kids are at the manor! If there's a serial killer loose in Trenton, who knows where this person—this killer—might be. He could be near the children, and they wouldn't even know it!" Her words came out in a rush, thick with fear.

"Okay, okay, calm down," James replied, his tone steady but laced with concern. He placed a comforting hand on her shoulder, trying to ground her. "We have the picture Michaels faxed over this morning. Thank God the fax machine still works. I'll send it to the kids with a note. If they decide to stay at the manor, they need to lock the place down until Michaels gets there. If they choose to come back, I want them here by tomorrow, no later."

He moved to the fax machine and pulled out the sheet that had come through earlier—a grainy black-and-white image of a man's face accompanied by a brief description. My mother leaned in to take a look, but the moment her eyes landed on the photo, she gasped sharply. Her face drained of color, and she swayed unsteadily before collapsing into James's arms, unconscious.

"Amy!" James shouted, holding her close. His eyes darted to the picture in his hand, then back to his wife, his mind racing. Whatever—or whoever—was in that photo had struck a deep chord of recognition. The hum of the fax machine filled the tense silence, a mechanical reminder of the urgency at hand.

Back at the manor, Ethan tried to shake off the unease from the garbled phone call. "We'll try calling her back later, Maeve. Don't worry. If Officer Michaels is heading this way, we'll wait for him to arrive," he said, his voice steady. Despite his calm tone, I could hear the tension just beneath the surface, barely concealed. He reached out, brushing his hand against my cheek with a small, reassuring smile. Then, without another word, he turned and headed toward the other living room to help Luke with whatever project they were tackling.

I lingered for a moment, staring after him. The way Mom's

voice had cracked, the urgency in her words—it didn't sit right with me. What exactly had she been trying to say before the call cut off?

"Huh," I muttered, glancing back at the phone. Following the cord to the wall, I saw it was still securely connected. "Maybe the line's just old," I reasoned aloud, though the explanation didn't ease the knot of unease in my chest.

Shaking off the thought, I moved toward the right living room where Ethan and Luke were dusting off old pillows and pulling open the heavy, moth-eaten curtains. Sunlight spilled in, cutting through the thick, dusty air and illuminating the room in golden beams. Before I could join them, the front door creaked open, and Mike stepped inside. I froze instinctively, my eyes locking onto his.

For a moment, neither of us said anything, the weight of unspoken words hanging between us like a storm cloud. Then, with a slight shake of my head, I brushed past him, heading toward Ethan and Luke. Mike stood there for a moment, his expression unreadable. Finally, he ran a hand through his hair and walked further into the house, his movements hesitant but deliberate. He scanned the room, his eyes flicking over the worn furniture and faded wallpaper, as if piecing together the stories held within these walls. Then, without a word, he joined us, his casual demeanor betraying a hint of unease.

"Maeve, can I talk to you for a moment?" Mike's voice called out behind me.

Ethan and Luke, mid-task adjusting the curtains, immediately turned their heads. Ethan's expression darkened, his shoulders stiffening.

"No, you can't speak to her," Ethan snapped, his tone sharp and unyielding.

I shot him a pointed look, tilting my head as if to say, *butt out*. Ignoring his overprotectiveness, I turned back to Mike, crossing my arms. "What do you want?" I asked, irritation creeping into my voice.

Mike gestured toward the door, silently asking me to follow. With a heavy sigh, I brushed past Ethan, making my way outside with Mike trailing behind. The crisp air bit at my skin as I leaned against the wooden railing of the porch. My eyes fell on the rusted metal gate at the edge of the property, its once-pristine scrollwork bearing the family name *Emersons* now dulled by time and decay. Despite its condition, a faint smile tugged at my lips, the sight stirring memories of what the manor used to be.

Mike stood nearby, fidgeting slightly before motioning toward the back of the house. "Can we talk over here? There's something I want to show you."

"What is it, Mike? What do you want to show me?" I asked impatiently, my tone laced with suspicion. Without a word, he turned and started walking, leaving me no choice but to follow. We rounded the side of the house, the ground beneath us crunching with every step. My footsteps slowed as we reached the backyard, and I froze.

The overgrown graveyard loomed ahead, its headstones leaning with age and shrouded in weeds. In the midst of it all was a man, his back to us, meticulously brushing dirt off one of the stones with a shovel. His wiry frame was silhouetted against the morning light, his battered hat shielding most of his face from view.

"Do you know him?" Mike asked quietly, his voice low, his unease mirroring my own.

I shook my head, a knot tightening in my stomach. "No... who the hell is that?"

As if hearing us, the man straightened and turned. His weathered face broke into a smile as he tipped his hat in our direction. Without hesitation, he began walking toward us, his casual demeanor only adding to my growing unease.

"ETHAN!" I shouted, my voice sharper than I intended. Panic crept in, tightening my chest. "ETHAN, GET OUT HERE!" The urgency in my tone echoed through the still air.

Heavy footsteps pounded against the porch as Ethan and Luke emerged from the house, their expressions immediately shifting to alertness. Ethan positioned himself in front of me, his broad frame a protective barrier. Luke stood beside him, his stance tense and ready.

"Hey!" Ethan called, his voice firm and commanding. "Who are you, and what are you doing here? This is private property."

The man stopped a few feet away, unfazed by the confrontation. He tipped his hat again, his smile oddly friendly. "Sorry if I gave you a scare there, young lady. Didn't mean to cause any fuss," he said, his tone warm but unsettlingly casual. "Name's Eric... Eric Andrews. Your mother hired me to keep up the property while you folks were away."

Ethan's eyes narrowed, his suspicion evident. "My mother never mentioned hiring anyone," he said coldly. "How did you get in here?"

"The gate was open," Eric replied with a shrug, leaning casually on his shovel. "I've been working here for a few months now. Your mom lets me stay in the shed out back while I'm on the job."

Ethan's expression darkened further, his voice growing colder. "I don't believe you. My mother would've told us if she hired someone to work here."

Eric shrugged again, his smile unwavering. "Maybe she forgot to mention it. Happens sometimes, doesn't it? Either way, I'll stay out of your way. You folks enjoy your visit." Without waiting for a response, he turned and strolled back toward the graveyard, whistling as though nothing unusual had happened.

I stared after him, my unease growing with every step he took. "Do you really think Mom hired him?" I asked Ethan, my voice low.

"Not for a second," Ethan muttered, his eyes fixed on Eric's retreating figure. "I'm calling her again as soon as we get inside." He turned to Luke, his tone firm. "No one lets him inside. No exceptions. If he's lying, I'll handle it."

Luke nodded, his jaw tight. "Got it."

Mike, leaning against the railing, watched Eric disappear behind the shed. His usual aloofness was gone, replaced by a rare seriousness. "Yeah," he said, his voice quiet, "there's something off about that guy."

Ethan exhaled sharply, addressing the group. "Stick together, and don't let him anywhere near the house. If anything seems off, you come straight to me."

Luke gave a firm nod, tapping his fist lightly against Ethan's in agreement. Tara and Gwen, who had been watching from the doorway, exchanged uneasy glances before retreating back inside.

Ethan lingered for a moment, his eyes scanning the yard and the distant graveyard. The tension in his posture was palpable, and I could tell he wasn't letting his guard down for a second. Finally, he turned and followed the rest of us into the house, his shoulders stiff with determination. The door shut with a heavy thud, sealing us inside as the weight of unease settled over us.

GHOSTS

THINGS WERE ABOUT to get even stranger at my parents' house. "James, calm down... calm down," lieutenant Michaels said into the phone, though his own voice wavered slightly. He had recognized the number immediately. James, my stepfather, had called in a panic, and Michaels braced himself for whatever bombshell was about to drop.

Lieutenant Michaels was parked with his SWAT team and a convoy of officers in a desolate lot, eight hours outside Trenton, just on the outskirts of Nebraska. They were preparing to head toward the town when the call came through—a call that felt like it could blow everything wide open.

"Is your wife near you?" Michaels asked, his voice sharp with urgency. "Let me speak to her, if she's able."

"My wife had a panic attack," James replied, his words shaky.

"She saw the picture of this man—said it was like seeing a ghost. She fainted. The house is full of officers and EMTs right now."

Michaels' grip on the phone tightened. "Listen carefully, James," he said, his voice dropping to a grave whisper. "That man has many aliases. He's extremely dangerous and likely armed. We've been hunting him for over twenty years. Does your wife know his real name?"

James switched the phone to speaker mode, carefully placing it into Amy's trembling hands. "Amy, it's lieutenant Michaels. Can you talk to him?"

Amy nodded faintly, her pale face drawn tight with fear. Her hands shook as she brought the phone closer to her ear.

"Amy," Michaels said firmly, trying to ground her. "I need to know if the kids made it to the mansion. Are they safe?"

Her breath hitched, and her voice cracked as she responded, "Lieutenant Michaels... please, you have to warn my children. You have to..." she broke down, sobs wracking her body as she crumpled under the weight of her fear. James held her close, his attempts to console her falling flat. The room was heavy with tension as an officer nearby gently took the phone from Amy's trembling hand, stepping aside to continue the call.

"Chief," the officer said, his voice low as he moved to a quieter room. "We've been digging into this guy since you left for Nebraska. He's slippery. Changes identities like clockwork. But there's more..."

Michaels clenched his jaw, his mind flashing back to the chaotic police conference room—the maps, photographs, and articles pinned across every surface. For two decades, they had chased a ghost, his crimes spanning states, leaving victims and confusion in his wake. Red string connected blurred faces and crime scenes to aliases—Eric Andrews, Derek Reed, Jonathan Clarke. Every name led them in circles. He was a master at disappearing, evading every trap.

And now, for the first time, they had a name. A real connection.

"Amy told us his name is Eric Stephenson," the officer continued, his voice cutting through the haze of Michaels' memories. "Her first husband. Maeve's biological father. He could be using a new alias now, but that's who we're dealing with."

The color drained from Michaels' face. Years of chasing shadows, and now, the man they had been hunting was tied to the very family he was trying to protect.

"Son of a bitch!" Michaels cursed, his frustration spilling over. He slammed his fist against the dashboard, making several officers outside glance over in alarm. He didn't care. The rage and urgency boiled within him.

"Get those kids out of that house!" he roared into the phone, his voice trembling with fear and fury. "I don't care how—call them, fax them, send smoke signals if you have to! Just get them out of there!"

The officer on the other end stiffened at the order, his own urgency now mirroring Michaels'. "Understood, Chief. We'll use every channel. We'll reach them."

Michaels took a ragged breath, his mind racing as he delivered his final command. "Do whatever it takes. That man is a monster, and if he's near those kids..." His voice faltered for a moment before hardening again. "God help them."

…

I couldn't stop laughing at the sheer stupidity of my brother, who, in all his brilliance, was trying to figure out why the massive TV in the living room wasn't working. If the idiot had bothered to glance just once to the side, he'd have noticed it wasn't plugged in. Problem solved.

Standing nearby with my arms crossed, I decided to enjoy the show. "Come on, boys, it's a TV. How hard can it be?" I teased, struggling to keep a straight face as they fumbled around like they were defusing a bomb. Ethan shot me an annoyed glance, clearly at his wit's end. "Fine, genius. Forty bucks says you can't get this baby working," he challenged, giving me a smug, almost daring smile as he folded his arms across his chest.

Challenge accepted, you big, brawny idiot.

Luke snickered, stepping back as if the task of plugging in a cord was too much for me to handle. Meanwhile, Mike leaned casually against the far wall, quietly observing the chaos. Every time Ethan and Luke bickered, his smirk grew wider, barely suppressing a laugh.

"No, you moron, the cords are plugged in," Ethan growled, his frustration mounting.

"Then why isn't it working, genius?" Luke countered, grinning as he threw his hands in the air like they were trying to solve an advanced algorithm instead of plugging in a TV.

I clapped my hands together, strolling over with an air of exaggerated confidence. "Step aside, boys," I said. Without another word, I bent down, grabbed the unplugged cord from where it lay pathetically on the floor, and plugged it in.

Mike couldn't hold back anymore—he burst out laughing, clutching his stomach as the whole room froze. Ethan crossed his arms tighter, biting his lip like he was physically restraining himself from snapping at me. That look he gave me? Priceless. It was the *"I dare you to rub it in"* face, and I wasn't going to waste the opportunity.

"I'll take my forty in two twenties, thanks," I said with a grin, patting Ethan on the chest as I sauntered past him.

Ethan stared after me, probably trying to think of a witty comeback but too flustered to say anything coherent. "You..." he muttered, his voice trailing off as I disappeared down the hall toward the kitchen.

Luke burst into laughter, shaking his head. "Man, she owned you," he said, punching Ethan playfully in the arm.

Ethan turned to him, his scowl deepening. "Oh, you think that's funny?" Without warning, he launched a playful punch at Luke's shoulder. In seconds, they were full-on wrestling, their voices bouncing off the walls as they rolled around like a pair of overgrown kids.

Mike, still leaning against the wall, shook his head, his amusement clear. "Well, at least the TV works now," he muttered to himself, his quiet chuckle the perfect punctuation to the scene.

"May, girlfriend… tell me, are you really okay with Mike being here?" Tara asked as I stepped into the kitchen. She stood by the sink peeling carrots, her brow furrowed slightly in concern.

I joined her at the sink, washing my hands. The kitchen was alive with activity as we prepped for a big dinner in the manor's massive dining room. With everyone pitching in, it felt chaotic but comforting. Grabbing a towel hanging from the stove, I dried my hands before picking up a knife to help chop the carrots. "I don't know," I admitted after a moment, keeping my focus on the cutting board. "I haven't really said much to him... we haven't talked at all, actually. I guess I still haven't forgiven him for breaking up with me." My words were calm, but the weight of them hung in the air between us.

Tara gave me a sympathetic look, resting her hand on my shoulder for a moment before walking to a cupboard. She pulled out a large, dusty bowl, its intricate China print barely visible beneath the grime. After rinsing it off, she placed it on the counter for the chopped carrots.

At the stove, Gwen was busy preparing the roast her mom had packed for us. She stared at the pressure cooker like it was some alien technology. "Is it one hour or two that I need to cook this thing for?" she asked, half-frustrated, half-amused. I couldn't help but laugh, rolling my eyes as I walked over. I grabbed the lid of the pressure cooker, placed it on the pot, and turned on the stove. "Two hours," I said with a grin.

Gwen threw her hands up in mock defeat. "Why didn't I know that?" she said with a laugh, before moving to the fridge to pull out lettuce and other ingredients for the salad.

As we worked, my eyes kept drifting toward the large kitchen window, drawn to the graveyard in the distance. Something about it unsettled me. When had it been put there? Who were those graves for? My gaze followed the man from earlier, still tending to the space like a caretaker, his movements deliberate as he shoveled dirt between the headstones. I became so lost in thought, watching him, that I didn't notice the knife slip until I felt a sharp sting. "Ouch! Oh!" I gasped, looking down to see a deep cut along my finger. Blood welled up quickly.

"Run it under water," Gwen said, noticing the blood.

I rolled my eyes in frustration, moving to the sink to let the cool water rinse the wound. The bleeding didn't stop, dripping steadily as I pulled my hand away.

"Crap," I muttered, grabbing a nearby towel to press against it. Rifling through drawers, I searched for Band-Aids, but they seemed to be nowhere in sight. Tara and Gwen, caught up in their conversation, paid no attention to my mini crisis.

"I'm dying over here," I mumbled sarcastically under my breath, though they remained oblivious.

"I have some," Mike's voice came from behind me, startling me. I turned to find him standing a few feet away, holding a box of Band-Aids. How long had he been there?

He stepped closer, pulling out a Band-Aid and unwrapping it. Without a word, he gently took the towel from my hand and carefully wrapped the Band-Aid around my finger. His touch was practiced and oddly familiar.

"There you are, kitten. All better," he said softly, his small smile unsettling. His hand lingered briefly on my chin—just like he used to.

Kitten. The pet name I hadn't heard in years. It stirred something in me, a mix of emotions I wasn't ready to unpack. I quickly stepped back, breaking the moment.

"Thanks," I mumbled, brushing past him on my way to the dining room. Tara and Gwen were already setting up the table, their laughter filling the space, oblivious to the tension that had just unfolded in the kitchen. As I walked through the large dining room doors, I felt Mike's gaze following me. But I didn't turn around.

...

Lieutenant Michaels paced inside the FBI station in Florida, his nerves fraying as he took a call from dispatch. The entire place was on high alert—SWAT teams, FBI agents, and officers from Nebraska were gathered, their faces tense as they worked around the clock. Time was running out.

"Cary, you better have some good news for me," Michaels barked into the phone, his frustration barely contained.

"We've uncovered something, sir," Cary replied, her voice strained but steady. "Eric Stephenson has an accomplice— someone who's been working with him for years. I'm sending the fax now."

Behind Michaels, the fax machine whirred to life, spitting out a grainy image. Officers clustered around a board pinned with maps and photographs, trying to trace Eric Stephenson's movements. Michaels snatched the paper the moment it emerged.

"I'll be damned," he muttered, staring at the photograph.

Cary continued, her voice calm but purposeful. "His name is Justin Shawn Smith. He's about 26 years old, and like Stephenson, he uses several aliases. He's extremely cautious."

Michaels felt a chill of recognition run down his spine. "I know this boy," he said, his brow furrowed. "He's from Nebraska..."

"Yes, sir. Remember the fire 20 years ago? His parents died in it—that's when Eric Stephenson left his wife and daughter. According to sealed records, Justin was placed in foster care after the fire. Eric took him in shortly after. He's been with Stephenson ever since."

The pieces were starting to fall into place, but the picture they painted was even darker than Michaels had imagined. "I'll be damned," he said again, shaking his head. "This boy... he's using the alias Mike—Michael Cory Smith."

There was a pause on the line before Cary asked, "Michael Cory Smith? Are you sure?"

Michaels nodded, even though she couldn't see him. "Cary, run that name. What do we have on him?"

Cary typed furiously, her voice quick. "Under that name? Nothing. No criminal record, no flagged activity. In fact, it looks like a spotless history—captain of the football team, straight-A student, well-known in Nebraska."

Michaels' gut twisted. "You're telling me this kid has no record? Nothing at all?"

"I'm sending you another photo now, sir. Hold tight," Cary said. Moments later, the fax machine buzzed again. Michaels ripped the paper from the tray and stared at it.

"Holy mother of Jesus," he breathed. The face staring back at him was unmistakably Mike—the same Mike currently staying at Aberdeen Manor.

"Cary," Michaels said, his voice sharp, "I need every lead you've got on this kid. Where is he now? Do we know his exact location?"

Cary's voice tightened. "No solid information yet, sir, but his last known location was... Florida."

"Florida?" Michaels repeated, his voice rising. His pulse quickened as the realization hit him like a freight train. "Maeve lives here. She attends university here. Are you absolutely sure?"

"Yes, sir," Cary replied. "We're tracking now."

"Get me his movements. Every single one. I don't care what it takes," Michaels growled, slamming the phone down.

He turned to the gathered officers, holding up the faxed papers like a battle flag. "Listen up! We've got an accomplice, and we've got a name: Michael Cory Smith. Someone get me a line to those kids—now!"

His voice boomed through the station as officers scrambled. Phones rang, keyboards clattered, and calls were made to anyone connected to Aberdeen Manor. The urgency was palpable.

Another officer pushed through the crowd and slapped a large blueprint of the house on the counter. "Lieutenant, according to the plans and what Amy and James confirmed, there are two phone lines inside the house. One in the living room and one in the basement. The living room line runs to a shed on the property—it's been cut. The basement line runs underground."

Michaels leaned over the plans, his mind racing. "I want the number for that basement line. I don't care how you contact those kids—call, fax, hell, send smoke signals if you have to. Just get them on the phone. Now."

Officers snapped into action. The station roared to life, everyone working frantically to establish a connection to the manor before it was too late. Michaels slammed his fist onto the counter. "Do whatever it takes," he growled, his voice trembling with urgency. "Eric Stephenson isn't just some run-of-the-mill killer—he's a goddamn lunatic! If he's anywhere near those kids…" Michaels paused, his voice breaking slightly as he struggled to contain his emotions. "God help them. God help us all."

...

"Don't you dare," Luke said, laughing as he pointed across the table at Ethan, who was midway through recounting one of their more reckless teenage escapades. He leaned back in his chair, his laughter barely contained.

Ethan grinned, refusing to hold back. "Oh, come on! Seriously, we were so drunk, we tried sneaking back into the house through the basement window—you know, the one right above the washer and dryer?"

Tara and Gwen, mid-bite, burst into laughter, covering their mouths to avoid choking.

"Yeah, and this idiot," Luke added, pointing at Ethan, "forgot how small that window actually was. Picture it—two teenage giants trying to squeeze through a window made for a cat. It was a disaster."

I bit into a piece of bread, tears forming in my eyes as I tried to contain my laughter.

Ethan smirked and ruffled my hair. "And this one," he said, motioning toward me, "she just stood there watching, arms crossed, not even trying to help us."

I couldn't hold it in any longer and let out a loud laugh. "You guys were so stupid! You really thought you could sneak in like that?"

"If you hadn't ratted us out, we might've pulled it off!" Luke chimed in, pointing at me with mock indignation.

The memory hit me like a tidal wave. I was fourteen at the time, and Ethan and Luke, both sixteen, were far from sober. I had stood at the window, watching them make fools of themselves, until one of them noticed me. I had bolted upstairs, yelling, "MOM! Ethan and Luke are drunk again!"

The memory was too much—I doubled over in laughter, clutching my sides as tears streamed down my face.

"You really thought you could fit through a basement window," I choked out between gasps.

Even Mike, who had been quietly observing from the end of the table, let out a few chuckles, shaking his head at the ridiculous story.

"My God, this is so good," Tara said, catching her breath as the conversation carried on. Laughter and warmth filled the room as everyone traded stories, lightening the air that had been thick with unease earlier.

But as the laughter continued, my mind began to drift. My gaze wandered toward the kitchen, and memories of childhood began to surface. I could see it clearly: my uncle standing by the sink, peeling apples, while Ethan and I stood on stools beside him.

I remembered singing "Old McDonald Had a Farm," my voice loud and full of glee, belting out "E-I-E-I-O" after every verse. My uncle would laugh, encouraging me, while Ethan stood quietly beside us, hands stuffed in his pockets.

"Come on, big brother, it's E-I-E-I-O," I had said, looking up at Ethan with wide eyes. It was the first time I'd ever called him "big brother" since he came into our family.

I'd never forget the way his face lit up—how his grin spread like he'd just heard the best news in the world. Then, laughing, he joined in, singing the chorus louder than me. Lost in the memory, my eyes remained fixed on the kitchen. That's when I saw him—my uncle. He was standing there, clear as day, looking at me from across the room. My heart stopped. How was this possible? He was gone. This couldn't be real.

I pushed back my chair so abruptly that it crashed to the floor.

"Maeve, you okay?" Ethan's voice cut through the haze, his hand reaching out to steady me.

I pointed to the kitchen, my hand trembling. "Does anyone see that?" I whispered, barely able to get the words out.

All eyes turned toward the kitchen. My uncle stood there, just like he used to—his brown button-down shirt neatly pressed, his hair combed to the side, and his pleated brown pants held up by his favorite belt. It *was* him. There was no mistaking it.

"What are you talking about, May?" Ethan asked again, his voice calm but concerned. His hand rested on the small of my back, grounding me.

I turned to look at him, then back to the kitchen—but the figure was gone. The space was empty, as though nothing had ever been there.

"Nothing... never mind," I muttered, my voice shaking as I bent down to pick up my chair. My heart was still racing as I sat back down, my hands gripping the edge of the table for support.

The warmth of the room, the laughter from moments ago, felt distant now. All I could think about was what I'd just seen— and the uneasy feeling that it wouldn't be the last.

Chapter 7

THE GRAVE KEEPER

IT WAS MID-EVENING, and the sun had begun to dip behind the horizon, painting the sky in breathtaking shades of orange and red. The fiery glow illuminated the manor's facade, casting a surreal beauty over its weathered exterior. Despite its haunting air, the house almost seemed to belong in this strange, vibrant sunset.

We sat outside the front door, huddled in blankets on the circular patio that wrapped around the manor. The old wooden planks beneath us creaked softly with each shift of weight. Tara, Gwen, and Luke were sharing a smoke and passing around a beer, their laughter carried away on the cool evening breeze. For a fleeting moment, everything felt almost normal—like a lazy summer evening spent among friends. Almost. The strange unease that had clung to the house all day lingered, refusing to let us fully relax.

The cigarette made its way toward me, the smoke curling lazily in the air. Ethan held it out with a teasing grin. "Dare ya," he said, his voice full of playful challenge.

He knew how much I despised smoking, how I'd always sworn I'd never touch the stuff. Ethan wasn't a smoker either, but every now and then, he'd take a puff or two just to mess around. Everyone's eyes were on me, their faces lit with expectant grins. Should I break my vow just this once?

Mike, sitting cross-legged on the floor in front of me, chuckled, his amusement evident as he waited for my decision. With a dramatic sigh, I snatched the cigarette from Ethan's hand, holding it up to my lips. I took in the smallest breath—and immediately regretted it. Smoke filled my lungs, burning and bitter, and I doubled over, coughing hard as it billowed out of my mouth and nose.

"She couldn't handle it!" Luke howled, slapping his knee as laughter erupted around the group.

Ethan grinned like a mischievous kid as he took the cigarette back. "Disgusting," I choked out, my voice raspy as I wiped my watery eyes. I pulled my blanket tighter around my shoulders, my face scrunched in disgust.

The laughter was still echoing when the mood shifted abruptly. Out of the corner of my eye, I saw movement. The grave keeper had come around the side of the house. But something was different this time. He wasn't carrying a shovel. Slung over his shoulder was a rifle.

A chill ran through me, sharp and immediate. I wasn't the only one who noticed. Ethan shot to his feet, his chair scraping loudly against the patio. His voice was sharp, cutting through the evening air. "Hey! No guns on the property!" His tone carried more anger than fear, but I could see the tension in his posture.

Mike stood as well, leaning against the railing, his eyes locked on the man.

The grave keeper paused, seemingly unfazed by the sudden attention. With a casual wave, he tapped the barrel of the rifle with his hand. "Aye, son, no need to worry. Gotta eat, right? Just hunting me some deer," he said, his chuckle low and unsettling. His eyes didn't match the warmth in his voice. Without waiting for a response, he turned and disappeared into the shadowy trees near the metal gate.

I stared after him, my pulse racing. Something wasn't right. As he vanished, my eyes caught something strange—the gate. Or rather, what seemed to be an opening near it. Had there always been a gap there? I couldn't remember seeing one before. The gate had always seemed solid, impenetrable.

Ethan sat back down, though his posture remained rigid. His eyes kept flickering toward the gate, his unease palpable.

"Since when is there an opening near the metal gate?" I asked, trying to keep my voice steady.

Ethan's jaw tightened. He shook his head slowly, his worry mirroring my own. "Since never," he replied, his tone clipped.

"How'd it get there?" My voice rose slightly, the question more pointed this time. I wanted an answer that made sense, something to put my mind at ease.

Ethan hesitated, glancing toward the gate again. "Maybe Uncle made it before he passed," he said, though his words lacked conviction.

It wasn't the reassurance I needed.

The entire time we sat outside, my eyes kept drifting back to that opening. Was it a gate we'd never noticed? A break in the brick wall? How could something like that just appear? And why hadn't we seen it before?

The more I stared into the growing darkness, the more the unease gnawed at me. The evening, which had felt so light moments ago, now carried an ominous weight. It felt like the house itself was alive, watching, waiting.

We had spent nearly the entire evening outside, lingering until the sky turned pitch black. Finally, Ethan insisted we lock the house down.

"Hey, so have we decided? Are we staying the full four days?"

I asked, curious if Ethan still wanted to leave early. Mom's phone call had clearly shaken him, and his anxiety had rubbed off on me. I wondered what he and Luke had finally settled on.

"Nah, we've decided to stay at least two days," Ethan replied calmly, flashing me a reassuring smile. "It took us twelve hours to get here, after all." He reached out, gently patting my head before standing up.

"Lockdown, ladies!" Luke declared, half-drunk and swaying slightly as he staggered to his feet. A half-empty beer bottle dangled from his hand, his grin as wide as ever. "Be in bed by 10 p.m.!" he added in a mock-parental tone, waving his arm dramatically.

"Wow, he's like my parents. 'Time for bed, Tara! Be home by 10 p.m., Tara!'" Tara mimicked sarcastically, standing up from her rocking chair. Despite her mocking tone, she couldn't hide her laugh. She pulled a blanket tighter around her shoulders and followed Gwen inside, both of them giggling. Luke trailed after them, calling out more faux-parental orders: "Don't forget to brush your teeth, ladies! That's an order!" Tara and Gwen threw back playful insults, laughing as they disappeared into the house.

Mike, leaning against the railing, glanced my way before addressing Ethan. "Lockdown sounds like a good idea," he said, his eyes lingering on me.

Ethan folded his arms, giving Mike a subtle but firm nod. Tilting his head toward the door, Ethan silently urged Mike inside. Mike hesitated for a moment before turning and walking through the door.

I was about to follow when Ethan stepped in front of me, blocking my way.

"What's your problem?" I snapped, trying to sidestep him, but he moved with me, planting himself in my path. His hands rested firmly on my shoulders.

"I don't want you near him. I don't trust him, Maeve," Ethan said quietly but with conviction. "Mike isn't a good guy. There's something about him... something off."

I sighed, pressing a hand to my forehead. "What, just because he was stuck in Trenton? Or because he's staying in this abandoned house with us?" My irritation was clear. Ethan's hand dropped from my shoulder, and he tilted my chin up, forcing me to meet his eyes.

"He called you 'kitten' in the kitchen," Ethan said, his tone serious. "I heard him. He used to call you that all the time, Maeve. I don't like it."

I swatted his hand away, stepping back. "I'm not a child, Ethan. You don't need to watch out for me or protect me," I said, my voice rising. "Mike and I are over. I don't care about him anymore. Stop this!"

I tried to move around him again, but he blocked me once more. His eyes softened, pleading now. "Maeve," he said gently, but I'd had enough. I shoved past him, harder than I'd intended, hitting his shoulder as I pushed by.

"I don't want you to get hurt again," he called after me as I reached the door. My hand froze on the handle for a moment.

Inside, I could see Tara, Gwen, and Luke leaning against the stair railing, laughing like everything was normal. Mike stood near the door, and for a fleeting second, I wondered if he'd overheard us.

"Stop, Ethan. Just leave me alone for the rest of the night," I said, my back still to him. My voice wavered, no longer angry but tinged with exhaustion. I didn't know why I was so upset with him—he was only trying to protect me, like he always had.

I pushed the screen door open and stepped inside, letting it close softly behind me. Ethan followed a moment later, closing and locking the front door. Mike shifted away from the entryway, heading toward the living room. Meanwhile, Luke, Tara, and Gwen moved through the house, latching windows and locking every exterior door.

I made my way to the kitchen and stopped at the basement door. The air around it always felt heavier, carrying an eerie stillness that set me on edge. I hated the basement—unfinished, full of strange noises, and cluttered with old toys, forgotten clothes, and family heirlooms my aunt and uncle had cared for. I quickly latched the door with the hook near the top and turned away, trying to shake the unease creeping over me.

"I'm taking the room down the hall," I announced as I walked toward the main living room. It was my mother's old room, with its queen-sized bed still draped in red-and-gold sheets, just as she had left it.

"I thought we were all sleeping in the living room?" Luke asked, his voice tinged with surprise. I raised an eyebrow, confused. When had they decided that?

"Well, not me. I'm taking Mom's old room," I said sharply, brushing past Ethan as I headed toward the stairs. My shoulder collided with his, causing him to spill some of the water he was holding.

"What's with her?" Gwen asked, glancing at Ethan as I stormed out of the room.

"We had a little disagreement outside," Ethan replied quietly, his eyes following me as I disappeared down the hall.

Tara, busy inflating air mattresses near the fireplace, glanced up briefly but said nothing. The others continued setting up the sleeping arrangements, their voices filling the house as I closed the bedroom door behind me. The heavy silence that followed was a stark contrast to their lively chatter.

Inside the bedroom, I flicked on the light and let out a breath I hadn't realized I'd been holding. Everything was exactly as I remembered it: the wooden closet wardrobe with its intricate carvings, the vanity with its beautifully ornate round mirror, and my mom's collection of China dolls still lined neatly along the top. Beneath it, the round, fluffy stool sat perfectly in place, untouched by time. A soft smile crept across my face as a wave of nostalgia washed over me.

I walked to the window and looked out toward the graveyard. My heart lurched as I caught sight of Eric, the grave keeper, dragging the body of a dead deer toward the shed. My stomach churned at the sight. I quickly locked the window, drawing the curtains shut to block out the unsettling view.

As I turned back toward the room, something unfamiliar caught my eye—a mirror I hadn't noticed before. It was mounted on the wall next to the bed, just by the door to the bathroom. Its plain brown frame didn't match the ornate decor of the rest of the room.

"Strange... I've never seen this before," I muttered to myself, stepping closer to examine it. I waved my hand in front of the glass and felt a chill crawl up my spine. Something about it felt... wrong. This wasn't an ordinary mirror.

It was a two-way mirror.

My heart pounded in my chest as panic began to rise. I leaned closer, trying to peer behind the glass. The realization hit me like a punch to the gut—this wasn't just decorative.

"ETHAN!" I shouted, my voice shaking as I pounded on the glass. "ETHAN!" Panic made my voice louder, sharper.

The door burst open as Ethan rushed in, followed by Luke, Tara, Gwen, and Mike. Their faces were filled with concern as they crowded into the room.

"What? Maeve, what's wrong?" Ethan demanded, moving toward me quickly.

"Look at the mirror," I said, stepping back. My voice trembled as I pointed at it. Ethan waved his hand in front of it, his expression darkening as he examined the glass.

Luke was the first to speak. "It's a two-way mirror," he said grimly, running his fingers along the frame. His tone was tense, his words confirming my worst fear.

"Tara, get my bat—it's by the front door," Ethan ordered sharply. Tara nodded and darted out of the room, returning moments later with the metal bat in hand.

"Stand back," Ethan warned, his voice steady but tight with anger. He motioned for everyone to move away from the mirror before gripping the bat and swinging it with all his strength. The glass shattered with a loud crash, shards scattering across the floor and revealing what lay behind it.

Behind the mirror was a small hole in the wall, and nestled within it was a camera. Its lens gleamed ominously, silently aimed at the bed.

"What the hell?" Luke muttered, stepping closer to inspect the device. He crouched down, careful not to cut himself on the broken glass, and examined the camera more closely.

Ethan leaned in beside him, carefully brushing away some of the larger shards with his foot. His voice was low, heavy with disbelief. "Someone's been watching us."

Luke's face paled as he looked back at me. "No," he said, his tone grim. "Someone's been watching Maeve."

My stomach twisted into knots as their words sank in. Ethan turned to me, his face pale and tight with anger. His eyes scanned me briefly, and I instinctively pulled my sweater tighter around my body, suddenly hyper-aware of my tank top and how ex-posed I felt.

"I'm not sleeping in here," I whispered, my voice barely au-dible. A wave of fear surged through me, making it hard to breathe.

"Did you guys know about this?" Tara asked cautiously, her voice breaking the heavy silence. She took a step closer to Ethan and Luke, her face etched with unease. "Were there cameras in this house before?"

Ethan shook his head firmly. "No. We never had anything like this here—not for any reason."

Luke flinched slightly as the camera lens flickered, shifting as though adjusting. He stared at it for a long moment, then stepped back, his jaw clenched.

"Yeah, you're definitely not sleeping in here tonight," Ethan said, his tone final and protective. He glanced at me, his eyes softening for a moment. "We'll figure this out, but you're staying with the rest of us."

I nodded numbly, stepping away from the bed as Gwen grabbed a broom and dustpan, sweeping up the shattered glass.

Meanwhile, Ethan and Luke worked to dislodge the camera from the wall, their movements deliberate and tense. The air in the room felt thick with unease, the sense of safety we had tried so hard to cling to now completely shattered.

"Where's it connected to?" Luke muttered, running his hand along the wall as he tried to trace the wiring. Ethan yanked hard on the camera lens, pulling it free from the plaster with a crack that sent small fragments of drywall scattering. Behind the hole, a thick black cable snaked deeper into the wall.

"Don't pull it too hard—let's figure out where it leads first," Luke said, gripping the wire cautiously. He began to tug at the cable, revealing its path as chunks of drywall crumbled away. The cord, wrapped in thick plastic casing, ran upward over the bathroom and then disappeared down the side of the wall behind the wardrobe.

"Help me move this," Ethan said, motioning to the wardrobe. He and Luke braced themselves against the heavy wooden furniture and pulled it away from the wall with a groan, revealing more of the cable as it snaked toward the doorframe.

Mike, standing by the door, reached up and yanked at the exposed cord above the frame. With a grunt, he pulled it loose, revealing a small hidden hole housing a power outlet.

"If it's plugged into power, then how is it recording? Who's watching the footage?" Ethan muttered, his frustration evident as he turned the camera over in his hands. His fingers found a small flap on the side of the device, and he flipped it open, revealing an SD card tucked neatly inside. As soon as he pulled the card out, the camera blinked off, the tiny red recording light fading into darkness.

"What the hell is going on?" Luke said, inspecting the camera with a mix of anger and confusion.

I stood behind Ethan, trembling as fear and confusion churned in my chest. My heart pounded, and I couldn't seem to shake the feeling of being watched.

"I brought my laptop," Tara suddenly spoke up, her voice

breaking through the tension.

Ethan's eyes lit up with urgency. "Perfect. We'll check what's on the SD card right now." He handed it to Tara, who immediately darted out of the room. Ethan followed close behind, his pace quick and determined.

I hesitated, lingering in the doorway, my mind racing with possibilities. Luke noticed and extended his hand toward me, his expression softening. "Don't worry, Maeve. We'll figure this out. We'll find whoever did this," he said firmly. His calm demeanor grounded me, and I nodded, letting him guide me out of the room.

Gwen trailed behind, her eyes darting back to the shattered mirror and the exposed wall. Mike and Luke stayed close, their presence oddly comforting as we made our way to the living room, where Tara had already set up her laptop. Ethan was pacing near the TV, his frustration visible as he connected the laptop to the larger screen.

The room was thick with silence as Tara inserted the SD card into the laptop. The screen flickered to life, and all eyes turned toward the TV. My pulse quickened as Tara clicked through the files, her fingers moving swiftly over the keyboard. A single video file loaded, and the room seemed to collectively hold its breath.

The footage began to play, grainy and distorted at first. Static crackled across the screen, and flashes of the room appeared. Slowly, the picture cleared, revealing the bedroom.

"That's today," Tara whispered, her voice tight with unease. The timestamp confirmed it—it was from just a few hours ago.

"Fast forward," Ethan said sharply, his voice laced with anger. Tara sped through the footage, and we all watched as moments from earlier played out on the screen. Time blurred, hours condensed into minutes, and for a while, nothing seemed out of the ordinary—until it did.

The camera zoomed in on me as I sat by the window, staring out at the graveyard. My breath hitched. The footage lingered on me for far too long, capturing every small movement. I felt a knot of dread tighten in my stomach.

"This is sick," Gwen muttered, her arms crossed tightly over her chest.

"There's more," Ethan said, leaning forward, his jaw clenched.

The footage flickered again. For a moment, the screen went black, and when it came back, the camera was focused on me again—this time while I was lying on the bed earlier that evening. My heart sank as the video lingered on the most vulnerable moments, the thought of someone watching me like that making my skin crawl.

"Who the hell would do this?" Luke asked, his voice simmering with fury.

No one had an answer. The room felt colder, heavier, the air thick with tension and fear. I wrapped my arms around myself, trying to shake off the creeping sense of exposure that clung to me like a shadow. Even though the camera was no longer recording, the feeling lingered—a violation, a gross invasion of my privacy and safety. Whoever had set this up had been watching us, unseen and unchecked.

Tara glanced at Ethan, her face pale. "There might be more cameras. We need to check the whole house."

Ethan's expression hardened. "We're not leaving anything unchecked."

We began a frantic search, tearing through every room in the house. No mirror, closet, or corner was left unexamined as we hunted for more hidden cameras. My nerves were on edge as I scoured the main bathroom on the first floor. Something felt wrong, like an unseen presence was lurking nearby.

I opened the vanity cabinet above the sink, my hands trembling slightly. A chill ran down my spine, and dread settled in my chest. I had an overwhelming sense that something was behind the mirror.

"ETHAN!" I called, my voice cracking with panic. Within

seconds, Ethan appeared in the doorway, his face serious and ready.

"Behind here," I said, motioning to the mirror. We had already pulled out the mirrors in other rooms without finding anything, but this felt different.

"Stand back," Ethan said firmly. He gripped the vanity, and with a sharp tug, ripped it from the wall. The sound of cracking plaster filled the room.

"Another one," Luke muttered, standing in the doorway, his voice tinged with alarm.

"No... oh my God!" Gwen stammered, her face going white. "I showered in here earlier!" Her voice rose, frantic and distressed. "We were making out in the shower!" she exclaimed, pacing back and forth in the hall.

Luke moved to her side, grabbing her shoulders gently. "Gwen, stop. Breathe, okay? We'll figure this out," he said, his tone calm but urgent. Gwen was too panicked to listen, her breathing shallow and erratic.

"This is insane! Who's watching us?" Ethan growled, yanking the camera from its hiding spot in the wall. The power to the device cut out with a sharp snap, leaving a hollow space where the camera had been. He flipped the device over, revealing a small compartment containing an SD card—identical to the first.

"Tara, take this," Ethan said, handing her the card. Tara grabbed it and bolted toward the living room, where her laptop was set up.

We gathered in the living room, the atmosphere heavy with tension. Gwen was visibly shaken, clinging to Luke for comfort, her hands trembling. Ethan's face was grim as Tara inserted the card into her computer. The screen lit up, and the footage began to play. The camera had been recording earlier that day. We watched as Gwen and Luke entered the bathroom, laughing and playfully teasing each other. Tara quickly averted her eyes, and the rest of us followed, feeling like unwelcome voyeurs. Tara fast-forwarded through the footage, her fingers moving rapidly across the keyboard until it reached the end.

"Nothing," Tara said quietly, her frustration evident. "There's nothing showing who set this up."

The footage ended abruptly after Gwen and Luke left the bathroom, leaving us with no leads, no answers—only more questions.

"I have a feeling..." Ethan said, his eyes narrowing as they flicked toward the kitchen.

"Ethan, no," I said, realizing what he was about to do. My heart raced as he grabbed the bat he'd left by my room and stormed toward the back door.

"Ethan! What are you doing?" I shouted, running after him.

He threw open the door, the screen door slamming against the wall as he stormed down the steps. We followed him in a frantic rush, our voices echoing in the night. Ethan didn't stop. His pace quickened as he headed straight for the shed in the yard.

"Ethan!" Luke shouted, sprinting to catch up. Mike followed closely, his face grim with concern.

Eric, the grave keeper, stepped out of the shed just as Ethan reached it. He looked calm, eerily so, and a smirk slowly spread across his face as if he had been expecting us.

"ARE YOU WATCHING US?" Ethan roared, his voice shaking with fury.

Eric didn't flinch. He stood there, clasping his hands together, his posture relaxed. "You think I set up cameras in yer house, boy?" he said, his thick Southern drawl dripping with mockery.

Ethan lunged, but Luke and Mike grabbed him, holding him back before he could get any closer to Eric.

"Ethan, stop it!" I cried, gripping his arm as tears of frustration and fear welled in my eyes. Tara and Gwen stood nearby, both on edge, their expressions mirroring my unease.

"GET OFF MY PROPERTY!" Ethan shouted, his voice

raw with emotion as he struggled against Luke and Mike's restraint. "You have until daylight to get the hell out of here!"

Eric chuckled, a sound so cold and unsettling it sent a shiver down my spine. Slowly, he removed his cap, running a hand over his short, graying hair before shaking his head. "Listen here, boy," he said, his voice unnervingly calm. "I've got a contract on this property. You don't have the authority to kick me off. Only yer mother does."

With that, Eric turned his back on us and walked back into the shed, the door slamming shut behind him with a loud, defiant bang.

"ETHAN!" I screamed, grabbing his arm as he tried to lunge forward again, straining against Luke and Mike's restraint. His muscles were rigid, and I could feel the rage radiating off him like heat from a fire.

"Ethan, stop!" Luke said firmly, stepping between him and the shed door. "We need to call your parents, stay the night, and get the hell out of here by morning. Going after him now isn't going to solve anything."

Ethan's furious glare met Luke's, and for a moment, I thought he might push past him anyway. But then, slowly, his shoulders sagged, and some of the tension drained from his posture. His jaw remained tight, though, and his eyes still burned with barely restrained anger.

"Fine," he muttered through gritted teeth. He turned to the rest of us, his voice sharp and commanding. "Check your phones. See if we can call home. Tara, try to get internet access out here. We're not leaving this place unchecked."

Tara gave a quick nod and hurried toward the house, her urgency matching Ethan's. The rest of us followed, our footsteps heavy as the oppressive tension hung in the air like a storm cloud about to burst.

My mind raced, the pieces of this horrifying puzzle tumbling over one another with no clear picture in sight. Why had Ethan lost it like that? Was he really ready to go after Eric? My chest tightened at the thought. As much as I hated to admit it, I didn't think Eric was behind the cameras. He was unsettling, sure, but this didn't feel like his doing. Could it be someone else—someone who had trespassed on the property? But why? And who?

As I stepped through the door into the house, I glanced back over my shoulder at the shed. The small structure stood eerily silent against the backdrop of the darkening night. My stomach churned with unease. Something about Eric felt off—too calm, too smug, like he knew more than he was letting on.

I followed Ethan inside, my thoughts spiraling as the gnawing fear in the back of my mind refused to let go.

Inside the house, Tara sat at her laptop, furiously clicking and typing as she tried to pick up any signal. The tension in the air was suffocating as we searched for any modem or device that could hint at an internet connection. Luke and Ethan were upstairs, combing through the remaining rooms, while Mike hovered by the kitchen door, his eyes fixed on me as I rifled through cupboards, drawers, and the pantry. Anything that could hide a modem or internet box was fair game.

"You're making me nervous. Why are you just standing there watching me?" I snapped, noticing the weight of his stare. It felt invasive, unsettling.

Mike stepped closer, slipping into the pantry with me, and suddenly, the space felt claustrophobic. He leaned casually against the doorway, blocking the only exit. His unease was palpable, though his eyes held a trace of something softer—regret, maybe.

"Sorry, kitten," he began, his voice low and tense, "I just... I don't know. I can't explain it."

I folded my arms, keeping my expression cold. "Stop calling me kitten," I said firmly, the irritation rising in my tone. "We're not together anymore. You don't get to call me that."

Mike hesitated for a moment, then reached out, brushing his hand lightly against my cheek. My pulse quickened, but not with the affection it once did. It was adrenaline—fear and anger. Without thinking, I shoved him back hard, creating distance between us.

"Don't you dare try to kiss me," I snapped, the words escaping before I could stop them. My voice was sharp, trembling with barely restrained fury.

Mike raised his hands in surrender, stepping back slightly but still blocking the doorway. "May, stop. Relax, okay? I'm sorry. I just wanted to apologize… for the way I ended things." His voice softened, his eyes pleading, but I wasn't having it.

"Stay away from me," I warned, the finality in my tone leaving no room for argument. My chest was tight with a confusing swirl of emotions—hurt, anger, fear. He stood there for a beat longer, as if debating whether to say more.

"May, can't you just forgive me?" he asked, his voice quieter this time, almost desperate.

Before I realized what I was doing, my hand flew up, and I slapped him hard across the face. The sound reverberated through the small pantry, sharp and definitive. Mike's hand moved instinctively to his cheek, his expression stunned.

Finally, he stepped aside, giving me enough room to storm past him. I barely registered the tears welling in my eyes as I bolted toward the kitchen. My chest ached with a mix of frustration and regret, but I pushed the feelings aside, focusing on something—anything—to distract myself.

My hand found the basement door. I yanked it open with more force than I intended, the hinge and lock snapping as the door swung wide. Without hesitation, I rushed down the stairs, the cool air of the basement hitting me like a slap to the face.

At the bottom step, I reached for the light string, pulling it on. The dim bulb cast long shadows across the space, amplifying its eerie atmosphere. The basement smelled of damp wood and mildew, its corners cluttered with forgotten boxes and dusty heirlooms. I forced myself to focus, scanning the room for anything that could explain the broken phone line—or the cameras.

That's when I saw it. A metal door stood slightly ajar in a bare-walled room next to an old, rusted bike and a dusty hope chest. My stomach twisted as I moved closer, pushing the bike aside to get a better look. I clicked on the light inside the room, and my heart dropped.

The fuse box was open, wires spilling out like entrails. My gaze zeroed in on one particular wire—severed, its ends frayed and exposed. It was the phone line. Someone had deliberately cut it.

"What the hell?" I muttered, stepping closer to inspect it. My fingers hovered over the cut wire, cold dread seeping into my veins. Whoever did this knew exactly what they were doing.

Before I could investigate further, a voice echoed from the top of the stairs. "WHAT? THE CBs ARE ACTIVE?" Gwen's shout jolted me out of my thoughts. Panic surged through me as I bolted up the stairs, leaving the basement and its unsettling discoveries behind.

I rushed outside, the cool night air hitting me like a wave. Ethan stood by his car, gripping the CB radio receiver tightly, his expression grim.

"Repeat that again," he barked into the radio, his voice edged with frustration. Luke was in the driver's seat, furiously turning the dials, his face tense as he worked to recapture the signal.

"What's going on?" I asked breathlessly, my fear barely concealed as I approached them.

"We don't know yet," Ethan said, his tone clipped. "We picked up something—static at first, but then a voice came through. Someone's transmitting."

He pressed the receiver button again. "Repeat your message. Who is this?"

The radio crackled, but only static answered him. Luke continued adjusting the dials, muttering under his breath. "It was clear a second ago. Someone was trying to reach us."

The static grew louder, cutting through the tense silence. My heart pounded in my chest as I stared at the radio, hoping—dreading—that the voice would return.

I glanced back toward the house, a shiver crawling up my spine. If the phone lines were cut and now we were getting strange signals from the CBs... was someone nearby? Watching us? Or was it all just a cruel coincidence?

"We need to figure this out fast," Ethan said, his voice full of determination. "We're not staying another night here without knowing who's watching us."

Suddenly, the crackling static on the CB was interrupted. A voice came through, distorted but unmistakable. "Hello, can anyone hear me? This is officer Michaels broadcasting to CB 18915 on Channel 9."

Ethan's hand trembled as he quickly clicked the receiver. "Channel 9," he repeated urgently, gesturing to Luke, who turned the dial with sharp focus.

"Can anyone hear me? I am reaching CB 18915 on Channel 9, emergency line," Michaels' voice broke through again, clearer this time though still tinged with static.

I moved closer to the car, my stomach twisting into knots. Something was wrong. I could feel it.

"This is CB 18915. I hear you, lieutenant Michaels," Ethan replied, his voice tense but steady. On the other end, there was an audible sigh of relief.

"Thank God, boy. We've been trying to reach you for the last hour. We're heading toward Trenton. You kids stay inside that house—DO NOT leave that house," Michaels said, his words laced with urgency.

The static hissed, but his message was clear enough to send chills down my spine.

"Lieutenant Michaels, are we in danger? We need more to go

on! Why should we stay?" Ethan's voice rose, desperation bleeding into his tone as he clutched the receiver tightly. Tara, Gwen, and I stood near the car, tension crackling between us like electricity. Michaels' next words were fragmented, broken by static.

"STAY in that house. We're on our way. Do not—I repeat—do not leave. Lock it down and stay there. There's a phone in the basement..."

The transmission fizzled out completely, swallowed by static.

"A phone in the basement?" Ethan muttered, his expression a mix of shock and determination. "Did anyone know about this?"

The CB dissolved into noise, and Luke slammed the side of the dashboard in frustration. "Signal's gone."

"Damn it!" Ethan growled, tossing the receiver back into the car. His eyes were wild with urgency. "There's a phone in the basement!" Without waiting for a response, he bolted toward the house, Luke hot on his heels. We all scrambled after them, adrenaline surging as Ethan flung the front door open and made a beeline for the basement.

"Everyone—search everything. Every wall, every corner. Find it!" Ethan barked, his voice sharp with command. There was no room for hesitation.

We scattered through the cold, dark basement. I rifled through dusty boxes and old furniture, shoving aside relics of our childhood and forgotten heirlooms. The unfinished walls loomed like skeletons in the dim light, and every creak and shadow set my nerves on edge.

"ETHAN!" Luke's shout shattered the tension. His flashlight beam focused on a small area near the fuse box. There, partially hidden in the cracked plaster, was a phone jack.

Ethan rushed over, his breath shallow and fast. "Where is it?" His trembling hands reached for the wall as if the phone jack might disappear.

"Is it even connected?" Luke asked, crouching near the base

of the wall. He traced the cord carefully, following its path along the plaster and down behind the fuse box. The wire snaked along the floor before vanishing behind the furnace.

"It stops here, behind the furnace," Luke said, his voice tense with frustration. "Is there some kind of hidden panel or trapdoor?"

Ethan and Luke pushed against the wooden paneling under the stairs, testing for any give, but the planks were solidly in place.

"Impossible... how can a phone cord just vanish into a wall?" Ethan muttered, his voice laced with frustration. He pressed his palms against the boards, his fingers searching for any hidden mechanism.

"It's connected underground," Luke said, crouching closer to inspect the cord's path. His voice dropped, realization dawning. "There's no phone—just the jack."

"That's insane," Tara said, her voice tight with unease. Then her eyes lit up as she remembered something. "Wait! We have a phone upstairs. Let's try plugging it in there."

Tara and I darted upstairs, racing to grab the old rotary phone from the living room. My heart pounded as I unplugged it from the wall and dashed back down to the basement, my breath coming in shallow bursts.

"Here," I said, shoving the phone into Ethan's hands. "Try this."

Luke quickly unplugged the wire from the fuse box and connected it to the phone. He picked up the receiver, his face a mask of skepticism. Then, suddenly, his expression changed.

"There's a dial tone!" Luke shouted, his voice breaking the tension like a hammer to glass. "It's alive!"

Ethan grabbed the phone from Luke, his hands shaking slightly as he clutched the receiver. This was it—a possible lifeline.

"Maeve, it's working," Luke said, the disbelief in his voice replaced with a flicker of hope. He quickly dialed the number for my parents, and we all held our breath, waiting.

The ringing tone hummed softly through the line, each ring stretching longer in my mind. Seconds felt like hours as we waited, the silence in the room charged with anxious energy.

GAMES

M Y BLOOD WAS BOILING, my pulse pounding so loudly in my ears it drowned out everything else. I was teetering on the edge of a full-blown panic attack, clinging desperately to whatever control I could muster. My breaths came in shallow bursts, my hands trembling as I glanced around at the others. Ethan paced near the furnace, clutching the phone tightly to his ear. "Come on, come on," he muttered under his breath, his anxiety seeping through as the number rang and rang.

"Voicemail," he finally said, frustration sharpening his tone. He quickly left a message: "Mom, it's me. We're still at the house in Aberdeen. I don't know the number to this line—maybe it'll show up on call display. We're okay—don't panic. We're locking down the house. Lieutenant Michaels contacted us through CB—" Before he could finish, the line abruptly went dead.

"What the...?" Ethan pulled the receiver away from his ear, staring at it with confusion.

"What's wrong?" I asked, my voice tight, betraying my growing fear.

"It's dead," he said, his voice heavy with unease. "But... at least I got the message out to Mom and Dad." His attempt at reassurance felt hollow. The air around us grew heavier, the silence almost menacing.

"Alright, let's lock it down like Michaels said," Luke interjected, his voice steady as he tried to take charge. "We'll keep the cars close in case we need to get out of here fast." He motioned for everyone to calm down, his hands moving in a steadying gesture. But it did little to ease the panic spreading through us like wildfire.

"Luke's right," Ethan said, snapping back into focus. "Let's grab what we need and set up in the living room." He slammed the receiver back onto the phone's base and tossed it to the ground with a loud thud. The sound echoed ominously in the room, like a final nail being driven into a coffin. We bolted upstairs, our footsteps reverberating through the empty hallways. That's when I noticed something off.

"Where's Mike?" I asked, my heart sinking.

"HEY, CUT THAT OUT!" Mike's voice rang out from the front yard, sharp with anger. My stomach dropped, and Ethan and Luke were already sprinting toward the door, their urgency pulling me along.

We burst outside to find Mike standing near the cars, his face flushed with rage. All four tires had knives sticking out of them, the blades catching the dim light from the porch. Ethan cursed loudly as he descended the steps two at a time. Mike stood near the open metal gates, breathless, his chest heaving as though he'd been chasing someone. The gates groaned as he pushed them shut, the sound grating against the tense silence of the night.

"DAMN IT!" Luke shouted, yanking a knife out of one of

the tires. His face was pale, his frustration palpable.

"WHO DID THIS?" Ethan yelled, his voice raw with fury as he sprinted toward Mike. His anger crackled like electricity in the air.

Mike stumbled back through the gates, slamming them shut with force. His eyes were wide, adrenaline coursing through him. But Ethan didn't slow down. Grabbing Mike by the collar, he shoved him hard against the hood of the car.

"ETHAN, STOP!" I screamed, rushing forward to grab his arm. This wasn't Ethan—this was something darker, something unhinged. I pulled at him, but he shrugged me off as if I weren't even there.

"SPEAK!" Ethan shouted, his voice filled with rage. "What happened? Did you see who did this?" He shook Mike violently, his knuckles white from the grip.

Luke was beside them now, trying to pry Ethan off. "Ethan, let him go! This isn't helping!" he barked, his voice urgent.

Mike coughed, grabbing at Ethan's wrist and managing to force his grip to loosen. "Calm down, man! I chased him off the property, alright? Got a description," he panted, his voice ragged. "A man in a black fedora hat and a trench coat."

Ethan froze, his grip slackening as the weight of Mike's words sank in. Slowly, he released him, taking a step back. His face went pale, and his eyes darkened with realization.

"What? He's here? That man's here?" I asked, my voice trembling, panic bubbling in my chest and threatening to spill over. The fear that had been lurking beneath the surface was now roaring, drowning out every rational thought.

"Everyone get inside. Lock down the house," Ethan barked, his tone sharp and commanding. Mike adjusted his shirt, brushing himself off as he moved away from Ethan, trailing behind the rest of us toward the house. Luke lingered, watching as Ethan strode to his car, his jaw set. Ethan popped open the glove compartment, pulling out a small box. He flipped it open, checking the barrel of his gun before slipping it securely into his waistband.

"We're stranded now," Luke said quietly, his eyes fixed on the slashed tires. "Whoever did this… they wanted us stranded."

Ethan's gaze darkened as it flicked toward the house, specifically to Mike, who was busy helping us gather the bags and supplies. "I have an idea who did this," Ethan muttered, his voice laced with suspicion.

"You think it was Mike?" Luke asked, his tone hushed but pointed. His eyes followed Ethan's to where Mike stood, his movements deliberate but calm. Ethan nodded, slipping the box of bullets into his back pocket. "Yeah, and I'm not about to let him out of my sight."

Luke sighed, running a hand through his hair. "If you think it was him, why keep him here? Kick him out—let him fend for himself."

Ethan's gaze didn't waver. "Because I need to keep him where I can see him," he said, his voice low and dangerous. "Something's off, and until I figure out what, he stays."

Luke exhaled heavily, clearly torn. He walked back to his own car and opened the trunk, pulling out a baseball bat and a handgun. Tucking the gun into his waistband, he held the bat over his shoulder. "Fine," he said, his tone resolute. "Let's lock this place down and hunker in the living room. Michaels will be here soon."

Together, they returned to the house, locking the door securely behind them. The air inside was stifling, thick with fear and uncertainty. Ethan and Luke didn't waste any time—they did a final sweep, ensuring every door and window, including those in the basement, were securely locked. No one was taking any chances.

As we gathered in the living room, the oppressive silence was broken only by the occasional creak of the old house. We were isolated, vulnerable, and whoever had done this clearly knew what they were doing. Tara had set up blankets and pillows in the center of the room, with enough food and water to last until Michaels arrived. Despite the small comforts, the looming sense of danger made the room feel cold and unwelcoming.

I sat on a mattress near the couch, my knees tucked against my chest, the weight of the day pressing down on me. Gwen moved quickly, her movements jerky as she closed the curtains. Ethan lit an old gas lamp he'd found in the kitchen, casting flickering, dim light across the room. Even the light felt uneasy, as if it, too, didn't want to be here. Luke sat near the fireplace, his phone in hand, still desperately searching for a signal. But we all knew it was pointless. We were too deep in the woods for any cell tower to reach us.

I pulled my blanket tighter around my shoulders, trying to fight the chill that had settled deep in my bones. But it wasn't just the cold—it was the anxiety, creeping in like a storm. The questions in my mind were relentless: Who slashed the tires? Why were the cameras set up? Was someone watching us right now? The fear twisted tighter and tighter until it became unbearable.

Before I knew it, tears began to spill down my face. I hadn't even realized I was crying until Ethan noticed. He was beside me in an instant, his hands gently rubbing up and down my arms. "Hey, hey, Maeve, calm your nerves," he whispered, his voice soothing but tinged with worry. He leaned closer, trying to steady me, but his touch wasn't enough to stop the spiral I was falling into.

Mike's usual smirk was gone, replaced with a look of genuine concern. He knelt beside me, his presence adding to the overwhelming swirl of emotions that threatened to pull me under.

"Where are her pills?" Tara's voice cut through the tension, sharp and urgent. She turned to Gwen, and the two of them rushed to the kitchen, where I'd left my purse. Their voices rose in frustration as they rummaged through its contents.

My breathing hitched, becoming shallow and ragged. I threw the blanket off me, gasping for air as my chest tightened, the weight of everything pressing down on me like a vice.

"No, Maeve!" Ethan's voice was firm, but I could barely hear him through the rush of blood pounding in my ears. He wrapped his arms around me, pulling me tightly against his chest. His grip was grounding, strong, but my panic had taken over, and I couldn't break free from it.

"Tara! Gwen! Did you find her meds?" Luke's voice was loud and desperate, cutting through the chaos. He bolted to the kitchen to help them search.

The pressure in my chest grew heavier, and my vision started to narrow. My body trembled uncontrollably as I felt the walls closing in. It was like the house itself was suffocating me.

"I'm right here, Maeve. I'm right here," Ethan murmured, his voice low and steady, a lifeline against the storm raging inside me. His grip tightened as his hands moved up and down my arms, trying to ground me, but it felt like nothing could break through the crushing panic.

Luke knelt beside me, his face close to mine, his voice calm but urgent. "Maeve, listen to me. Where are your pills? Do you remember where you left them?"

I couldn't speak; my throat was locked tight, and it felt like every breath was a battle. Instead, I raised my trembling hand, pointing toward the other living room. My jacket—I'd tossed it over the armchair when we first got here. The pills were in the pocket.

"The other room!" Mike's voice cut through the chaos like a whip. He shot to his feet, already moving. "THE OTHER LIV-ING ROOM!" he shouted to Tara and Gwen, urgency propelling them into action. They sprinted toward the living room, searching my jacket with frantic hands until Gwen pulled the small bottle from the pocket.

Ethan rocked me gently, his voice a constant murmur in my

ear. "You're okay, Maeve. You're okay. I've got you." But his words barely pierced the suffocating haze. My body was locked in fear, every nerve screaming as I tried to hold on.

Gwen ran back, the bottle clutched tightly in her hand, her fingers fumbling to open it. Ethan grabbed a pill from her, his hands steady despite the tension etched into his face. He brought it to my lips, his voice soft but firm. "Take this. Just one swallow, Maeve."

I obeyed, swallowing the pill as quickly as I could, though my whole body still trembled uncontrollably. Ethan held me closer, his warmth pressing against me as he stroked my hair, whispering reassurances that finally began to cut through the suffocating fear.

"I've never seen her like this," Mike said, his voice uncharacteristically subdued. The color had drained from his face, and the cocky demeanor he always carried was gone, replaced by a genuine worry that felt almost foreign coming from him.

"She's had severe anxiety for years," Ethan said quietly, still holding me. His fingers brushed a strand of hair from my face as he continued, "Anything can trigger it, especially... situations like this."

I exhaled deeply, the air rushing out of my lungs like a dam breaking. My muscles began to loosen, the tight coil of panic slowly unwinding. My vision cleared, and for the first time in what felt like forever, I could think straight again. But then my gaze drifted toward the hallway.

And that's when I saw him.

My uncle.

He stood at the end of the hall, faint but undeniably there. His expression was a mix of worry and sorrow, his eyes fixed on me as though he had been watching the entire time. He looked exactly as I remembered him—his brown button-down shirt, his pleated slacks, the same gentle presence he'd always had. But now, there was something heavier in his gaze, a pain that wasn't there before.

His lips moved, forming words I couldn't hear. But I knew what he was saying.

"Come on, Maeve. Get up. Get up."

A cold wave of realization crashed over me. I was seeing my uncle's ghost.

I sat frozen, staring at him, my breath catching in my chest again. My aunt—his wife—used to claim she could see "earthbound spirits," a gift passed down from her grandmother. She would tell stories of seeing lost souls, trapped between worlds. I'd always thought they were just that—stories. Even my grandmother had spoken about it, though it had skipped over my mother. I never believed it. Not really.

Until now.

He didn't disappear. He just stood there, waiting. His eyes, so filled with pain and worry, locked on mine. I wanted to look away, to close my eyes and pretend it wasn't real. But I couldn't. I was rooted to the spot, unable to move as he stared back at me, silent but desperate for me to understand.

Finally, my body gave in. I closed my eyes and let myself sink back against Ethan, my breath slowing as exhaustion took over. Even as my body relaxed, the image of my uncle stayed burned in my mind, his presence lingering like the chill of the night air.

After my nerves finally settled, exhaustion pulled me under, and I fell into a deep sleep. I vaguely felt Ethan draping a blanket over me, his movements careful and protective. The quiet murmurs of his voice mingled with Luke's as they whispered in the corner of the living room, their words a faint hum against the stillness. Tara and Gwen slept beside me, their soft, rhythmic breathing lulling me further into unconsciousness.

But even in sleep, I heard a voice—a whisper close to my ear. It wasn't loud, yet it was clear and unmistakable. A man's voice, soft and familiar. A chill ran down my spine, though the sound didn't frighten me. Instead, it wrapped around me, strangely comforting.

In the haze of my dream, I saw him—my uncle. He knelt beside me, his presence cool yet warm in its familiarity. A gentle breeze seemed to brush my forehead, as though his hand rested lightly there. His voice, distant yet distinct, drifted through the stillness.

"May... that's my girl, May," he whispered, his tone soothing and full of affection. "You can control these anxiety attacks. Don't let them overpower you. You're stronger than you realize."

It was undeniably his voice. Even in the dreamlike state, I could feel it—the familiarity of his touch, the warmth of his words. They felt real, more real than any dream I had ever experienced. Though I knew no one else could see him, it didn't matter. He was there with me. For the first time in days, the tightness in my chest eased, my muscles relaxed, and my mind quieted. His words seemed to chase away every dark thought and fear.

I slipped deeper into sleep, feeling safe under his watchful presence. That night, for the first time in nearly a week, I slept without nightmares.

No shadows. No running. Just stillness.

It was peaceful, quiet, and unbroken.

Even in that restful sleep, faint voices reached me. Ethan and Luke were talking again, their whispers threading through the edges of my dreams. Though muffled, I caught fragments of their conversation.

"How long are we staying here?" Luke's voice, tinged with worry, broke through the quiet.

"As long as it takes for Michaels to get here," Ethan replied, his voice low but resolute. "I've got this gut feeling someone's out there, watching us. Waiting."

I could sense movement in the room. Mike wasn't asleep either. I could feel him sitting on the far side of the room, his posture tense as he listened intently to their conversation.

Luke hesitated before speaking again. "Do you think this has something to do with your uncle's death? They never caught the killer."

Ethan nodded slowly, the weight of his words hanging thick in the air. "I don't know for sure... but that man in the fedora? What if it's him? What if he's the one who killed my uncle? I can't shake the feeling. Ever since we first saw him, something about him felt... wrong. Terrifying, even. If he is connected to my uncle's death, and now he's on our property, we need to be a step ahead of him. We can't afford to wait for him to make the next move."

The tension in his voice sent a chill through the room, sharp enough to pierce even my half-conscious state. Luke didn't answer right away. I could almost feel him shifting uneasily, his silence heavy with the weight of Ethan's words.

Maybe that's why Michaels had ordered the lockdown. Maybe the man in the fedora—the one Ethan believed might have killed our uncle—wasn't done.

Maybe he was hunting us now.

And that had to be it.

Just then, I heard my uncle's voice again, clear as day in my mind: "Yes!" he said, firm and certain. The word jolted me, startling me awake—well, almost. Was he answering Ethan's question? Was he confirming it?

I wanted to open my eyes, to ask, but I couldn't. It was like I was caught between two worlds—hovering in that strange, dream-like space between sleep and wakefulness. I could hear everything around me, every whisper and creak of the old house, but I was trapped. Why couldn't I move? Why was his voice so clear?

"May, I know you can hear me..." my uncle's voice came again, softer this time, urgent but soothing. "You're the only one who can. Stay in the house. Do not leave it."

The words were a command, not a suggestion, and they resonated deep within me. Just as quickly as his voice had come, it faded again, dissolving into silence. Yet, in its wake, I felt something unexpected—an overwhelming sense of safety, as though he was still watching over us, shielding us from whatever was coming.

After that, I drifted into true sleep. The voices faded, the invisible presence I'd felt before gone, leaving only stillness. The tension that had gripped the house for hours seemed to finally loosen its hold. Even Ethan and Luke, who had been on edge for so long, eventually succumbed to the pull of sleep. The quiet that settled over the house felt strange, almost unsettling, broken only by the soft, rhythmic sound of our breathing.

Meanwhile, in the shed, Eric leaned over the battered fax machine, the dim, swaying bulb above casting eerie shadows across his face. "Uh-huh, a fax," he muttered to himself, his lips curling into a wicked grin. He'd had the machine hooked up there the entire time—hidden away where no one could have guessed. No wonder nothing had ever reached the house.

Eric adjusted the light, squinting as the machine churned out a message, the faint hum and click breaking the silence. A moment later, the paper slid out. He snatched it, his grin widening as his eyes scanned the stark black text.

The note read:

Kids, it's Michaels.

The image I sent you is of the man who killed your uncle. Ethan, hear me, son—this man is Maeve's estranged father, Eric Stephenson. He's in Trenton, and we believe he's looking for you kids. Your mother does not want Maeve to know about this—Ethan, do not tell her. Your mother's worried about her anxiety.

Stay locked indoors and don't you dare go anywhere. Keep yourselves protected at all costs. We're six hours away from you. We need time to contact the local stations near Trenton, and it may take us an extra day. We may not reach you until late the next day—or even the third day.

Hunker down.

Eric let out a low, sinister laugh as he finished reading, the sound filling the cramped shed like a warning. "Eric Stephenson..." he muttered to himself, the irony of the message too rich to ignore.

Without hesitation, he grabbed the paper and ripped it in half. The pieces fell to the floor, but he wasn't done. He tore them again, and again, until they were nothing but tiny fragments scattered like dead leaves around his boots. The light above swung gently, casting shadows that seemed to move with a life of their own as Eric's laughter echoed into the night.

"Well, they ain't getting that," Eric sneered, his voice low and venomous. "Too late for that now, lieutenant Michaels. The kids'll be dead before you even reach them, and I'll have Maeve... I'll take her from her mother. She was mine to begin with." His words dripped with a sinister finality as he pocketed the shredded message.

Whistling softly, Eric switched off the fax machine and stood, his movements deliberate and almost ritualistic. He reached for the black fedora and trench coat draped neatly over the single bed in the corner. Both were worn with age but felt as familiar to him as his own skin. With practiced ease, he slipped them on and turned out the dim light, plunging the shed into darkness.

By the door hung a long, cruel-looking hook—its design more like a weapon than a tool. The main shaft was thick and sharp, with two smaller hooks branching off near the base, and a heavy cord was wrapped tightly around the handle. Eric grabbed it, coiling the cord around his torso like a serpent. He tucked the hook beneath his trench coat, ensuring it was concealed, and stepped outside.

The night air was still—unnaturally so. His steps were eerily silent as he approached the house, his dark silhouette blending seamlessly into the shadows. He moved like a predator, his eyes fixed on the back stairs. Through the window, he could make out our sleeping forms in the living room. The faint flicker of the oil lamp cast long shadows, painting the room in dim, golden light.

Eric circled to the patio, the brim of his hat casting his face into shadow. Reaching the living room window, he paused. The darkness inside seemed to swallow everything, but he could see us clearly—vulnerable, unaware. His grin widened as he slowly drew the hook from beneath his coat.

Then, with deliberate precision, he began tapping it against the wooden railing.

Tap... tap... tap.

The sound cut through the stillness of the night, sharp and deliberate, its rhythm both slow and unsettling. Inside, Ethan and Luke jolted awake, their bodies tense as their eyes darted around in alarm.

"What the hell was that?" Ethan muttered, his voice rough from sleep. He rose to his feet, his movements quick and deliberate. Luke followed, rubbing the sleep from his eyes, his expression shifting to one of confusion and fear as the tapping continued.

Tap... tap... tap.

Ethan flung the curtains open, and there he was—Eric, standing motionless just beyond the window. His black fedora obscured most of his face, but his cold, gleaming eyes pierced through the faint light. His figure was a shadow against the darkness, and the sight sent an icy shiver down Ethan's spine.

"Who's out there?" Ethan barked, his voice sharp and commanding. The sound jolted me awake, followed by Tara and Gwen, who sat up abruptly, their expressions mirroring the fear and confusion in the room.

"What's going on?" Tara asked, her voice shaky, clutching her blanket tightly.

"There's someone outside," Ethan said, his words clipped. His eyes never left the window, even as he tried to reassure us. "No one's going out there."

"How do we stop him?" Luke asked, his voice cracking slightly as he glanced nervously between Ethan and the window.

Ethan grabbed the oil lamp and raised it, holding it close to the glass in an effort to see the intruder more clearly. The faint light flickered, briefly illuminating Eric's face. The shadows from his hat only made his expression more menacing, his eyes glinting with cold malice.

"It's him," Ethan whispered, his voice tight. He yanked the curtains shut as though the act could block out the growing sense of danger. The tapping stopped, but the silence that followed was somehow worse, hanging heavy in the air like the calm before a storm.

For a fleeting moment, the light illuminated the man's face—Eric. The brim of his fedora cast long shadows over his eyes, but what little could be seen gleamed with cold, predatory intent. A chill raced down Ethan's spine as he jerked the curtains shut instinctively.

"CLOSE THE CURTAINS!" Ethan shouted, his voice taut with urgency. Luke didn't hesitate, pulling the heavy fabric closed, cutting off the horrifying image of Eric from view.

Ethan rushed to the door, snatching the metal bat he had left propped against the entryway. Luke grabbed his own bat from the living room, the tension in the air thickening with every passing second. Each movement felt loaded, deliberate, as though the weight of what was outside bore down on us all. Mike, who had been lounging by the fireplace, stood up slowly, his expression calm but his body betraying a flicker of unease. A smug smile tugged at his lips, though it didn't quite reach his eyes.

"Bats? Really?" he scoffed, his voice tinged with mockery. "What's the big deal? Who's even out there?" His tone carried an air of indifference, but his gaze darted toward the curtained window, betraying his uncertainty.

Ethan ignored him, his grip tightening on the bat. He crouched next to me, his face set with grim determination. Beside me, Gwen and Tara clung to each other, their fear evident in their wide eyes and trembling hands. Luke positioned himself in the shadows near the window, his breathing shallow but controlled, his eyes darting toward the front door. Then, we saw it— the shadow. A dark silhouette stretched across the windows, tall and menacing as it moved deliberately around the house. Each slow, measured step sent waves of dread rippling through the room.

"He's trying to get in!" I screamed, my voice cracking with panic. I clamped my hand over my mouth, but it was too late— the sound echoed through the room. My heart pounded in my chest, so loud it drowned out everything else. Tara and Gwen gripped me tighter, their pale faces etched with terror.

"He's playing games," Ethan growled, the anger simmering just beneath his voice. His frustration was a palpable force in the room, building with every tap of the hook outside. The sound was relentless, deliberate—a predator toying with its prey.

Suddenly, Ethan straightened, his movements sharp and decisive. He planted himself near the door, bat raised, crouching slightly in preparation. "If he gets in, we swing," he said through clenched teeth, his voice a steady edge of resolve.

Luke nodded, gripping his bat tightly. "Swing hard." Mike's earlier confidence had crumbled. He glanced nervously around the room, his voice shaky as he muttered, "I'm unarmed."

Luke pointed toward the fireplace. "Grab the fire pokers," he said in a hushed but firm tone.

Mike obeyed, his hands trembling as he reached for the sharpest poker. His bravado was gone, replaced with stark fear as reality settled over him like a weight.

The house fell into a suffocating silence. The presence outside—the tapping, the deliberate circling—was an oppressive force, hanging in the air like a storm about to break. My gaze flitted around the room, each shadow more threatening than the last. The man outside was pacing the patio, his hook tapping against the windows, as though daring us to confront him. Each tap felt like a countdown, a taunt designed to push us to our breaking point.

Unable to sit still any longer, I slipped away from Tara and Gwen and moved quietly toward Ethan. My legs felt heavy, every step measured as though walking through water. I reached Ethan's side, gripping his arm for balance.

And then I saw him—my uncle.

He stood beside Ethan at the door, his presence so clear it stole the breath from my lungs. My steps faltered as I stared at him. His familiar face turned toward me, his eyes filled with urgency. He was just as I remembered him, yet there was something otherworldly about him now, something commanding.

"Tell him not to open the door or leave the house," my uncle said, his voice low and steady, carrying the weight of a warning that chilled me to the core.

"Don't open it, please, Ethan!" I whispered, my voice barely audible as I tugged at his arm. Ethan's hand hovered over the door handle, his whole-body tense, ready to spring out at the man outside. He glanced at me, holding a finger to his lips, signaling for silence. Tears welled in my eyes as I looked between Ethan and my uncle.

My uncle's ghostly figure stood between us, his expression one of desperate warning, as if he could read Ethan's every move.

"Tell him not to make a move, Maeve," my uncle whispered again. "That man out there—he'll kill him. You have to protect him."

I grabbed Ethan's hand, my grip firm. He turned his head slightly, his eyes narrowing as he listened to the faint tapping outside. Eric continued to circle the house, his hook scraping along the glass and the walls. Every few steps, he whistled a slow, haunting tune, each note more chilling than the last.

"Please don't make a move," I pleaded, my voice trembling. Ethan's jaw clenched, his anger and fear warring within him, but he stayed where he was, silent.

Then, we heard it—a deep, sinister laugh that rumbled from behind the door. Ethan jerked back, startled. The sound reverberated through the walls like a threat, palpable and cold. Luke and Mike stood frozen near the windows, their faces pale, their hands shaking. Eric began to rattle the doorknob, testing it to see if it was unlocked.

"OPEN THIS DOOR, YOU STUPID KIDS!" Eric bellowed from the other side, his voice booming. I screamed, terror ripping through me as I hid behind Ethan. He raised the bat higher, his face set in a grim expression.

Tara and Gwen, trembling, clutched the last two fire pokers tightly. Their hands shook, but they stood firm, eyes wide with fear.

"COME OUT, COME OUT, WHEREVER YOU ARE!" Eric called again, his voice dripping with malice. A dark, twisted laugh followed his words, reverberating through the walls. It wasn't just a game to him—it was a hunt. A sick, twisted hunt.

I stifled another scream, pressing my hand against my mouth. I couldn't let him know how terrified I was, but my entire body shook with fear. My uncle's figure stood beside me again, his face contorted with worry. He placed a finger to his lips, urging me to stay quiet. I nodded, holding back my panic.

Then, in a soft whisper, my uncle leaned in close, his voice barely a breath in my ear. "Upstairs, in the third room on the right, there's a hidden hatch in the floor under the bed. He didn't know about it. It's loaded with rifles and ammunition. Tell Ethan and protect yourselves."

His figure dissolved into the shadows, vanishing into the kitchen, leaving me standing there with the weight of his words. My knees wobbled, but I leaned against Ethan's back, trying to stay calm. The tapping outside grew louder, more deliberate—an assault on our nerves, a reminder that time was running out.

"FINE, YOU KIDS. DON'T WORRY—I WON'T BE FAR. SUNRISE IS COMING!" Eric's voice bellowed again, a sinister laugh trailing behind him as his heavy boots stomped down the stairs. The sound of his footsteps echoed in the silence, fading into the distance.

Luke carefully pulled the curtain aside, his heart racing as he watched Eric's shadow fade into the night. "He didn't go back to the shed. He's heading toward the gates," he whispered, his voice tight with unease.

Ethan leaned against the door, his knuckles white as he gripped the bat. He peered through the small window. "He went into that opening near the metal gates," he murmured, his tone low and deliberate.

Outside, the first crack of sunlight began to creep over the horizon, casting long, eerie shadows across the yard. As the faint light pushed back the night, Ethan let out a breath, his posture relaxing slightly. He lowered the bat, the tension in the room easing as the others slowly lowered their makeshift weapons. But the fear didn't dissipate—it lingered, heavy and suffocating, clinging to us like the night's damp air.

Ethan turned to me, his gaze softening, concern etched into his face. "Are you okay?" he asked, his voice gentle but filled with urgency.

I couldn't answer. My hand remained clamped over my

mouth, shaking my head as tears streamed down my face. My thoughts spiraled, chaotic and relentless. First, my uncle's ghost had appeared again, warning us, shielding us from danger. Then Eric—the man in the fedora—prowled like a predator, taunting us, feeding off our fear. My mind screamed under the weight of it all, a cacophony of terror and disbelief.

I collapsed to my knees, my body trembling uncontrollably. The cold wood of the floor pressed against my legs, but I barely felt it. Everything blurred, the world shrinking until all that remained was the crushing fear. Ethan was beside me in an instant, pulling me into his arms, holding me tightly.

"May, no. Don't—calm yourself," he urged, his voice heavy with worry, his hands rubbing my back in steady, grounding motions. He was afraid I was slipping into another panic attack, but this wasn't panic.

This was terror—pure, raw, unrelenting terror.

My chest tightened, and my throat burned with the scream building inside me, desperate to escape. All I wanted to do was scream—loud enough to drown out the fear, loud enough to shatter the oppressive silence that had settled over the house like a curse.

But I couldn't. I was frozen, trapped in my own fear, unable to release the sound that clawed at my throat.

...

"This is lieutenant Michaels broadcasting on emergency Channel 9 to all police stations in and around the Trenton area. I don't care where you are—we need backup and immediate assistance. We are a day away from Trenton. Five kids are on lockdown at Aberdeen Manor. I repeat: five kids at Aberdeen Manor. Proceed to the property and await further instructions," Michaels' voice cut through the static, tight with urgency as he sped down the highway. Behind him, a convoy of squad cars, SWAT units, and FBI vehicles trailed in formation, their lights flashing ominously against the darkened landscape. Overhead, a helicopter sliced through the night sky, its searchlights scanning the ground below like razor-edged blades.

"Michaels, this is Station 9101. Sergeant Steven Esparada of the New Port Police Station," a voice crackled through the radio. "We received a fax from your department in Nebraska regarding a man named Justin Shawn Smith—or, as he's been known here, Michael Cory Smith. Sir, this man is an accomplice to a serial killer. He's been on our radar for over five years."

The words hit Michaels like a gut punch, the air in the car suddenly feeling heavier. His grip tightened on the steering wheel, his knuckles turning white. Accomplice? His worst fears were materializing. This wasn't just about Eric Stephenson—it was far bigger, far deadlier.

"Come again?" Michaels barked, his voice sharp with disbelief, his mind racing to connect the pieces.

"The name Mike," Esparada continued, his tone steady but grim. "He's been living in New Port under the alias Michael Cory Smith for the last five years. But his real name is Justin Shawn Smith. He's wanted in connection to a string of deadly murders here in New Port. Sir, are you certain the man you're focused on is Eric Stephenson?"

Michaels' stomach churned as the horrifying realization dawned on him. This wasn't a coincidence. These men were working together. "I'll be damned," he muttered under his breath, his mind racing to connect the dots. He snatched the radio, his voice sharper now. "Sergeant, listen carefully: Eric Stephenson and Justin Shawn Smith are connected. Mike—Justin—has been using this alias to cover his tracks. They're likely collaborating. Eric might even be protecting Justin or vice versa."

A tense silence followed as Esparada digested the implications. When he spoke again, his voice was tinged with urgency. "Roger that, lieutenant. Copy. I'll have my men positioned near the property in nine hours. Sir, that's the absolute fastest we can get there."

"Nine hours?" Michaels hissed, frustration bubbling beneath his calm exterior. Nine hours could be too late. His mind flashed to the kids—Maeve, Ethan, Luke, Tara, and Gwen—vulnerable, trapped, and completely isolated while two ruthless killers prowled closer.

"I don't care how fast you have to drive—just get there," Michaels barked into the radio, his tone cutting through the static like steel. "And listen to me: do not approach the manor. Both men are likely armed and dangerous. We still don't have Justin Shawn Smith's exact location. He could be lurking nearby, waiting for his moment, or he could already be with Eric Stephenson. If your team finds anything—any lead on either man—broadcast it to all units immediately."

The radio crackled with a brief response before falling silent, leaving only the low hum of dispatch chatter in the background. Michaels leaned back in his seat, his eyes fixed on the road ahead, the weight of the unfolding nightmare pressing down on him like a vice. The clock was ticking, and time was running out.

UNCLE JOE

THE HOUSE WAS EERILY SILENT, the tension thick and suffocating, pressing down on all of us. I wasn't sure if I should tell Ethan that Uncle's ghost was here with us—watching, guiding, warning. My eyes tracked Ethan and Luke as they moved through the house, barricading every door, including the basement entrance. Tara and Gwen worked quickly, taping the curtains shut to make it harder for anyone to see inside or break through. In the kitchen, Mike rifled through drawers, gathering knives, scissors, and anything else sharp we could use to defend ourselves. His movements were frantic, almost chaotic.

I sat at the table, still trembling from the terror that had seized me earlier. My breaths were shallow, my body tense, as if the fear had burrowed deep into my muscles. I tried to calm myself, but the heavy air in the room refused to let me breathe easily. My gaze drifted, unbidden, to the kitchen, where Uncle's ghost stood, his face etched with concern. He watched everything, his brow furrowed as if he were calculating our every move.

Why could I see him? Why could I hear him? Was this some latent ability I'd inherited, something I never knew existed? Uncle's wife wasn't related by blood, but she had been able to see spirits. Maybe it had nothing to do with bloodlines. Maybe it was just... fate.

Ethan passed by Uncle's ghost, oblivious to his presence, but Uncle muttered in frustration, shaking his head. "No, Ethan. This won't do," he said, his tone firm yet tinged with worry. I clenched my hands together, unsure of whether to say anything. What would Ethan think if I told him our uncle was standing right here? Would he believe me, or would he think I was losing my mind?

"Maeve, darling," Uncle said, his voice soft but insistent. He turned his worried gaze on me. "Tell him. He can't barricade the back door like that. Tilt the chair so it rests under the handle— like I showed him. He needs to do it right."

I hesitated, my heart pounding. This was something Uncle had taught Ethan long ago, something only we would remember. If I repeated it now, would Ethan question me? How could I possibly explain this?

Taking a deep, shaky breath, I rose from the table and crossed the room to the back door. My hands trembled as I reached for the chair Ethan had placed against it. He turned to me immediately, confusion flashing across his face.

"What are you doing, Maeve?" he asked, his voice sharp but uncertain.

I tilted the chair forward, angling it until the backrest slipped perfectly under the door handle. "Uncle taught you to do it this way," I whispered, my voice barely audible. I avoided his gaze, afraid of what I might see in his eyes.

Ethan froze. His gaze flickered from me to the chair, then back to me, his expression shifting from confusion to something deeper. Slowly, he knelt down and adjusted the chair himself, securing it exactly as Uncle had taught him when we were kids. The chair locked neatly under the handle, bracing the door with a firm hold.

I watched as the memory washed over Ethan's face, a wave of recognition hitting him like a force. I could almost feel it my-self—a warm summer evening, years ago. Uncle had crouched next to Ethan, his voice serious yet gentle as he demonstrated the technique. "If you're ever in trouble," he'd said, "this will give you enough time to get out. Remember this, Ethan."

Ethan stood, his hands lingering on the chair, his eyes distant. The memory hung heavy in the air between us, an unspoken connection that neither of us dared to break. Uncle's ghost stood nearby, nodding in approval, but his face remained tight with worry.

Then Uncle moved swiftly toward me, his presence startling in its intensity. I hadn't realized how close he was until he was right there, his figure looming. I gasped softly, clutching my chest as a shiver ran through me.

"Maeve," Uncle whispered urgently, "the man who killed me—there's something you need to know about him."

Just as he was about to say more, Mike walked into the dining room. The atmosphere shifted immediately, heavy and tense. Uncle's expression darkened, and then the lights overhead flick-ered. A strange, palpable energy pulsed through the room. I knew it was Uncle causing it.

"What…" I whispered, my voice trembling. The flickering lights unsettled me, though I understood spirits could manipu-late electronics. Why now? Was Uncle angry? Was he trying to warn me?

Ethan, Luke, Tara, and Gwen froze, their heads snapping up to the ceiling as the lights flickered again. The tension in the room grew thicker, suffocating.

"Stop it," I whispered faintly, hoping Uncle would hear me and calm down.

Mike, oblivious to the subtle interactions between Uncle and me, eyed me suspiciously. His gaze lingered for a moment, as though he could sense something off, but he said nothing. The lights steadied, but the tension didn't ease. Uncle's figure remained beside me, his face shadowed with anger as he glared at Mike. The energy in the room felt almost dangerous, charged with emotions I couldn't yet understand. There was something Uncle wasn't saying, something he knew.

"Maeve," Mike interrupted, setting a box down on the table with a dull thud. "We found some batteries, flashlights, and... flares," he said, holding up a flare gun with a smirk. The sight of the flare gun sent a ripple of unease through me. Ethan was on him in an instant, crossing the room in long strides, his eyes fixed on the flare gun. At the same time, Uncle's voice echoed sharply in my mind: "Where did he find this?"

"Where did you find this?" Ethan demanded aloud, his voice tight, overlapping with Uncle's ghostly echo. Both of them had the same urgency, the same pointed suspicion.

Mike shrugged, casually placing the flare gun back in the box. "Upstairs. Third room on the right of the hall," he said nonchalantly.

My heart dropped. Uncle's box. This was why he made the lights flicker—he was trying to warn me. "That's my box, May," Uncle whispered urgently, stepping closer. "I had it hidden in the bottom of the closet. There are enough flares in there for three shots." I forced myself to stay calm, acting as if I hadn't heard him. I didn't want to tip Mike off. Uncle's eyes bore into me, brimming with concern.

"He didn't find the guns, did he?" Uncle murmured. His figure flickered like static before vanishing, leaving a cold gust of air behind. The temperature in the room dropped instantly, enough to send shivers down my spine.

"Did someone leave a window open?" Ethan asked, frowning as his eyes scanned the room. Everyone shook their heads, though no one had an explanation for the sudden chill.

As Ethan inspected the box and Tara passed flashlights around, I moved quietly. I reached into the box, my fingers brushing against the smooth, cold cylinders of the flares. Without hesitation, I slipped three of them into the pocket of my jacket, which hung loosely over my chair. My heart pounded as I leaned back, trying to mask the movement.

No one seemed to notice. The room stayed tense, with the faint hum of the lights above and the distant, haunting silence from outside.

"Okay, the flare gun seems to be functional, but where are the flares?" Ethan said, rummaging through the box with growing frustration. I kept my face calm, though my heart raced, knowing exactly where the flares were hidden.

"Damn, none in the box," Ethan muttered, slamming the lid shut. Mike, now digging furiously, pulled out an old, thick plaid fishing jacket from the bottom. It had belonged to my uncle, and as Mike carelessly tossed it aside, a sharp pang of anger shot through me.

"They were in there! I swear I saw them rolling around at the bottom," Mike insisted, sifting through the remaining items without a care. Watching him handle Uncle's jacket so thoughtlessly felt like a slap to the face. Before I could stop myself, I reached out and snatched it from him.

"Mike, this is my uncle's!" I shouted, my voice trembling with a mix of anger and grief. I clutched the jacket tightly to my chest, the fabric a tangible connection to Uncle's memory. The familiar scent of his cologne and the faint trace of fish brought an overwhelming wave of emotion crashing over me.

The room fell silent. Everyone turned to look at me, their movements slowing as they registered the raw emotion in my voice. Ethan stepped forward, his hand resting gently on mine.

"Maeve, it's okay," he said softly, his tone laced with concern. But it wasn't okay—not to me. Mike had been about to discard the one thing that still felt like Uncle, and the thought twisted something deep inside me. Ignoring their stares, I yanked my own jacket off the chair and layered it over Uncle's coat. Without a word, I spun on my heel and stormed upstairs, my boots thudding heavily against the wooden steps. My vision blurred with tears, and I could feel Ethan's eyes boring into my back as I disappeared down the hall.

"Maeve, wait! What's wrong?" Ethan called after me, his voice distant as I slammed the door shut behind me. Leaning against the door, I pressed the jacket closer to my chest, inhaling deeply as if it could somehow bring Uncle back to me. My breaths were shallow, uneven, as the tears finally spilled over. I wiped at my face, but my hands were shaking too much to stop the flood.

"Maeve."

The voice was soft but urgent, and it froze me in place. I opened my eyes to see Uncle standing next to the bed, his figure calm yet resolute. He pointed toward the floor, his gaze locking onto mine.

"Here, Maeve. Move the bed," he said, his tone commanding but not unkind. I stared at him, my voice caught in my throat. The ache in my chest deepened as I took a shaky step forward. "Uncle..." I whispered, my voice breaking. I wanted to reach out, to touch him, but I knew better. He wasn't really here, no matter how real he seemed. My heart shattered all over again, the grief as fresh as the day we'd lost him.

He gestured again, more insistent this time. "Move the bed, Maeve. There's something you need to see."

I nodded, brushing away the tears as I braced myself against the heavy wooden frame. I pushed with all my strength, but it barely budged. My feet slid against the floor, and frustration bubbled up inside me.

"Get Ethan," Uncle urged, his voice firm but compassionate.

"He'll help you. Tell him."

I sank down beside the bed, my forehead resting against the cool wood. "What am I supposed to tell him?" I asked weakly. "That I can see you? That you're guiding me to some hidden hatch?" The idea felt impossible, ridiculous. But Uncle crouched beside me, his presence as steady and reassuring as it had always been.

"Tell him the truth, Maeve," he said gently, his eyes filled with understanding. "He might not believe you at first, but once he opens that hatch, he'll know. Trust me."

I exhaled deeply, the weight of his words pressing down on me. I knew he was right, but the thought of explaining everything to Ethan sent a fresh wave of panic through me. Would he think I was crazy? Would he believe me?

When I finally stood, Uncle was gone. The room felt colder, emptier without him, but his words lingered in the air, heavy with purpose. I pulled Uncle's jacket closer around me, letting the familiar scent anchor me. It smelled just as it had on that winter morning so many years ago when he'd gone fishing with Ethan and James. The memory flashed vividly in my mind—the warmth of his laugh, the kindness in his eyes as he tickled me, promising to bring back fish for dinner.

Uncle had always worn—the thick, plaid coat that had once protected him from the harsh winters. I pulled it closer around me, lifting the collar, it still smelled like him. That familiar musk mixed with the faint scent of fish from his last fishing trip clung to the fabric, bringing back memories of when he'd worn it before.

I closed my eyes, letting the memory wash over me. I was ten years old. It was a freezing winter, and Uncle had planned a fishing trip with Ethan and James, my stepfather. I had pouted, huffing in disappointment when Uncle had said I couldn't come along.

"But that's not fair! Why can't I go?" I had asked, crossing my arms and stamping my foot like a stubborn child.

Uncle had smiled, his kind eyes twinkling with amusement. He bent down and touched my chin gently. "My sweet little Maeve, men bring home the food for their families. So, my precious Maeve can fill her tummy when we get back," he said, tickling me until I laughed.

The thought brought a small, fleeting smile to my lips. I rolled up the long sleeves of the coat, feeling its comforting weight on my shoulders. It was like he was still protecting me, even now. Steeling myself, I opened the door and headed back downstairs. The quiet murmur of conversation filled the living room as everyone picked at the food Tara had laid out. To them, it seemed like nothing had happened. But for me, everything had changed.

I marched over to Ethan, who was casually leaning against the fireplace, eating a sandwich. Arms crossed, I tapped my foot impatiently. He glanced up at me, still chewing, and mumbled through his bite, "Yes?"

"Chew. Swallow. Are you finished?" I asked, my voice frantic, betraying my urgency. He raised an eyebrow, clearly curious about why I was so worked up. He swallowed, the lump visibly sliding down his throat.

"Okay, good." Without waiting for him to respond, I grabbed his arm and yanked him away from the fireplace.

"Uh… okay," Luke said, his face a mix of confusion and amusement as he watched me drag Ethan into the kitchen.

Once inside, I slammed the door leading to the living room and then slid the wooden doors to the dining room shut with a loud thud. Ethan stood there, sandwich still in hand, staring at me like I'd lost my mind.

"Uh-huh," he said, raising an eyebrow, clearly entertained by my manic behavior. He took another bite of his sandwich, watching me pace like I was a wind-up toy on the verge of breaking. "Alright, what's going on?" he asked, his voice muffled by his chewing, though I could tell he was more intrigued now than amused.

"I don't even know how to say this," I started, pacing back and forth, my nerves jangling like loose wires. Ethan just stood there, waiting, occasionally nibbling on his sandwich as if this was just another quirky Maeve moment. I ran my hands through my hair, trying to find the words, but my thoughts were a tangled mess.

"Right, so… you know how Grandma and Great Aunt had the ability to see, uh… earthbound spirits?" I finally blurted out, the words tumbling out in one breath.

Ethan froze mid-chew, his sandwich hovering near his mouth. He lowered it slowly, his expression shifting from casual curiosity to wary disbelief. "Wait, hang on a second," he said, putting the sandwich down on the counter. His tone was sharper now, his posture straightening. "Do not tell me you're seeing earthbound spirits too."

"Just listen!" I hissed, slapping a hand over his mouth before he could say another word. His muffled protests were ignored as I took a deep breath, muttering to myself, "Oh, just come out with it."

"I've seen Uncle's ghost," I said, my voice barely above a whisper. "He's attached to this house… and he's here. With us."

Ethan's eyebrows shot up, and for a moment, he just stared at me. Then, a small, incredulous smile tugged at the corners of his mouth. He chuckled, shaking his head like he couldn't believe what he was hearing. "Okay, Maeve. Sure. I believe you," he said, rolling his eyes. Just as he reached for his sandwich again, a sudden gust of air swept across the kitchen, knocking the sandwich off the counter. Ethan's eyes widened as the sandwich landed on the floor with a soft splat. "Oh man," he muttered, bending down to pick it up. "It hit the floor. That sucks."

I stood frozen, my eyes locked on Uncle's ghost, who was standing by the door, his hand outstretched. He had knocked it down. "No, Ethan. Uncle knocked it off the counter," I whispered, my gaze fixed on the spot where Uncle's figure loomed.

Ethan glanced up at me, following my line of sight. His skepticism faltered as he saw the seriousness in my face. "You're not joking," he said, his voice quieter now. He couldn't see Uncle, but the sudden chill in the room—and the sandwich on the floor—made him hesitate.

"He's standing by the door. He wants you to believe me," I insisted, my voice firm. Ethan exhaled deeply, his expression a mix of doubt and growing unease. "Seriously, Maeve?"

"Follow me," I said sharply, grabbing his arm before he could argue. I pulled him toward the kitchen door, practically dragging him up the stairs.

"Maeve, what the hell are you doing?" Ethan protested, trying to pull away, but I didn't let go. My grip tightened as I hauled him to the third room on the right. Shoving the door open, I yanked him inside and slammed it shut behind us.

"Help me move the bed," I demanded, not bothering to explain. Ethan blinked at me, his confusion deepening. "What are you—?"

"Just do it," I snapped, cutting him off. I braced myself against the bedframe, ready to shove with all my strength.

Ethan crossed his arms, skepticism written all over his face. "Why? What's under it?"

"Just move it," I snapped, my tone edged with urgency. I pushed against the bed frame, but it was too heavy to budge on my own. Ethan stared at the bed for a moment, still confused, but after a second of hesitation, he sighed and stepped forward. With one swift motion, we shoved the heavy frame aside, revealing a hidden hatch beneath.

"What the hell is this?" Ethan muttered, his voice low as he knelt down and opened the latch. The creak of the wood made my skin crawl, and I held my breath as the hidden door revealed its secrets. Inside was a collection of guns and ammunition neatly tucked beneath the floorboards.

"Uncle told me this was here," I explained, my voice breathless, trembling with the weight of what I was saying. "He said inside was everything we'd need to defend ourselves."

Ethan's eyes widened as he stared down at the cache. Slowly, he reached in and pulled out a rifle, his disbelief melting into awe. His fingers traced the wood grain of the weapon until they stopped at a carved detail on the handle. His initials—E.A.

"Wait, I remember this," Ethan whispered, his voice soft with reverence. "This was mine. The rifle Dad and Uncle gave me when we went hunting that first time."

I watched him, my chest tight as memories seemed to flood over him. His grip on the rifle was firm but tender, as if it were an old friend.

It was twelve years ago before uncle disappeared—a cold autumn morning. Ethan had been so excited about his first hunting trip with Uncle and his dad. He had been barely old enough to handle a rifle, but Uncle had insisted that it was time. They packed up early, heading out to the woods, the cold biting at their faces. Ethan, full of nerves and excitement, had gripped the rifle tightly.

"I thought I lost this," Ethan murmured, his voice distant as the memory consumed him. "When those bears charged us..." His words trailed off as his brow furrowed. I knew the story. They had gotten too close to a family of bears, and in the chaos of retreating to the trailer, Ethan had dropped the rifle. He'd thought it was gone forever.

"Uncle must've found it," I said softly. "And he hid it here."

Ethan stood there, staring at the rifle like it held the answers to questions he hadn't dared ask. Uncle's presence was palpable, watching over us, satisfied that Ethan had rediscovered this piece of his past.

"So... he's here? Right now?" Ethan's voice was quiet, almost fragile, as if speaking too loudly would shatter the moment. "Can he hear us?"

I nodded, glancing at the door where Uncle stood, smiling

faintly, his expression filled with both pride and worry. "Yeah," I whispered. "He's here."

"Good girl, May," Uncle's voice echoed faintly in my ears. I froze, goosebumps prickling my skin. Ethan, oblivious to Uncle's words, bent down to examine something else in the hatch.

"He saw it," Uncle's voice whispered near the door, making my heart pound.

Ethan pulled out a three-way walkie-talkie, the kind we used as kids. Recognition flickered in his eyes as he turned it over in his hands. "The other one's at Mom and Dad's house—on the mantel," he muttered, almost to himself. These weren't just toys. They were military-grade, capable of picking up nearby signals and broadcasting to vast distances. Ethan and Dad used to play with them all the time.

A faint smile tugged at his lips as he checked the battery. "It's full," Uncle's voice whispered again, sending a shiver down my spine.

"Uncle says it's full," I echoed without thinking. Ethan stiffened, his head tilting toward the door, his eyes wide with disbelief.

"This is insane," Ethan muttered, glancing at the empty space on the bed beside him. "He's actually here." Without hesitation, he clipped the walkie-talkie to his belt, making sure to keep it out of sight. No one downstairs could know—not Mike, not anyone. It was too dangerous.

"So, Uncle," Ethan said quietly, almost as if he were testing the waters, "if you can hear me… what's going on here? Why all of this?"

Uncle chuckled softly, the sound faint but unmistakable. His figure moved from the doorway, sitting down beside Ethan on the bed. I couldn't take my eyes off him.

"He's sitting next to you," I said gently, watching Ethan's reaction. He glanced at me, then at the empty space beside him, a flicker of uncertainty crossing his face.

"What's going on?" he whispered, his voice laced with both

disbelief and fear.

Uncle's voice came through again, this time more serious. "Maeve, Ethan... the reason I bought this house from your mother ten years ago wasn't because I wanted to maintain or protect it," he began, his tone low, as though revealing a long-buried secret. I relayed every word to Ethan, my voice shaking.

Ethan's gaze flicked to the spot where Uncle sat, confusion clouding his face. "Why would you need to buy the house, then?" he asked, glancing between me and the empty space beside him.

"I bought it because..." Uncle's voice strained, heavy with hesitation. His figure paced the room, his ghostly presence radiating unease. He stopped mid-step, turning to me, his expression tense, like he knew the truth would shake us to our core. "How can I tell you this, May..."

The air in the room thickened, pressing down on me. My heart pounded, the weight of his words filling the silence. Whatever Uncle knew, it was bad. I could feel it in the way his presence shifted, like he was preparing to shatter the fragile sense of safety we clung to.

"Uncle, please, tell me! What do you know? What happened? How did you die?" My voice trembled, the questions spilling out uncontrollably. I didn't know if I wanted the answers—but I *needed* them.

His voice came back, sharp and direct, slicing through the air. "The man out there in the shed... he wasn't hired by your mother, May—"

Before Uncle could finish, Luke's voice exploded through the air, cutting him off.

"ETHAN! You better come see this, quick!" Luke's urgent shout echoed down the hallway, followed by heavy pounding on the door.

Ethan jerked upright, his eyes darting toward the sound. Without hesitation, he shut the hatch, latched it tightly, and bolted for the door. I followed, my pulse racing, panic already clawing at my chest. Ethan flung the door open, and we sprinted after Luke, who was halfway down the stairs, his face pale and drawn like he'd seen something he couldn't unsee. By the time we reached the living room, Uncle was already there, standing by the large patio window. His expression was grim, his ghostly form casting a faint chill over the room. Tara and Gwen were frozen in place, staring at the glass, their faces pale with shock.

Luke pointed toward the window, his hand trembling violently. "What kind of sick joke is this?" he muttered, his voice a mix of anger and fear. As I approached the window, everyone turned to look at me, their faces twisted in an unsettling combination of confusion and dread. Behind their mock bravery, I saw something else—real terror. The kind that grips you and doesn't let go.

Ethan moved closer to the window, his fingers trembling as they traced the edge of the glass. My stomach churned as I followed his gaze. There, taped to the outside of the glass, was a picture of me—16 years old, wearing my high school cheerleading uniform. Ethan's eyes locked onto mine, wide with unspoken questions. His face had drained of color, and fear tightened every feature. He didn't need to say it—I knew what he was thinking. This picture… this exact picture… shouldn't be here. It had been taken years ago, in the family home, and no one else had a copy. No one except Ethan and my parents.

And yet, here it was, taped to the glass like a macabre message meant just for me.

The room felt like it was collapsing in on itself. The air turned thick, suffocating, heavy with something dark and oppressive. My knees went weak, but I forced myself to stay upright, every nerve screaming for answers I didn't have.

"How did this get here?" Ethan asked, his voice low and tight, like he was trying to keep it together but barely succeeding. I opened my mouth to answer, but no words came out. My gaze stayed glued to the picture, the edges taped with precision, almost deliberately perfect. A sick chill crawled up my spine, spreading through every inch of me.

Someone had been watching me. Not just recently—but for years. Someone who knew every detail of my life, someone who had access to this intimate piece of my past. And more terrifyingly—someone who wanted us to know how much control they had.

"What the hell is this?" I whispered, my voice breaking as panic surged through me.

Ethan turned back to the room, his hand still on the glass. "Whoever did this… they're not just messing with us. They're *inside* our lives." His words hung heavy in the air, making the silence even more unbearable.

Uncle's voice came through faintly, almost drowned out by the weight of my panic. "May… don't let this break you. You're stronger than they think."

But as I stared at the picture, my strength faltered. Whoever this was—they weren't just watching. They were hunting.

PHONE CALL

EVERYONE STOOD STILL, staring at me like I was some kind of foreign object in their midst. No one said a word about the picture taped to the glass. The silence stretched thin, like the air had been sucked out of the room.

"What? Why is everyone looking at me like that? This has to be some kind of sick joke," I said, my voice rising with panic. I stepped forward, reaching for the patio doors to pull the picture off the window, but I froze. There, just beyond the wooden railing, stood the man in the fedora.

"AHH!" I screamed, stumbling back into Ethan as cold fear washed over me, my heart racing. Everyone whipped around, their eyes snapping to the window.

"He's outside, damn it," Ethan muttered, his voice low and tense. The daylight outside felt wrong, too bright for the terror that now seeped into every corner of the room. Despite the sunlight, the air seemed thick with dread, pressing in on all sides. It was only mid-afternoon, the second day of being stuck inside Aberdeen Manor, yet it felt like the walls were closing in on us. There was no way out—our cars had flat tires, and none of the CB radios were working.

I turned to Ethan, who was gripping the curtains tightly, his knuckles white. Everyone stood frozen near the window, staring out at the man who loomed just beyond the glass, his face hidden beneath the shadow of the fedora. The brim dipped low, casting an eerie darkness where his features should have been. And then we saw him. Mike. Standing right beside the man, hands folded calmly in front of him, as if he were part of this twisted nightmare.

"MIKE, THAT SON OF A BITCH!" Ethan erupted, his voice raw with fury.

In a fit of rage, he broke every rule we'd set about keeping the house on lockdown. He yanked at the curtains, tearing through the tape that sealed them shut, and forcefully slid open the patio door. The sharp sound of the door rolling back pierced the silence like a gunshot.

"ETHAN!" I screamed after him, panic clawing at my chest. Tara and Gwen were already in a frenzy, their voices high-pitched with fear as they tried to make sense of the chaos.

Without thinking, I rushed after Ethan, my mind spinning. Luke grabbed a fire poker from the hearth and followed, his eyes wide and grip tight. The moment we stepped outside, the air seemed to shift. It hung heavy, as though the very world was holding its breath, waiting for the inevitable. My heart pounded in my ears as we stepped onto the porch. The man stood motionless by the railing, Mike at his side, watching us with an unnatural stillness.

Every instinct in me screamed that this was wrong—something terrible was about to happen. Ethan jumped over the patio railing, and Luke followed, both landing swiftly in front of Mike and the man in the fedora. The man slowly removed his hat, revealing his face.

"You..." Ethan muttered, his voice tinged with recognition. He was the gravekeeper—the same man we had seen tending the graves behind the house.

Ethan turned toward Mike, his expression boiling with rage, ready to confront him. But before he could get a word out, the gravekeeper stepped forward, blocking his path.

"Hang on there, boy," Eric said, his tone firm and assertive. He held up a hand, pressing it lightly against Ethan's chest to stop him.

"I'm going to pound your face in, Mike, you traitor! You snake!" Ethan snarled, pacing in tight circles near Eric and Mike. Luke stood close by, ready to hold Ethan back if things escalated further. The tension crackled in the air, sharp and ready to snap.

Inside, the patio door hung wide open. I could hear every word as I stood frozen just beyond the threshold, clutching Ethan's bat in my hands, hiding it against my leg.

"What the hell do you want? Why are you playing games with us?" Luke demanded, his voice sharp and angry as he directed his fury at Eric.

"Calm down now, calm down," Eric said, his voice slow and condescending as Ethan lunged toward him, only for Luke to hold him back.

"Lookie here," Eric said, gesturing toward the metal gates with a slow, deliberate point. "Y'all can leave… see that gap over there? That road'll take ya right off the property. But I want one thing in return…"

Ethan and Luke glanced toward the gap before snapping their attention back to Eric, their expressions hardening. Ethan's fists clenched at his sides, his pacing becoming more erratic.

"Whatever the hell both of you want, you're not getting it. Let us leave... the cops are on their way—" Ethan began, his voice tight with anger, but Eric cut him off with a sharp gesture.

"There ain't no cops comin', boy," Eric said, his voice dripping with confidence. "By the time they show up, I'll have everything I need."

Ethan froze mid-step, his jaw tightening as he darted a glance at Luke. Eric's words hung heavy in the air, suffocating the space around us.

"What the hell do you want? We're not in the mood to negotiate," Luke said, standing firm beside Ethan, his voice sharp with defiance.

Eric chuckled, the sound slow and mocking. He folded his arms and began pacing deliberately, his boots scuffing the dirt as his gaze dropped to the ground. Then, with a deliberate slowness, he raised his eyes, locking them with Ethan's.

"How much do you love that stepsister o' yours, boy?" Eric sneered, his lips curling into a twisted grin as he waited for a reaction.

Ethan's expression tightened, his anger boiling just beneath the surface. "Stay the hell away from Maeve—and all of us. Do you not understand that?" he growled, his voice cutting through the still air.

Eric smirked, his low chuckle sending shivers down my spine. "I thought I made myself clear... Y'all can leave, but all I want in return is her." He stopped pacing and pointed directly at me. His cold, unrelenting gaze bore into mine, freezing me where I stood. Fear surged through me, immobilizing me as my chest tightened painfully. Tara and Gwen gripped my arms, trembling as much as I was.

"We have no deal," Ethan snapped, his voice firm and unyielding. Beside him, Luke's eyes stayed locked on Mike, whose smug smirk never faltered. He stood motionless, his arms folded as though none of this chaos fazed him.

As Ethan and Luke began to turn back toward the house,

Eric's voice lashed out, sharp and venomous. "Listen here, boy. I don't negotiate. You've got 'til tomorrow… Leave her here, walk out that gate, and go," he snarled.

Ethan spun around, his rage erupting as he lunged at Eric. Luke grabbed his arm, trying to hold him back, but Ethan was relentless. "Get your hands off me!" he barked, struggling against Luke's restraint. Mike, standing nearby, stepped forward, his calm demeanor finally cracking as he moved to intervene.

"What the hell do you want with Maeve?" Ethan shouted, his voice shaking with anger and desperation. He yanked his arm free from Luke's grip, breathing heavily as he glared at Eric.

"What I want with her is none o' your business, boy. Y'all just think on that," Eric said coldly, his tone dripping with malice.

"You can go to hell. We're leaving," Ethan snarled. He turned sharply toward the house, shouting for us to grab whatever we could. But before he could take another step, Eric reached into his trench coat and pulled out a long, gleaming metal fisherman's hook. The sight of it made my blood run cold, the sharp edges catching the faint light like a predator's teeth.

"ETHAN, LUKE, LOOK OUT!" I screamed, panic choking my voice as I rushed toward them, trapped by the patio railing. Ethan and Luke spun around in unison, their movements swift as they both drew their guns from under their shirts, aiming them directly at Eric and Mike.

Eric hesitated for a moment, his eyes narrowing as he measured their resolve. Slowly, he lowered the hook but kept it in his hand. "We ain't done here, boy," he said, his voice low and threatening. "You've got 'til tomorrow's light, ya hear me?"

Ethan and Luke didn't waver, their guns trained on Eric and Mike as they carefully backed up the steps to the patio. Their movements were deliberate, every step taken with precision, their gazes never leaving the men in front of them.

"Get inside," Ethan ordered sharply, his voice cutting through my panic. I scrambled back into the house, Tara and Gwen following closely behind, their faces pale with terror.

"MORNING'S LIGHT! YA HEAR ME?" Eric's voice thundered from outside, his words ringing in my ears even as Ethan slammed the patio door shut and latched it firmly. His eyes burned with fury as he turned to us.

"Get your things. Now!" he barked, his tone brooking no argument. His chest heaved as he struggled to regain control of himself, but the rage in his eyes hadn't dimmed.

Luke stepped forward, placing a steadying hand on Ethan's chest. "Ethan," he said softly, his voice low and firm, trying to ground him. But Ethan was barely holding it together, his whole body trembling as his breaths came in harsh, uneven bursts.

"Where the hell are we going to go?" I demanded, my voice rising in fear and frustration. "The tires on the cars are blown, and we have no way to get out of here, ETHAN!" My panic spilled over, the words tumbling out before I could stop them.

Ethan's jaw clenched as he turned his wild eyes toward me, his frustration mirrored in my own. But he didn't answer. Instead, he shoved past Luke and began pacing the room, his hands clenched into fists. Tara and Gwen rushed around the house, grabbing bags and stuffing them with whatever they could find, their movements frantic and disjointed.

"MAEVE, MOVE!" Luke barked, snapping me out of my paralysis. His voice jolted me into action, but the fear inside me didn't subside.

Ethan was unraveling, the weight of the situation pressing down on him like a crushing tide. His breathing grew harsher, more desperate, as he tried to piece together a plan in the midst of chaos.

"They're gone," Luke muttered, glancing out the window, scanning the empty yard. Eric and Mike had disappeared from sight, leaving an eerie silence behind. But the quiet was worse than their presence—it was heavy, oppressive, and full of unspoken threats. We were alone now, trapped in the house, with two dangerous men lurking somewhere on the property.

"Maeve, now!" Luke snapped, his patience clearly thinning as he tried to get me moving. My feet felt rooted to the floor, fear wrapping around me like a suffocating fog. No matter how fast we packed, no matter how ready we were to leave, there was nowhere to run.

"I told you to move and get your things," Ethan barked, his frustration boiling over as he stormed toward me. He grabbed my arm, his grip tight and unyielding, pulling me roughly through the house. His touch wasn't gentle—it was forceful, almost angry.

"ETHAN, STOP!" I shouted, trying to yank my arm free, but he didn't loosen his grip. He dragged me through the kitchen before finally letting go, his chest heaving as he turned to face me.

"We're leaving. You're not staying here… none of us are," he said, his voice hard, his words clipped. Tara passed him a bag, and he shoved it into my arms, the motion sharp and impatient.

I stared at him, my heart pounding. Ethan had always been the calm one, the protector. But now, his anger and fear made him almost unrecognizable. For the first time, I felt more terrified of him than anything outside this house.

"Ethan, stop!" I shouted again, my voice cracking under the pressure. That's when I heard it—a faint sound, barely audible above the chaos. I froze, unsure if it was real or my imagination.

"Everyone, quiet!" I yelled, cutting through the noise. My sudden outburst startled everyone into silence. I strained to listen, my heart hammering in my chest.

Then I heard it again. A phone ringing.

Without thinking, I bolted toward the basement door.

"Maeve! What the hell are you doing?" Ethan shouted, his voice laced with frustration as he chased after me. Luke followed close behind, their footsteps echoing as we raced down the stairs.

The ringing grew louder with each step. At the bottom of the stairs, beside the furnace, I saw the phone we'd left there earlier.

Standing next to it was Uncle's ghostly figure, pale and translucent, his expression urgent as he pointed at the phone.

"ANSWER IT! HURRY!" Uncle's voice thundered in my head, his command clear.

I snatched the phone off the ground, my hands shaking as I pressed it to my ear.

"Hello?" I gasped, my voice barely audible.

"Maeve." The moment I heard my mother's voice, tears filled my eyes. My chest tightened, and a sob escaped before I could stop it. Everyone turned toward me, alarmed by my sudden breakdown. Ethan rushed to my side, his face a mix of concern and confusion.

"Mother?" I cried, my voice trembling.

"Listen to me, Maeve. Listen. Don't speak," my mother said, her voice shaky and full of urgency. I could hear James, my stepfather, murmuring in the background. The fear in her voice was palpable, raw, and it sent a chill down my spine.

"You... your brother... your friends... you must leave the property immediately. Officer Michaels is on his way," she continued, her words frantic and rushed. Ethan leaned closer, trying to grab the phone, but I pulled away, clutching it tighter.

"Stop crying, listen…" My mother's voice cracked. I wiped my tears, forcing myself to focus as Tara, Gwen, and Luke stood frozen, their faces etched with worry.

"I need you to listen," she repeated, her tone rising. "Eric Stephenson... is your father, Maeve."

Her words hit me like a freight train. The room spun, and the world seemed to collapse around me. My grip on the phone faltered, my breath hitching as the weight of her revelation crashed down on me. Eric… my father? The man outside—the one tormenting us—was my father?

"I—" I started, but my voice failed me. I stumbled back, my legs giving out as the realization sank in. Ethan caught me by the shoulders, steadying me as I struggled to process what she'd just said.

"Give the phone to Ethan," James's voice cut through my spiraling thoughts, firm and commanding. Numbly, I handed the phone to Ethan, my hands trembling. I stumbled away, pacing near the furnace as my mind raced. Eric Stephenson… my father? How? Why? None of it made sense.

Ethan pressed the phone to his ear, stepping away from me and lowering his voice as he spoke to James. I caught fragments of the conversation, but each piece only made my stomach sink further.

"…Don't say anything to Maeve or your friends," James was saying, his tone urgent. "Listen carefully—Eric Stephenson… he's the man who killed your uncle."

Ethan froze, his posture stiffening as the words hit him. My heart sank as I watched his face pale, the shock and anger contorting his features.

James continued, his voice steady but grim. "He's been evading the police for years, using aliases, staying off the radar. Mike—no, Justin—is his accomplice. They've been working together, Ethan. Eric isn't at the manor by accident. He's here for Maeve."

Ethan's hand tightened around the phone, his knuckles white. His breaths grew heavier, each one labored as he processed the truth.

"Do you understand? You need to leave or lock down the house and wait for Michaels," James said. "Eric wants Maeve. Your mother has had a restraining order against him for years. He tried to kidnap her when she was two… planned to leave the state with her."

Ethan's jaw clenched, his fury barely contained. "Our tires are slashed. We're stuck here," he said, his voice low and tense. James's response was chilling. "Then you're exactly where he wants you. Be ready, Ethan. Protect Maeve at all costs."

Ethan's heart pounded against his ribs, his face pale as he processed the revelation. Slowly, he turned his head to look at me, his eyes filled with an unreadable mix of emotions—fear, guilt, and something darker. I stood with Tara and Gwen, trying to explain the pieces of what I understood from my mother's frantic call.

"Eric Stephenson is a serial killer, Ethan," James said, his voice low and grim through the phone. "He's been killing for over twenty years, ever since he and Amy split."

Ethan's grip on the phone tightened, his knuckles white. "We're getting the hell out of here," he muttered through clenched teeth.

"NO, SON! Listen to me," James shouted, his voice cracking. "There's a hidden underground bunker. It's in the blueprints of the house—a storm shelter. It's outside, behind the shed, concealed by the brick wall, you can't see it from the house. There are wooden doors in the ground. Lock yourselves in there. Michaels will reach you before we can."

Panic welled in Ethan's throat. "Dad, we can barely move out here—Mike—Justin—and Eric are still outside. We're trapped!" His voice cracked, each word a struggle against the mounting terror.

"Ethan, you can figure this out, son. You have to. Get to that bunker and stay there. We're already on our way from Nebraska, but it'll take twelve hours. Michaels is closer—he's only a few hours out. Hold out until then," James urged, his voice thick with desperation.

The line went dead.

Ethan stared at the phone, the dull tone ringing in his ears like a funeral bell. Slowly, he lowered it and set it down on the floor behind the furnace. When he turned to face us, I froze. His face was drained of color, his expression hollow and haunted. It was as if the weight of everything had crushed the life out of him, leaving only a shadow of the brother I knew.

"Ethan?" I called out, my voice trembling, reaching for him as if I could pull him back from whatever dark place his mind had gone. But he stepped away, his eyes distant, lost in the storm of thoughts that consumed him. Without a word, he turned and hurried upstairs, his movements unsteady, almost like he was running from the truth.

Luke glanced at me, his brow furrowed with worry before he bolted after Ethan. "ETHAN!" he shouted, his voice echoing through the house.

Panic gripped me, tightening around my chest like a vise. Tara, Gwen, and I scrambled up the stairs after them, our movements frantic, our breathing quick. The house felt like a suffocating labyrinth, the walls pressing in as we rushed from room to room. But Ethan and Luke had disappeared into the shadows, their voices lost in the maze.

Upstairs, Ethan grabbed Luke by the arm and yanked him into Uncle's old room. The door slammed shut behind them, the sound reverberating through the house. Inside, the air was thick with tension, the faint, ghostly presence of Uncle looming like a silent witness.

"Ethan, what is it? What did your parents say?" Luke asked, his voice sharp with urgency, his eyes darting around the room as if he expected danger to burst through the walls.

Ethan didn't answer right away. Instead, he strode to the center of the room, his movements swift and purposeful. He knelt down, removing the latch on the hidden door in the floor and pulling it open with a sharp creak. The sound echoed in the still room, sending a chill down Luke's spine. Without hesitation, Ethan pulled out a couple of rifles and shoved one into Luke's hands, along with a box of bullets.

"Woah, woah, hold on!" Luke stammered, gripping the rifle like it might bite him. His voice wavered, barely masking his growing fear.

"We're not letting that monster anywhere near Maeve," Ethan growled, his hands moving deftly as he loaded the rifle. The sharp *click* of the chamber locking in place sliced through the tense silence like a warning shot.

Luke raised a hand, trying to calm him. "Hang on. What is going on? What did your parents say?" His voice cracked, the strain in the room pushing him to his limits.

Ethan's jaw tightened, his fury barely contained. "That man outside... Eric... he's a serial killer. He's the one who murdered my uncle. And..." Ethan hesitated, his words catching like they physically hurt to say. "He's also Maeve's biological father."

The words hit Luke like a physical blow. His eyes widened in shock, his hands trembling as he held the rifle. "What?" he whispered, the weight of the revelation sinking in. "That's why he's after Maeve..." His voice trailed off, the full horror of their situation dawning on him.

Ethan's face darkened further, his rage bubbling beneath the surface. He grabbed another rifle, slamming the butt against the floor as he checked the chamber. "We're not letting him take her. Not while I'm breathing," he said, his voice low and deadly.

Luke nodded slowly, his movements shaky but resolute as he began loading the rifle in his hands. "Alright," he said, his voice steadier now. "We hold the line. No matter what."

Ethan, his anger rising to the surface, quickly recounted everything his father had told him—the murders, the restraining order, and the underground bunker hidden behind the brick wall outside. Luke listened in stunned silence before his brow furrowed in worry. "Don't you think Eric and Mike—Justin—whatever his name is, have already checked the property? What if they've already found the bunker?"

The realization hit Ethan like a physical blow. His heart dropped into his stomach. The weight of Luke's words sent a chill racing down his spine. He froze, staring at Luke as if the floor had just fallen out from beneath him.

"Shit," Ethan muttered, his voice rough and hollow, barely more than a whisper.

The room seemed to shrink, the air too thick to breathe. Every second felt like a ticking bomb, counting down to an inevitable confrontation. They were trapped—surrounded by a deadly killer, with nowhere to hide.

Downstairs, my hands trembled violently as I rifled through my mother's old room on the property. Every creak, every distant sound felt like Eric or Mike closing in on us. My heart pounded in my chest, and my breaths came quick and shallow. I yanked clothes off hangers, shoving them haphazardly into the duffle bag. My fingers fumbled so badly that I could barely zip the bag, but I forced it closed. I didn't care what I left behind—survival was all that mattered now.

As I turned toward the wardrobe, something caught my eye—a shoe box wedged tightly into the bottom left drawer. I hesitated for a moment, but then, with a sharp tug, I yanked it free. The wood scraped harshly against the edges, the sound grating in the oppressive silence. The box fell to the floor, its lid popping off on impact. Pictures spilled out, scattering across the hardwood like ghosts demanding to be seen.

I crouched down, instinctively reaching for the photos, my hands trembling as I gathered them. As I flipped through the first few, my breath hitched. My fingers froze mid-motion, and the air felt like it had been sucked out of the room.

"What… what the hell?" I whispered, my voice barely audible. My chest tightened as I picked up two of the pictures, holding them in shaking hands. The images stared back at me—horrific, grotesque. My stomach churned, and a wave of nausea rolled through me. The realization struck like a thunderclap, and before I could stop it, a scream ripped from my throat.

"AAAAAH! AAAAAAAH!" The sound was raw, primal, echoing through the house. I screamed again, the images searing themselves into my mind. Women, bound and tortured, their faces twisted in agony. Some were mutilated beyond recognition, their bodies bearing evidence of unimaginable suffering. Others hung lifelessly from metal pegs, their forms limp and dehumanized in what looked like a dimly lit basement.

Tears blurred my vision, but I couldn't stop flipping through the photos, each more horrifying than the last. My mind raced, desperately trying to make sense of what I was seeing. But deep down, I already knew. These weren't random photos. These were *his* victims. Eric Stephenson—my father—had done this. The man outside, the monster who wanted me, had taken these women's lives.

I collapsed against the dresser, my knees buckling beneath me. My hands flew to my mouth, trying to stifle the relentless sobs that tore from my chest. The room tilted, spinning in a disorienting blur. The box, the photos—they felt like living proof of the evil that surrounded us, the evil that had shaped my existence.

"Maeve!" Tara and Gwen burst into the room, their eyes wide with panic. They froze in the doorway for a split second before rushing to my side, their faces twisting in horror as they saw the photos scattered around me. Gwen dropped to her knees, reaching out hesitantly to pick up one of the pictures. The moment she processed what she was looking at, she screamed—a raw, piercing sound that joined mine, filling the room with an unbearable cacophony.

"Oh my God…" Tara gasped, her hands covering her mouth as tears streamed down her face. Her whole body trembled as she knelt beside me, unable to tear her gaze from the horrifying images.

Ethan and Luke appeared in the doorway, drawn by our screams. Ethan's eyes darted from me to the scattered photos on the floor, his expression hardening as the realization hit him. His jaw clenched, and his entire body tensed as he stepped further into the room.

Luke, his face pale, reached down to pick up one of the photos. His hands trembled as he held it, his usually composed demeanor shattering. "Oh my God…" he whispered, his voice barely audible, choked with disbelief.

Ethan crouched beside me, his movements slow and deliberate, as if trying not to break the fragile tension in the room. "Maeve…" he murmured, his voice low and pained. He reached out, pulling me into his arms. His embrace was firm, protective, but I could feel the terror radiating off him, the anger boiling just beneath the surface.

He knew—we both knew—that my father had done this. The man who had tormented and killed all these women wasn't just some faceless monster. He was blood. The realization sat like a lead weight in my chest, choking me with its cruel reality.

Tara, her hands trembling violently, reached for one last photo buried beneath the pile. As she turned it over, her body froze. Her lips parted, but no sound escaped. The color drained from her face, leaving her pale and ghostly. Tears streamed freely down her cheeks, and her breaths came in shallow, uneven gasps. I didn't want to look. Every fiber of my being screamed at me to stop her, to rip the photo away before it could do any more damage. But it was too late. I saw her expression shatter, her hands trembling so badly that the picture nearly slipped from her grasp.

And then I saw him—my uncle's ghost. He stood silently in the corner of the room, his face etched with sorrow, his translucent figure almost shimmering in the dim light. His voice came through like a whisper, soft but heavy with urgency: "No, May… no. Don't look. Don't look."

Ethan stepped forward, his jaw clenched as he reached for the photo in Tara's hands. She let it go without resistance, her arms falling limply to her sides as she collapsed into Gwen, who was sobbing uncontrollably. Ethan turned the picture over, and the moment his eyes landed on it, I squeezed mine shut. I couldn't look—I *wouldn't* look.

Ethan's breath hitched audibly, and I heard the faint, sharp intake of air as his body stiffened. He sank to the floor beside me, still holding the picture. The weight of what he'd seen seemed to pull him down, his shoulders trembling as he stared at the image in stunned silence.

I couldn't bear to open my eyes. Whatever it was, I didn't want it burned into my memory like the rest of those images. But I could feel the shift in the room—like the air itself had turned to stone, pressing down on us, suffocating and inescapable.

Tara and Gwen's sobs grew louder, uncontrollable, breaking through the heavy silence. Luke, usually composed, knelt beside us, his head bowed, his hands gripping his knees as if he were trying to ground himself. No one spoke. There were no words for what we were feeling, no way to make sense of the horror that had overtaken us.

Ethan's hand found mine. His grip was firm, but I could feel the tremor in his fingers as he held onto me, as if trying to keep us both anchored. I finally opened my eyes, glancing at him through my tears. His face was pale, his expression blank except for the raw, unfiltered pain in his eyes.

And then I saw the picture in his hand.

It was my uncle. The last victim in Eric's twisted, grotesque game. He was bound and lifeless, his body displayed like the others, but it was the look in his eyes—frozen in his final moments of fear and agony—that sent a fresh wave of nausea rolling through me. I couldn't look anymore. I buried my face in Ethan's shoulder, my body trembling violently as sobs wracked my chest.

The room around us felt like it had collapsed, the weight of our collective horror pressing down with suffocating force. Ethan held onto me tightly, his arm wrapping protectively around my shoulders as if he could shield me from the unbearable truth.

The only sound was the soft, broken cries of all of us— trapped in a nightmare we could no longer escape.

And then the final piece of reality hit me, sharp and unforgiving: my father was the notorious Nebraska murderer.

ERIC STEPHENSON
(Part: 1)

1984, Nebraska.

E RIC STEPHENSON stood on the crowded platform, ready to board a train bound for Delaware, when his eyes fell upon her—a striking woman standing alone near the edge of the platform. She had short, dark hair that framed her delicate features, and she was wrapped in a long brown coat that draped down to her shoes. There was something about her—something that drew his attention immediately. She stood with an air of quiet confidence, her posture straight, her gaze fixed on the approaching train.

Eric felt an inexplicable pull toward her. It wasn't just her appearance—there was an aura around her that intrigued him, stirred something deep inside him. Without thinking, he began weaving his way through the crowd, his eyes never leaving her. His footsteps quickened as the train pulled in, its doors sliding open with a soft hiss.

The woman moved toward the train, stepping inside with the other passengers. Eric hesitated for a fraction of a second, then made his decision. He followed her.

The doors closed behind him, and the train lurched forward, carrying them into the dimly lit tunnels. The woman stood near the door, her hand gripping the overhead strap, her dark eyes gazing ahead as the world outside the train blurred past. Eric found a spot not far from her, close enough to observe but not yet ready to speak. He took a moment, watching her, studying her—there was a quiet elegance in the way she held herself, completely unaware of his presence.

After a beat, Eric decided it was time. He straightened his posture, putting on the charming smile that had always served him well. He had always known how to strike up a conversation, how to draw people in. This time would be no different.

"Excuse me," he said in a gentle, almost warm voice, projecting just the right amount of casual politeness.

The woman turned her head slightly, her eyes meeting his for a fleeting second before returning to the view outside the window, as if weighing whether to engage. Her response was subtle—a flicker of acknowledgment, but distant, as if she were lost in thought.

Undeterred, Eric pressed on. "My name is Eric Stephenson," he continued, his voice soft yet confident. "I couldn't help but notice... how gorgeous you look." He let the compliment linger in the air, watching for her reaction.

A small smile tugged at the corners of her lips, soft but unmistakable. Slowly, she turned to face him fully, her eyes now fixed on his, appraising. There was a spark of amusement there, perhaps even intrigue of her own.

"Amy Emerson," she said, her voice light and easy, yet tinged with curiosity. "Pleasure to meet you, Eric." She extended her hand, slender and graceful, and as Eric took it, he brought it to his lips, brushing it with a gentle kiss.

The moment lingered. There was something electric in the air, a tension not of fear or anxiety but of possibility. The kind of moment where paths cross, and futures are rewritten in the most subtle of gestures.

"And where might such a stunning woman like you be heading off to at this hour?" Eric asked, his tone playful, his smile effortlessly disarming. "These trains aren't exactly suited for someone as posh as yourself."

He gently released her hand, his fingers lingering just long enough to leave an impression. His smile was warm, easy, and inviting, and Amy couldn't help but blush. She tucked a loose strand of hair behind her ear, her cheeks flushed with a mix of flattery and caution.

"I live here in Nebraska," she replied, her voice soft yet measured. "I'm on my way to my brother Joseph's house. It's not far from the station." She mentioned her brother deliberately, signaling she wouldn't be alone after this encounter. Eric's magnetism intrigued her, but she wasn't ready to drop her guard entirely.

Eric's smile didn't falter. He seemed undeterred by the mention of her brother, leaning into the conversation with effortless charm. "I see. Well, do you think your brother would mind if I took you out for a drink before you pay him a visit?" His tone was light, teasing, but with a clear interest that hung in the air.

Amy hesitated for a moment, glancing at the clock inside the train car. It was 7:00 p.m., and she wasn't expected at her brother's until 9:30. The idea of a quick drink didn't seem too forward. Besides, there was a spark between them she couldn't deny. She smiled, her eyes meeting his, her guard lowering just a touch.

"Well, maybe a drink," she conceded. "There's a nice little shop along the way, not far from where I should be."

Eric's smile broadened, his eyes glinting with satisfaction. "Perfect," he said smoothly, his tone persuasive without being pushy. "A drink at this little shop near your brother's sounds just right."

Amy let out a light laugh, covering her mouth briefly with her hand. "That sounds quite alright," she said, her tone brighter now. Her initial wariness began to dissolve, replaced by a growing ease in Eric's presence. There was something about him—disarming, magnetic. It felt oddly natural, even if she couldn't quite explain why.

As the train continued its journey, Eric and Amy spent the rest of the ride talking, their conversation flowing easily. Eric listened intently to everything she said, asking just the right questions to keep the conversation lively, while revealing only snippets about himself. Amy found herself leaning in, more drawn to him with each passing moment, though she remained careful to keep the conversation light.

When the train finally began to slow, an announcement came over the intercom, stating their upcoming stop. Amy adjusted the belt on her coat, straightening the collar as the doors slid open with a soft hiss. She caught Eric's eye again, smiling as she stepped off the train, walking backward, her gaze still locked on his.

"Careful now, don't trip," Eric said, laughing softly as he watched her playful exit.

Amy giggled, turning around quickly, her footsteps light as she descended onto the platform. There was a lightness in the air between them, the kind of effortless connection that felt almost too good to be true. Eric followed close behind, walking beside her as they moved through the train station, the crowd bustling around them, yet it felt as though they were in their own little world. As they reached the stairs leading to street level, Eric matched his pace with hers, his presence steady, but not over-bearing. Amy glanced at him, her heart fluttering slightly as they climbed the stairs together, their footsteps in sync.

It wasn't often that she found herself so drawn to someone so quickly, but there was something about Eric—something that felt different, though she couldn't quite place why. When they emerged onto the street, the cool night air brushed against Amy's cheeks, refreshing after the warmth of the train. She smiled up at the evening sky, feeling the anticipation of what the night could bring. Eric walked beside her, his gaze focused, but re-laxed, as if this moment was exactly where he wanted to be.

"Here we are," Amy said, leading Eric to a quaint Italian café nestled on a quiet street corner. The small shop, with its warm light spilling onto the sidewalk, had always been one of her fa-vorite spots. She loved their lattes—creamy and topped with del-icate chocolate flakes that melted into the foam. It was her go-to place for comfort and familiarity.

"How lovely," Eric remarked as they stepped inside, taking in the cozy atmosphere. The warm scent of coffee and freshly baked pastries filled the air. After placing their orders, Eric re-quested a table outside, and a cheerful waitress guided them to a small table on the patio. The evening air was crisp, and the soft glow of the café's outdoor lights made the setting feel intimate.

As they sat down, Amy unbuttoned her coat, revealing a beautiful black dress that fell elegantly to her knees. The dress was simple but sophisticated, with a round collar that added a touch of modesty to her look. Eric leaned back in his chair, a smile playing on his lips as he admired her effortless elegance.

"Tell me, Amy, is there a party at your brother's house to-night? You're certainly dressed... modestly," he teased with a gentle chuckle.

Amy glanced down at her dress, smiling faintly at his playful remark. "Oh, yes. My brother and his wife are hosting a celebra-tion for his business's success," she explained, her tone meas-ured, giving just enough detail without revealing too much. She'd always been cautious with strangers, and Eric was no exception, despite his disarming charm.

Amy was the type of woman who carried herself with grace and confidence. She was poised, well-spoken, and came from a wealthy family. She knew how to navigate conversations with care, and if a man ever tried to cross a line with her, she could stop him in his tracks with just her words. Eric could sense this about her—the way she moved, the way she spoke, all spoke to a life of privilege and education.

He noticed the small details about her—the expensive watch that glimmered on her wrist, the sleek designer purse she carried with her. Her entire appearance reflected someone who was not only comfortable in her own skin but also accustomed to a certain lifestyle. This intrigued Eric. His interest wasn't solely in Amy as a person but in the life, she seemed to represent. There was a subtle allure in her refinement, her unspoken elegance.

The waitress soon returned with two beautifully crafted lattes, each one crowned with a generous swirl of foam and a dusting of chocolate. "Thank you," Eric said warmly as the waitress set the cups down on the table.

Amy's eyes lit up as she took in the familiar aroma, her hands instinctively reaching for the cup. "I've always loved their lattes," she said, her tone soft, almost affectionate. She took a sip, smiling as the rich flavors warmed her from the inside out.

Eric watched her, his curiosity deepening. There was something about Amy—an understated charm, a quiet strength—that intrigued him more with every passing moment. He lifted his cup and took a sip, savoring not just the taste but the company he now found himself in.

That evening, Amy found herself pleasantly surprised by how effortlessly the conversation flowed with Eric. There was something charming, almost magnetic, about the way he spoke. His words were polished, and every detail he shared seemed to pique her interest. Eric talked about his college days, his pursuit of a law degree, and how he had inherited a sizable fortune from his parents—a backstory that intrigued Amy, though she would later learn that every word had been carefully fabricated.

"How interesting you are, Mr. Stephenson," Amy said with a smile, holding her latte close as she spoke. The warmth of the cup in her hands seemed to mirror the warmth she felt in their exchange, though a small voice in her mind reminded her to remain cautious. "But I'm afraid I must cut our time short," she continued, glancing at the clock inside the café. "My brother's house is just a short walk from here."

Eric gave her a knowing smile, nodding in acknowledgment. He reached into the pocket of his sleek black trench coat to retrieve his wallet, his movements measured, deliberate.

"Oh no, please," Amy interjected, her tone polite but firm. "Allow me. I did invite you, after all." She opened her purse and quickly slipped out a crisp twenty-dollar bill, tucking it neatly under her plate. It was more than enough to cover the cost of their lattes, leaving a generous tip for the waitress. It was a simple gesture, but it spoke volumes about her upbringing—graceful, considerate, and quietly generous.

"My, my, you are quite the lady," Eric said with a playful glint in his eyes, leaning forward slightly. "Tell you what... how about the next one is on me?"

Amy smiled, her fingers brushing the delicate earring at her lobe, a soft blush rising to her cheeks. "Well then," she replied, her tone light and playful. From her purse, she retrieved a small, elegant business card, its neat lettering reflecting her poised nature. She handed it to him with a subtle nod. "Do call."

Eric accepted the card, glancing at it briefly before meeting her eyes. "I certainly will," he said, rising to his feet as she stood.

As they prepared to leave, Eric moved to her side, gesturing toward the sidewalk with a courteous flourish. "A lady shouldn't be walking alone at night," he said smoothly, his voice warm yet insistent. "How about I walk you to your brother's?"

Amy hesitated for just a moment, her mind weighing the offer. She didn't want to appear ungrateful, but at the same time, she wasn't entirely comfortable with Eric knowing exactly where her brother lived. Her instinct for caution hadn't disappeared completely, even if the evening had been pleasant.

"I appreciate the offer," she said with a polite smile, "but perhaps you can walk me part of the way."

Eric's expression didn't falter, his charm remaining as steady as ever. "Halfway it is," he said with a slight bow, gesturing toward the path ahead.

Amy nodded slightly, a quiet understanding passing between them. Together, they began walking, side by side, down the bustling city street. The lamplights above cast a soft glow over the pavement as they strolled, their conversation lighter now, filled with idle comments about the city and the evening.

As they walked, Amy glanced up at him occasionally, her mind reflecting on the unusual ease of the night. She still didn't know much about Eric, but there was something compelling about him, something that made her feel drawn in. She couldn't quite put her finger on it—whether it was his stories, his charm, or the way he carried himself—but there was a part of her that was intrigued, even if her natural caution hadn't completely faded.

When they reached a point close enough to her brother's house to feel safe but far enough to keep its exact location private, Amy stopped. She turned to face Eric, her posture relaxed but resolute. "This is where I'll part ways," she said softly, her voice carrying a note of finality. "Thank you for the company— and for the conversation."

Eric smiled, bowing his head slightly. "The pleasure was all mine," he replied, his tone smooth, his eyes lingering on hers with a warmth that seemed genuine.

Amy returned his gaze for a moment longer before nodding and turning away. Her footsteps were steady, her thoughts still turning over the events of the night. She couldn't help but glance at the business card she had handed him, wondering if he would actually call. Something about him lingered in her mind—something she couldn't quite place but that made her pulse quicken with both intrigue and unease.

Eric stood on the sidewalk, his eyes following Amy as she crossed the street in a hurry. Her steps quickened as she reached the opposite side, her focus locked on her destination. Two houses down the block, she ascended the stairs to a modest home, her pace even faster now, as though she could feel his gaze lingering.

She didn't look back—not once. It was as if she wanted to put as much distance between them as possible without being impolite. Eric's lips curled into a faint, knowing smile as he slipped her business card from his pocket. He studied it for a moment, running his thumb over the clean edges, before tucking it back into the folds of his coat.

Whistling softly to himself, Eric turned and continued walking down the block. His steps were unhurried, deliberate, the faint echo of his tune fading into the crisp night air.

●●●

The next day, Amy found herself juggling a flurry of phone calls in her cozy home office. Sunlight streamed through the large windows, casting a warm, golden glow on her neatly organized desk. Amy, a paralegal finishing her final internship, was working remotely for a prestigious firm. Her days were a whirlwind of legal documents, court filings, and conference calls—each task moving her closer to her dream of launching her own paralegal company. The vision was clear: a future where she would be her own boss, managing clients from the comfort of a beautifully furnished office.

"Hello, Amy Emerson speaking," she answered, balancing the phone between her shoulder and ear while typing diligently on her computer.

Suddenly, a voice she hadn't expected made her fingers freeze on the keyboard.

"Well, if this voice is like ice, my heart will shatter…" Eric's smooth tone flowed through the phone, catching her completely off-guard. A bright smile spread across Amy's face, and she stopped typing, her attention fully on him. Absentmindedly, she twirled the phone cord around her finger, her heart skipping a beat.

"Mr. Stephenson! Such a surprise," she replied, her voice carrying a trace of excitement she tried to keep in check. She couldn't deny the thrill that he had actually called.

Eric chuckled on the other end, clearly pleased with her reaction. "Well, Amy, I was calling to see if you might have time for dinner tonight—my treat, of course."

Amy's smile deepened, and she nearly bounced in her seat, her fingers tapping lightly on the desk. She was intrigued by him, far more than she had been by anyone else in a long time. There was something about his voice, smooth and confident, that sent a pleasant thrill through her.

"Yes, my schedule is open," she said, aiming for composure despite the excitement bubbling inside her. "How about 8:00 p.m.?"

"That sounds perfect," Eric replied warmly. They exchanged details, and Amy gave him her address.

After hanging up the phone, a surge of anticipation coursed through Amy. Her apartment, though small, was elegant—a reflection of her refined taste. Located in an upscale neighborhood, the building boasted polished marble floors, high ceilings, and large windows offering a stunning view of the city. With a concierge and regular security patrols, it provided an added sense of safety and privacy. Amy's thoughts briefly wandered to her future plans. She hoped to move closer to her brother's home— a stunning property with sprawling gardens, expansive windows, and a perfect blend of modernity and timeless charm. It was the kind of home she dreamed of for herself, a place where she could start a family and build the life she envisioned.

For now, though, she was happy in her current place. The neighborhood was quiet and upscale, and her apartment was everything she needed while she focused on building her career. At 22, Amy was on the verge of achieving everything she'd worked so hard for—a promising career, a beautiful lifestyle, and the independence she'd always craved. But there was still something missing.

As she straightened her desk, smoothing the papers and closing her laptop, she thought of Eric. He was different from the other men she had met—polished, charming, and attentive. She couldn't help but wonder if he might be the man who could give her the family she had always dreamed of. A husband, a home, and children—these were the things she longed for, though she had been cautious, not rushing into relationships lightly. Yet, with Eric, there was a sense of possibility. She imagined him fitting perfectly into the future she envisioned for herself—a strong, capable partner who would not only share her life but also add to the fulfillment she sought.

There was a flicker of hope in her heart as she stood by the window, looking out at the city below. Tonight, would be the start of something new, something that felt exciting and full of potential. She smoothed her dress, mentally preparing for what could be a perfect evening, the promise of something deeper lingering in the air.

• • •

After their first date, Amy realized with certainty that Eric was the one she was meant to be with. Days turned into weeks, weeks into months, and within just three months of their whirlwind courtship, Eric got down on one knee and proposed. It felt like something out of a fairytale—his charm, his charisma, the way he made her feel as though they were destined for each other. Love-struck and full of excitement, Amy accepted without a second thought.

And now, on this day, the wedding of her dreams was unfolding before her eyes.

The ceremony was intimate yet lavish, hosted at a grand, historic château nestled in the countryside. The venue was nothing short of breathtaking—ornate chandeliers hung from high, gilded ceilings, casting a warm, golden glow across the room. White roses, lilies, and blush peonies adorned every corner, their delicate fragrance perfuming the air. Every detail had been meticulously planned, perfectly tailored to Amy's vision of elegance and grace, as if plucked straight from the pages of a storybook.

Fifty guests had gathered—an unexpected but intimate number. It was a blend of generations, with Amy's family dating back to her great-grandmothers, grandmothers, and her mother all present. Her brother, Joseph, stood proudly beside his wife, beaming with joy as he watched his sister prepare for the happiest day of her life. Amy's father's side of the family was also in attendance, their smiles and tears of happiness adding to the magic of the day.

Eric, on the other hand, hadn't invited many. He had told Amy that most of his family had passed on long ago, leaving only a few close connections. The only person from Eric's life who stood by his side was a young boy, four-year-old Justin Shawn Smith—a child Eric had taken in from foster care, a boy he referred to as his half-son. Justin, dressed in a tiny, perfectly fitted tuxedo, looked on curiously at the scene unfolding around him, unaware of the grandness of the occasion.

Amy, unbeknownst to her family, was pregnant. She and Eric had kept this secret between them, cherishing the new life they were creating together. At three months along, she had started to show just slightly, enough that her custom-made wedding dress had been meticulously designed to flatter her growing figure. The gown was a masterpiece—silk satin with delicate lace detailing, hugging her body in all the right places while allowing her to move gracefully. The bodice, adorned with tiny pearls, accentuated her elegance, while the soft drape of the fabric flowed down to the floor, creating a perfect silhouette.

In the private room of the château, Amy stood before a large, ornate mirror as her mother and grandmother helped dress her. The room was quiet, filled with the gentle rustling of fabric and the faint scent of flowers from the arrangements nearby. Her mother's hands were gentle as she fastened the final pearl buttons on the back of the dress, and her grandmother carefully placed the delicate lace veil over her hair. Amy gazed at her reflection, her heart swelling with happiness.

Beaming with joy, she took in the sight of herself—radiant, glowing, and surrounded by love. The dress fit her like a dream, the custom design subtly concealing her pregnancy while highlighting the elegance she had always imagined for her wedding day. The soft sheen of the silk caught the light from the chandelier above, making her look as if she were glowing from within.

"You look breathtaking, Amy," her grandmother whispered, her voice thick with emotion as she smoothed the veil over her shoulders. "Just like an angel."

Amy's eyes sparkled as she smiled, her hands instinctively resting on her stomach for a brief moment before she pulled them away, not wanting to give anything away to her family just yet. This day was perfect, and soon, the secret she shared with Eric would become part of their new life together.

As she prepared to walk down the aisle, Amy's thoughts turned to Eric. He was waiting for her at the end of that grand, flower-lined aisle—her future, her partner, the father of her child. The thought filled her with warmth, her heart fluttering with anticipation.

Outside, the guests began to take their seats in the château's beautiful garden, where the ceremony would take place under an arch of cascading white flowers. The gentle breeze carried the sweet scent of roses and peonies through the air, mingling with the soft notes of classical music played by a string quartet. The scene was picturesque—perfect in every way.

As Amy made her way toward the entrance of the garden, arm-in-arm with her father, her heart swelled with love and gratitude. Every step felt like a dream, each moment a memory she would hold onto forever. The soft chatter of guests faded into the background as she locked eyes with Eric at the end of the aisle, his expression one of awe and devotion.

The sun began to dip lower in the sky, casting a golden light over the scene. The entire moment felt timeless—suspended in beauty, joy, and love. This was the wedding Amy had always dreamed of, and with Eric by her side, her future felt as bright as the warm glow surrounding them. As they exchanged vows, the world seemed to fall away. It was just them, promising forever to one another in a moment that was as intimate as it was grand.

The wedding was everything Amy had ever dreamed of—grand, beautiful, and overflowing with love. From the elegant ceremony to the lavish reception, every detail had been perfect, a reflection of the life she and Eric were about to build together. The laughter and smiles of Amy's family filled the air throughout the day, and as the evening began to wind down, the last of the guests departed with joyful goodbyes and warm embraces. Eric, ever the romantic, had a surprise in store for his new bride. He had bought her a small, cozy cottage home in Nebraska, a few miles away from the hustle and bustle of city life. It was meant to be their peaceful retreat, a place where they could start their new life together, surrounded by nature.

As the banquet hall slowly emptied, Eric turned to Amy, his eyes sparkling with excitement. Without saying a word, he took her hand and, with a playful grin, began to pull her toward the doors. The remaining guests laughed and clapped as the couple ran hand in hand through the hall, their smiles infectious. It was a scene of pure joy—love radiating from them, lighting up the room as they made their way outside.

Waiting for them was a sleek car, its door open, ready to whisk them away to the next chapter of their lives. Little Justin was already sitting in the backseat, his small legs swinging as he listened to cartoons on the phone Eric had given him. The moment he spotted Eric and Amy, his face lit up with a wide, toothy grin.

"Hi, Miss Amy!" Justin called out, his voice filled with the excitement only a child could have, his words slurring together in his eagerness.

Amy laughed, her heart swelling at the sight of him. She had grown fond of the boy, and the sound of his voice felt like another piece of this perfect day falling into place. She squeezed Eric's hand before they both climbed into the back seat of the car, joining Justin as the driver prepared to take them to their new home. As the car slowly pulled away from the hall, the last of Amy's family gathered outside, clapping and cheering for the newlyweds. The air was filled with the sound of joy, the warmth of family, and the promise of a new beginning. Amy leaned against Eric, her heart brimming with happiness as the city began to fade into the distance behind them.

As they left the city behind, the scenery changed dramatically. The bright lights and tall buildings gave way to open skies and sprawling fields. The further they drove, the more peaceful the world seemed to become. Nature surrounded them—endless green fields, tall trees swaying gently in the evening breeze, and the golden light of the setting sun casting a soft glow over the landscape. It was serene, almost magical, and Amy couldn't help but feel a deep sense of contentment wash over her.

Soon, the cottage came into view. Nestled at the edge of a quiet road, the small house stood proudly in the middle of a barren plot of land, yet to be touched by fertile hands. The white picket fence surrounding it added a touch of charm, a promise of the life they would build here together.

Amy laughed, her eyes lighting up as they approached. "Oh, it's lovely!" she exclaimed, her voice filled with genuine delight.

The driver slowed the car and pulled into the gravel driveway, the tires crunching softly as they came to a stop in front of the cottage. There was something so charming about its simplicity, the promise of what it could become with time and care. The house wasn't grand or elaborate, but it was theirs—a place where they could build a life, a family, a future.

Eric smiled at Amy, the excitement still gleaming in his eyes. "Welcome home, Mrs. Stephenson," he said softly, his voice filled with warmth.

Amy looked at him, her heart swelling with love. This was the beginning of everything—her life as a wife, soon as a mother, and all the dreams she had ever hoped for. She couldn't help but feel as though she was stepping into a fairytale, one where she and Eric would write their own happy ending.

They stepped out of the car, Justin running ahead, his small legs carrying him toward the front door with eager anticipation. "This is where we're going to live, Miss Amy?" he asked, his voice filled with childish wonder.

Amy knelt down beside him, ruffling his hair gently. "Yes, Justin, this is home now," she said, her voice soft and full of affection.

As the sun set behind the horizon, painting the sky in hues of pink and orange, Amy stood beside Eric, her hand resting gently in his. Together, they looked at the cottage, their home, the future unfolding before them like a beautiful, untold story.

· · ·

ERIC STEPHENSON
(Part: 2)

IT HAD BEEN SIX MONTHS since Amy and Eric moved into their new home. What had once been filled with excitement and hope now felt lonely and barren, the warmth drained from the walls. Amy found herself in the kitchen, preparing a simple meal for herself—a daily ritual that had become an echo of her new, solitary routine. The house, though quaint and charming, felt emptier with each passing day.

Ever since their wedding, Eric had changed. Gone was the attentive, loving man who had swept her off her feet. He still smiled, still played the part of the doting husband at times, but there were now secrets between them—things he kept hidden behind closed doors. His "businesses," as he called them, took him away for days on end. He never told Amy the full extent of what he did, and she had long stopped asking. Each time she pressed for details about his supposed law firm, he would brush her off with vague reassurances.

Eric always took Justin with him on these trips, leaving Amy behind. It was as if he didn't trust her mothering instincts, a subtle, unspoken judgment that cut deeper than words. She was about to become a mother herself, now nine months pregnant with a girl, and yet she felt more alone than ever.

That evening, like so many others, Amy sat at the small kitchen table, her hand resting on her swollen belly. She had prepared a meal, but the appetite that once came with excitement for Eric's return had faded. She ate alone now—every day since Eric had taken on these mysterious jobs that required all of his time.

The day had been a long one. Eric had called earlier, telling her once again that he'd be late—stuck at the office, supposedly finalizing some deal with the law firm he claimed to be partnering with. It was the same excuse as always. Amy had never seen this firm, never even heard the name of it. It was as if it didn't exist. With a sigh, Amy sat down at the table and picked up her fork, staring at the meal she had prepared. She was about to take a bite when a knock came at the door. Startled, she set her fork down, her heart fluttering with surprise.

"Oh, what is this?" she huffed, pushing herself up from the table, her hand bracing her lower back as she waddled to the door.

When she opened it, a wave of relief and happiness washed over her. Standing there was her brother Joseph, a familiar face she hadn't seen in far too long. His warm smile lit up the evening, and without hesitation, they embraced. In that moment, all the loneliness that had weighed on her seemed to melt away.

"Joseph!" Amy exclaimed, hugging him tightly. Her heart swelled with joy at the sight of him.

Joseph smiled warmly and held out a plush teddy bear. It was soft and sweet, with a custom-made tag that read, "For baby Maeve."

"I had this made for her, thought she might like it when she arrives," Joseph said, his voice full of affection as he handed her the bear.

Amy beamed, her heart filled with gratitude. "Oh, Joseph, it's absolutely lovely!" She hugged him again, feeling the weight of all her unspoken emotions rise to the surface. It was a small gift, but it meant the world to her—someone was thinking of her, of her baby, of the family she longed to build.

Joseph glanced around the small, quiet home, the absence of Eric noticeable. "Where's that husband of yours?" he asked, his brow furrowing as he took in the empty space. The only sound was the low hum of the television playing softly in the background.

"Busy with work," Amy replied, her voice carrying a hint of weariness as she tapped her brother on the shoulder. She returned to the table, and Joseph joined her, the two of them settling into the comfortable familiarity of siblings. The house, once filled with silence, now felt alive again with his presence.

"How's little Maeve doing today?" Joseph asked, a broad smile lighting up his face as he gently placed his hands on Amy's belly.

Amy laughed, the tension in her shoulders easing as she leaned back in her chair. "She's moving, lively—and I think ready to come out! I've been having contractions all day," she said, her voice a mix of excitement and anticipation.

Joseph's eyes widened with delight, his hands tapping the table in excitement. "I have to meet her—tell her to hurry up!" he laughed, his joy infectious.

Amy smiled at her brother's enthusiasm. In that moment, all the uncertainty and loneliness that had been creeping in since Eric's absences faded into the background. Joseph's presence was a reminder that she wasn't truly alone. Her family was still here, still supporting her—even if Eric wasn't.

As the evening wore on, Amy and Joseph sat together, talking, reminiscing, and sharing their excitement for the baby. The ticking clock, the warmth of the room, and the bond between them gave Amy a sense of peace she hadn't felt in months. Even though Eric was absent, even though his presence had become more of a shadow than a comfort, Amy knew she had people who loved her—people who would be there for her and for her baby.

And though she didn't know it yet, it would be Joseph, not Eric, who would stay by her side when she finally gave birth to May—her daughter, Maeve. It was Joseph who would hold her hand, comfort her, and welcome her baby into the world, while Eric remained distant, consumed by secrets and a life Amy had yet to fully understand.

"Well, my dear Amy, it's late, and I must head home," Joseph said, standing up from the couch, stretching his arms after a long evening. Amy, who had been lounging with him, shifted uncomfortably to her feet, her heavily pregnant belly leading her movements.

"Oooh!" she gasped, her hand instinctively flying to her stomach as she felt a sharp twinge.

Joseph's eyes widened, concern immediately crossing his face. "Amy?" he asked, his voice laced with both worry and excitement.

A knowing smile spread across Amy's face. "I think Maeve is ready to come out and meet the world," she said, laughing softly through the discomfort.

Joseph's panic was instant. "Okay, uh, okay, let's go! Get a bag... a bag! We need a bag, right?" he stuttered, running his hands through his hair as he frantically looked around, clearly trying to get a grip on the situation.

Amy, amused by her brother's nervous energy, chuckled despite the contractions starting to take hold. "Joe, Joe, calm down," she said, her voice gentle and reassuring. "She's not here yet, and I already packed my bag. It's by the door, ready to go."

With a firm tap on his shoulder, Amy guided Joseph back to a calmer state. He looked at her, wide-eyed and flustered, but followed her lead. He grabbed the hospital bag by the door, throwing it over his shoulder as he helped Amy navigate her way out of the cottage, carefully supporting her as they stepped into the cool night air.

The excitement was palpable. The stars above twinkled like tiny celebrations waiting to happen, as if the universe itself knew a new life was about to enter the world.

Joseph helped Amy into the car, and they set off toward the hospital. But in his nervous haste, Joseph's foot pressed a little too hard on the gas pedal. The quiet roads soon turned into a blur of trees and distant headlights as they sped down the highway.

It didn't take long before flashing red and blue lights filled the rearview mirror. Joseph groaned, his panic rising again. "Oh no, oh no…"

Amy, sitting in the passenger seat, looked at him with amusement, unable to hold back a laugh. "Joseph, really?" she said, her voice a mixture of disbelief and humor. "You didn't have to speed! Maeve's not here yet."

The officer approached, but after hearing the situation—a heavily pregnant woman on her way to the hospital—the officer let them off with a warning, urging them to drive safely. As the officer waved them back onto the road, Joseph exhaled a sigh of relief, the tension visibly leaving his shoulders.

Amy burst out laughing as they pulled away. "Well, that was quite the adventure!" she said, still shaking her head at the ridiculousness of the situation. It was exactly what she needed to keep her mind off the building contractions—a moment of lightheartedness before the real work began.

"Not funny, Amy!" Joseph retorted, gripping the wheel tighter, but a smile tugged at his lips despite his words. "This is a big deal—Maeve is coming into the world! I just want to make sure it happens in a hospital, not the back of this car!"

Amy laughed again, but soon, her breathing deepened as the contractions became stronger. Joseph kept glancing over, his concern growing, but Amy stayed calm, instructing him to follow the speed limit this time as they made their way to the city.

When they finally arrived at the hospital, Amy was admitted, and the medical team whisked her into the maternity ward. Joseph stayed by her side, his earlier nerves calming as the hospital staff took over. The excitement of the moment began to settle in—a mix of joy, anticipation, and wonder at the thought of meeting baby Maeve.

Hours passed in a blur of breathing exercises, comforting words, and the steady support of Joseph at Amy's side. She squeezed his hand, and he did his best to keep her spirits up, offering jokes to ease her through the pain, though his eyes held nothing but admiration for his sister's strength.

And then, as the first light of dawn broke through the hospital windows, the most joyful sound filled the room: the tiny, perfect cry of a newborn.

Tears welled up in Amy's eyes as the nurse gently placed Maeve in her arms, her little face scrunched up, her soft cries a beautiful melody to Amy's ears. "Hello, Maeve," Amy whispered, her voice filled with awe and love. In that moment, everything else faded away—the loneliness, the long days, the uncertainty. All that mattered was this tiny life, the beautiful baby girl she had brought into the world.

Joseph stood beside her, his eyes shimmering with tears of his own. "She's perfect, Amy," he said softly, leaning in to get a closer look at his niece. He wiped at his eyes, overcome with emotion, as he marveled at the little girl who had already captured all their hearts.

Amy looked up at him, her heart full. "Thank you, Joe," she whispered, knowing she couldn't have done this without him. He had been there, when no one else had, and his presence meant more to her than she could ever express.

Joseph grinned, reaching out to gently touch Maeve's tiny hand. "Welcome to the world, Maeve," he said, his voice thick with emotion. "We've been waiting for you."

Eric had called that evening, just after Joseph left the hospital. Filled with excitement, Joseph had returned home to share the joyful news of Maeve's birth with their family. Amy, still basking in the glow of her daughter's arrival, was to spend three more days in the hospital. She had expected Eric to rush to see his newborn daughter, but he didn't. Instead, he called, promising that he would come by tomorrow. His voice on the phone was excited, almost too much so, as he told her he had a special gift for Maeve.

"Oh, Eric, you have to come meet her," Amy said, her tone a mix of sternness and longing. It had been a full day since Maeve was born, and still, Eric had not shown up. In fact, when Amy thought about it, it had been three days since she had last seen him at all. A sinking feeling began to take hold in her chest—doubt creeping in. She was starting to lose faith in him, starting to question everything he said.

"Bring little Justin with you," she added, trying to lighten her voice. "He should meet his lovely half-sister—"

Before she could finish her sentence, Eric cut her off with an anger that startled her. "Justin is no longer your business," he snapped. "I will not bring him."

His tone was sharp, aggressive—nothing like the man she had married. Amy froze, the phone pressed against her ear as the words sank in. He had never spoken to her like this before. His sudden outburst left her confused, her mind spinning in disbelief.

And then, without another word, Eric hung up.

Amy sat there, staring at the phone in her hand, her heart pounding. Her thoughts raced as she tried to make sense of what had just happened. This wasn't the Eric she knew—or rather, the Eric she thought she knew. Slowly, she placed the phone down on the small hospital counter beside her and turned to look at Maeve, sleeping peacefully in her bassinet.

Smiling softly, she reached out and touched her baby's tiny hand, the warmth of her daughter grounding her in the moment. But even as she smiled, her mind churned with unease. "There's something very strange going on with your father, Maeve," she murmured softly. She spoke to her baby as though confiding in her, trying to make sense of her own thoughts.

"He was once this wonderful man—charming and charismatic," Amy continued, gently stroking Maeve's delicate fingers. "But now, my dear one, I'm beginning to question who he really is. Well, let's see if he even arrives tomorrow, as he says."

Amy tried to push the troubling thoughts aside, focusing on Maeve's soft coos and the way her tiny lips twitched as she slept. Every little sound her daughter made filled her with joy, a welcome distraction from the growing worry festering in her mind. But deep down, Amy couldn't shake the feeling that something was terribly wrong. Eric had been distant, secretive, and now this outburst—what was really going on?

That night, as Maeve slept beside her in the small hospital bed, Amy's mind raced. She couldn't rest, couldn't let the nagging suspicion go. She had to know the truth. If Eric had been lying to her, she needed to find out—no matter what it took.

Determined, she reached for the hospital phone, the old rotary-style device still attached to a phone book. Her fingers flipped through the thin pages, scanning the list of law firms. Eric had always told her he was working on his law degree, that he had partnered with a firm in Nebraska. Yet she had never seen it, never been introduced to anyone he worked with. Now, that doubt had taken root, and it was growing fast.

She dialed the first number. "Hello, could you tell me if you employ a man named Eric Stephenson?" she asked the receptionist at Scott & Schmidt Law Office, trying to sound casual. The receptionist transferred her to a man—possibly Scott or Schmidt—and Amy waited on the line until a voice finally answered.

"I'm sorry, ma'am, unless you're looking for a lawyer, I cannot disclose employee information," the man on the other end replied, his voice formal and guarded.

Amy quickly adapted. "Well, yes, actually I am. I heard Eric Stephenson was the best, and I'm looking to hire him."

There was a brief pause on the line, followed by the sound of typing. "No, ma'am, we have no one by that name working here," the man said, his voice final. Then the line went dead.

Amy stared at the phone, her heart sinking. This was only the first call, but already her suspicions were deepening. One by one, she called firm after firm, each time receiving the same answer. No one had heard of Eric Stephenson, no law firm had employed him, and her heart began to race as the reality of it all started to set in.

By the time she reached the thirtieth listing in the yellow pages, she was beginning to feel sick. Was everything Eric had told her a lie? Was he even a lawyer at all? The doubts that had once been whispers were now shouting in her mind.

Amy took a deep breath as she dialed the last number on the list. "Kramer and Johnson," came the cheery voice of a receptionist.

"Oh, hello," Amy said, forcing a smile into her voice. "I'm looking to hire a lawyer. Could you tell me if Eric Stephenson works for your firm? I've heard wonderful things about him."

There was a pause, then the sound of typing on the other end. "I'm sorry, ma'am, we don't have anyone by that name employed here," the woman said.

Amy's heart sank again, but before she could hang up, the receptionist continued. "However, we do have a client named

Eric Andrews, though he doesn't work as a lawyer. I can't disclose details about his case though."

Amy's breath caught in her throat. "Eric Andrews?" she repeated, the name foreign on her tongue. Had Eric been using an alias this whole time?

"Yes, ma'am, but I can't say more than that," the woman said apologetically before ending the call.

Amy sat there in silence, the phone still in her hand. The world around her seemed to spin. Who was this man she had married? The lies had become too many to ignore, and now she knew for certain—Eric wasn't who he said he was.

Everything she thought she knew about her husband was crumbling, and with it, her trust. Her mind raced with possibilities—what else had he lied about? And what was he hiding? The realization hit her like a tidal wave: the man she had married, the father of her child, was a stranger.

...

As the soft light of dawn filtered through the thin hospital curtains, Amy stirred awake to the sound of her daughter's sweet cooing. Blinking away the remnants of sleep, her vision cleared to see her hospital room filled with familiar faces. There, gathered around her, were her brother Joseph, his wife Mary, her mother, and her grandmother, all beaming down at little Maeve.

"Oh, how wonderful! Everyone's here to meet Maeve," Amy said, her face lighting up with joy as she took in the loving scene. It was as if the room had become a bubble of warmth, family, and love.

Maeve, oblivious to the excitement surrounding her, was being passed from arm to arm, each relative taking turns admiring her. Laughter filled the air, especially when Maeve, with perfect timing, decided to introduce herself to her uncle Joseph in a less-than-ideal way—by promptly throwing up all over his shirt.

"Agh, no, no, Maeve!" Joseph mock-scolded, his tone light

as he reached for a white baby cloth folded neatly on the bedside table. "This is not how you introduce yourself to family, young lady," he said, shaking his head but smiling as he dabbed at his now-drenched shirt.

Amy couldn't help but laugh, watching Joseph's playful attempts at cleaning himself up. The room was alive with laughter, banter, and the joy that only a newborn could bring. It felt like a perfect moment, her family showering Maeve with love and attention.

Amidst the chatter, a young doctor entered the room, his presence drawing everyone's attention. He was tall, with a warm, easy smile, holding a folder in his hands. A nurse stood beside him, but it was the doctor who spoke.

"Well, Mrs. Stephenson," he began, glancing at the notes in his folder, then looking up at Amy with a kind smile. "I see little Maeve was born yesterday. Congratulations!"

Amy blushed, her heart skipping a beat at the sight of the doctor. There was something about his easy charm and the softness in his voice that caught her off guard. She hadn't expected to find herself flustered, but there it was—a moment of warmth between them.

"Thank you, Doctor," she said softly, smiling back.

"We just need to borrow Maeve for a little bit," the doctor continued, his tone gentle. "Take some tests, measurements, and check her heart and lungs."

Joseph, still laughing from the earlier incident, carefully stood and passed Maeve back to Amy. "Ah, man," Joseph said, glancing down at his shirt with a sigh. "Doctor, is there any chance there's a place around here where I can get a fresh shirt?"

The doctor chuckled, clearly amused by Joseph's predicament. Amy's mother and grandmother laughed too, their voices light as they teased Joseph. "Oh, Joseph dear, the gift shop is downstairs," their mother chimed in.

"Well, guess I'll be making a trip then," Joseph said with a grin, throwing a mock-salute as he left the room, still shaking his head at his luck.

As he walked out, the room seemed to settle, the lively energy dimming just a bit. The doctor stepped closer to Amy, still smiling. "Your family is certainly… lively," he remarked with a twinkle in his eye.

Amy laughed, nodding. "They're something, aren't they?"

The doctor looked down at Maeve, his expression softening. "Well, I think we can do all the tests right here," he said, glancing at the nurse beside him. "This little one doesn't need to go anywhere."

Amy smiled gratefully as the doctor took a seat beside her on the hospital bed, pulling out his stethoscope. There was something comforting about his presence, the way he handled everything with such care. The cold metal of the stethoscope touched Maeve's tiny chest, and the doctor listened intently, his expression one of focus and warmth.

After a few moments, he glanced up at Amy and smiled, their eyes meeting briefly. There was a softness in his gaze, something unspoken yet present, a small connection that made Amy's heart flutter.

"She's perfect," the doctor said softly, his words simple but full of reassurance.

"Thank you, Doctor…" Amy paused, realizing she didn't know his name.

"James. James Adams," he introduced himself, his smile widening just a little.

"Well, thank you, Dr. Adams," Amy said, her smile matching his. She couldn't help but feel a small spark, something that felt… different. She brushed it aside for now, focusing on Maeve, but the thought lingered.

As Dr. Adams finished the check-up, he stood, giving Maeve one last gentle look. "We'll keep an eye on both of you, but so far, everything looks great," he said with a nod. "And, if you need anything at all, just let me know."

"Thank you, I will," Amy replied, her heart still fluttering slightly. There was something about him—something kind, steady, and warm.

As he left the room, Amy's thoughts lingered on the encounter. She looked down at Maeve, smiling as her baby girl blinked up at her with curious eyes. Life had become so much more complicated with the questions surrounding Eric, but for now, she felt a strange sense of calm.

Dr. James Adams. It was just a name, just a brief meeting, but Amy couldn't help but wonder if this was the beginning of something more.

"Well, Maeve, it looks like your father hasn't shown up yet," Amy said softly as she gently touched her baby's tiny hands. There was a hint of disappointment in her voice, but she pushed it aside, focusing on the sweet innocence of her daughter.

Just then, the sound of hurried footsteps echoed down the hall, followed by a sudden burst of energy as a young boy barged into Amy's hospital room, skidding to a stop beside her bed.

"Hi!" the boy said, his eyes wide with excitement as he stood there, slightly out of breath. Startled, Amy looked up at the unexpected visitor, but she quickly smiled, charmed by the boy's lively presence.

"Hello there, young man," she greeted him warmly, her curiosity piqued. He was full of energy, clearly up to something.

The boy's eyes drifted to Maeve, his expression softening as he tilted his head toward the door. "I'm hiding," he whispered, as though sharing a secret.

Amy laughed, holding her hand to her mouth to stifle the sound. "Oh, hiding, are we? And who are you hiding from, little one?" she asked, her voice playful.

The boy let out a deep sigh, shaking his head with exaggerated frustration. "My dad," he said with a little laugh, his mischievous smile lighting up his face.

He then leaned in closer, extending his hand gently toward

Maeve, his fingers brushing the top of her head. His eyes widened with amazement as he took in her tiny size. "She's soooo small! Wow, how can she even fit into your arms like that?" he asked in awe, completely mesmerized by the tiny baby cradled in Amy's embrace. Amy chuckled at his innocent wonder. There was something heartwarming about the way he was drawn to Maeve, his curiosity pure and sweet.

Before Amy could respond, a familiar voice called out from the hallway. "ETHAN! Ethan Adams!" Dr. Adams' voice echoed from just outside the door. Moments later, he appeared, his arms folded as he gave his son a half-amused, half-exasperated look. "I am so sorry, Mrs. Stephenson," James said, shaking his head with a smile.

"Ethan has been running around the hospital all day, and I've been chasing him ever since. Looks like he found his way here before I could catch up." Ethan stood still for a moment, his face a perfect picture of serious concentration, as though deciding whether to acknowledge his father or keep playing the part of the runaway. Eventually, he stuffed his hands into his pockets and walked slowly around James, heading toward the door as if nothing had happened.

James sighed, rubbing the back of his neck. "Please forgive my son's intrusion. Ever since his mother's death six months ago, he's been... difficult. He never listens to a word I say." There was a note of sadness in his voice, but he smiled at Amy, trying to brush it off.

Amy's heart softened. She shook her head gently. "That's quite alright. He's a sweet boy," she said, her smile warm as she glanced at Ethan, who had paused by the door, casting one last look at Maeve before pretending not to care.

James tapped his forehead lightly, clearly a little flustered. "Well, please let me know if there's anything you need," he said, turning to leave.

"Oh, Doctor," Amy called after him, stopping him in his tracks.

He turned, tilting his head in her direction, his brow raised in curiosity. "Yes, Mrs. Stephenson?"

Amy smiled at him, her voice soft. "Since I'll be here for the next couple of days, if young Ethan wants to hang around and visit with Maeve, he's more than welcome to." She cast a glance toward Ethan, who was still hovering by the door, pretending not to listen.

James's face lit up with appreciation. "That's very kind of you. I'll let him know." He gave her a grateful nod, then turned to his son. "Ethan, did you hear that? You can visit Maeve for the next two days if you want."

Ethan, ever serious, said nothing in response, but there was a flicker of interest in his eyes as he glanced back toward Maeve. Without a word, he turned and walked slowly down the hall, his small footsteps echoing off the hospital walls.

Amy watched him disappear around the corner, a soft smile playing on her lips. There was something endearing about the quiet connection between Ethan and Maeve, even in those first moments. As she cradled her daughter in her arms, she couldn't help but wonder if this was the beginning of something special between them—a bond that could grow into something meaningful.

For now, though, she let the thought rest, simply enjoying the peace of the moment, her heart lighter than it had been in a long time.

. . .

Amy hummed softly to Maeve as she shifted herself out of bed, her hands moving gently as she dressed her squirming, giggling baby. Maeve was a bundle of energy, wiggling on the hospital bed as Amy reached for a fresh diaper. Just as Amy slipped the clean diaper under her, Maeve squealed and promptly peed all over the new one.

Amy burst out laughing. "Well, that saves me time changing

you again," she said with amusement, shaking her head. She replaced the soaked diaper with a fresh one, taping it securely around Maeve's tiny waist. Smiling down at her daughter, Amy spoke gently. "Now, do you think you can hold off for a few hours and not soil this one, please?" Maeve cooed and giggled, her toothless smile lighting up the room.

Just then, a familiar voice cut through the air. "HI!" Ethan's voice chimed from behind Amy, startling her.

"Oh, dear boy, you startled me," Amy said, turning to face him with a smile. Ethan stood there, hands tucked into his pockets, nodding to her without smiling, a serious expression on his face. Amy chuckled and touched his head affectionately before she turned around to dispose of the diaper in the bathroom garbage. "Can you watch her for a moment, young man?" she asked over her shoulder.

Ethan shuffled closer to Maeve, his serious face still in place as he leaned over the tiny baby. Maeve made some strange, gurgling noises, and Ethan's brow furrowed in confusion. "Why does she make weird noises like that?" he asked, genuinely curious.

Amy laughed as she returned to the bed, sitting beside Maeve. "She's still a baby, Ethan. She won't talk for a long while yet," Amy explained, brushing Maeve's soft hair with her hand.

"Oh," Ethan said, surprised. His eyes flicked back to Maeve as he seemed to consider this information. After a beat of silence, he grinned and began telling Maeve his mischievous tales. "You know what I did, Maeve? I hid in the nurse's lounge behind this big ol' plant, and every time a nurse came in, I'd jump out and yell 'Boo!'" He laughed, shaking his head. "They screamed every time! But then my dad caught me, and let's just say, I wasn't the only one doing the yelling."

He paused, watching baby Maeve coo, then continued with a playful smirk, "Oh, and you should've seen me with these shoes I had. They had wheels on the heels—coolest thing ever. I'd zoom down the hallways, dodging beds and doctors like I was in some kinda race. The nurses called me 'the little rocket.'"

Maeve was completely unfazed by his stories, cooing and laughing as if she already adored him, her wide eyes fixated on him like he was the most entertaining person in the world. Amy couldn't help but laugh as she watched Ethan's animated storytelling, enjoying the carefree moments in a place that had been filled with so much anxiety. She had spent the last two days at the hospital, making frantic phone calls—trying to track down any information about Eric, about Justin, about the lies she had uncovered. There were no records of Eric Stephenson being a lawyer, no trace of Justins's existence in any foster home or orphanage. Everything Eric had told her was unraveling, and it only deepened the pit of dread in her stomach.

Ethan had been in the room for about half an hour, still chatting away to Maeve, when Amy's attention was pulled toward the door. She heard raised voices and footsteps approaching rapidly. Her body stiffened, and she instinctively placed a protective hand over Ethan's head, pulling him closer to her side as she shifted toward Maeve.

The door flew open, and there stood Eric, with a man in a suit by his side. Behind them was Dr. Adams, his face tense and his posture rigid.

"ERIC?" Amy gasped, her eyes wide with shock. It had been days, and he hadn't called or shown up—and now he barged into the room unannounced? Her heart raced.

"Excuse me, sir," Dr. Adams said, stepping forward, his voice firm and assertive.

"Back off, Doctor," Eric barked at him. His tone was cold, menacing, nothing like the man Amy once knew.

The man beside Eric stepped forward and pulled a folded piece of paper from his pocket, handing it to Amy. She stared at it, bewildered, her hands trembling as she opened it.

"What is this?" she asked, her voice unsteady.

"It's a court order," the lawyer said coolly. "Eric has been granted full custody of Maeve, and we are here to take her immediately."

Amy's world spun. Her heart pounded in her chest as she clutched Maeve tighter to her body. "WHAT?" she shouted, throwing the paper to the ground as her entire body trembled with disbelief. This couldn't be happening.

Eric's eyes were cold as he stepped closer. "I've filed for divorce, Amy. Maeve—who will now be called Josephina—is legally mine," he said with a calm cruelty, reaching toward her and Maeve.

Amy burst into tears, her grip on Maeve tightening as the baby began to wail in response. Dr. Adams moved swiftly to intercept, his voice sharp. "HEY! Back off!" he barked, standing protectively between Amy and Eric.

Ethan, who had been silently watching the scene unfold, clenched his fists. He couldn't stand seeing Amy so upset, and the idea of Eric taking Maeve away made his blood boil. As Eric reached toward Amy again, Ethan sprang into action. With a swift movement, he kicked Eric hard in the knee, causing him to flinch and stumble back.

"YOU CAN'T HAVE HER!" Ethan shouted, his voice filled with fury as he planted himself firmly between Amy and Eric, his small fists balled up, ready to defend Maeve.

Eric stared at the boy in shock, while Dr. Adams quickly called for security. Within moments, hospital security rushed in, taking hold of Eric and the lawyer.

"I want this man arrested and thrown out of the hospital," Dr. Adams ordered as he bent down to retrieve the court order. He handed it to the security officers. "And this document needs to be verified immediately," he added, his voice steady but filled with authority.

As Eric and his lawyer were escorted out, Amy collapsed into sobs, clutching Maeve close to her chest. The shock and fear of what had just happened overwhelmed her. She couldn't believe Eric had gone this far, that he had tried to take her daughter away.

Ethan, still standing by her side, placed a gentle hand on Maeve's tiny fingers. His face was calm now, his voice soft. "He won't take her," he said with quiet determination. He looked up at Amy, his eyes full of sincerity. "I won't let him."

Amy, tears streaming down her face, looked at Ethan, her heart swelling with gratitude. This young boy had stood up for her and Maeve in a way she hadn't expected.

The next day, after Amy had been discharged from the hospital, she was filled with dread. She feared that Eric might still find a way to take Maeve. The thought of losing her daughter consumed her. As she packed her things to leave, Dr. Adams approached her gently. "Amy," he said softly, "I know you're worried about what Eric might do. I have a home in the city, a safe place where you and Maeve can stay, hidden away from him. You'll be safe there."

Amy looked up at him, her eyes filled with uncertainty, but she trusted him. Dr. Adams had been there for her when Eric hadn't. He had protected her. With a nod, she agreed.

Over the next two years, Amy and Dr. Adams grew closer. What began as a relationship built on trust and safety soon blossomed into something deeper. They fell in love, and on Maeve's second birthday, they were married. Maeve grew up happy and protected, with Ethan treating her like a little sister.

But Eric wasn't done. On the day James and Amy moved into their dream home, Eric resurfaced, threatening to kidnap Maeve again, throwing Amy's life into turmoil. Dr. Adams, determined to protect his family, hired the most powerful lawyer he could find. Together, they fought Eric in court, winning full custody of Maeve and securing a restraining order against him.

Eric, enraged by the outcome, vowed revenge. 'I'll destroy you, Amy, and I will take her… you hear me?' he spat, his eyes burning with fury. But as Amy stood with Dr. Adams and Ethan by her side, she knew that no matter what Eric tried, they would face it together. Their love, their family, was stronger than anything Eric could throw at them.

Chapter 13

GWEN

2000, Nebraska (Maeve, 17 years old. Gwen, 16.)

GWEN SAT ON MY BED, flipping through a *Teen Vogue* magazine—the same one I always read. "You've got to be kidding me. *Luke*... Luke Greyson? *The* Luke Greyson?" I said, wide-eyed. I spun around, staring at her in disbelief. She just grinned, completely smitten, hugging one of my fuzzy pillows tightly to her chest.

"Oh my God, you're insane!" I laughed, rummaging through my closet for something to wear. I held up a shirt, checked myself in the mirror, then tossed it aside, reaching for another.

"He's so hot," Gwen gushed, dragging out the word. "Like, *really* hot. You should see how those biceps flex every time he moves his arms." She sighed dramatically, completely lost in daydreams of Luke.

I raised an eyebrow, glancing over my shoulder. "Gwen... Luke is practically part of the furniture in my house. He lives two doors down, and you're telling me you're dating *Luke Greyson?*" I said, both shocked and slightly intrigued. I mean, Luke was fun, but the guy barely scraped through school and partied like there was no tomorrow.

Gwen just blushed harder. That's when it hit me. I dropped the shirt I was holding. "Wait, wait—*no way*. Do *not* tell me you started dating him after that party at your parents' house," I said, throwing my hands up in the air, my voice climbing an octave.

She nodded sheepishly.

"You've got to be kidding me!" I practically shouted. Slamming the door shut, I dove onto the bed next to her. Her face lit up like Christmas as she recalled every detail.

"Oh my God, Maeve, you should've seen him coming out of my pool. His shirt was totally soaked, *see-through*, and his chest—*mmm!*" She mimicked swooning, biting her fist to muffle her giggles.

I rolled my eyes so hard I thought they might stay stuck.

"Gwen... LUKE GREYSON?!" I cried out again, completely exasperated. She just nodded, laughing like the total lovesick teenager she was.

...

My mother's room in Aberdeen Manor suddenly felt ice cold. The air thickened with a chilling dread as we all sat there, paralyzed, still shaken by what we had just uncovered in that old shoebox. Over a hundred photos—women, so many women... and then, the last image: my uncle. The only man. The final victim of my father, Eric Stephenson.

Ethan dropped the photograph he had been holding, his hand trembling. His heart still pounded like it was trying to escape his chest. The entire room was suffocatingly still, the only sound an eerie hum—our own ragged breaths and muffled sobs filling the silence. Ethan stood abruptly, running a shaky hand through his hair, desperately trying to pull himself together. I couldn't bring myself to move. My eyes were squeezed shut, my hand clamped over my mouth, stifling the scream clawing at my throat.

"Get up. We need to leave. *Now*," Ethan said, his voice barely masking the panic beneath it. Tara was the first to react, her hands running over her fear-stricken face as she staggered to her feet. Gwen followed suit, her legs wobbling beneath her as she clung to Luke's arm for support.

Luke's face was set in stone, but I could see the cracks in his composure. "We need to get the hell out of here. Right now!" His voice was thick with fear, shaking with a barely contained fury. I thought for sure the strain in his voice would break him. Gwen gripped Luke's arm tighter, her terror palpable. He glanced at her, acknowledging her fear with a brief nod before turning back to the door.

I forced myself to move, slowly, pulling myself up from beside the wardrobe. My fingers were ice as I wiped the tears from my eyes. "What do we do with these images?" I asked, my voice hoarse, barely audible.

Ethan looked at me, eyes hollow, shaking his head. "They stay here. If Michaels is coming with the cops, he'll need to see them." Without glancing at the photos again, he knelt and shoved them all back into the shoebox, sliding it deep under the wardrobe until it hit the wall.

"We need to arm ourselves," Ethan said, his voice steadying with resolve. "When night falls, we make a run for it—through the forest behind the manor. It'll take us to a dirt road west of here." His words were laced with the remnants of a memory, a survival plan he had heard from Uncle Joe, who had once shown him the hunting trails around the manor.

I glanced toward the large patio windows. Uncle Joe stood there, his silhouette barely visible in the fading light. He nodded, as if to confirm what Ethan had said. "Yes, Ethan. Take the path behind the house and run. Don't stop. Don't come back," Uncle Joe's voice echoed in my mind. I knew no one else could hear him, could see him. Only me.

I swallowed hard, nodding back, and slipped toward the door behind Luke and Gwen. Tara grabbed my arm, pulling me close, wedging me between her and Gwen. The sense of urgency thrummed in the air. Without another word, we bolted from the room, Ethan close behind us.

As we tore out of the room and into the living room, Ethan and Luke dashed upstairs toward Uncle's old room. The sound of their footsteps thundered above, mingling with the hollow echo of drawers being yanked open, metal clanging, and boxes being thrown into duffel bags. I could hear the unmistakable sound of rifles being cocked, followed by their low, urgent voices. Ethan was gathering all the guns Uncle had stashed away.

My heart raced, pounding in my ears as I rushed to the kitchen. My hands were shaking as I yanked open the box we'd left on the counter—our last-ditch arsenal: flashlights, the flare gun, anything that could give us an edge if this nightmare got worse. Without a second thought, I grabbed flashlights, tossing them to Tara and Gwen. They caught them, their faces pale, eyes wide with barely contained panic. In a frantic motion, they shoved them under their shirts, as though concealing light could protect us from what lurked in the shadows.

But my mind was already elsewhere. My hands dove back into the box, rifling through its contents—batteries, keys, an old clock—my breath growing shallower with each passing second.

"No," I muttered, the panic bubbling in my throat as I flung things aside, my movements becoming increasingly erratic. Gwen looked over, her face tightening as she sensed the terror rising in me. She moved toward the table, watching as I dumped the entire box, scattering everything across the surface. "What is it?" she asked, her voice thin and strained, barely masking the fear that gripped her.

"The flare gun," I snapped, my voice trembling, frustration

mixing with raw panic. "Where is it?" My hands raked through the mess, items clattering to the floor, as if the flare gun would somehow emerge if I just tore through fast enough. "No, no, no—*where is the flare gun*?!" I shouted, my voice splintering under the weight of fear.

Gwen's face blanched as the realization sank in. She began frantically sifting through the clutter with me, her fingers moving just as desperately, but every movement felt like a lifetime.

I clutched at my jacket, my fingers brushing the weight of the flares in my pocket—a cold comfort. I shoved them deeper into Uncle's old fishing jacket, the sudden heaviness of their presence gnawing at my nerves. Useless. Without the gun, they were useless.

"I have the flares," I gasped, trying to steady my breathing, but it came out shaky. "But where's the gun?" My voice was barely a whisper now, panic tightening around my throat like a vice. I ripped open the drawers, every slam echoing like a countdown, a ticking clock. I yanked open the cupboards with force, pulling everything out, my mind spinning. Where could it be?

Tara burst into the kitchen, her eyes wild, sweat beading at her temple. Without a word, she joined the frantic search, tearing through the pantry, tossing aside cans and boxes like her life depended on it. Gwen was beside her, her breath shallow, her hands trembling as she emptied drawer after drawer.

From the hallway, Ethan's voice cut through the chaos like a knife. "What's happening?" His voice was sharp, strained, as though he could feel the tension suffocating the air.

"The flare gun! Where *is* it?" I shouted back, nearly choking on the desperation in my voice. My eyes darted to Ethan and Luke as they appeared at the doorway.

For a second, everything froze. The world seemed to hang in silence. Ethan and Luke exchanged a look—one that spoke volumes. Slowly, Ethan turned toward me, his face pale, his voice low and thick with dread.

"Maeve," he said quietly, every word weighted with fear,

"Mike was the last person who had it."

The room tilted. Time seemed to slow as the reality of his words sank in. I stopped, my fingers clutching the edge of the drawer, knuckles white, my heart hammering in my chest. I turned slowly, my pulse deafening in my ears. It was gone. The flare gun was gone.

And so was our last chance.

. . .

Night had struck us quicker then we anticipated, the entire time we were panicking over the flare gun, we let it go—Mike now had it. He had our last chance of signaling for help. Ethan and Luke had spent the time teaching us how to load the rifles, how to aim and shoot if we had too.

I was still shaking from the lesson, I never ever handled a gun in my entire life, and I knew now, in this very moment, I might have to use it.

"Justin," Eric called out, his voice low but commanding. Justin turned to face him, giving his full attention.

"Listen, boy, I don't want you mixed up in this mess. Your job was to get me information, and you did that. You knew Maeve would show up here," Eric said firmly. Justin's expression shifted, a mix of confusion and conflict playing across his face.

Justin had never crossed the line into violence. His role had always been that of a private investigator for Eric, gathering intel on everyone Eric had targeted. Eric had made it clear—Justin wasn't supposed to get his hands dirty.

"Eric… you're not planning to hurt Maeve, are you?" Justin asked, his voice calm but laced with worry.

Eric's eyes darkened. "She's my daughter, Justin. It's her mother who's going to pay. I'll take Maeve away, and her mother will never see her again," he said, slamming his fist against the small table in the shed.

Justin sat on the edge of the cot, his eyes drifting to the monitors lined up on the wooden table. Hidden cameras had been set up all over the house, in places none of us would have thought to check. He leaned forward, scanning the screens. "Looks like they've got guns… and they're talking about leaving," Justin muttered, listening closely to our conversation through the audio feed. He twisted the dial on the recorder to catch more of what we were saying.

Eric turned in his chair, his gaze steady on Justin. "I told you since you were a kid, I'd take care of you," he said, tapping away at the keyboard of his laptop. After a moment, he turned back to Justin. "I've just deposited enough money in your account to last you a couple of years. You'll be fine."

Justin's jaw tightened, and he crossed his arms. "So that's it? You want me to leave? Come on, Eric, we're in this together. You said I could help," he argued, his frustration evident.

Eric shook his head, raising a hand to silence him. "I told you, Justin—your job is to gather information, not spill blood. You're not built for that. I've been doing this for twenty years. When I want something, I get it. And right now, I want my daughter," he said, his gaze cold as it returned to the screens.

Justin narrowed his eyes, watching the monitors closely. "Eric, they're making a move," he said, leaning forward to listen more intently to what we were saying. Eric's eyes flicked to the screen.

"Now I make mine. Stay in the shed," Eric ordered, his voice firm. He stood up, walked to the door, and grabbed the black fedora hanging from a peg. He put it on, followed by a long black trench coat, and then took hold of a long metal hook. Wrapping a thick cord around his waist, he concealed the hook under his jacket.

"Keep yourself safe, boy," Eric muttered before leaving the shed.

Justin kept his focus on the screens. His hand reached up to a small shelf above him, where a metal box sat. He opened it, revealing a handgun inside. He hesitated for a moment before taking it out.

...

"Ethan, we can't just walk out. Eric will find us," I whispered, my voice trembling as Ethan checked over the rifle he held. He took a flashlight from Tara, tucking it under his shirt and into his belt.

"Ethan's right, Maeve. We can't just sit here and wait for the cops. Either way, we have to move. There's five of us and only two of them," Luke added, slipping his own flashlight under his shirt.

"Fine," I muttered, doing the same, though instead of hiding mine, I tapped it, making sure it was working.

"Alright, listen," Ethan said, his voice low but urgent. "We leave through the back door, past the graveyard, then through the metal gate. Once we hit the trees—run."

I nodded, swallowing hard as my pulse quickened. The gravity of what we were about to do sank in, and my chest tightened with panic. My breathing grew shallow, the edges of another anxiety attack looming. I reached into the pocket of my uncle's jacket and found my medication. With shaky hands, I unscrewed the cap and quickly swallowed a pill.

Ethan's eyes stayed on me, concern etched in his face. "You good?" he asked, his voice softer now.

I nodded, exhaling a shaky breath. I closed my eyes for just a second, trying to calm the storm inside me—then I heard it. My uncle's voice, right beside me, as clear as if he were standing there.

"Be careful, May... you and Ethan are precious to your parents. Don't let him get any of you," my uncle's ghostly whisper warned. I froze but nodded slightly, acknowledging his presence. Ethan must've sensed something, his eyes scanning the room as if trying to catch a glimpse of my uncle's ghost, himself.

As I moved closer to Ethan, Tara suddenly grabbed my arm, yanking me aside, pulling me away from everyone. Her grip was tight, urgent.

"I have to tell you something," she whispered, her voice trembling, eyes darting around as if checking for unseen ears. I glanced over my shoulder at Ethan, Gwen, and Luke, who were huddled in the dining room, deep in conversation. We were alone in the dim living room, the oppressive silence of the manor bearing down on us like a weight.

Tara let out a shaky breath, leaning in closer until her lips almost brushed my ear. "Maeve… two days ago, I found out… I'm pregnant." Her hand drifted protectively to her stomach, her fingers trembling as they rested there. Her eyes flicked toward Ethan, filled with dread. She was terrified he would overhear.

My hand flew to my mouth, my heart plummeting. Tears stung my eyes, blurring my vision.

"Tara, no…" My voice came out strangled, and I fought to keep the panic down. "You have to tell Ethan. You have to tell him right now!" My whisper was fierce, almost too loud, but the others were too distracted. Ethan, Luke, and Gwen were still caught up in their frantic discussion, debating which part of the woods was the safest and how to reach the road. They had no idea what was happening—none of them did.

Tara shook her head wildly, gripping my hands now, her fingers cold and trembling. She pressed her forehead against mine. "No, Maeve… listen." Her voice cracked as she held me there, forehead to forehead, her breath coming in quick, shallow bursts. "I'm two months pregnant. If anything happens to me… if I don't make it out of here… please—please, tell him I'm sorry. Tell him I wanted to name her April."

I gasped, tears slipping down my cheeks as the weight of her words sank in. She pulled me into her arms, muffling my sobs, her body shaking as much as mine. April. The name echoed in my mind like a bell tolling in the distance—haunting, inevitable. I clutched her tighter, imagining Ethan's face if he knew, how his eyes would light up at the thought of being a father.

But then the cold grip of reality clawed at me. If we leave this house, there are only two endings: we make it to the road, or... Eric finds us.

The thought hit me like a punch to the gut. Eric. He was still out there, somewhere in the dark, waiting. And Tara... Tara couldn't run. She couldn't keep up. My entire body began to tremble uncontrollably, the fear coursing through me like electricity. We were all vulnerable, but Tara... she was carrying a life inside her, and it made everything so much more fragile.

"Shh, sshhh... it's okay," Tara whispered, but her voice was cracking, and I knew it wasn't okay—not even close. She hugged me tighter, her desperation seeping into my skin like cold rain. "I might not have the strength to run, Maeve. That's why I'm telling you this." Her voice was barely audible now, just a breath against my ear. "If something happens to me, please... please, May, you have to tell Ethan."

I couldn't speak. The lump in my throat was too thick, choking me. My knees buckled, and I fell to the floor. Tara fell with me, still holding me close, her arms around my head, muffling my sobs so Ethan wouldn't hear. I buried my face in her shoulder, biting my lip so hard I tasted blood, trying to keep the panic from spilling out in loud, hysterical cries.

This situation has now gotten even more serious, we were not only surrounded by Justin and a sadistic serial killer who was my own biological father. Tara was vulnerable, delicate, weak. This changes the entire situation.

Eric was somewhere outside, and every second we stayed here, he was getting closer. Tara was two months pregnant, and she wouldn't survive if we had to run. I knew it. I knew it deep down in my bones. Her body would give out, and I would lose her—and Ethan would lose everything.

After what felt like an eternity, I forced myself to breathe, to steady my shaking hands. Tara gently loosened her arms around me, her eyes glistening with unshed tears as she pulled away.

"I'm sorry, Tara. I'm so, so sorry…" I whispered, my voice barely holding together. I was apologizing because I knew, deep down, I couldn't save her. Any more stress, any more fear, could break her—and take April away forever.

"Okay," I whispered, but the word felt hollow, as if saying it would make me believe in something I didn't. I tried to compose myself, but the weight of it all pressed down on me like a vice. My breath trembled as I wiped the tears from my face, forcing myself to be strong. I had to be strong. I nodded, repeating it more for myself than for her. "Okay, okay!"

Tara smiled faintly, a fragile attempt at reassurance, but I could see the cracks beneath her determination. I could feel her fear, and it fed into my own like a wildfire. I reached out, touched her stomach—April's name whispered on my lips—and for a moment, the world seemed to stop. A life, so delicate, so helpless. How could we protect her when we could barely protect ourselves?

Tara exhaled slowly, gently removing my hands from her stomach. "We have to go, Maeve. We can't stay here," she said, her voice low but steady. "Ethan's right. We have to leave."

Her words pulled me back into the present. The reality of the situation hit me like a freight train, a crashing realization that everything was spiraling out of control. It wasn't just about survival anymore. It was about sacrifice. I knew, deep down, what needed to be done. Tara knew too, but she wouldn't say it. She wouldn't let herself go there, not yet. I nodded again, though my throat was closing up. How could she be so calm? My heart raced in my chest, hammering against my ribs like it was trying to escape. I wanted to scream.

Tara squeezed my hand, pulling me into the dining room where Ethan, Luke, and Gwen were making their plans. The air was thick, suffocating. The dim light barely cut through the shadows, and every creak of the old house made me jump, my nerves on fire. It was too quiet. Too calm. Like we were all waiting for the axe to fall.

Ethan's eyes met mine, and for a moment, I saw it—the fear he was trying so hard to hide. His hand rested on my head, a silent comfort, but I could feel the lie in it. We weren't going to be okay. None of us were. Not if I didn't do something.

"Okay, back door. Let's do this," Luke said, his voice rough with forced confidence. He picked up a rifle, checking it mechanically. Gwen followed suit, though her hands shook so violently I wondered if she'd even be able to hold the gun, let alone fire it. We were just kids playing with matches in a house made of kindling.

I hovered near them, my mind racing. My father—Eric—was out there, somewhere, hunting us down like animals. I could almost feel his eyes on me, lurking in the dark. This was all because of me. Because he wanted me, and he wouldn't stop until he had me. I was the reason they were all in danger.

I turned my back to the group, my decision made. I couldn't let them die because of me. I grabbed my rifle, my flashlight tucked into the pocket of my uncle's jacket, the one that smelled faintly of dust and memories I didn't want anymore. This jacket was supposed to keep me safe, but it felt more like a shroud.

Tara pulled Ethan aside, and I watched as she kissed him, her hands gripping him like he was her lifeline. His arms wrapped around her in response, his lips moving softly against her forehead. I could feel their love, their hope, and it tore me apart. They were planning for a future they might never get to see.

"I'm sorry, Ethan," Tara whispered, her voice trembling. I could see the way her body shook, the way her fingers clung to him like he was her last tether to the world. Ethan rested his forehead against hers, whispering promises I knew he couldn't keep.

We weren't all getting out of here.

My throat tightened as I looked away, the weight of what I was about to do crashing down on me. This was my fault. The fear, the panic, the way Tara's body seemed to break under the strain of it all. I felt like I was suffocating, my breath coming in short, frantic gasps as I moved behind Luke and Gwen.

The plan. The stupid plan to run. They thought we could make it, but I knew better. I knew what was waiting out there in the dark, the cold hands of death that would claim us one by one if we tried to flee. Eric was out there. My father was out there.

And he wouldn't stop until he had me. And I won't let him hurt them.

I gripped the rifle tighter, the metal cold against my skin, and in that moment, the only thing I knew for certain was that I had to run. I had to make him chase me. I had to be the bait.

I stepped back, inching toward the door, the noise of the others fading into the background as my heartbeat pounded in my ears. Everything felt surreal, like I was floating outside my body, watching myself make a decision that couldn't be undone. I didn't care what happened to me. I couldn't let him hurt them. My hand found the doorknob, shaking violently as I twisted it open. But then, the flashlight slipped from my fingers.

Clatter.

The sound was like a gunshot in the dead silence.

"Maeve?" Ethan's voice shot through the air like a knife. No. Not now. Not yet.

I dropped to my knees, fumbling for the flashlight, my heart racing as I grabbed it, my fingers trembling uncontrollably. I had to go. I couldn't hesitate, couldn't let them stop me. If I did, we'd all be dead. I yanked the door open and bolted. The cold night hit me like a slap, stealing my breath away, but I didn't stop. I couldn't.

"MAEVE!" Ethan's voice roared behind me, but I didn't dare look back. If I did, I might lose my nerve.

Everyone inside was yelling, their voices frantic, but they were fading behind me as I ran down the steps, the flashlight bouncing wildly in my hand. My lungs burned as I sprinted across the yard, past the graveyard, the dark stones blurring into shadows. I felt like a ghost myself, already dead and running from the inevitable.

"MAEVE!" Luke and Ethan shouted in unison, their voices chasing after me, but I pushed harder. I wasn't going to let them die for me.

I reached the small, rusted gate at the edge of the property, my hands numb as I forced it open with a loud creak. I was out of time. He was out there, and I knew it. I didn't stop. Not even when I heard them screaming my name, their flashlights cutting through the dark like beacons. I ran, faster and faster, because I knew what was coming.

Eric.

Wanted me.

He was waiting for me. And I had the responsibility to protect everyone I loved.

Before I thought I had gotten far enough away from the house, I felt Ethan and Luke closing in on me. Of course they were faster. They had always been stronger, quicker. I could feel the ground slipping away beneath my feet as they drew nearer, and before I could react, Ethan tackled me.

The impact was brutal. I hit the ground hard, the breath knocked from my lungs as I felt the rifle tumble from my grasp. The deafening crack of a gunshot ripped through the night, echoing in the trees like thunder.

"WHAT THE HELL ARE YOU THINKING?" Ethan's voice boomed, full of rage, panic. I gasped for air, my chest heaving, but all I could see was his face, inches from mine, furious and terrified all at once. Luke was behind him, wide-eyed, his breath coming fast.

Ethan hauled me to my feet, his grip tight, fingers digging into my arms. "What are you doing, Maeve? What's wrong with you?" His voice shook with barely contained anger. His eyes bored into me, demanding an answer. But I couldn't speak. I couldn't even breathe. Everything inside me churned, my mind spinning, my stomach twisting. All I could do was look past him—look into the thick, black forest that seemed to close in around us, suffocating, endless. I felt like I was drowning.

Luke stepped forward, his voice softer, but just as bewildered. "Why, Maeve? Why did you do that?" His words cut through me, but I still couldn't answer. How could I explain? How could I make them understand that running was the only thing I had left—that I would rather die than watch them get slaughtered because of me?

Ethan shook me again, his rage spilling over. "ANSWER ME! Maeve, what the hell were you thinking, you stupid—" He hurled a torrent of curses, his frustration boiling over, his words hitting me like physical blows.

I opened my mouth, the word barely escaping my lips. "Bait..."

But then, the scream.

A shrill, gut-wrenching scream tore through the air, slicing through the dark like a blade. I froze. My blood turned to ice in my veins, my heart stopping for a fraction of a second. It was Gwen.

Ethan released me instantly, his head whipping toward the sound. Luke's flashlight beam shot through the trees, wild and frantic, searching for her.

"GWEN!" I screamed, my voice cracking as terror gripped me.

"GWEN!" Luke echoed, his voice full of panic.

We ran.

We bolted toward the scream, our feet pounding the earth, the cold night air cutting into our lungs. I could feel the dread sinking into my bones. Gwen's voice kept cutting through the darkness—bloodcurdling, desperate, and full of terror. She was in pain. She was in agony. We crashed through the trees, the flashlight beams flickering wildly, illuminating nothing but shadow. And then we saw it.

Eric.

He was there, standing in the clearing like some twisted nightmare brought to life. He had her.

The long, thick fishing hook—sharp, rusted, and brutal—was embedded deep into Gwen's torso, the metal glistening with blood. He had swung it at her like a hunter snaring his prey, hooking her like she was nothing more than an animal. She screamed again, her body convulsing as Eric yanked on the rope, dragging her backward across the forest floor. The sound of her flesh tearing made my stomach turn. She reached out toward us, her fingers trembling, her face twisted in pain and horror.

"NO!" I screamed, my voice breaking as I surged forward, but Ethan grabbed my arm, pulling me back. Luke pushed past us, raising his rifle, trying to get a clear shot, but Eric was already disappearing into the trees, dragging Gwen behind him like she was nothing more than a rag doll.

"GWEN!" Luke's voice cracked, his sobs tearing through the night as he watched her vanish into the shadows. The night swallowed her whole.

We ran after them, our legs burning, our lungs screaming for air, but no matter how fast we ran, we couldn't catch up. Gwen's screams grew fainter, more desperate, and then suddenly—they stopped.

The silence was deafening.

"GWEN!" Luke screamed her name again, his voice hoarse and broken. He staggered, his legs buckling beneath him as he collapsed to the ground, his face twisted in anguish. We couldn't see her anymore. We didn't know where Eric had taken her— what direction, what hell he was dragging her toward.

I shoved past Ethan, my heart pounding, my mind blank with terror. I had to find her. I had to stop him. Eric was going to kill her—he was going to kill us all if I didn't do something.

"Maeve!" Ethan's arms wrapped around my waist, yanking me back. I kicked and thrashed against him, desperate to break free, desperate to chase after Gwen.

"NO! LET ME GO!" I screamed, my voice raw, tears blurring my vision. "We have to get her! We have to save her!"

And then, the scream.

It cut through the air like a blade, sharp and gut-wrenching. Gwen's scream. Loud. Piercing. Final. And then—silence. We froze. The world stopped. Every sound, every thought, every breath was consumed by the horrifying quiet that followed.

"No... no... no..." Luke's voice cracked as he dropped to his knees, his flashlight slipping from his grasp and clattering to the ground. His body shook, and then his voice erupted—a desperate, heart-shattering roar. "GWEN!"

His scream echoed through the suffocating darkness, swallowed by the void. But there was no answer. Nothing. Only the relentless silence, only the crushing truth: Eric had her. Gwen was gone.

We ran, all of us, stumbling blindly through the trees, calling her name, tripping over roots and crashing into branches. The woods stretched endlessly around us, a maze of shadows and hopelessness. Eric had vanished, dragging Gwen with him. And we were powerless to stop it.

"Where did he take her?" Ethan's voice was barely above a whisper, thick with dread, as we stood in the clearing. Our breaths came in harsh, ragged gasps, our bodies trembling.

We didn't know. We didn't know where Eric had taken her. But one thing was certain—he wasn't finished. He was coming back for us.

Chapter 14

TARA

ETHAN PACED AROUND the jewelry store counters, his eyes scanning for the perfect ring. He had something specific in mind—a two-carat round diamond set in a gold mount, with smaller diamonds surrounding the basket. A solitaire, a flawless symbol of his six-year, on-again, off-again relationship with Tara. You might be wondering why a ring for a relationship like that? Well, this time, Ethan was convinced they were serious—really serious.

Tara, on the other hand, was usually the one who ended things. She often felt like Ethan didn't spend enough time with her or give her the attention she needed. I tapped my hands over the glass showcase, I was so bored waiting on Ethan to find the perfect ring. Ethan works as a nurse practitioner in the hospital where our father works. So, he definitely has a stable enough income to be able to find the perfect ring.

I rolled my eyes twirling around in the round stool.

"Did you find it yet, we've been in here for over two hours," I protested. Ethan smirked, touched a hand to his nose and tapped his nose, signifying he found it.

I smiled and jumped up from the stool.

The man who had been following Ethan around the store smiled when Ethan sat down on the stool in front of the lab grown diamond section. I pranced over to him and pulled a stool up next to him.

"Okay show me," I said excited.

"This one please," he said to the man behind the counter. The man smiled, opened the glass cabinet, pulled out a perfect 2 carat round solitaire and held it out to Ethan.

Ethan inspected the ring closely, the diamond sparkling under the store's lights. I stood there, hands over my mouth, trying my hardest not to squeal in excitement. Meanwhile, Luke was off in the mall with Gwen and Tara, expertly keeping Tara distracted so Ethan could shop for the perfect ring.

"A perfect two-carat, sir," the jeweler said, carefully taking the ring from Ethan's hand—only to turn and extend it to me. Ethan shot him a confused look as if to say, *What on Earth are you doing?* But before either of us could say anything, the jeweler gently took my hand and slid the ring onto my finger. I tried even harder not to scream.

"Just perfect for your excited lady here. You can tell how much she loves it," the man said with a proud smile.

Wait, was he talking about *me*? Did he think I was with Ethan? I blinked, trying to keep a straight face. Oh boy. Ethan glanced at me with a twinkle in his eye. I know my brother—he's going to run with this.

"Isn't it just *gorgeous* on her?" Ethan said, taking my hand and giving me his best 'romantic' look. I shot him a death glare, biting my lip so hard I almost burst out laughing.

Ethan held up my hand, pretending to admire the ring. I

wanted to yank it off, shout *I'm his sister, not his girlfriend!*—but I decided to let him have his fun. Let's see where this goes.

"So, have you two set a date yet?" the jeweler asked, eyes gleaming with excitement. *Oh no,* I thought. *Please, Ethan, end this now.*

"Not yet," Ethan replied, far too casually. *Wait, does he actually not realize the jeweler thinks I'm his girlfriend?* I bit my lip harder. Yep, I definitely tasted blood.

"Well, congratulations to both of you!" the jeweler exclaimed. That's when the lightbulb finally flickered on for Ethan. He looked at me, then at the ring, then back at the jeweler.

"Wait... you think..." Ethan pointed to me and then to himself, clearly flabbergasted. "...you think we're *together?*"

The jeweler's face fell, realizing his mistake. He gave a sheepish nod.

"Oh, HELL NO!" Ethan yelled, loud enough to turn heads across the entire store. "She's my *sister!* My actual sister!"

And that was it—I couldn't hold it in any longer. I burst out laughing so hard my sides hurt. It had taken him long enough to figure it out. What an idiot. The jeweler's cheeks flushed red as he stammered an apology, but Ethan was already glaring at me. "Oh, you think this is funny, don't you?" he muttered, yanking the ring off my finger.

"Absolutely," I wheezed, struggling to catch my breath. "You—moron!"

Ethan groaned, shaking his head as he handed the ring back to the jeweler. "Just box it up," he muttered. "Before she breaks a rib laughing."

Moron.

...

"ARGH!" Luke screamed, hurling his rifle to the ground with such force I thought it might shatter. His fist slammed into the dirt, again and again, his body trembling with rage.

"GWENNNNN!" His voice echoed through the woods, bouncing back at us, mocking us with its emptiness. There was no answer. Only the cold, cruel silence of the night.

Tears blurred my vision, streaming hot and fast down my cheeks. Everything felt like it was spinning, like the world was collapsing in on itself. I turned in frantic circles, desperate, my eyes scanning the impenetrable darkness around us. There was nothing—no sign of Gwen, no sign of Eric. Just shadows, stretching on forever.

"No, no, no…" Tara's voice broke through my panic, shaky and full of fear. She was unraveling, her breaths coming in short, sharp gasps. I rushed toward her, my hands shaking as I tried to pull her into some kind of embrace. The last thing we needed was Tara losing control—April's life depended on her staying calm. But Tara was losing it. Her eyes were wide with terror, her face pale.

"HE'S PICKING US OFF!" she screamed, her voice cracking under the weight of her fear. "HE'S GOING TO PICK US OFF, ONE BY ONE!" Her words ripped through the air, full of desperation and panic. She pressed her hands to her face, her fingers digging into her skin as if trying to wake herself from the nightmare. Then, she screamed—a raw, guttural sound that tore through the night. "GWEN!"

Ethan rushed to her side, his arms wrapping around her, holding her tight as she sobbed against his chest. But even he couldn't hide the fear in his eyes.

"Okay, okay, we'll find her," Ethan said, his voice trying and failing to sound steady. He glanced at me, his expression full of silent desperation. He didn't know what to do. None of us did.

Tara's sobs wracked her body, and Ethan tightened his grip on her. "We have to keep it together. We have to find her," he whispered, more to himself than anyone else. Then, louder: "Luke, get up! We need to go back to the house and find Gwen. We'll find her." His voice was shaking, but it was all we had to hold onto.

Luke wobbled to his feet, his eyes hollow, his face twisted with fury. He looked like a man on the edge of losing everything. He snatched his rifle from the ground, dirt clinging to his palms, and stormed off in the direction of the house—or at least, what he thought was the direction. None of us were sure anymore. Eric had pulled us so far into the trees that the house felt like a distant memory.

"I'm not letting him get away with this," Luke growled, his voice rough and hoarse, like he'd screamed so much it had torn something inside him. He wasn't thinking straight. None of us were.

I stumbled after him, the weight of everything pressing down on my chest, suffocating me. I had nothing. No rifle, no flash-light—just the crushing realization that I'd run after Gwen without thinking, without preparing.

And now? She was gone.

"Luke," I called out, but my voice barely made it past my lips, weak and trembling. He didn't hear me. He was too far gone, driven by rage and desperation. Ethan, still holding onto Tara, hurried after him, and I found myself trailing behind them all, my heart pounding in my throat, my breath coming in shallow, panicked gasps.

We were lost. I could feel it in every step. The forest was pressing in around us, the trees looming like dark sentinels, their branches reaching out like skeletal fingers. I could feel Eric out there, watching, waiting for his next move. He wasn't done with us. Not by a long shot.

Tara's sobs echoed behind me as Ethan tried to calm her, his words growing more frantic as her panic escalated. We were falling apart, all of us. Gwen was gone. We didn't even know where.

And now we were heading back toward the house, back toward where we thought we'd be safe, but Eric had already proven there was no safety anymore. He was out there, hunting us, picking us off—just like Tara said.

We kept moving, but every step felt wrong, every second

stretched on like an eternity. The trees all looked the same, the night swallowing us whole.

"Where is she?!" Luke barked, his voice rising in desperation, his grip on the rifle tightening. His pace quickened, as though he could outrun the nightmare chasing us.

But there was no escaping.

I glanced around, heart hammering in my chest, my eyes darting between the darkened branches, the rustling leaves, the flicker of shadows. Every noise sounded like him. Every breath of wind felt like he was right there, breathing down my neck.

"Maeve..." Ethan's voice called out, quiet, shaky. He didn't have to say anything more. We all knew.

We were being hunted.

"Tie her to the hooks, boy," Eric drawled, his thick southern accent heavy with command. His voice was low, menacing, each word dripping with authority as he nodded toward Justin—or Mike, as we knew him. Justin smirked, the flicker of cruel amusement dancing in his eyes as he moved to close the wooden doors of the bunker behind Eric.

Gwen's body slumped lifelessly in Eric's grip, her limbs heavy and unresponsive. She wasn't moving, barely conscious, and every step down the bunker's stairs caused her body to thud against the wooden steps with a dull, sickening rhythm.

Thump. Thump. Thump.

Once inside the bunker, the door sealed shut behind them, swallowing the scene in oppressive silence. The air in the underground space felt thicker now, more stifling, as if the earth itself had trapped them down here, cut off from the world above.

Justin moved swiftly, almost practiced, as he grabbed Gwen by the arms, his hands harsh against her skin. Eric, without so much as a flicker of hesitation, ripped the hook from her chest, where it was now embedded. A sickening squelch filled the air, but Gwen didn't scream.

She didn't make a sound.

Justin worked quickly, his hands steady as he fastened her wrists into the cuffs that hung from long, rusted chains affixed to the ceiling. The chains creaked as they were pulled taut, lifting Gwen's arms high above her head. Her knees dangled inches from the concrete floor, her body limp, like a marionette whose strings had been severed.

She was silent. Eerily silent. Her voice had been stolen, taken by the pain, by the terror of Eric's hook or maybe she had succumbed to the horrific gaping hole in her chest. Her head hung forward, her blonde hair matted to her forehead, blood soaking her once-clean clothes. The pool beneath her grew steadily, a slow, crimson drip that splattered against the cold concrete.

Eric stood back, his arms crossed, admiring the macabre display with a calm indifference. To him, she was just another catch—a prize he could dangle like a fish on a hook.

The bunker itself felt alive with a different kind of horror. Its walls seemed to close in around Gwen, trapping her in a tomb of concrete and decay. The space was wide, cavernous, but it felt smaller now, suffocating, the chill of the underground seeping into every breath.

Along the walls, rusted metal shelves stood empty, a reminder of a time when this place had been used for survival. Now, though, it was nothing but a husk—abandoned, forgotten, left to rot. The single dim bulb above flickered occasionally, casting uneven shadows across the room, each one dancing like specters waiting for the inevitable.

In the corner, the narrow bed sat untouched, its sheets stiff with age, yellowed and crumbling at the edges. There was no comfort here. No escape. The bunker was a tomb now, a place where hope went to die.

The stillness was oppressive, wrapping around the scene like a suffocating blanket. Every breath felt heavy, thick with fear and the scent of blood. The only sounds were the faint dripping of moisture from the ceiling and the creak of the chains as Gwen's body swayed ever so slightly, her feet never quite reaching the ground.

Eric took a step back, surveying his handiwork with cold satisfaction. To him, Gwen wasn't a person anymore. She was just a body.

"I warned them kids, I warned them," Eric's voice was horse and sadistic as he watched Justin rattled the chains behind Gwen making sure they were still supported to the thick metal rings that were hooked deep within the concrete.

"IF THEY WON'T GIVE ME MAEVE, I WILL TAKE EACH ONE OF THEM UNTILS I GET HER," Eric said angrily, he grabbed his hook still dripping from Gwen's blood and dragged it along the concreate floor, and up the wooden stairs. Before he opened the wooden doors of the bunker he heard our voices in the yard near the house.

"GWEN!" Luke shouted as the silhouette of the manor came into our view. We ran towards it the small metal gate still opened from when I had bolted out of it. We ran through the graveyard and towards the house. Stopping near the back stairs of the wraparound porch. We looked around the yard cautiously. Tara was behind Ethan, her hand intertwined with his, she was breathing heavily—her hand rested against her stomach. I looked at her and let out a deep breath in worry over her condition.

"Quietly, we go inside…" Luke whispered as he crept up the stairs of the porch. The lights in the house were on. We hadn't left them on. We had deliberately avoided attracting attention when we were here earlier, but now… someone else was inside.

I followed Luke, Ethan right behind me, his hand firm against my back, guiding me. Tara shifted nervously, clinging to Ethan, her steps shaky as she stayed close to him.

"Shh," Luke warned, as he slowly pushed the back door

open. We stepped into the kitchen, our footsteps barely making a sound. I let Ethan and Tara slip ahead, lingering behind, cautious, my heart pounding in my chest. Luke scanned the area, his eyes darting to the dining room. The house was eerily quiet.

"He's playing games with us," Luke muttered, frustration etched across his face. Ethan released Tara's hand and positioned himself near the wall, peering into the living room, his body tense. I stood frozen near the door, my senses on high alert, when suddenly—a soft creak. The door clicked shut behind me. My heart dropped, and I spun around.

There he was.

Eric. He stood right next to the door, leaning against the wall, his fedora's brim casting a shadow over his face. My stomach lurched as my voice broke free.

"ETHAN! LUKE!" I screamed, stumbling backward, crashing into Tara. Luke swung around, lifting his rifle, and Ethan followed, both of their weapons now trained on Eric. But Eric didn't move. He didn't even flinch. Instead, he began to whistle—a low, eerie tune that sent chills crawling up my spine. We exchanged terrified glances, the air thick with fear.

"WHERE'S GWEN?" Luke demanded, his voice a raw mix of anger and desperation. Eric remained motionless, the haunting whistle the only response. Ethan's knuckles whitened as he cocked his gun, his patience gone.

"We're done with your sick games. Where is she?" Ethan's voice was sharp, filled with hatred.

Eric pushed off the wall, tilting his hat back just enough for his cold eyes to meet ours. His lips curled into a smirk.

"I warned ya, boy... warned all of you. You could've walked right out, I wanted nothing to do with any of ya," he drawled, his voice dripping with malice. Ethan immediately shifted in front of me, shielding me from Eric's view. But Tara... Tara was exposed. In the chaos, Ethan hadn't pulled her with him. Eric's eyes gleamed as he took notice, his grin widening.

"I told you, leave Maeve here, and the rest of you can go. It wouldn't have come to this. But none of you listened." Eric's voice rang out, louder this time, his arms folding across his chest.

"And I told you... you can't have her," Ethan growled, his voice hoarse with rage. I clung to him, trembling as I tried to make sense of the terror unfolding.

Then, in an instant, everything exploded.

Eric moved faster than any of us could react, swinging his fishing hook from around his body. The deadly arc sliced through the air, aiming straight for Tara.

"TARA!" I screamed, as the hook buried itself into her chest. Her scream was cut short—a horrible, strangled sound. She went limp, her body slumping to the floor.

"ETHAN!" I screamed, my voice breaking, but it was too late. Justin—Mike—had lunged from the pantry, wrapping his arms around my neck, yanking me back. Ethan and Luke were both momentarily distracted, their attempts to save Tara stalled by the chaos. Ethan ran at Eric, but Eric yanked Tara so hard towards him that he left a trail of blood along the wooden floors.

"ETHAN!" Tara's voice gurgled, but her cries faded as Eric dragged her out the back door. Her body thudded lifelessly down the wooden steps, each impact echoing through the house.

"GO AFTER TARA—HE'S TAKING HER TO GWEN!" I shouted desperately. Ethan hesitated, torn between protecting me and saving Tara. His eyes locked with mine for a split second before he bolted out the door, chasing after her.

Luke swung his rifle toward Justin, his hands trembling as he aimed the barrel at him. "Let her go, Mike—Justin—whatever the hell your name is," Luke demanded, trying to steady his voice. Justin's grip around my neck tightened, his breath hot against my skin as he held a gun to my head.

"I don't think so. Put the rifle down, Luke, or I'll put a bullet through her," Justin threatened, his voice low and menacing. Luke glanced at me, his eyes full of desperation, torn between lowering his weapon and trying to save me.

Tara's muffled scream came from outside, her voice barely a whisper. Luke's resolve cracked. He looked at me, then back at Justin. Slowly, reluctantly, he lowered his rifle.

"Go outside, Luke," Justin barked, pushing me forward, making me stumble. Luke took a step back, raising his hands in surrender, his eyes never leaving mine.

"Let her go, man. Walk away from this. Don't end up like Eric." Luke's voice softened, pleading. Even now, Luke—the eternal optimist—was trying to reach the part of Justin that he hoped was still good, still someone we once knew. But Justin's sneer only deepened, his grip on the gun tightening as he pressed it harder against my skin.

"WALK OUT THE DOOR, LUKE!" Justin snapped, shoving me closer to him. The cold barrel of the gun bit into my cheek, and I felt my panic rising, my breaths coming in ragged gasps.

"LUKE, just go! Please, go... go find Gwen," I pleaded, my voice shaking, but he stood there, frozen. He wouldn't leave me. Not like this. Luke hesitated for a moment too long, and Justin's patience snapped. He shoved me harder toward the backdoor, and with no choice left, Luke backed up, his eyes filled with helpless fury.

As Luke bolted out the door, his heavy footsteps thundered against the wooden porch steps, fading quickly into the night. Then—silence. Complete and suffocating silence.

"Well, now that I have you here, Maeve," Justin said, his voice unsettlingly calm as he loosened his grip from around my neck. His hands spun me around roughly, gripping my wrists with a vice-like hold. "Don't do anything stupid, okay?" he added, his tone casual, almost conversational, as though we weren't standing on the edge of chaos.

He reached into the pantry, his movements deliberate but far too relaxed for the situation and pulled out a length of rope. Without hesitation, he began tying my hands together, the coarse fibers biting into my skin. I watched him closely, trying to appear frightened, compliant. He was tying a fisherman's knot—something my uncle had taught Ethan and me years ago during summers spent on the lake.

Then I heard my uncle's voice, clear and steady beside me, a ghostly whisper cutting through my fear. "Remember, Maeve—he's sloppy. Two knots, not tight enough. You can work your hands free when the moment's right." His tone was reassuring, familiar, and it sparked a flicker of hope in me. Justin's attempt at restraint would prove his weakness.

Justin stood back, inspecting his work. The knot was amateur at best. He either underestimated me, or he thought fear alone would keep me from fighting back.

"Why are you with him, Mike—I mean, Justin?" I asked, my voice steady despite the adrenaline pumping through my veins. I kept my gaze locked on his, searching for cracks in his resolve.

He finished securing the rope and tucked the gun back into the waistband of his jeans. Then, with an almost mocking gentleness, he tapped my chin. "Because he raised me, Maeve," he said, his tone eerily calm, his words laced with conviction. "Eric is a father to me."

My stomach churned, a mix of anger and despair tightening in my chest. "Why are you doing this?" I demanded, my voice sharp but deliberate, refusing to let him see how much his words rattled me. "Leave, Justin. You don't have to do this. Help us. You can stop this—you can go back from this." I leaned into the vulnerability in my voice, desperate to find the part of him I thought I knew.

He crossed his arms, his gaze steady but distant, as if weighing my words. Then, with a small nod, he replied, "My job is to keep you in my sight until Eric—your father—is done with his plan." The way he said "father" was devoid of warmth, like the word carried no meaning beyond the man who had turned him into this.

Justin stepped back, his eyes raking over me like I was an object, not a person. I held still, my mind racing. Running wasn't an option—not yet. I needed answers. "What's his plan, Justin?" I asked, keeping my tone calm, measured, despite the storm building inside me.

He didn't answer immediately. Instead, he continued to study me, his expression unreadable. The room felt impossibly small, the silence pressing in as I waited, every second stretching longer than the last. If I could just get him to talk—to falter—I might still have a chance to save Gwen and Tara.

He leaned forward, his hands pressing firmly against my waist as he pulled me closer. Calmly, almost mockingly, he whispered near my ear, "He's going to take each and every one of them out until he gets you… he did all of this for you," Justin's words sent an icy shiver crawling up my spine. I tried to step back, my breath hitching, but Justin held me close, his grip unyielding.

He looked down at me with a smug smirk, his tone almost casual. "Your mother, Amy, stopped him twenty years ago when you were two, playing outside with Ethan. He had you in his arms. If it wasn't for Ethan… God, I hate that guy… seriously, if it wasn't for him, your dad wouldn't have had to resort to all this trouble to find you and take you," he said, his smirk deepening as he finished.

The words rattled me, and for a moment, my mind was a whirlwind of confusion and dread. My voice caught in my throat as memories long buried began to surface. I tried to piece it together, my uncle's voice echoing in my thoughts, guiding me back to that day.

"No, no, May, like this," Ethan's childlike voice echoed in my mind. He was about four, his face lit with excitement as he showed me how to carefully remove a block from our Jenga tower. The two of us sat on the grass in the front yard, surrounded by the pristine white picket fence of our newly bought home—the house my mother had always dreamed of.

"Yay! I did it!" I exclaimed as I slid a block free without toppling the tower. Ethan clapped his hands, grinning widely. "See? Told you! You just have to be gentle and careful," he said, his young voice filled with pride.

That's when I heard the sound of tires crunching on the driveway gravel. A sleek black car pulled up to the curb. I didn't pay much attention, too focused on my game, but Ethan stiffened. I glanced up, following his gaze, and saw a man stepping out of the driver's side. A young boy, no older than Ethan—possibly six years of age, peered at us from the back seat, his small face pressed against the window.

The man walked toward the fence, his footsteps deliberate. "Well, there you are," his voice was calm and unsettlingly gentle. He stopped at the gate, his eyes locking on me. I glanced up at him, confused but curious.

"How's my little girl doing today?" he asked with a softness that belied the sharp tension in his presence.

Ethan's small hands balled into fists as he stood protectively. He knew who this man was. He had heard the hushed arguments, the stories of why we couldn't leave the house alone. "I'm not supposed to talk to strangers," I said shyly, pulling a strand of hair behind my ear.

"Good girl," the man replied, smiling in a way that didn't reach his eyes. Then, with an ease that turned my world upside down, he reached over the fence and scooped me into his arms.

"HEY! YOU CAN'T TAKE MY SISTER LIKE THAT!" Ethan's voice erupted, sharp and filled with rage far too big for his tiny frame. He stumbled on his feet, his face red with anger.

I screamed, the suddenness of it all hitting me like a cold wave. "MOMMY!" My voice broke as I kicked and thrashed in his grasp.

"There, there, my little one," the man—Eric—said soothingly, his hold on me tightening. "Don't worry. We're just going to take a little trip."

"DAD! UNCLE JOE!" Ethan's desperate screams cut

through the air. His small fists pounded against the man's leg. "LET HER GO!"

In the chaos, James and Uncle Joe came rushing out of the house. James's face twisted with rage, his steps quick and deliberate. Uncle Joe wasn't far behind, his voice booming. "ERIC! PUT HER DOWN!"

Eric turned, his expression calm but defiant. "She's my daughter. I have every right—"

Before he could finish, Ethan lunged forward, pushing against Eric's thigh with all the strength his small body could muster. The unexpected force made Eric stagger, his grip loosening just enough for me to tumble out of his arms and into Ethan's. My brother caught me, his arms wrapping tightly around me as I sobbed into his shoulder.

My mother appeared next, her face pale, her eyes wide with terror. She ran to us, scooping me up and holding me close, tears streaming down her face. "Oh my baby, my sweet girl," she cried, her voice trembling as she kissed the top of my head.

James advanced on Eric, his hands clenched into fists. "You crossed the line, Eric," he growled, his voice low and dangerous. "We're putting a restraining order on you. You come near my daughter again, or my family—"

Eric's calm façade cracked, his face twisting with fury. "Your daughter?" he spat, his voice venomous. "She isn't yours. She's mine. And I'll have her. I'll take her, and none of you will ever see her again."

James lunged, his fist raised, but Joe grabbed his arm, holding him back. "James, don't. He's not worth it." Joe's voice was steady but firm. He turned his sharp gaze on Eric. "This is your final warning. If you don't leave this property right now, I'll have you arrested. And if you ever touch May again, you won't just be dealing with James."

Eric's eyes burned with rage, but he didn't move. His chest heaved as he glared at James and Joe, his fists clenched at his sides. Finally, he stepped back, his lips curling into a dangerous smirk. "This isn't over," he muttered before turning and walking away.

The black car roared to life as Eric climbed back inside. The boy in the back seat glanced out the window, his expression unreadable. The car sped off, disappearing down the road.

Mother held me tightly, her tears soaking into my hair as she whispered reassurances. James knelt beside us, his hand resting gently on my back as he vowed softly, "He'll never touch you again, May. I swear it."

Ethan stood near us, his small fists clenched at his sides, his young face twisted with determination. He watched as our mother held me close, her sobs shaking both of us. Slowly, Ethan extended his hand to rest on my head. "He won't have you... I won't let him," he said firmly. It was something he had said before—and something he would say again.

I exhaled deeply, my mind snapping back to the present as the memory faded. My body trembled in Justin's grasp, his hands still wrapped tightly around my waist. His words echoed in my ears like a sinister lullaby.

"Either way, Maeve, I did what I had to do. He needed information, so I gave it to him," Justin said, loosening his grip just enough to make me feel the slightest bit of freedom. His voice was calm, but the smug smile playing on his lips made my stomach churn.

"What information?" I asked, my voice shaking as I fought to maintain composure, desperate to reach any shred of reason in him.

Justin's smile widened, cold and cruel. "I broke up with you for a reason. Not because Luke told me to, but because it was part of your father's plan." He leaned closer, wagging a finger in my face like he was scolding a child. "I never moved to New Port. No, instead, we both moved to Florida. Right after you decided to leave Nebraska."

My stomach dropped. "What?"

"How do you think he always knew where you were? Every move you made?" Justin chuckled darkly. His hand reached behind him into the pantry, pulling out an old shoebox. He opened it, revealing a thick stack of photographs, and let the box drop carelessly to the floor between us. Slowly, he began flipping through the pictures, holding them up one by one for me to see.

My breath hitched as the images burned into my mind. Pictures of me—eating ice cream sloppily with Gwen, walking to class, sitting in coffee shops. Gwen, being my roommate, was in almost every picture. There were shots of Tara and Luke during one of their visits, their expressions carefree, oblivious to the watchful lens. Ethan appeared too—dropping by to pick me up for our trip to the manor. The photo showed him standing by his car, phone in hand, moments before realizing I had taken the bus instead. That was the trip we were supposed to take together, the one that ended in his accident. Every moment was captured in eerie detail.

"How? Why, Justin? Why?" I stammered, my voice breaking as tears welled in my eyes.

Justin smirked, holding up another photograph, letting the others fall carelessly to the floor. "That night you and Ethan traveled here... you remember the accident, don't you?" His tone was mocking, almost playful. "Eric blew the tire. He caused it. Damn idiot should've died that night, but no... Ethan just had to survive." He rolled his eyes as if annoyed. "Pissed Eric off when the ambulance came to save him. That's when Eric decided to wait."

My body froze, my breathing shallow as Justin continued.

"Eric was at the bar after the accident. He watched that man Jake, assault you. Don't worry, though. Eric dealt with him." Justin laughed, the sound cold and devoid of humanity. "Kept him alive for a few days. Tortured him. Thought you'd like to know."

My stomach twisted painfully as Justin pulled out another photograph, holding it up with pride. It was a picture of Jake, the man who assaulted me that day in the bar, his body limp and battered, blood pooling beneath him in a dark, windowless room. The horror on his face was unmistakable—he had been alive in the photo.

"Recognize him?" Justin sneered, tossing the picture at my feet. "That corpse the police found? My genius work. It wasn't him. That was another victim's body. We just used his teeth so the cops could find the evidence they needed to identify him. I knew they'd bite." He let out a cruel laugh, throwing another handful of pictures onto the floor like they were nothing more then confetti.

The air in the room felt suffocating, the weight of his words pressing down on me like a vice. My vision blurred as tears streamed freely down my face. "Why? Justin, why?" I choked out, my voice barely audible.

Justin ignored me, holding out more photos and letting them fall one by one. Pictures of Ethan, Gwen, Tara, Luke. So many pictures. Each one a stolen moment, a haunting invasion of our lives.

I gasped for air, my chest tightening as if the room were closing in around me. I wanted to scream, to cry out, but the terror in my throat silenced me. The realization hit me like a tidal wave: we had been watched, hunted, manipulated—all for the sick games of my father and the man standing before me.

Justin leaned in close, his voice low and mocking. "You should've stayed put, Maeve. Would've made things a lot easier. But hey, I'm not complaining. Watching him go through all this trouble to get you? Kinda impressive, don't you think?"

My knees buckled, and I stumbled backward, the weight of it all crashing down. My tears blurred the horrifying images scattered at my feet, but their sharp edges cut deeper than any blade could.

Justin's grin widened as he watched me crumble, his expression dripping with satisfaction. "You should've known, Maeve. This was never going to end any other way."

I staggered to my feet, planting them firmly against the wooden floor as my uncle's voice echoed near me. "Now's your chance, May. You need to run. Help Ethan and Luke—find them!" His tone was urgent, pushing me to act before it was too late.

Justin stood by the pantry, watching me with a smug grin that twisted my stomach. "Where do you think you're going?" he taunted, stepping closer. His confidence only fueled my desperation. I tugged hard at the ropes binding my hands, ignoring the sting of the coarse fibers cutting into my skin.

"You won't be able to get out of that…" Justin said, his tone dripping with mockery as he noticed my hands shifting and moving against the poorly tied knot. He took another step forward, his smirk growing.

"One thing you didn't notice, Mike—" I spat his name like venom as my hands twisted free. "Your fisherman's knot is sloppy." I dropped the rope to my feet and straightened, my eyes locked on his.

Before he could react, I bent quickly, reaching into my long boots. My fingers curled around the handle of the hunting knife I had tucked there earlier. I had taken it from the stash, knowing I'd need it.

In one fluid motion, I swung the knife just as Justin lunged at me. The blade sliced through the air, embedding itself deep into his right shoulder.

"Ah, shit! MAEVE!" Justin shouted, staggering back. His hand flew to the knife buried in his flesh, blood blooming and soaking through the fabric of his shirt. His face contorted in pain and rage as he glared at me.

I didn't waste a second. My chest heaved as I backed away, my trembling hands raised defensively. "One thing you need to learn, Justin—you can't control me," I said, my voice steady despite the fear surging through me.

His lips curled into a furious snarl. "You think you're smart, don't you? Don't go out there, Maeve. Eric wants you alive, not dead. You'll only make this worse for yourself," he stammered, his voice laced with anger and pain.

"RUN, MAY!" my uncle's voice thundered near me. It was all the push I needed. I turned on my heel and bolted for the back door. I flung it open, the night air slapping me in the face as I descended the steps two at a time.

Once in the yard, I paused briefly, gasping for air, my heart pounding so hard I thought it might burst out of my chest. I scanned the dark expanse, trying to think through the panic clawing at my mind. "ETHAN!" I screamed his name, my voice cracking as it tore through the stillness.

A gunshot rang out to my left, followed by another. My head snapped in the direction of the sound, and I screamed again, desperation lacing my voice. "LUKE! ETHAN!" I ran toward the graveyard, my feet pounding against the ground as the night closed in around me. My mind raced, torn between finding them and staying out of Eric's grasp.

But just as I reached the middle of the yard, two arms wrapped around me, slamming me to the ground with brutal force. The air rushed from my lungs as I hit the cold, damp grass.

"AAH, GET OFF!" I shouted, kicking and thrashing. Justin was on top of me, his weight pinning me down. His shoulder was wrapped in a blood-soaked gauze, and his face was twisted into a mask of fury and triumph.

"Bad move, Maeve," he sneered, leaning in close. His breath was hot against my ear, sending shivers of revulsion down my spine. I thrashed harder, but his grip was iron, his arms locking mine against the ground. My nails clawed at his arms, but he didn't flinch.

"I told you. Bad move." His voice was low, venomous, and laced with sadistic amusement. His knees pinned my legs as he used his full weight to immobilize me. I could feel the cold grass pressing into my back, the weight of him suffocating.

He leaned closer, his lips curling into a sinister grin. "Eric told me I could have my time with you. Do whatever I wanted." His words were slow, deliberate, each one cutting like a blade. "Since you stripped me of that chance years ago... well, now's the time to fix that."

My heart stopped, a wave of dread crashing over me. "You're lying," I spat, my voice trembling but defiant.

"Am I?" Justin's smirk deepened, his eyes dark with intent. "You've never given yourself to anyone. Not to me. Not to anyone. You were always so... precious. But now, Maeve, there's no one here to stop me."

My stomach churned, my chest tightening as panic gripped me. I struggled harder, muscles burning with effort, but his weight bore down on me like a suffocating force. My vision blurred with tears of desperation as my screams cut through the night.

"Get off me!" I cried, thrashing wildly. My voice echoed into the emptiness around us, but Justin didn't waver. His hands pinned mine to the ground, his face inches from mine. "No one's coming, Maeve. It's just you and me."

Tears streamed down my face as I pushed back against him, my breath hitching in sobs. The cold night air stung my skin, and I fought with everything I had left. My mind raced for a way out, for something—anything—to stop him. I felt powerless, trapped in a nightmare I couldn't escape.

And then, cutting through the darkness, a voice. "MAEVE!"

Ethan. His voice rang out like a lifeline, piercing through the suffocating terror. Hope ignited within me like a match struck in the dark.

I screamed again, louder this time, pouring every ounce of fear and desperation into my voice. "ETHAN! HELP!"

Justin's head snapped up, his grip faltering as he turned toward the sound. That brief moment of distraction was all I needed. I thrashed with renewed strength, trying to break free. His hands tightened again, his eyes narrowing in frustration, but my screams continued to tear through the night.

The sound of footsteps—pounding, fast—came closer. Justin hesitated, and for the first time, I saw doubt flash across his face. "Shut up!" he barked, his voice sharp with panic. But it was too late. Ethan's voice grew louder, closer.

"Maeve! Where are you?" Ethan shouted.

Tears blurred my vision as I sobbed, my voice breaking with desperation. "HERE! ETHAN, HELP ME!"

Justin looked down at me, his expression twisted with rage and frustration. He hesitated, as though weighing his next move, but the sound of Ethan closing in forced his hand. He shoved me roughly to the ground and bolted, disappearing into the shadows.

I lay there trembling, my breath coming in shallow, ragged gasps. The fear and helplessness began to recede as Ethan's voice drew nearer. Moments later, his arms were around me, pulling me into a protective embrace. I clung to him, my body shaking uncontrollably.

"It's okay," Ethan murmured, his voice low and thick with emotion. "I've got you, May. You're safe now. I'm right here."

But even as I sobbed into his chest, the lingering terror remained, etched deep into my bones. Justin's words echoed in my mind, a haunting reminder of how close I had come to losing everything.

CONTACT

I SCREAMED INTO ETHAN'S CHEST, my cries muffled by the fabric of his blood-soaked shirt. He held me tightly, rocking me in his arms like he was trying to shield me from the horrors of the world. My fingers gripped his shirt so fiercely I thought I'd tear through the fabric. I couldn't bring myself to look at him, couldn't even process that he was injured—my fear, my anguish, and the terror of what Justin had nearly done consumed me.

"He didn't touch you, did he?" Ethan's voice trembled, raw with desperation. He had arrived just in time to stop Justin, and the realization that it could have been far worse tightened my chest. My pants were unbuttoned, my sense of security shattered, but Justin hadn't managed to go any further. I shook my head, unable to speak, as fear bubbled inside me—not just of Justin, but of Eric, who was still out there, hunting us.

I gasped for breath, forcing myself to calm down as I buried my face in Ethan's chest. "Luke," I finally whispered, my voice breaking. "What happened to Luke?"

"He… he's gone," Ethan said, his voice cracking. "We chased Eric into the woods. We shot at him—I'm sure we hit him—but…" He trailed off, his hand resting on the back of my head. His body trembled as he sat on the cold ground, holding me, trying to regain his composure as much as I was.

I pulled away, noticing the deep crimson soaking through his shirt. My breath hitched. "Oh my God, Ethan. You're bleeding."

He glanced down at his side, lifting the hem of his shirt to reveal the makeshift bandage he'd tied around the wound. "I took care of it," he said, his voice firm, though his pale complexion betrayed his pain. "Ripped my shirt and wrapped it. It's not bad."

"What happened to Luke?" I asked, trying to steady myself. My voice quivered as I looked into Ethan's haunted eyes. He let out a heavy sigh, his gaze distant as he recounted what had happened.

"LEFT, ETHAN! That bastard's to our left!" Luke's shout echoed through the oppressive darkness of the woods. The trees pressed in around them, their thick trunks and gnarled branches forming a labyrinth that swallowed the light.

"I told ya, didn't I? I warned ya kids!" Eric's voice boomed through the night, chilling and almost mocking as it reverberated off the trees.

Ethan and Luke both raised their guns, their breaths coming in ragged gasps. They fired into the darkness where the voice had come from. A sharp cry rang out, followed by a guttural groan.

"We hit him! I'm sure we hit him," Luke said, his chest heaving as he tried to catch his breath.

Fueled by adrenaline and pure fury, Ethan spun in a tight circle, his eyes darting frantically to every shadow that moved. The woods seemed alive, every creak and rustle amplifying the tension.

Without warning, Eric burst through the underbrush, his hulking figure illuminated briefly by the faint moonlight that filtered through the canopy. His hook swung in wide arcs, the air hissing with its menacing trajectory.

"ETHAN, WATCH OUT!" Luke shouted, but before either of them could react, Eric's hook sailed through the air with deadly precision. It struck Luke in the back, the barbed metal burying itself deep into his flesh.

"LUKE!" Ethan shouted again, sprinting after him as Eric reeled the rope, dragging Luke through the underbrush with terrifying speed. Luke clawed at the ground, his breaths labored as his body slammed against tree trunks and rocks.

"Shit!" Luke panted heavily, his hands fumbling to grab the thick rope attached to the hook. He knew he might not make it out of this situation. With every ounce of strength he had left, he pulled on the rope, trying to relieve the pressure so the hook wouldn't rip deeper into his body. His fingers tightened around the rope, desperate and trembling.

Then, a horrifying realization struck him. "Shit... I can't feel my body," he muttered, his voice barely above a whisper. Panic surged as he realized the impact of being dragged had left him paralyzed from the waist down. The sharp agony in his back dulled into a terrifying numbness.

Despite the fear clawing at him, Luke kept pulling at the rope, his movements growing frantic as Eric's relentless strength continued to drag him deeper into the dense, unforgiving woods.

"ETHAN, GO! GO BACK FOR MAEVE!" Luke yelled, his voice raw with pain as Eric reeled him in. Luke clawed at the rope, trying to loosen its grip, but his strength was failing. Each yank dragged him further into the dense trees, his body colliding with trunks and branches, leaving him battered and bloodied.

"I'M NOT LEAVING YOU!" Ethan screamed, his voice breaking as he sprinted after his friend. But then he froze, hearing a piercing scream—my scream—echoing from the direction of the house.

"LUKE!" Ethan called again, torn between his best friend and his sister. He hesitated for a moment, his fists clenched tightly around his gun. "I'll come back for you!" he shouted, his voice trembling with rage and helplessness. Ethan turned and ran, my cries drawing him back toward the house.

"He's gone, Maeve," Ethan said, his voice hollow. "Eric dragged him into the woods. I chased him, but I couldn't catch up. Luke… Luke told me to come back for you." His words cracked under the weight of guilt.

Tears streamed down my face as I clapped my hands over my mouth, my sobs muffling into my palms. "We have to go after him," I stammered. "We can't just leave him out there."

Ethan pulled me to my feet, his grip firm but shaking. "We will," he said, his voice strained. "But I have to clean this wound first. I can't help Luke if I pass out from blood loss."

His words were sharp, but I could see the pain etched into his features—not just from his injury but from the impossible choices he'd been forced to make. My legs felt weak beneath me, but I nodded, swallowing hard. "Okay," I whispered. "But we can't let him die out there, Ethan. We can't."

He squeezed my hands, his voice low and resolute. "We won't. I promise."

As he guided me back toward the house, the weight of Eric's shadow loomed over us, suffocating and inescapable. The woods behind us seemed to hum with menace, the distant echoes of Luke's shouts haunting the silence. Ethan's grip on my hand was unrelenting, as though letting go for even a second would mean losing everything.

And deep down, I feared he might be right.

...

Inside the house, Ethan was on red alert, his every movement calculated but strained. He stumbled into the kitchen pantry, searching for the first aid kit. I stood outside, my body taut as a lookout, my eyes darting between the back door and every shadow in the room, listening for any creak or distant sound that might signal danger.

Ethan emerged moments later, clutching the kit in one hand while his other pressed firmly against his wounded side. He moved to the kitchen counter and set the kit down with a thud, flipping it open with one hand. I followed, watching as he pulled out a fresh pad, tape, gauze, and a bottle of alcohol.

"You're not going to..." I began, my voice trailing off as I saw his bloody, trembling fingers unscrew the bottle. He peeled off his torn shirt and unwound the makeshift bandage, revealing the angry, gaping wound.

"I am a nurse, Maeve. I don't have anything else to work with right now," he said, his voice tight but resolute. Taking a deep breath, he grabbed a clean towel from the edge of the stove and soaked it with alcohol.

I froze as I watched him press the cloth firmly against his side. His body tensed, a guttural sound escaping his throat. "Agh!" he grunted, his lips pressing together in a thin, determined line. His face twisted in pain, beads of sweat forming along his brow as the alcohol did its brutal work.

"This is similar to cauterizing a wound," he explained through clenched teeth, his voice uneven. "It burns through the veins, arteries, or muscles that are cut, sealing them so they won't bleed." His tone was almost clinical, as if explaining the process to detach himself from the pain.

I couldn't tear my eyes away as he held the cloth there a moment longer before pulling it off, the bleeding mercifully slowed.

Letting out a deep, ragged breath, he reached for the clean pad and placed it over the wound. Using his teeth, he ripped strips of white tape and secured the pad, then grabbed three rolls of gauze and wrapped them tightly around his torso, ensuring the dressing stayed firmly in place.

"Are you sure that's enough?" I asked, my voice barely above a whisper. My worry was etched across my face, but Ethan didn't respond right away. Instead, he closed the kit with a decisive snap and turned toward the living room. I followed closely, my heart pounding.

"Ethan?" I pressed, trying to draw his attention. He finally stopped, his expression hard yet weary. "For now, Maeve, it'll have to be enough. It could start bleeding again if I move wrong or if…" He paused, his jaw tightening. "If I get stabbed again."

My stomach twisted at his words.

"Eric got me before Luke caught up to us," he added, his voice low, almost bitter. He dug through one of the duffle bags we had dropped in the living room, pulling out two shirts. He layered them quickly, as if building armor, before slipping on his jacket.

He turned to me, his gaze sharp and unwavering. "Listen to me," he said, stepping closer. His hands came to my face, his palms warm despite the cold tension between us. "We're going out there to find Luke. But you do not leave my sight. You stay next to me the entire time. Do you understand me, Maeve?"

I nodded, my breath hitching as his words sank in. "I under-stand," I whispered.

Ethan exhaled deeply, his forehead pressing against mine in a rare moment of vulnerability. The warmth of his skin against mine grounded me, even as the storm of fear churned in my chest. His breath was steady, but his eyes held a flicker of unease that mirrored my own.

"You stay close to me, Maeve. No matter what happens," he said, his voice low but resolute, each word carrying the weight of both worry and fierce determination.

I nodded, swallowing hard, my resolve solidifying as I met his gaze. Whatever lay ahead, we would face it together.

...

"Shit!" Justin cursed as he stumbled toward the bunker, his steps unsteady. He threw open the heavy door and maneuvered himself inside, the wood creaking as it closed behind him. His breaths came shallow and strained, blood dripping steadily from the wound in his shoulder.

"Justin, what happened?" Eric demanded, securing the rope tightly around Luke's body. Luke was bound to a chair, his hands tied behind his back, his mouth muffled with a cloth. He was pale, his chest heaving as blood stained his shirt from the deep wound inflicted by Eric's hook.

"I got stabbed," Justin muttered, his voice tight with frustration as he gingerly touched his shoulder. The wound, aggravated during his scuffle with Maeve, had worsened. Her frantic blows to his injured shoulder in her desperate attempt to escape had reopened it, causing fresh blood to seep through the fabric.

Eric turned away from Luke, his expression unreadable. "Come here, son," he said in a calm but commanding tone, walking toward a small room in the bunker designed as a makeshift bedroom for emergencies. He grabbed a first aid kit from its hook by the door and motioned for Justin to follow.

Leaning against a wooden shelf near the door, Justin kept his eyes fixed on Luke, whose bound body trembled in the chair. "I thought you hooked him," Justin said, disappointment creeping into his tone as he watched Luke's labored breaths. Justin slid his arm out of his sleeve, exhaling deeply, his gaze never leaving Luke.

"I did," Eric replied, unscrewing the cap of a bottle of alcohol. "Apparently, this one's got more fight in him than I thought. But he'll bleed out soon enough. Shame, really—I was looking forward to watching him suffer a bit longer." Eric's tone was casual, almost conversational, as he poured the alcohol over Justin's wound without warning. Justin clenched his jaw, a guttural grunt escaping as he bit back a cry of pain. Eric's hands moved with a detached efficiency, methodically cleaning and wrapping the wound with practiced coldness. Tossing the empty bottle back into the kit, Eric added, "Which one of those kids did this to you?"

Justin hesitated, his lips tightening before he finally muttered, "Maeve." Letting out a slow, frustrated breath, he carefully slid his injured arm back into his shirt, his movements deliberate but strained.

Eric's eyes darkened, and a slow, cruel smile crept across his face. "Maeve," he repeated, savoring my name like a twisted triumph. "Well, ain't that something. That's my girl." He chuckled low and deliberate, shrugging off his fedora and long black coat before hanging them neatly on a peg.

"She's tougher than I thought." Justin replied as he stepped away from the shelves. Justin shifted uncomfortably, his gaze moving toward Gwen and Tara, their lifeless bodies still hanging limply from the chains. Luke's muffled cries grew louder as he tried to twist against his restraints, tears pooling in his eyes as he looked at the grim scene before him.

"What are you planning to do with these two?" Justin asked, gesturing toward Gwen and Tara. His tone was almost casual, though his eyes betrayed a hint of unease.

"Same as usual," Eric said, rolling up his sleeves and moving with unnerving precision. "Get me the Polaroid and the tools."

Justin nodded, a faint smirk tugging at his lips as he circled Gwen's body and approached a nearby shelf. He picked up an old Polaroid camera and a long wooden box, his movements deliberate. Luke's muffled protests grew louder, more desperate, as Justin handed the items over to Eric.

He set the tools on a nearby table, unrolling a collection of sharp, gleaming instruments. The air grew thick with tension as he ran a bloodstained cloth over one of the larger blades, inspecting its edge.

"Can't leave any evidence," Eric remarked, snapping open the wooden box to reveal its contents—tools polished to a cold shine, their purpose grim and undeniable. Justin raised the camera, pointing it at Luke first.

Kneeling before Luke, Justin smirked. "See, Luke," he said mockingly, "you get to watch while Eric works. That pretty little girl of yours? We'll start with her. Maybe we'll leave Tara for Ethan—give him something to look forward to."

Luke thrashed against the ropes, his muffled screams tearing through the bunker. His eyes darted to Gwen's lifeless form as Eric approached her, the blade glinting in the dim light. With a slow, deliberate motion, Eric began his gruesome work, each cut precise and methodical.

"Good idea, boy," Eric said, holding up one of the tools, its sharp edge glinting in the dim light. "We'll save her for Ethan." His voice was cold, detached, as though he were discussing a routine task rather than human lives. Justin raised the camera again, capturing each horrific moment as Eric turned his attention to Gwen.

Eric's hands moved with an eerie calm, his focus unshaken. The sound of metal against flesh filled the room, punctuated by Luke's muffled cries and the wet thud of discarded remains hitting the floor. The metallic scent of blood permeated the air, mixing with the damp, musty smell of the bunker.

"Don't worry," Eric said, his voice dripping with malice as he glanced back at Luke. "You'll be next... but not before I make sure you've seen enough to haunt you forever."

Luke's body trembled violently, his breaths ragged and uneven as he fought against the unbearable pain and the crushing weight of helplessness. His tears blurred his vision, but the horrifying reality remained clear: Gwen was gone, and Eric was reveling in every second of his torment.

The bunker was silent except for the muffled cries, the wet

sound of Eric's work, and the occasional click of the camera. Every moment was a waking nightmare, each second carving a permanent scar into Luke's soul.

...

I watched carefully as Ethan loaded a rifle, his movements deliberate and tense. He handed it to me, then passed me a handgun, his jaw tight. I slid the gun under my shirt, tucking it into my waistband with shaking hands. Ethan grabbed a knife in its sheath, strapping it firmly to his belt. Every motion screamed urgency, his body coiled like a spring ready to snap.

"Stay close to me—no matter—" Ethan's words cut off as his head jerked toward the front door. The static-filled screech of the CB radio broke the heavy silence, sharp and grating. He moved swiftly, yanking the door open and bounding down the steps, the sound of his boots on the wood like gunfire in the night. I followed close behind, adrenaline surging through my veins.

"Ethan Adams, Ethan Adams!" a voice cracked over the CB, distorted but urgent.

Ethan froze, his face twisting with shock and recognition as he leaned through the open car window to grab the receiver. "This is Ethan Adams! Who's calling? Who is this?" His voice trembled with panic and hope.

"Been tryin'… contact you… four days…" The voice cut in and out, barely intelligible beneath the static.

"It's the bartender!" I shouted, my voice taut as I scanned the yard for any movement.

"Are you from the bar?" Ethan barked into the receiver.

"Yeah… Trenton Bar… danger... listen carefully…" The man's words broke apart, fragments of static swallowing most of the message.

"We need help! We're at Aberdeen Manor—sign 1524 South of Trenton. The road says, 'PRIVATE PROPERTY!'" Ethan shouted, desperation bleeding into every word.

"I hear ya—" The voice crackled before plunging into complete silence.

Ethan stared at the receiver, then slammed it into the car in frustration. "Damn it!" he yelled, his fist pounding the car's roof. The whole vehicle shuddered under the force of his anger as he leaned heavily against the door frame, his body trembling with rage and exhaustion.

"Ethan," I whispered, placing a hand on his arm. But he was lost in the moment, shaking the car and muttering curses under his breath.

Earlier, three hours before…

"This is lieutenant Michaels, broadcasting on emergency channel 9 to all compounds in the Trenton area. Anyone copy?" His voice came through the CB, strained but commanding.

Inside the Trenton Bar, a customer—a husky man with tattoos and a weathered biker jacket—glanced toward the bartender. The once lively crowd, a mix of hardened bikers and locals enjoying the rowdy atmosphere of biker night, fell silent.

"Roger, the CB in the backroom," the man said, pointing toward the device as he moved.

Roger, the bartender, grabbed the receiver, his thick fingers turning the dials as the bar's patrons crowded around him. The air was heavy with unease.

"This is Roger. I run the bar on South 40 before Trenton. I hear you," he said, his voice steady but grim.

"Thank God," Michaels replied, his relief palpable. "We've been trying to reach anyone for hours. There are kids at Aberdeen Manor—we lost contact with them last night. They're in grave danger."

The bar erupted in murmurs. Roger's face darkened as Michaels continued, his words striking a chord of urgency. "Eric

Stephenson is there—a sadistic serial killer. He's hunting them, and we're running out of time. Those kids need help. The boy's name is Ethan Adams, his sister's Maeve…"

Roger's hand tightened on the receiver. "Michaels, they were here three days ago. I told them if they didn't come back in four days, I'd go after them myself."

"Then get to them now!" Michaels shouted, his voice sharp. Static followed.

Roger turned to the crowd of men gathered around him. "We can't leave those kids out there. Let's move!"

Chairs scraped against the floor as the bikers sprang into action. Some grabbed shotguns from their trucks, while Roger reached under the bar, pulling out two of his own. The gravel outside crunched under boots as engines roared to life, headlights cutting through the darkness as the convoy assembled.

"It'll take an hour to get there," one man called to Roger through an open window.

"Don't care how long it takes—pedal to the floor!" Roger shouted back, his truck screeching onto the highway with a cloud of dust trailing behind.

In the back of one of the trucks, three men clutched their weapons, their faces grim and resolute. "No one gets left behind," one of them said, chambering a round.

Another truck blared its horn, and a voice shouted above the roar of engines, "Let's get to them!"

Roger grabbed the CB receiver in his truck, twisting the dials in a desperate attempt to reach Ethan. "Hold on, kids," he muttered under his breath. "We're coming."

…

"Ethan," I said again, my voice trembling as my hands tightened against his arm. He was still cursing, shaking the car in frustration, his anger spilling out in waves. His body radiated fury, but as I spoke his name again, he turned his head toward me. For a brief moment, his posture relaxed, his chest heaving with the effort to rein in his emotions.

Then, without warning, he grabbed me and pulled me into a fierce hug.

"Ethan! We have to find Luke, Tara, and Gwen," I reminded him, my voice urgent. His head pressed against my shoulder, and for a heartbeat, the only sound was our ragged breathing. I wrapped my arms around him, holding him tightly.

"If anything happens, and we get separated—you run," he said suddenly, his voice low but intense, his words laced with desperation. His hands cupped my face, forcing me to look at him. "You get the hell off this property. That guy from the bar, if he's coming, he'll reach you before Michaels does. You find him, and you escape. Don't look back. Don't come for me or Luke. You just run."

"Shut up!" I snapped, my voice cracking under the weight of his words.

"LISTEN TO ME!" he shouted, his tone sharp and commanding. His grip on my face tightened slightly, his eyes blazing with determination. "You run, Maeve. You don't come for me. You don't look back. You run!" His forehead pressed firmly against mine, his breath hot against my skin as his words hung heavily in the air.

"SHUT UP!" I yelled, shoving him back with trembling hands. "We have to find Luke!" My voice wavered, but I held my ground, my heart pounding in my chest.

Ethan stared at me for a moment, his jaw tightening, his hands dropping to his sides. His knuckles whitened as they curled into fists. Then he nodded, his expression hardening.

"Let's find Luke," he said finally, his voice like steel. "And get the hell off this property."

Without another word, I grabbed my rifle off the hood of the car, the weight of it grounding me as I stepped away from Ethan. He watched me for a second, then picked up his own rifle that rested against the car. With a swift motion, he cocked it, the sound sharp and final in the cold night air.

The tension between us hung thick, unspoken fears crackling like static. Together, we moved forward into the suffocating darkness, the shadows of the trees closing in around us like a noose.

Ethan moved ahead of me, his steps deliberate and cautious. I followed closely behind, gripping my rifle tightly. "Where are we looking?" I whispered.

"The woods. That's where we were last," Ethan replied, his voice low. Neither of us even thought to check the bunker—it hadn't crossed our minds that the property even had one.

As we circled the house and approached the graveyard, a faint glow caught our attention, emanating from the shed nearby. Ethan's pace slowed, his body tense. He cocked his head toward the shed, signaling with a finger to his lips for silence. Then, with a slight tilt of his head, he gestured for me to follow.

We crept toward the shed, our steps slow and deliberate, each one feeling impossibly loud in the stillness of the night. Ethan reached out, his hand hovering over the metal handle before he grasped it carefully. The wooden door creaked loudly on its hinges as he eased it open.

"It's empty," I whispered, peering inside.

Ethan didn't step in right away. His eyes darted to the edges of the doorframe, scanning for anything—tripwires, traps, anything out of place. Satisfied, he cautiously stepped into the doorway, standing just inside.

Inside the shed was a small, grimy bed shoved into one corner and two long wooden shelves lined with old TVs and a recording device. The faint hum of electronics filled the air.

"He's been watching us," I murmured, stepping in after Ethan, my voice tight with unease. "I thought we found all the cameras."

"Shit," Ethan muttered under his breath, his eyes glued to the flickering monitors. "He's been watching us this whole bloody time."

The screens displayed various parts of the house and property—empty, devoid of movement. Ethan's eyes narrowed as he studied the footage, then suddenly, a thick white mist flashed across one of the screens.

"Holy shit! What was that?" Ethan stumbled back, his heel catching on a wooden chair. He gripped the edge of a shelf to steady himself, his face pale.

I leaned closer, my eyes widening as the mist began to coalesce into a figure. "Uncle," I breathed, my voice trembling. The shape solidified briefly, his full figure visible within the swirling white light.

Ethan's gaze snapped to me. "That's Uncle? You can see him?" He pointed at the screen, his voice a mix of awe and disbelief.

"Yeah," I said quietly, my eyes glued to the screen. "Recording devices can pick up orbs of deceased people if they're still lingering."

Ethan shook his head, his panic rising. "Why do you see him clearly and I only see... that?" He gestured to the white orb on the screen.

"Because I have the ability to see earthbound spirits," I replied, my voice calm despite the tension in the air. "I already told you this."

The orb pulsed faintly, then vanished in an instant, leaving the screen dark once more.

Ethan's expression hardened as he turned to me. "Oh my god. We have to go now, May. Find Luke and get the hell out of here." He grabbed my arm and yanked me toward the door. The shed door slammed hard against the frame as we stumbled out.

"You think I'm crazy, don't you?" I said, struggling to keep up as he dragged me toward the graveyard.

Ethan stopped abruptly, releasing my arm. He turned to face me, his expression grim and resolute. "If you're seeing Uncle, that means he didn't cross over. That means he's bound to the house." He paused, cocking his gun. "Which also means Eric killed him."

"And now…" Ethan's voice grew cold, his jaw tightening. "We find Eric, and I put a bullet in him for what he did to Uncle."

I tightened my grip on my rifle, my knuckles white. The weight of everything pressed down on me, but in that moment, a surge of determination coursed through me. Ethan and I exchanged a look, both of us steeling ourselves for what was to come.

Without another word, we turned and ran, the open gate behind us leading straight into the darkened woods. The trees swallowed us whole, their shadows deep and unrelenting as the hunt began.

"Justin, let's go, son! We have two more to find," Eric barked, wiping his bloody hands on a rag. He tossed it onto the table, the fabric sliding over his bloodied tools. "When we find Maeve, do not harm her. Bring her to me."

Justin snapped one last picture with the Polaroid, the camera's mechanical click slicing through the heavy air. As the photo developed, he pulled it free, examined it, and then tossed it onto Luke's lap.

"Try not to go anywhere," Justin sneered, his voice dripping with mockery as he turned to face Luke. Luke's shirt was soaked with blood, his body trembling from exhaustion and pain. His eyes, glassy with unshed tears, glared at Justin with a fierce determination. He mumbled something into the gag, his voice muffled and guttural.

"What was that?" Justin taunted, leaning closer, cupping his hand around his ear with exaggerated amusement. He yanked the gag down, exposing Luke's bloodied lips.

"I'm going to kill you… you and Eric," Luke rasped, his voice weak but venomous. "And I'll enjoy watching the life drain from your—"

Before Luke could finish, Justin shoved the gag back into his mouth, silencing him with a rough motion. "Good luck with that," Justin said with a cruel smirk, tapping Luke's cheek in a condescending gesture.

Eric stood nearby, his expression unreadable as he adjusted his trench coat and grabbed the hook off the peg. "Let's go, Justin," he said, his tone calm but commanding.

Justin straightened, grabbing his gun and checking the clip with practiced ease. "Got it," he replied, falling in step behind Eric as they ascended the creaking wooden stairs. Luke's muffled gasps echoed in the dim confines of the bunker, his struggles futile against the ropes that bound him.

Justin paused outside, leaning against the weathered wooden frame of the shelter doors. He reloaded his gun with meticulous care, the metallic clicks echoing in the still night air. Beside him, Eric coiled the thick rope tightly around his waist, the infamous hook gleaming briefly before disappearing into the folds of his trench coat.

"They're more than likely in the woods," Justin said, his voice steady and low as he snapped the clip into place.

Eric smirked, his fedora spinning idly between his fingers before he placed it neatly on his head. "Do as you please to Ethan, but you leave Maeve to me," he said, his voice laced with cold authority.

Justin chuckled, a sharp grin spreading across his face. "Alright," he replied, slipping his gun back into his waistband.

Eric stopped at the top of the bunker stairs, his hand resting on the heavy wooden doors. He cast a final glance back into the darkened shelter. Luke's muffled cries and labored breaths filled the space, a haunting sound in the otherwise suffocating silence.

"Don't worry, boy," Eric said with a dark chuckle. "You'll have company soon enough."

Luke thrashed in his chair, his desperate cries rising in volume. Justin pulled the Polaroid camera from his side, snapping one final picture before tossing it into the open shelter. The photograph fluttered down the stairs, twisting and turning in the air before landing near Luke's feet. With a low groan, the thick wooden doors swung shut, the sound of the latch clicking into place echoing like a death knell. The oppressive darkness of the bunker enveloped Luke completely, his muffled screams fading into the void.

Ethan pulled me close, his grip firm on my hand. "Stay quiet, and stay with me," he whispered, his voice low and urgent.

I nodded, following him as we moved cautiously through the dense woods. The trees loomed around us, their gnarled branches twisting like skeletal fingers. Each step we took felt impossibly loud, the crunch of leaves and twigs beneath our boots echoing in the eerie silence.

"This is where we were last," Ethan murmured, his eyes scanning the ground. A dark, wet trail of blood led through the grass, dragging toward the tree line.

"We follow this, then," I said, pointing to the trail.

Ethan exhaled deeply, his grip tightening on his rifle. Just as we were about to step forward, a pale figure materialized before me. "Uncle," I whispered, startled by the sudden appearance.

Ethan froze, his head snapping to me. "What? What's wrong?"

My gaze locked onto the spectral figure. My uncle's face was drawn with worry, his translucent form glowing faintly in the dim light. "Maeve, no. You and Ethan have to leave. Leave now!" his voice pleaded, his urgency palpable.

Tears welled in my eyes. "We can't, Uncle," I whispered. "We have to find our friends. We can't leave them."

Ethan's gaze darted between me and the empty space he couldn't see. "What's he saying, May?"

I placed a hand against Ethan's chest, silencing him as I focused on our uncle.

"Please, Maeve," my uncle begged. "Don't make me beg.

Your lives are too precious. Leave now before it's too late!"

My voice broke as I answered, "We can't leave them. I won't leave them."

Before my uncle could respond, his head snapped toward the rustling bushes nearby. His form flickered, and he vanished as quickly as he had appeared.

"Someone's coming," Ethan hissed, stepping in front of me and raising his rifle.

A low whistle pierced the silence, chilling me to the bone.

"I warned ya, didn't I?" Eric's voice called out, his thick drawl slicing through the night. "And look what happened..."

Ethan's body tensed, his eyes scanning the darkness.

"I took those girls, Ethan. Both of them," Eric continued, his tone dripping with malice. "Saved one for you, though. The other? Well, Luke had a front-row seat to her final moments. Let's just say it was... *unforgettable!*"

His cruel laughter echoed through the woods, followed by another low whistle.

"Show yourself, you bastard!" Ethan snarled, his rifle aimed and ready. The trees around us swayed, and the air grew heavy with anticipation. Then, without warning, a hook whistled through the air.

"ETHAN!" I screamed as he shoved me to the ground. The hook struck him square in the chest, its barbed point tearing through flesh and emerging from his back.

Ethan staggered but remained standing, his breaths labored. "Shit!" he growled, one hand gripping the hook as blood poured from the wound.

Eric emerged from the shadows, the rope in his hands, his expression smug and triumphant. "Thought I'd give you a front-row seat, Ethan," he sneered. "Your girl and your best friend? They'll be the grand finale."

"ETHAN!" I screamed again, tears streaming down my face as I scrambled to my feet.

"NO, MAY!" Ethan shouted, his voice strained but commanding. "It didn't hit anything vital. I'm fine. RUN!"

I hesitated, torn between staying and fleeing.

"GO NOW!" Ethan bellowed, his voice filled with desperation as he gripped the hook, fighting to keep Eric from pulling it further.

Eric grinned, tightening his hold on the rope as he stepped closer. "Go ahead, girl. Run. I'll deal with you soon enough."

My heart shattered as I turned and ran, my sobs choking me as I disappeared into the darkness of the woods. Ethan's voice echoed behind me, his defiance cutting through the night.

I slowed down, my legs trembling as I stopped far from the house—far from Ethan. The air was heavy, the silence pressing down on me. I turned back, desperately searching for any sign of him. Nothing. No movement. No sound.

My knees buckled, and I collapsed to the ground, tears streaming down my face. "AAAAH! Ethan!" I screamed, the sound tearing from my throat like a primal cry. I clenched my hands over my ears, trying to block out the deafening silence. "Stupid! Stupid!" I shouted, slamming my fists against the dirt.

"Damn, you run fast," a voice drawled, startling me.

I jerked my head up and froze. Justin was standing a few feet away, his smirk curling into something darker as he caught his breath. "Could barely keep up with you," he said, his tone laced with mock amusement.

Before I could react, he lunged forward, grabbing my arms in one swift motion and yanking me to my feet. His grip was like iron, unyielding and suffocating.

"This time don't even think about screaming or trying to run," he growled, his voice low and dangerous. He pulled a length of rope from his belt and began tying my wrists. This time, he used a hitch knot, tightening it until the rope bit into my skin. He yanked hard, forcing my bound hands closer to his chest.

"Well, now that I've caught you," he said, his smirk returning, "why don't we go watch the show?" He jerked me toward him, his breath hot and acrid against my face.

I clenched my jaw, my breath shaky but steady enough to spit directly into his face. "I'm not going anywhere with you," I hissed, my voice trembling with defiance.

Justin froze, his expression darkening as he wiped the spit from his face with deliberate slowness. He let out a long, sharp exhale and shook his head. "You really shouldn't have done that, Maeve," he said, his tone icy and controlled. "Not a smart move."

With a sudden, violent tug, he dragged me forward, forcing me to stumble alongside him. His grip on the rope tightened painfully as he pulled me closer to his body, his smirk fading into a look of grim determination.

"Let's go," he muttered, his tone leaving no room for argument. I resisted, trying to plant my feet in the dirt, but it was futile. His strength was overwhelming, and every attempt to fight back only seemed to amuse him.

My chest heaved with panic as the house loomed closer with each reluctant step. My mind raced, desperately searching for a way out, but the rope around my wrists burned, and Justin's grip was unyielding. The shadows of the house swallowed us whole as he dragged me back toward the nightmare I had tried so desperately to escape.

As the house loomed closer, I fought harder against Justin's grip, my heels digging into the dirt as I resisted with everything I had. He grunted, his teeth clenched, dragging me inch by inch. "Stop that!" he snapped, yanking me forward with renewed force.

Then I saw it: the storm cellar. Wait... the storm cellar? How did we miss this?

The wooden doors creaked open violently, the sound reverberating through the still night. "Take it easy there, boy. Don't harm her," Eric's voice called out from below, his tone calm but chilling. I thrashed even harder, my feet scrabbling against the ground, but Justin was relentless. With one last powerful yank, he wrenched me to his side and half-carried, half-dragged me toward the wooden stairs descending into the dark cellar.

"No! Let me go!" I screamed, my voice raw with desperation as the doors slammed shut behind us.

The air in the cellar was cold and heavy, a damp, suffocating chill that seemed to seep into my bones. Ethan was bound to a chair in the center of the room, his arms tied behind his back, a gag muffling his furious shouts. His eyes locked onto mine, wide with fear and determination. Beside him, Luke slumped in another chair, his head hanging low, his breaths shallow. When he heard my voice, his head lifted slightly, his gaze dull but aware.

"LUKE! ETHAN!" I screamed again, struggling harder, but Justin only smirked. Without warning, he threw me down onto the cold concrete floor. The impact sent a jolt of pain through my knees and hands as I hit the unforgiving surface.

"Jeez, she's a feisty one," Justin muttered, wiping his face as though I had physically exhausted him.

Eric descended the stairs swiftly, his boots thudding against the wooden steps, and approached me with a calm, almost soothing demeanor that made my stomach churn. "There, there, Maeve," he said, crouching beside me. His voice was low, smooth, almost gentle. It was the kind of tone someone used to calm a frightened animal, but it only made my fear spike higher. "No need to worry."

I flinched as he grabbed my bound hands, his grip firm but oddly careful. He began pulling me along the cold floor, the friction scraping against my legs as I tried to resist. "Stop it!" I shouted, twisting my wrists against the rope, but his strength was overwhelming.

Justin had positioned himself in front of Ethan and Luke, dropping into a chair like he didn't have a care in the world. He leaned back, casually observing them as Ethan thrashed in his restraints, muffled curses spilling from behind the gag. Luke's head sagged again, his breaths shallow and uneven.

Eric tugged me into the small side room, his grip firm and unyielding. With a sharp pull, a single bare bulb flickered to life, casting a harsh yellow glow over the space. "Maeve, I am so sorry it had to resort to this," he said, his voice dripping with mock regret as he hoisted me into a chair.

The room was stark and eerily tidy—a queen-sized bed, perfectly made, stood in the center, flanked by two dressers against one wall. A large round carpet lay in the middle, its edges curling slightly, as if untouched for years. The air was cold and heavy, the space hauntingly domestic, as though it had been preserved for this moment.

This was the room my father, James, had built in case of emergencies—a place meant to protect us from the storms outside. Now, it felt like a cruel parody of its purpose. Instead of safety, it held nothing but me and the man standing before me... my real father.

"Here we are, precious," Eric said, crouching in front of me, his dark eyes locked onto mine. "Now, let's talk."

I glared at him, defiance burning through the fear that threatened to consume me. "Let me go. Right. Now!" I shouted, my voice shaking with rage.

Eric shook his head slowly, a small, pitying smile tugging at his lips. "I can't do that, Maeve. Not yet." He held up a hand as if to calm me, his voice maddeningly steady.

I clenched my teeth, pressing my lips into a tight line. I didn't want to hear anything he had to say—I didn't care about his plans or his twisted motives. My focus was on one thing: getting Ethan and Luke out of here alive.

My body tensed, every fiber of my being screaming to fight, to resist. My eyes darted to the door, searching for an escape, but Eric's cold gaze held me in place. "I know you don't want to hear it," he continued, his voice soft but unyielding, "but you're going to listen."

Behind him, I could hear Justin taunting Ethan and Luke, his voice laced with cruelty. The faint sounds of Ethan's muffled shouts and Luke's labored breathing seeped into the room, a grim reminder of the danger we were all in.

"Now Maeve," Eric began, pacing in front of me, his boots clicking against the cold concrete floor. His thick Southern drawl was heavier now, almost suffocating as he spoke. "I know you're going to hate what I'm about to say, but you see… that boy out there, Ethan…" He paused, letting the name hang in the air like a taunt. "I can't let him walk out of here alive."

My breath caught in my throat, but I kept my face stone still, refusing to give him the reaction he wanted.

"Well," he continued, smirking, "he can't really walk much since I hooked him, now can he? Him and that Luke boy—both got it good." His laughter was low and bitter, the kind that sent shivers up my spine. He stopped pacing and turned to face me, studying me as if expecting me to break. My mind raced, searching for a way to escape, but I forced myself to stay calm.

"I want Ethan to watch," Eric said, leaning closer to me, his tone dropping into something cold and venomous. "I want him to see me cut up his precious girl. Then I'll do the same to his friend… nice and slow so he can hear every single second of Luke's final moments."

The words were a slap to the face, but I held my ground, even as the chair beneath me seemed to shrink with the weight of his threat. He crouched down, his face inches from mine, and reached for my cheek. I jerked my head away sharply, my body tensing like a coiled spring.

"Just once," he whispered, his voice eerily calm, "I'd love to hear you call me Dad, Maeve. Just one time… I am, after all, your father."

"You're not my father," I said through gritted teeth, my voice trembling with rage.

Eric exhaled heavily, his calm mask slipping for a moment. His hand shot out, grabbing a fistful of my ponytail and yanking my head back painfully. I cried out, the sharp pull sending tears streaming down my face.

"Just once," he growled, his voice rough with frustration. "Call me Dad, and I'll end all of this. Then I'll take you away. Anywhere you want to go—you pick."

My scalp burned under his iron grip, and the pressure felt unbearable. "My dad…" I choked out, my voice breaking. A slow smile spread across Eric's face, the kind that made my stomach turn.

"Yes, precious," he cooed, his grip tightening. "That's right. I know this is hard for you."

I gritted my teeth, anger bubbling up like a boiling cauldron. "My dad," I screamed suddenly, my voice cracking with fury, "IS JAMES ADAMS!"

Before he could react, I drove my knee up hard between his legs. Eric let out a guttural cry, releasing my hair as he stumbled backward, clutching himself in agony. He fell to the ground, his face contorted in pain.

"Screw you! Screw both of you!" I shouted, adrenaline surging through me as I sprang from the chair.

Justin leapt into the room, his face twisted in both anger and disbelief. "Hey, that wasn't nice," he sneered, grabbing me before I could make it past him. "You can't go around kicking people like that, Maeve."

"Let go of me!" I screamed, thrashing against his grip. His hands clamped around my tied wrists as I fought him with everything I had. My breath came in ragged gasps, and my heart thundered in my chest as I struggled to pull free.

Eric groaned, rolling onto his side as rage overtook his pain. With a snarl, he pushed himself to his feet, his eyes blazing with fury. "Enough!" he roared, his voice reverberating off the walls.

In two long strides, he reached Justin and yanked me out of his grasp. His hand came down hard across my face, the impact sending me sprawling to the floor. Stars exploded in my vision, and the world spun violently as I hit the cold concrete. Darkness seeped into the edges of my consciousness, threatening to pull me under.

Eric loomed over me, his breathing ragged and his presence suffocating. "You think you're smart, don't you?" he hissed, his voice low and venomous. "But this... this is just the beginning."

And then everything faded to black.

"Tie her up. I don't want any more of her surprises," Eric growled, his voice low and seething with rage. His words echoed in my ears as Justin yanked my hands with brutal force, the rope biting into my skin. It was the last thing I heard before the darkness swallowed me whole.

Chapter 16

JUSTIN SHAWN SMITH

JUSTIN ADJUSTED HIS JERSEY, his reflection staring back at him from the cracked mirror in their small apartment. He ran a hand through his short-cropped hair, exhaling sharply. "Don't forget, boy," Eric's voice cut through the silence, gruff and commanding. "Maeve attends that high school. Get close to her, win her over, and get me the information I need."

Justin's jaw tightened as he looked over his shoulder at Eric, who lounged in the corner with a cigarette dangling between his fingers. "Yeah, yeah, I got it," Justin replied, grabbing his book bag from the chair. "Don't worry, Eric. I'll win her over and get you what you're after."

Eric's nod was curt, his eyes cold and calculating as Justin walked out the door. The small, dingy apartment in Nebraska had become their hideout, a place where Eric plotted while Justin carried out his plans. He lived in Nebraska, close enough to keep us in his sight without my family ever suspecting. He slipped into my life like a shadow, unnoticed until he was already too close. He transferred to my high school, and from the moment he walked in, he was impossible to ignore.

When he walked into the high school that first day, Justin's confidence was palpable. He moved through the halls like he belonged there, blending in seamlessly with the other jocks. He was older than most of the students—two years older than Ethan and four years older than me—but with his athletic build and easy charm, no one questioned him. He was quickly recruited to the football team, his skills on the field earning him instant popularity.

As he strode down the crowded hallway, the familiar bravado of high school athletes surrounded him. The football players greeted him with loud slaps on the back, their laughter echoing off the metal lockers.

"Yo, Mike!" one of them called out, tossing him a football. He caught it effortlessly, grinning as the group erupted into cheers. Their macho behavior dominated the space, roughhousing and shoving each other in exaggerated displays of testosterone. The scent of sweat and cheap cologne filled the air as they postured and joked, their voices a cacophony of adolescent arrogance. It wasn't just his team who always noticed him, it was the girls who noticed him too—how could they not? He was tall, confident, and had that easy, cocky smile that seemed to disarm everyone in his path.

I remember the first day I saw him. My laugh echoed lightly down the hallway as I walked into the school with Gwen, the sound carefree and unguarded. Justin's eyes locked onto me the moment I passed him, heading toward my locker with my books clutched tightly to my chest. There was something in his expression—an unguarded smile that spread across his face, not calculated, but instinctive, as if he hadn't expected to react that way. He cleared his throat, snapping himself out of the trance. "Excuse me, gentlemen," he said, raising a hand to pause his group. With an almost theatrical gesture, he pointed in my direction. "See that little brunette there? She's mine."

The guys erupted in a chorus of cheers and whistles, their hands slapping against his shoulder in encouragement. "Go get her, Mike!" one of them shouted, laughing.

"Show her how it's done!" another added.

I froze, feeling the weight of his words before I even realized they were about me. Gwen nudged me with her elbow, and I looked up just in time to see him pointing in my direction. He left his group of teammates, who were cheering and clapping him on the back like he'd just scored a touchdown and started walking toward me.

I couldn't look away. He was tall, his jersey fitting just right, and that cocky grin was aimed directly at me. My face flushed instantly, and I buried it behind my books, trying to hide how red I'd turned.

"Hey, gorgeous," he said, leaning casually against the locker next to mine. His voice was smooth, like he'd rehearsed it, but there was something about the way he looked at me—like I was the only person in the room.

Gwen was no help. She was grinning ear to ear, clearly enjoying my sudden embarrassment. "I—uh, hi," I stammered, my voice barely above a whisper. My hands tightened around my books as I tried to focus on anything but him.

This was how I met Michael Cory Smith. Or, as I'd eventually learn, Justin Shawn Smith—the boy who had been sent to infiltrate my life, all under Eric's orders. At that moment, though, all

I saw was a boy who made my heart race in a way I didn't understand yet.

...

My head throbbed as I blinked my eyes open, the dim light of the storm cellar swimming into focus. I was tied to a chair, my arms and legs firmly bound. The ropes cut into my skin, and my mouth was gagged, silencing my screams. Warm blood trickled down my forehead, and I felt its sticky heat. Eric crouched in front of me, the first aid kit open at his side. His hand pressed a damp pad against the wound on my head, the sting sharp enough to make me flinch and mumble against the gag.

"I'm sorry I hit you like that, Maeve, but you need to learn what happens when you cross me," Eric said, his tone sickeningly calm as he smoothed a large bandage onto my forehead. He stood, his shadow looming over me as I scanned the room. My eyes landed on Tara's lifeless body, hanging naked from the chains. A chill ran through me, but I forced myself to look away, my gaze shifting to Ethan.

Ethan's tear-filled eyes were locked on Tara, his face a mask of panic and devastation. His gaze lingered on her small, rounded stomach—a protruding bump that hadn't been there before. My heart shattered as I realized the truth: Tara had been pregnant. Ethan's expression said it all—the shock, the grief, the crushing realization of what had been taken from him. His chest heaved with muffled sobs, curses spilling from behind his gag.

Luke sat slumped in his chair next to Ethan, his breathing shallow but steady. Blood stained his shirt, and his head hung low, but he was alive—for now.

"Alright, boy, let's finish this," Eric said, his voice dripping with malice. He grabbed Ethan's chair and yanked it forward, scraping it across the concrete floor until it faced Tara. "There. Now you've got a front-row seat," he said with a sneer, clapping his hands together. Ethan thrashed against his restraints, his muffled curses rising in volume, but Eric and Justin paid him no attention.

Justin chuckled as he circled Ethan, the Polaroid camera in hand. Leaning over Ethan's shoulder, he raised the camera. "Smile for the scrapbook, buddy. We like to keep little souvenirs," he said, snapping a photo of Tara. The flash illuminated the horror in the room for a brief second before fading back into the dim light.

Eric dragged his wooden table closer, the legs scraping loudly against the floor. He began selecting tools from his collection, each gleaming blade and saw more sinister than the last. I struggled violently against the ropes, screaming into my gag, but the bindings wouldn't budge. Tears streamed down my face as I fought harder, desperate to stop what was coming.

And then, through the thick tension of the room, a faint sound broke the silence: honking, followed by distant shouts.

"MAEVE! ETHAN!" Roger's voice echoed faintly from outside.

Eric froze, his head snapping toward the stairs. "What the bloody hell is this?" he growled. Justin immediately set the camera down and grabbed his gun, his movements quick and cautious.

"They found us?" Justin muttered, his voice laced with tension as he checked the clip in his gun.

Eric cursed under his breath as he threw on his trench coat and grabbed the rifle he'd taken from me earlier. "Let's go, boy," he said, his voice steady but sharp. He reached for his fedora, placing it firmly on his head before ascending the wooden stairs. Justin followed close behind, both of them moving quietly but with purpose. The heavy wooden doors creaked open as they slipped outside, closing them with a muted thud.

Outside, the property was surrounded. Trucks and motorcycles formed a barrier around the manor, their headlights slicing through the dark. Roger stood by his truck, a flashlight in hand, his voice cutting through the still night. "MAEVE! ETHAN! DO YOU HEAR ME?"

Men spilled out of the vehicles, moving in coordinated groups. Guns were cocked, and the metallic clink of ammunition being loaded filled the air.

"Keep it tight, men. Do not harm the kids," one of the bikers ordered, his voice low but commanding. He adjusted the shotgun slung over his shoulder as he led his group toward the house. The gravel crunched under their boots as they fanned out, some approaching the front steps while others circled around to the back.

Roger's voice barked orders as he gestured to two men. "Steve, Tony, take the left and right. The rest of you, stay alert. Any movement, take it down—but make damn sure it's not one of the kids."

The men split up, moving silently through the property. The back group entered through the rear door, their steps careful but deliberate. At the front, Roger, Steve, and Tony ascended the wooden porch steps, the boards creaking under their weight. Each man's flashlight cut through the darkness, sweeping over the yard and the house's exterior.

The air was thick with tension, every sound amplified as they closed in on the manor. Inside, Eric and Justin moved with equal caution, their weapons ready as they prepared to face whatever waited for them above ground.

. . .

My gaze shifted to Ethan, who was furiously fighting against his restraints. The ropes were cutting into his skin, but he didn't care—his entire focus was on freeing himself. I twisted my head, working to loosen the gag until it slipped from my lips. "ETHAN!" I shouted, my voice shaking.

Ethan froze for a moment, his head tilting slightly toward me. He heard me. I knew he did. "I'm sorry," I stammered through my tears, my words tumbling out. "Tara told me before… before all this happened. I'm sorry!" My voice broke as I sobbed, unable to look at Tara's lifeless body hanging from the chains, her small, rounded stomach a heartbreaking reminder of the life she once carried.

Luke's head lifted weakly, his gag hanging loose from his mouth. His voice was barely above a whisper. "Maeve," he croaked, his breathing labored. "There's… a knife… to your left."

I whipped my head to the side, and there it was—a hunting knife resting on a low shelf. The same knife I had stabbed Justin with earlier.

"Use it… May," Luke gasped, his words strained.

"No, Luke," I said, my voice shaking as tears blurred my vision. "You stay awake. Keep talking to me."

I shifted my weight, inching the chair back toward the shelf. The legs scraped against the cold, hard floor, each movement agonizingly slow. My back pressed against the shelf as I leaned into it, stretching my fingers desperately toward the blade. My wrists burned as the sharp edge nicked my skin, but I ignored the pain and managed to grasp the hilt.

Ethan cursed under his breath, his furious struggles intensifying. "Ethan, stop!" I cried. "You're going to cut yourself to pieces. Let me free myself, and I'll cut you loose."

But he wouldn't listen. His tear-filled eyes were fixed on Tara, his desperation pouring out in every frenzied movement as though sheer determination could bring her back.

I dragged the blade over the ropes binding my wrists, sawing furiously. My hands bled, but I didn't stop. Finally, I heard the satisfying snap of the ropes giving way.

"Good… Maeve," Luke rasped, his voice faint.

"If you lift your arms, you'll be able…" Luke breathed, his words broken by a cough. "To free those!" he added, his voice barely audible.

I followed his advice, lifting my arms to loosen the ropes that wrapped around my chest. They slackened immediately, and I managed to pull them off. With shaking hands, I bent down and started cutting the ropes binding my legs. Each stroke of the knife made the fibers fray until, with a final snap, the ropes fell away.

I let out a deep breath and stood up as soon as I was free. My knees wobbled, but I steadied myself and moved toward Luke. "Okay, I'm getting you out of here," I said, crouching down to cut the ropes around his legs and waist.

"No, Maeve… you need to leave," Luke stuttered, his breath shallow. "I can't move. I can't go anywhere."

I froze, my heart sinking.

I hadn't noticed Ethan had freed his gag until his voice broke through the suffocating silence. Ethan's voice cut through the air, raw and filled with anger. "Eric struck his spine," he said, his jaw clenched. "He can't feel his legs."

I froze, the knife slipping slightly in my hand as I turned to look at him. "What? NO!" My voice cracked, and my knees gave out as I fell back onto the cold concrete floor. My chest heaved with sharp, panicked breaths as the weight of his words settled over me.

"Get out of here, May," Ethan demanded, his voice sharp and filled with an anger I hadn't heard from him before. "Find those men. Get the hell out of here."

Tears blurred my vision as I crawled toward him, the knife trembling in my hands. I pressed the blade against the ropes binding his hands and began to saw through the thick fibers. "No, Ethan," I sobbed. "I can't leave you. I can't leave either of you."

He yanked his freed arms forward, his wrists raw and bleeding. "I SAID GET THE HELL OUT!" His voice thundered through the room, shaking me to my core. He shifted his chair, jerking it away from Tara's lifeless body, as if the sight of her was unbearable.

"I can't do it," I cried, gripping his knees, my tears soaking into the fabric of his jeans. "I won't leave you both here. Please, Ethan. Let me help—"

"You can't help us!" he bellowed, his voice cracking with both rage and desperation. "You need to leave! Right now, May. Go find those men and get out of here before Eric comes back!" He moved the chair again, forcing distance between us.

Luke's ragged breathing filled the room, his head hanging low as he fought to stay conscious. I turned to him, his pale face a grim reminder of how dire this was. My hands shook as I picked up the knife and scanned the room for something—anything— I could use as another weapon. But the room was barren, empty of anything that could offer us an advantage.

"He took all the weapons out of here," Ethan growled, his jaw tight. His fiery gaze locked onto mine. "Now take the knife, get the hell out, and don't look back."

I hesitated, torn between the urge to fight and the terror of leaving them behind.

"GO!" he shouted, jerking his chair closer to Luke.

Fresh tears streamed down my face as I staggered to my feet. My legs wobbled beneath me as I turned toward the wooden stairs. Each step felt like a betrayal, my heart breaking with every movement away from them.

As I reached the top, voices filtered in from outside—the unmistakable roar of motorbikes, shouts, and orders being barked through the night. I paused, gripping the knife tightly in my hand, my pulse pounding in my ears. Slowly, I lifted one side of the cellar doors and peeked out into the chaos.

Men were scattered across the property, their flashlights cutting through the darkness. Trucks and motorbikes surrounded the manor, engines growling and headlights beaming through the night. I hesitated, my heart racing, unsure of who these men were or if they were even here to help. With a shaky breath, I slid out of the door and gently lowered it behind me, the wood creaking in protest.

I locked it hesitantly, sealing Ethan and Luke inside the storm cellar. My fingers lingered on the latch for a moment, my throat tightening with guilt and fear. The knife felt heavy in my hand as I crouched low, the cold night air biting at my skin. My tears hadn't stopped, but I swallowed my sobs, silencing myself as I crept toward the source of the voices. Whoever these men were, they were my only hope now.

It was up to me now. I only prayed I wasn't too late.

As I stood, steadying myself against my legs, I let out a shaky breath, readying myself to wave my arms and call out for help. But before I could, a hand clamped over my mouth, and an arm wrapped tightly around my waist, yanking me backward away from the cellar doors. I screamed against the muffling hand, struggling and clawing at the arm restraining me.

"Shut it!" Justin's voice hissed in my ear, his breath hot and laced with frustration. He dragged me backward, away from the yard and into the thick cover of the trees. The yard, now filled with trucks and men shouting orders, became a distant blur as Justin maneuvered through the shadows, unseen by the rescuers.

As we broke through the edge of the trees, Eric was waiting. He glanced at us, his face calm and menacing. "Keep her quiet," he growled.

Justin tightened his grip on me, pressing his hand harder against my mouth as I thrashed in his grasp. "How the hell did they get here?" Justin asked, his voice tense.

I twisted in his hold, managing to knock his hand slightly away from my face. Taking a desperate breath, I screamed, but Eric lunged forward, cutting me off. "Enough!" he snapped, yanking me roughly from Justin. In one fluid motion, Eric pulled a chloroform-soaked cloth from his trench coat and pressed it firmly over my mouth and nose.

I squirmed, kicking wildly, my muffled cries dissolving into frantic gasps. My vision blurred, and my body weakened as the chemicals took hold. The last thing I heard before everything went dark was Eric's low, mocking voice. "Sorry, Maeve, but you gave me no choice."

He hoisted me over his shoulder as I went limp, turning to Justin. "So how do we get past them?" Justin asked, glancing nervously toward the chaos erupting near the house.

"With bait," Eric replied with a smug grin, his eyes gleaming with malicious intent.

From the rear of the yard, Justin emerged, his hands raised in a show of surrender. "You there, boy!" one of the bikers shouted, directing a flashlight beam at him. Three men raised their guns, stepping cautiously toward him.

"Don't shoot!" Justin's voice trembled, feigning fear. He kept his hands high, his eyes darting between the men.

Roger approached, his gun trained on Justin. "What's your name, boy? What are you doing here?" he demanded, trying to place the face. There was something familiar about him, but the adrenaline clouded Roger's memory.

"It's Mike," Justin said quickly, his voice wavering. "I joined Ethan and Maeve after they got here. I'm on your side, I swear."

Roger's eyes narrowed, suspicion evident in his gaze. "You better not be lying to me," he warned, his grip tightening on his weapon. "Where are Maeve and Ethan?"

Justin's smirk was faint, but before Roger could react, Justin reached under his shirt and pulled out a gun. In one swift motion, he fired two shots, grazing two of the men.

"Crap!" Roger shouted, ducking for cover as chaos erupted. The wounded men stumbled back, clutching their injuries, while others raised their weapons, shouting orders to contain the situation. Justin bolted into the darkness, disappearing before anyone could fire back.

"Shit!" Ethan cursed, his voice sharp as the sound of gunshots echoed above them. He whipped his head toward Luke, urgency tightening his features. "Luke!" he called, his voice trembling with equal parts fear and determination.

With a swift, powerful motion, Ethan yanked his arms forward, the ropes biting into his already bloodied wrists. He grit his teeth, forcing the fibers to snap under the strain. Blood smeared against his hands, but he didn't stop. Leaning forward, he broke the ropes binding his legs, his movements deliberate and intense.

But he didn't stand. Not yet.

"Luke, I'm getting you out of here," Ethan growled, his voice low and resolute. "Then I'm grabbing May, and we're gone." He shifted in his chair, reaching toward Luke. His hands shook from the strain, but he managed to loosen the ropes around his friend's arms and waist.

Luke groaned, his voice faltering. "Ethan… I can't move. You can't carry me…" His words stuttered, heavy with defeat.

Ethan ignored him, slipping an arm around Luke's waist and hoisting him up. The effort sent a surge of white-hot pain through Ethan's back, forcing a sharp cry from his throat.

"Aaarrghh!" he gasped, staggering forward. His left leg buckled beneath him, the injury to his spine sending shocks of agony through his entire body. He clenched his jaw, his breath ragged as he struggled to steady them both.

"We can't, Ethan," Luke murmured, his voice barely audible. "You'll… you'll hurt yourself worse…"

Ethan panted heavily, sweat dripping from his brow. His eyes darted toward the floor, spotting the first aid kit beneath the shelf. "Stay with me, Luke," he rasped, carefully lowering his friend back down. With a grimace, Ethan twisted his body, dragging himself toward the kit. His knees scraped against the hard concrete, every movement a fight against the searing pain.

...

I felt my head swimming as I tried to make sense of the muffled voices around me. My vision blurred, but I could just make out Justin standing nearby, reloading his gun with quick, deliberate movements. "Damn," I heard him mutter as he turned toward Eric, who was crouched beside me.

"Is she okay?" Justin asked, his voice tense but controlled. His eyes darted toward the house, where the commotion of men and trucks echoed through the yard.

"She's fine," Eric replied, his tone sharp and detached. "I won't keep her exposed out here." He stood up, towering over me, and brushed the dirt from his trench coat. His cold eyes scanned the chaos before him as he cocked the rifle in his hands with a chilling precision.

"Listen here, Justin," Eric said, his voice dropping into something darker, almost gleeful. "Let's hunt some men." He raised the rifle, pointing it toward the house like he was surveying prey.

Justin smirked, gripping his gun with both hands. "Let's do it," he said, his voice carrying a smug confidence that made my stomach turn.

Eric's rifle was steady in his hands, his aim precise. Without hesitation, he fired twice, each shot splitting the night. Two bikers went down—a sharp cry from one struck in the arm, and a guttural grunt from the other hit in the thigh. Both crumpled to the ground as chaos erupted near the house.

"FALL BACK!" Roger's voice bellowed, his hand waving furiously through the air. His command echoed across the yard as the men scattered, retreating to the trucks parked on the other side of the wall. The walkie-talkies crackled with frantic voices.

"Gunshots! Men down to the left!" one of the bikers called, his voice strained with urgency. "Either fire back or fall back!"

Justin's smirk deepened as he squeezed the trigger again. Gunfire lit up the night, shattering what little calm remained. Three more bikers dropped, their groans of pain cutting through the chaos. Though none were fatally injured, their comrades wasted no time. They hoisted the wounded into the backs of the trucks, tires screeching as they pulled back toward the edge of the property.

Roger's truck skidded out of the driveway, joining the others just beyond the metal gates. "Damn it!" he shouted into the walkie-talkie. "We can't get to those kids if we're being pinned down!"

Another voice crackled through the receiver, calm but calculating. "I think there's something near the back—looks like a cellar or a bunker. Wooden doors. Maybe that's where they're keeping them."

"Hold tight, regroup. Let's figure out a plan to get in and get them out," Roger barked in response.

Eric chuckled darkly as he watched the convoy retreat to a safer distance. The yard now lay barren, quiet but surrounded. The headlights of trucks and motorbikes pierced the darkness, their engines rumbling faintly in the background.

"They're still out there," Justin said, his eyes scanning the perimeter as he checked his clip.

Eric gave a low, guttural laugh. "Yes, but far enough to be of no concern. You'll keep them at bay. I just need time to finish this," he said, his voice cold and deliberate. "Once I have Maeve in the backseat of the car, I don't care if this place goes up in flames."

I gasped as I regained full consciousness, the sharp sting of reality hitting me like a freight train. Eric tilted his head toward me, crouching down. His face, so close to mine, was a mask of false regret. "Sorry, Maeve," he said, his tone almost patronizing. "But you wouldn't keep quiet."

My voice shook as I stuttered through the tears streaming down my face. "Let me go, please… just let me go."

Eric's expression hardened, his voice calm but terrifying. "I can't do that, Maeve. There's still work to be done. That girl. Luke. And lastly… Ethan." His words, measured and deliberate, sent ice through my veins.

I pressed my trembling hand over my mouth, stifling a scream as his arms hoisted me off the ground and slung me over his shoulder like I weighed nothing.

"Eric, do you want me to stay out here?" Justin called, his gun poised as his eyes scanned the property for movement.

Eric didn't look back. "Aye, boy. You stay out here. Take the rifle, and if anything moves… kill it. I don't care who it is."

Desperation swelled inside me as my thoughts raced. The men from the bar—the bikers—they were here! They could help. But before I could open my mouth to scream, Eric yanked me off his shoulder and clamped his hand over my mouth, his grip iron-tight.

"Now you listen," he growled, his voice low and venomous. "I don't care if you think I'm your father or not. I don't care if you acknowledge it. But if you so much as scream, if you dare make a sound…" His face loomed closer, his eyes dark and unrelenting. "I'll make you watch as I cut your brother into pieces and send his remains to his father. IN. A. BODY BAG."

The weight of his threat crushed any defiance I had left. Tears streamed down my face as I nodded silently, my lips trembling against his palm.

"Do you understand me?" he hissed.

I nodded again, too terrified to do anything else.

•••

"Keep quiet!" Ethan whispered harshly to Luke, pressing a hand over his lips as Luke clenched his teeth around the gag still hanging loosely from his mouth. Ethan let out a deep breath and tipped a full bottle of alcohol over Luke's wounded chest.

Luke flinched violently, groaning as his body jerked forward in pain. He panted heavily, struggling to catch his breath, his hands trembling against his knees.

"Sorry, Luke!" Ethan said quickly, his voice tight with guilt as he wrapped gauze tightly around Luke's chest, careful but efficient.

Luke stuttered out, his voice thin, "Ethan… I'm so sorry about Tara…" His words faltered with the weight of grief and pain, his breath hitching with each word.

Ethan paused, the air between them heavy and suffocating. His jaw clenched as he exhaled hard through his nose. "Gwen, I'm sorry—" he began, but Luke's hand shot out, gripping Ethan's arm with surprising strength.

"What he did to her… what I had to watch him do…" Luke gasped, his voice trembling, raw with anger and anguish. "I want to do it to him. To make him *suffer* for what he did to Gwen." His words cracked as tears streamed down his face.

Ethan's expression hardened, his fury barely contained as his nostrils flared. "I promise you, Luke," he said firmly, his voice a low growl, "I'm getting you out of here first. But after that? I'll make Eric pay. I'll make him feel everything he's done to you, to me, to Tara… and to Gwen."

Luke nodded weakly, his breathing labored. "If I don't make it out of this… you make him *suffer*, Ethan. You kill him slow," Luke rasped, his hand falling away limply.

Ethan grabbed Luke's arm, his determination steel-like. "You're making it out of here," he said, his voice resolute. He hoisted Luke out of the chair with an agonizing grunt, the sudden motion sending a searing pain through his own back and legs. Ethan's left leg gave out slightly, but he gritted his teeth, forcing himself upright, balancing on his right leg as he held Luke tightly by the waist.

"Ethan, you can't—" Luke stuttered, his voice ragged. "You can't seriously think you can move me like this. Not in your condition."

"I don't care if I paralyze myself even worse," Ethan snapped, his breath sharp and labored. "I'm getting you off this property."

He dragged Luke slowly, step by painstaking step, toward the wooden stairs. Luke tried to shift some of his weight onto his feet, but every attempt sent a blazing pain coursing through his back.

"ARRGH! ETHAN, STOP! STOP, WAIT!" Luke shouted, his voice strangled with agony.

Ethan halted immediately, his chest heaving as he steadied himself against the wooden railing. He lowered Luke onto a step, his face pale and lined with worry.

"I can't... I can't move like this," Luke gasped, his voice a rasping whisper. "Every step—it feels like my back's being ripped apart."

"Damn it," Ethan muttered, running a hand over his face, his mind racing as he scanned the small bunker for anything he could use. His eyes fell on Tara's lifeless form hanging from the chains. His breath hitched, grief clawing at his throat, but he forced himself to look away. He couldn't afford to break now.

"Wait, hang on," Ethan said suddenly, a spark of determination igniting in his eyes.

He steadied himself, gripping the shelves as he dragged his body toward the bedroom door. Each step was a battle, his injured leg barely able to hold his weight. Inside the bedroom, he looked around frantically until his eyes fell on the closet. Throwing open the doors, he found old wooden slats that had been stored there, likely leftover pieces James had stashed for emergencies.

Ethan grabbed the slats, testing their strength with his hands. They were sturdy enough. He then rummaged through the shelves until he found some thick fabric and a length of rope. It wasn't much, but it was enough.

Dragging the materials back to Luke, Ethan shifted to his knees and began working quickly, his hands trembling but steady. "I'm making you a stretcher," he said, his voice hoarse but resolute. "We'll attach these slats to your legs—they'll act like crutches. You can use them to balance and move while I help carry you."

Luke blinked at him, tears pooling in his eyes. "You're insane, Ethan," he said weakly, his voice cracking with emotion.

"Damn right I am," Ethan replied, not looking up from his work. "And it's what's going to get us out of here."

With swift, deliberate movements, Ethan secured the wooden slats to Luke's legs using the fabric and rope. He wrapped the fabric tightly around Luke's thighs and calves, ensuring the makeshift crutches were stable. Once finished, he hoisted Luke to his feet, guiding his hands to grip the slats.

"Now, lean on me. We're getting out of this hellhole," Ethan said, his voice a growl of determination as he prepared to lead them up the stairs.

Chapter 17

LUKE

I T WAS A MONDAY MORNING, or so I thought, when I dragged myself out of bed to get ready for school. As I passed Ethan's room, I caught the sound of muffled voices—Ethan and Luke. *Oh great, he's still here,* I thought, rolling my eyes so hard I was surprised they didn't get stuck. I had just turned sixteen three days ago. Luke's parents, Gwen's parents, even Tara's parents—along with Gwen and Tara themselves—had come over for my birthday party.

It was nice and all, but Luke? Luke is a whole different story. When he comes over, it's like he becomes part of the furniture. Ethan sometimes spends days—*days*—at Luke's house, but when Luke crashes here, he practically moves in. And guess who's overstaying his welcome because his parents had to go to Missouri for a family emergency? Yep. Luke Greyson.

"Aren't you gone yet? Like, seriously?" I barged into Ethan's room without knocking. Luke turned to me, smirking as I stormed in, while Ethan barely glanced up from his computer screen.

Ethan leaned back in his chair, sighed dramatically, and chucked a book in my direction. "Ever heard of knocking?" he said, annoyed.

I crossed my arms and shot him a glare. "It's not like you two were in here making out or anything," I said with a snort.

Ethan rolled his eyes. "What do you want, May?"

"It's Monday. SCHOOL DAY. That means you both need to get your lazy butts ready," I said, throwing my hands in the air as I turned to leave.

"Yeah, so don't be late," Ethan called after me, his voice dripping with sarcasm.

I froze in the doorway, an evil grin forming on my face. "I'm going to tell Mom and Dad you two are slacking off and not going to school," I said, one foot still in the room.

"Go ahead," Ethan said without even looking at me.

I turned around, glaring at them both. Luke sat at the computer, grinning as he moved the mouse. Ethan still leaned back in his chair, looking far too relaxed for someone who should've been panicking about the time.

"SCHOOL DAY?" I repeated, louder this time.

Ethan nodded, still nonchalant. "Yeah, and you're going to be late."

"WHAT THE HELL, ETHAN? Why aren't you and Luke freaking out and getting ready for school?" I asked, tapping my watch for emphasis and folding my arms in irritation. They both stayed silent, their mouths pressed into thin lines, ignoring me as they leaned closer to the computer screen.

"HELLO? It's Monday?" I said, stepping toward them. They didn't even flinch.

"Give it about ten more minutes," Luke said casually, typing something on the keyboard. I rolled my eyes so hard it hurt. Huffing, I stood beside the computer desk, determined to break through their act.

"You're seriously going to make us all late," I said, tapping my foot in annoyance.

Ethan sighed, finally breaking the silence. "You're the one wasting time. Go get ready."

Just as I was about to lose my temper, our father's furious voice boomed from downstairs.

"ETHAN ADAMS! LUKE GREYSON! BOTH OF YOU, GET DOWN HERE RIGHT NOW!"

I tilted my head toward the door, smirking. "Oooh, what brilliant display of stupidity have you two cooked up this time?" I said smugly.

Luke chuckled as he stood up, giving Ethan a high five. "Time to face the music."

Before they could make a break for it, Mom stormed into the room like a whirlwind. She grabbed them both by their ears, dragging them out of their chairs.

"OW! MOM!" Ethan yelped, trying to escape her grasp.

"Mrs. Adams, I don't even *live* here!" Luke protested, wincing as she dragged him along.

"Changing all the clocks in the house and the calendar to make us think it's Monday? Really? Your father almost had a heart attack thinking he was late for work!" Mom scolded, her voice echoing through the house.

I stood there, stunned for a moment, before the full absurdity of their prank hit me. My jaw dropped, and frustration bubbled up. *They tricked me! They made me think I was late for school!* I stomped after them, barely able to keep from shouting. But as I reached the top of the stairs, I saw Dad waiting in the living room, his arms crossed and a very unimpressed look on his face.

On the table beside him were all the alarm clocks from the house, the kitchen wall clock, and a makeshift printed calendar with completely wrong dates. The scene was so ridiculous I almost burst out laughing.

"Come here, both of you!" Dad barked, waving a finger at Ethan and Luke. I pressed my lips together to keep from laughing as Dad started lecturing them, pacing back and forth as he listed all the ways their prank had disrupted the household. Ethan and Luke stood there sheepishly, trying to look sorry but clearly holding back grins.

Despite my initial annoyance, I couldn't help but admit it: this was probably the best prank they'd pulled in years.

...

Aberdeen Manor, once a proud family home passed down from my mother to Uncle Joe, was now nothing more than an eerie, silent graveyard. A place that had claimed two more lives and was now surrounded by a convoy of desperate men.

My entire body quivered as I crouched low, my hand trembling against my mouth, muffling my ragged breaths. My eyes stayed locked on Eric as he dragged the bloody carcass of a deer through the woods, the dull thud of its lifeless body echoing in the stillness.

"You and I are going to take a little trip," Eric said, his voice cold and deliberate. "Just as soon as I finish off Luke and Ethan. Once my work here is done… I'm taking you far away." He crouched next to the deer, his hands steady as he began gutting it with precision.

I clamped my hand tighter over my mouth, fighting the bile rising in my throat. The acrid smell of blood and flesh filled the air, and I couldn't bring myself to look at what he was doing. Instead, I focused on Justin, standing just within view, his hands wrapped tightly around his gun, his eyes scanning the manor property for any movement. I stared at him, desperate to distract myself from the grotesque sight in front of me.

"Using this as bait," Eric continued, his voice heavy with that drawl that made my skin crawl. "It'll lure those men away from the property. The trick is to cut the deer in just the right places—

make the pieces look human. By the time they find this mess, they'll think I've already cut you kids up good. Those fools will either flee or head back for reinforcements. Either way, by the time anyone useful shows up, I'll be long gone." He didn't stop his gruesome work as he spoke, his words as calculated as the movements of his knife.

The sound of flesh tearing hit my ears, wet and nauseating, and I couldn't hold it in any longer. I lurched forward, vomiting violently onto the forest floor, my knees sinking into the dirt and soil beneath me.

"You're a sick, twisted, evil sociopath. You monster," I spat, struggling to catch my breath, my voice trembling with disgust and fury.

Eric stopped, tilting his head toward me, his expression darkening. "Now that's a very disrespectful thing to say to your father, Maeve," he said, his tone dripping with mock offense. "I thought Amy raised you better than that... or was it James who taught you to have such a filthy mouth?" He smirked before resuming his gruesome work, the sound of his blade slicing through flesh making my stomach churn all over again.

"No need to worry," he added after a long pause. "Once we leave this state together, I'll make sure you never speak a foul word again." His voice was calm, measured, as though we were discussing a family outing instead of his horrific plan.

I stared at the ground, my hands pressed into the damp earth, trying to steady my breathing and keep myself from breaking down. *Think, Maeve. Think.*

I couldn't scream—if I did, I'd put Ethan and Luke in immediate danger. I couldn't run—Eric or Justin would catch me, and if they didn't, a bullet likely would. My options were few, and each felt more hopeless than the last.

Eric's knife continued to cut, each wet, tearing sound a reminder of how close I was to danger. I clenched my fists, the dirt caking my skin, and forced myself to focus.

I needed to find a way out. I needed to think of something—

anything—to escape this nightmare.

...

"Okay, Luke, we're going to try this," Ethan said, his voice firm but strained as he secured the second plank of wood against Luke's legs. The makeshift stretcher was crude at best, fashioned to act like crutches. If it worked, it might allow Luke to balance his paralyzed legs on the wood slabs just long enough for Ethan to semi-carry him up the stairs.

Luke leaned heavily against Ethan for support as they tested the contraption. The planks distributed Luke's weight awkwardly, his dead legs dragging but at least supported enough to prevent complete collapse. Ethan tightened his grip around Luke's waist. "Yeah, okay," Ethan grunted, adjusting his footing on the first step. He reached for the wooden rail, bracing both himself and Luke as they inched upward.

Luke gasped, shifting his grip to the opposite rail. "Okay... yeah... I don't feel any pain," he panted, his voice tight with exertion. They moved painstakingly slow, one step at a time. Ten wooden stairs stretched before them like an impossible climb to freedom. Each movement was deliberate, cautious, and agonizing.

"Shit!" Luke cursed, noticing the fabric securing the planks beginning to unravel.

Ethan immediately bent forward, releasing Luke's arm for just a moment to re-tie the fabric. His hands worked quickly, tightening the knot before Luke could tip backward. "Got it," Ethan said, pulling Luke back into position and resuming their ascent.

"We're unarmed," Luke rasped, sweat beading on his forehead. "How the hell are we getting through that yard without being shot at?" His breathing grew heavier, and Ethan stopped, bracing them both as he took a moment to catch his breath.

Without a word, Ethan lifted his shirt slightly, revealing two handguns tucked into his waistband. "I've got this. Eric didn't check me before he tied me up," Ethan said, letting the shirt fall back into place.

Luke's eyes narrowed. "Stop, Ethan. I can't do this. It's putting too much strain on me," he said, his voice weaker now, tinged with pain and frustration. Blood had begun to seep through the bandage on his chest again, despite Ethan's earlier efforts.

Ethan paused, glancing at Luke's wound. His jaw clenched. "We're almost there, just three more steps," he said, his voice filled with determination.

Luke shook his head, collapsing onto the stair and leaning heavily against the railing. "Get Maeve… and just go!" he said, his voice breaking with desperation as his breathing became more labored.

Ethan sat down beside him, running a hand through his hair in exasperation. "We're almost out, Luke. I can't leave you like this," he said, his tone softening but still resolute.

Luke pushed him away, his face twisted in anger. "I said no! Get your sister and GET THE HELL OUT OF HERE!" he shouted, his voice raw and filled with fury.

Ethan's eyes flashed with defiance as he shook his head. "Shut the hell up, you jerk! I'm not leaving you!" he snapped. His voice cracked under the weight of his emotions. "I already lost Tara. I'm not losing my best friend, too."

Ethan stood abruptly, his entire body trembling with pain and exhaustion, and forcefully hoisted Luke back up. He threw Luke's arm around his shoulder again, grunting under the strain. "We're doing this. Together," he said, his tone daring Luke to argue.

Luke growled, anger bubbling to the surface. "You're a goddamn nutcase, Ethan! Just GO!" he shouted, but his protests were weak against Ethan's sheer stubbornness.

Step by agonizing step, Ethan dragged them both upward. The effort sent waves of fire through his injured body, his left leg barely holding under the strain. Luke's breathing grew more labored, every gasp sharp and shallow, but Ethan refused to stop.

Finally, the faint outline of the wooden doors loomed above them. Ethan could feel the rough texture of the wood against his fingertips as they reached the top step. Luke was slumped heavily against him, his breaths ragged and uneven.

Ethan paused, his muscles trembling from the effort. "We made it, Luke," he whispered, his voice hoarse. But his eyes carried the steely resolve of someone who refused to give up, no matter the cost.

As Ethan pushed the wooden doors open, a chilling silence greeted him. No voices, no trucks, no footsteps—nothing but the oppressive stillness of the night. The convoy had moved so far back that the cellar and its surroundings were now eerily deserted. Ethan dragged Luke out with him, their combined weight collapsing onto the cold, damp ground as they hit the surface.

"Shit," Ethan muttered, his breath ragged. "I think my back's about to give out." His entire body screamed in agony, fire surging through every nerve. His right leg twitched and tingled uncontrollably, the pins-and-needles sensation nearly unbearable. He pressed a hand against his thigh, trying to force blood flow back into it.

"Leave me here," Luke gasped, his head tilted back to face the starless sky. His chest heaved with every labored breath, and a deep, hacking cough racked his body as blood seeped through his bandages. "Find May… just find her."

Ethan sat up, his chest rising and falling heavily, his breaths labored as he locked eyes with Luke. Reaching under his shirt, he pulled out a handgun and pressed it firmly into Luke's trembling hands. "Five rounds," Ethan said, his voice low but resolute. "You keep this. I'll find her, and then I'll come back for you."

Without waiting for a response, Ethan threw his body

around, rolling onto his stomach with a sharp groan. "Argh!" he hissed through gritted teeth, letting out a shaky breath. "Hoo, that was not good," he muttered, pain radiating through his battered frame.

Slowly, he began shifting his body like a snake, dragging himself along the grass. His arms strained with each pull, inching him farther away from the cellar in agonizing movements. The silence around him felt deafening, every rustle of grass beneath him amplifying the tension in the air.

Luke nodded weakly, clutching the gun to his chest. "Be careful, Ethan," he whispered hoarsely, his voice barely audible. He shifted slightly, throwing himself onto his stomach, the makeshift wooden slabs strapped to his legs anchoring him to the ground. "Don't let them get her…"

Ethan didn't reply. He turned his focus back to the task at hand, forcing his body to move. His legs were nearly useless, but his arms pulled him forward, dragging his frame across the damp grass. Every inch was a battle against the searing pain that threatened to overwhelm him. Behind him, Luke groaned softly, struggling to stay conscious, his breathing uneven.

From my position on all fours near the wooded area, I froze. My eyes locked on a faint, shifting figure about ten feet away, slithering slowly through the grass. It moved with a shimmying motion, side to side, as if trying to stay as low and undetected as possible. My breath hitched. A feeling deep inside me whispered that it was Ethan—or maybe Luke—trying desperately to reach safety.

I bit down hard on my lip, my gaze darting to Justin. His sharp eyes scanned the property with predatory precision, his gun raised and ready. He was close to the gate, close enough that if he caught any movement, he'd have a clear shot. My heart pounded in my chest as I silently prayed, *Please, please… stay hidden. Stay safe, Ethan. Luke.*

Eric continued his grim work nearby, hunched over the carcass of the deer. His trench coat lay discarded on the ground, now smeared with blood and draped with the severed parts he planned to use. I bit my lip hard, trying to keep the bile from rising again as he stood, his bloody hands coming together with a soft, wet clap. The grotesque sight was almost enough to shatter my composure, but I forced myself to focus.

As he bent down to pick up his trench coat and begin wrapping the organs in it, I seized the moment. "Uh, I'm hungry!" I blurted out, my voice louder than intended, desperate to distract him from noticing anything else.

Eric turned his head sharply toward me, his expression softening into a strange semblance of concern. "Is my precious girl hungry? Okay, well, let's get you something... I, uh, yeah, so hold on," he stammered, waving his hands as if trying to conjure a solution on the spot. His nervous fumbling was almost comical, but the weight of the situation kept my nerves taut.

He glanced toward the house, then to the bunker. "The house, yeah. There's food there," he mumbled, nodding to himself as though confirming his plan. After a few moments of thinking, he turned back to me with a grin, his bloodied hands resting on his hips. "I'll get you something from there. Just wait."

That's when I noticed the figure stop moving. My stomach tightened, and I bit my lip hard enough to draw blood. Worry clawed at my insides. What if that was Luke and he'd passed out from blood loss? Or worse—what if it was Ethan, and he was struggling to move? Panic churned in my chest, and I blurted out, "Never mind, I don't want anything," my voice shaking.

The figure remained motionless in the grass, and the fear of Eric heading toward the house gnawed at me. I couldn't risk him noticing it. "Maeve, no, please..." Eric's voice pulled me back to him. He dropped his trench coat near me, the fabric wrapped tightly around the organs. Kneeling down beside me, he reached out, his bloody hands cold against my face as he turned my gaze to meet his.

"If you're hungry, I'll get you something," he said softly, his calm tone undercut by an eerie, sadistic edge that made my skin crawl.

I shook my head, forcing my voice to remain steady. "Cutting up that deer made me queasy. I can't eat anything," I said quickly, trying to keep his focus on me and away from the direction I had been looking.

"Crap!" Ethan groaned, rolling onto his back, his chest heaving with labored breaths. The wounds on his chest and side had reopened, blood soaking through his shirt and pooling onto the ground beneath him. Pain burned through his body, and his breaths came in ragged gasps. He clenched his fists, striking the ground in frustration. "Crap, crap!" he hissed under his breath. "Shit! I can't keep going like this. I can't even stand. If someone sees me, I'll get a bullet in me…"

He muttered to himself, forcing his mind to focus despite the haze of pain. He could hear distant voices and the faint static of walkie-talkies, but the surrounding darkness concealed any movement. He couldn't pinpoint where the men were. The eerie silence pressed down on him, heightening the tension. It felt like a waiting game—a deadly stalemate where everyone was poised to strike but no one dared to move first.

Roger and his men were out there somewhere. Ethan knew they hadn't left; their silence and darkened vehicles were a calculated strategy, meant to deceive Eric and Justin into thinking they'd withdrawn. It was smart. No lights, no sounds—just waiting for the right moment.

"Crap!" Ethan growled again, his trembling hand pressing against the bleeding wound at his side. "Shit! I'm bleeding bad," he whispered, forcing himself to breathe through the pain.

His mind raced for options. He wasn't far from the bunker, maybe two meters at most. It wasn't much, but even that short distance felt impossible. With a grimace, he rolled back onto his stomach, letting out a pained grunt. "Mmmph," he bit down hard on his tongue to stifle the sound, his teeth grinding together.

Using his elbows and forearms, he began to drag himself along the ground, inch by inch. Each movement sent jolts of agony through his chest and side, the rough earth scraping against his skin. His right leg was completely numb now, trailing uselessly behind him, and every shift of his body made his wounds bleed more. Still, he kept going, gritting his teeth and pushing through the pain.

"I just need to get back to Luke," he muttered, his voice barely audible as he dug his elbows into the ground and heaved himself forward. Sweat dripped down his face, mixing with the dirt and blood. Every inch felt like a mile, but he didn't stop. He couldn't stop.

Finally, after what felt like an eternity, the bunker came into view again. With one final swing of his body, Ethan dragged himself closer, his arms trembling from the strain. He lifted his head, letting out a shaky breath as he braced himself for the next step.

"Ethan, why are you back?" Luke asked, his voice strained as he watched Ethan drag himself closer. Ethan rolled onto his back, his chest rising and falling heavily, his face twisted in pain.

"I couldn't go any further," Ethan replied, his voice filled with frustration. "My entire body feels like it's on fire. God, Luke, I have to find May, but I can't even move." He clenched his fists and slammed them against the ground, his anger and helplessness spilling over.

Luke, still lying on his stomach, was silent for a moment before an idea struck him. "These wooden slabs have kept my legs and hips stable enough that I don't feel much pain," he said, his voice shaky but determined. "I'll go find her. I'll go after May."

He shifted his weight onto his arms, attempting to push himself forward. Ethan lifted his head, his eyes narrowing as he took in Luke's labored breathing and blood-soaked chest. "No,"

Ethan said firmly. "You're bleeding worse than I am, and you're not even breathing right. You won't make it across the yard."

Luke let out a deep, frustrated breath, his jaw tightening as he shook his head. "I don't care," he muttered, his resolve unshaken. "I'll find her."

He began to drag himself forward, his movements slow and uneven. Ethan turned quickly, flipping onto his stomach to reach out and grab the slab of wood strapped to Luke's right leg. "Shut the hell up and stop!" Ethan snapped, his voice low but commanding. "Just breathe for a moment. Let's think this through and figure it out."

Luke froze, his body trembling as he caught his breath. He let himself collapse back onto the ground, panting heavily. His chest rose and fell with labored breaths as he glanced down at Ethan.

"See? I told you—you can barely breathe," Ethan said, running a hand over his face in exasperation. Both of them lay there in the quiet, the weight of their situation pressing down on them. The silence stretched as they struggled to gather their thoughts and find a way forward.

"Roger, we've got to move in. We've wasted enough time sitting here in the dark waiting for movement," Steve, one of the bikers, said urgently to Roger. They stood behind the metal gates, peering into the property with rifles loaded and ready.

"Steve, Tony, Roy," Roger called out to the men near him, his voice steady despite the tension. The walkie-talkie crackled to life, and Roger clicked it, ensuring everyone stationed around the property could hear.

"Listen up," Roger said into the device. "I've got a hunch those kids are hiding in the woods. I saw movement through there—something dragging, but I couldn't make out what."

"You mean one of the kids—or all of them—might be taking shelter in the trees?" came the response from a biker stationed near the bunker area, far enough away that he couldn't see Luke and Ethan.

"Exactly," Roger replied, his tone grim. "But here's the thing—I think that killer, Eric or whatever his name is, isn't working alone. When the gunshots rang out earlier, there were too many bullets flying for it to be just one guy."

Steve, standing next to Roger, nodded in agreement. "Yeah, makes sense. Here's what we should do: split the convoy. We'll stay here and keep an eye on the front of the house and the yard. We've got full view of the property. But the others…" He gestured toward the opposite side of the house, behind the brick wall. "They should go through the woods on foot. No lights, no bikes—just them and the walkies."

"That's a solid plan," said one of the bikers from the far side of the wall, his voice crackling through the walkie-talkie. "We'll split into two groups. Ten of us will head into the woods on foot, and the remaining eight will stay here with the vehicles, keeping watch on the exterior perimeter."

"Good. Stick to the plan, and don't take any unnecessary risks," Roger instructed. "Be cautious, and keep your eyes peeled."

The walkie-talkies went silent, leaving only the faint hum of engines in the distance and the weight of anticipation hanging in the air.

ESCAPE

As Eric rambled on about fetching food from the house, I tilted my gaze toward Justin, who had shifted uneasily on his feet, his gun lowered but still ready. He wasn't looking at me—his sharp eyes scanned the surrounding trees.

"Eric!" Justin called, his voice low and urgent as he stepped closer, his back turned toward me. "I heard something—movement. Shoes rustling against the ground in the trees."

Eric's head snapped up, his calculating gaze narrowing. He reached for the rifle Justin offered him. "Them men split up, eh? Decided to go in on foot?" Eric chuckled coldly, cocking the rifle. "Not their brightest idea. Idiots."

I remained still, sitting on the cold ground, my heart racing as I pieced together my next move. Eric and Justin were distracted, focused on some phantom sound in the woods. It was now or never. I needed to create chaos, noise—anything to draw their attention away from Luke and Ethan.

"Keep yer eyes sharp, boy," Eric muttered, his tone all command as he raised the rifle. "Anything that moves, you shoot it." Justin nodded, shifting his position, his rifle raised and his steps slow, calculated. They had moved just far enough from me, their focus entirely elsewhere.

This was my chance.

Without hesitation, I pushed myself to my feet, ignoring the sting of cold air against my scraped palms. I didn't think; I just ran—sprinting toward the house with every ounce of strength I had.

"Shit! Maeve!" Eric roared, his voice cutting through the night like a blade. His head whipped toward me, his furious glare searing into my back as I bolted toward the property's looming brick wall. "GET HER BACK HERE!" he bellowed at Justin.

"I got her!" Justin growled, his voice vibrating with raw frustration as he took off after me.

The night erupted into chaos.

Gunfire ripped through the air, bullets slicing past me and tearing into the earth as the bikers at the perimeter fired blindly toward the noise. The sharp reports of gunfire echoed, sending shivers down my spine, but I didn't stop. I couldn't.

With the gate too far away, I threw myself at the wall, my fingers scrambling for purchase against the rough brick. My arms screamed in protest as I hauled myself upward, the bricks scraping at my palms and forearms. My foot slipped, but I clawed my way higher, adrenaline overriding pain.

Behind me, Justin was closing in fast, his boots pounding against the ground. "Maeve!" he barked, his voice dripping with rage. I ignored him, throwing one last desperate pull over the top of the wall before tumbling down the other side.

The landing was brutal.

I crashed hard onto the jagged edge of a crumbling tombstone, my body slamming into the cold earth. Pain shot through my arm like lightning, and I screamed, clutching it instinctively to my chest. I knew it was broken—I could feel the unnatural twist beneath my hand.

Justin's shadow loomed above me as he climbed the wall. "You're not going anywhere!" he snarled, crouching as he prepared to jump down.

Ignoring the agony coursing through me, I staggered to my feet, blood dripping from my palms, and ran. Each step sent sharp jolts of pain through my body, but I pushed forward, the sprawling backyard stretching endlessly before me. My lungs burned, and my broken arm throbbed as I cradled it against my chest.

"ETHAN!" I screamed, my voice breaking, desperation tearing through me as I ran. "ETHAN!"

From somewhere behind the house, Luke stirred, his head snapping up at the sound of my voice. "That's Maeve!" he rasped, his weak, labored breaths barely audible over the distant gunfire.

Ethan remained slumped against the cold ground, his body limp, exhaustion having claimed him. He didn't react, his chest rising and falling shallowly.

"ETHAN!" Luke shouted, his voice hoarse as he struggled to push himself up. Panic etched across his pale, blood-streaked face as he craned his neck to look toward the sound of my cries. His breathing hitched, his battered body trembling with the effort, but he refused to give up.

"Come on, Ethan," Luke muttered, his voice trembling as he pushed his palms into the dirt, trying to shift his weight. "Get up. Get up!"

But Ethan's eyes remained closed, his body motionless against the freezing ground.

Luke's gaze flicked desperately toward the direction of my

voice, his heart pounding as he realized he had to do something—anything—to reach me.

"I'm coming, Maeve!" Luke growled through clenched teeth, his voice a mix of determination and pain. Gritting his teeth, he planted his hands firmly on the cold ground, forcing his battered body upward. With one powerful thrust, he propelled himself into a shaky, upright position. The wooden planks tied to his legs shifted awkwardly, dragging his limp feet inches above the ground.

"AURGH!" he roared, his entire body convulsing as searing pain shot through him like wildfire. His breaths came in harsh, ragged gasps, but he didn't stop. He tightened the fabric around the wooden slabs, securing them tightly against his legs. They were his makeshift limbs now—his only chance to get to me.

But it wasn't enough. He needed balance.

Luke scanned the ground desperately, his eyes darting in every direction. Then, just to his left, he spotted it—a thick, heavy stick, probably an old broom handle, lying abandoned near the wooden doors of the bunker.

"Come on," he muttered, swallowing the lump of fear and frustration in his throat. He bent down carefully, his trembling fingers wrapping around the stick. His body screamed in protest, but he pushed through, forcing himself upright once more.

"I'm coming, Maeve," he whispered fiercely, gripping the stick like his life depended on it. Using it to steady himself, he threw his makeshift legs forward, one painful step at a time. Each movement was excruciating, the wooden slabs dragging across the ground with a jarring scrape. But he kept going.

Gunfire erupted in the woods, a deafening cacophony that sliced through the night. Men shouted, their voices frantic and angry. "MAN DOWN!" one of the bikers bellowed, the words carrying across the yard. "GET THAT BASTARD!" another screamed, their fury focused on Eric.

Adrenaline coursed through Luke's veins, numbing the agony in his body. The world around him blurred into a haze of noise and pain, but he moved forward, throwing his legs left and right in a crude, unsteady rhythm. The stick wobbled beneath his grip, but he clung to it like a lifeline, dragging himself closer and closer to the metal gate.

Finally, he reached it. With a guttural groan, Luke collapsed near the gate, his strength nearly spent. His makeshift legs sprawled uselessly behind him as he lay there, gasping for breath. But he wasn't done yet.

"I can't stop now," he muttered, his voice barely audible over the chaos. Summoning what little energy he had left, he pressed his palms to the ground and began crawling, his body trembling with exertion. Each pull of his arms dragged him closer to the house, to Maeve, to safety—or so he hoped.

The gunfire continued to crackle through the night, the shouts of men blending into the sounds of chaos. But Luke didn't care. He kept moving, every inch forward a small victory against the pain and hopelessness threatening to consume him.

"I'm coming," he whispered again, his voice breaking. "Just hold on, Maeve. I'm coming."

"AAAHHH!" I screamed, my voice tearing through the night like a siren.

"Roger, the girl—I see her!" Steve shouted, his gun raised as I came into view, sprinting frantically around the house. My chest heaved, my legs burning, but before I could make it any farther, Justin lunged at me from the shadows, tackling me hard to the ground.

"Shut your mouth!" he hissed, flipping me over with force. My breath whooshed out, but I didn't stop. I clawed and swung wildly, aiming for his injured shoulder where I had stabbed him before. He didn't flinch this time. His hands locked around my wrists like steel bands.

"I said, shut your mouth, Maeve!" he growled, his weight pinning me down as I thrashed beneath him.

Panic surged through me as I fought harder, my hands clawing at him, but then I saw it: Justin's hand going for his gun, lying just inches away from us. Before I could react, he grabbed it and leveled it at me.

"Stop fighting!" he barked, pressing the cold barrel against my chest. My hands froze mid-swing, my breaths coming out in shallow gasps.

"I don't care if Eric wants you alive," Justin said, his voice dark, his eyes like ice. "You open your mouth again, and I'll shut it for you."

My gaze locked with his, my mind racing. I panted heavily, my chest heaving against the gun. "Go ahead, Justin," I said, my voice shaking but defiant. "All I have to do is scream, and those men out there will light this place up. Neither of us will survive."

His head jerked toward the gates, where Roger and his men were motionless silhouettes in the black night. "Maeve! Maeve Adams!" Roger's voice bellowed, cutting through the tension.

"Like I said, Justin," I whispered, my voice laced with a taunting edge.

Justin's jaw tightened, his hand trembling slightly on the gun. Then, without warning, he cocked it, the sound loud and final. My heart stuttered. His finger tightened on the trigger.

Before the shot could ring out, a battered form hurled itself into him with a guttural cry. Luke.

"LUKE!" I screamed, watching as his broken, bloodied body collided with Justin, knocking him off me. They hit the ground hard, Justin scrambling to regain his footing. Luke flung himself onto his back, his chest heaving as he gasped, "RUN!"

I froze for a split second, torn between saving him and fleeing.

"I don't think so," Justin snarled, his voice venomous as he pushed himself to his feet, his gun swinging up and aiming squarely at Luke's chest.

"No!" I screamed, my voice raw. Without thinking, I lunged at Justin, my body colliding with his arm just as he steadied his aim. Pain shot through my broken arm, but I didn't care. I slammed my fist into him, clawing at his shoulder, trying to throw him off balance.

Justin's head snapped toward me, his face twisted with rage. "You just don't quit, do you?" he spat, his arm jerking back as he prepared to strike me.

"DON'T YOU DARE!" I shouted, my voice a mix of desperation and fury. Luke's gun was still in his hand, but his strength was fading. I could see it—this might be his last chance.

"MAEVE, STOP IT!" Justin roared, his voice sharp and furious, cutting through the chaos. His focus shifted entirely to me, his gun swinging away from Luke and leveling in my direction. The deafening crack of the gunshot shattered the night. The bullet slammed into my shoulder, the force spinning me around before I crashed to the ground. A second shot followed, striking my already broken arm. A searing, unbearable pain engulfed my entire right side, spreading like wildfire through my body.

A scream tore from my throat, raw and piercing. Pain exploded through me as I clutched my shoulder, warm blood seeping between my fingers.

The men at the gate froze for a heartbeat, my scream cutting through the darkness, followed by the rapid exchange of gunfire.

Luke, trembling but defiant, lifted his gun with trembling hands and fired. Two shots rang out, each finding their mark in Justin's back and leg. "ARGH, YOU JACKASS!" Justin bellowed, stumbling but refusing to go down. He twisted around with a snarl and returned fire, his bullets striking Luke in the arm and chest. Luke let out a wet, gurgling sound, his body crumpling to the ground as I screamed his name, my voice a broken plea against the chaos.

Justin collapsed nearby, groaning and writhing in pain, his weapon slipping from his grip for just a moment. My vision blurred with tears, but through the haze, I could hear the men shouting, their voices rising as they sprinted toward us. The distance from the gate to the graveyard felt insurmountable, and I knew they might not make it in time.

"MAEVE!" Ethan's voice cut through the noise, hoarse and desperate. I turned my head, barely able to focus, and saw him forcing himself upright, using sheer will to push past the agony of his battered body.

From the shadows of the woods, Eric emerged like a specter, his gun already raised and trained on Ethan.

"Dammit, boy, you and Luke escaped? Well, that won't do at all," Eric sneered, his voice low and venomous.

Ethan, shaking with rage, yanked his gun free, his breaths coming in shallow, ragged gasps. "Over my dead body, you sadistic monster!" he snarled, his voice trembling with fury.

Without hesitation, Ethan fired. The first shot hit Eric in the shoulder, the second in the chest. Eric staggered, blood blossoming across his shirt as he struggled to keep his footing.

"This one's for TARA, YOU SON OF A BITCH!" Ethan roared, firing again. Each bullet ripped through Eric, sending him stumbling backward. The sound of pounding boots echoed around us as bikers closed in from the forest, their shouts mixing with the crackle of gunfire.

Eric dropped his rifle, his knees buckling, but Ethan wasn't finished. "AND THIS," Ethan shouted, his voice breaking as he took aim one final time, "IS FOR LUKE, AND THIS ONE…" He fired, the shot landing with lethal precision, "… IS FOR WHAT YOU DID TO GWEN!"

The last shot was deafening, silencing the night as Eric's lifeless body crumpled to the ground, Ethan's voice rose again, trembling with fury and determination. "YOU CAN'T HAVE HER… YOU WILL NEVER TAKE MAEVE!" Ethan shouted, his final words cutting through the night like a blade, leaving no doubt in Eric's mind as the light faded from his eyes. Ethan, spent and shaking, let the gun slip from his grasp as he collapsed forward onto the dirt. His chest heaved with heavy, ragged breaths as men surrounded him, their voices calling out urgently.

Then, the sound we had been waiting for but didn't dare hope to hear. Sirens. Wailing and growing louder, cutting through the night like a promise of salvation.

"Stay with me, come on, girl, stay with me," Roger's voice urged beside me, his hands firm but gentle as he pressed against my wound. My vision blurred, the world spinning, but I could hear it all: the thrum of a helicopter overhead, its spotlight cutting through the darkness, and amplified voices commanding the chaos below.

Three officers descended from the helicopter, landing near the house, while police cruisers pulled up behind the trucks and bikes.

"THE GIRL NEEDS HELP!" Steve's voice boomed as he waved frantically toward the officers. Bikers scrambled, some moving their motorcycles to clear a path for the approaching ambulances. The headlights illuminated the broken battlefield of the yard, revealing bodies, blood, and the remnants of a brutal fight for survival.

Through it all, I stared up at the black sky, my mind reeling with one thought: we were alive. For now.

"Maeve, I'm lieutenant Michaels," he said, kneeling beside me, his voice steady but urgent. "You're safe now. We've got you." He placed a reassuring hand on mine, but his words barely registered. My entire body trembled as tears streamed down my face.

"ETHAN!" I screamed, the force of my voice shaking through me. "Find him! Find my brother!" My plea echoed into the chaos. Michaels' jaw tightened, and he barked orders to the officers swarming the property.

"Get the boy and the other kids! Check the bunker—move now!" he shouted into his shoulder radio. Officers scrambled, their voices overlapping as they relayed commands and spread out across the property.

"LUKE!" I screamed again, trying desperately to lift my head, but the pain in my shoulder was blinding. My vision blurred as I searched for any sign of him. Justin lay nearby, still alive but barely, his gasps audible even over the commotion. Luke, though—Luke was silent.

"SAVE LUKE! PLEASE!" I cried, my voice breaking. "TARA AND GWEN—THEY'RE IN THE BUNKER!"

"I got you, okay? Sweetheart, stay still," Michaels said, his tone softening as he pressed me back down. Then, with a sharp turn, he stood and shouted orders. "Find that son of a bitch! Search the bunker! Now!"

The world around me spun into chaos. Shouts rang out—officers yelling commands, boots pounding against the dirt, the crackle of radios blending with the deafening roar of the helicopter overhead. Everything blurred together into an overwhelming storm of noise and movement. I couldn't stop screaming, the sound ripping from my throat, raw and primal, as if somehow it could fix what had been broken.

Through the cacophony—my screams, the officers' shouts, the clipped voices of dispatch over CB radios—everything froze. Time seemed to slow, stretching each second into an eternity. My vision blurred, tears clouding my eyes, and for a fleeting moment, I saw him.

Uncle Joe.

He was kneeling beside me, his face etched with the familiar kindness I'd known all my life. "Maeve," he said softly, his voice steady and warm despite the chaos around us. "Stay awake, my sweet girl." His words felt like a tether, pulling me back from the edge of despair.

I felt it then—a cold sensation against my hand. Was he holding it? I couldn't tell. My chest heaved as I blinked, trying to clear my vision. His form wavered, shimmering like a reflection on water, and then, as quickly as he had appeared, he was gone.

"No!" I screamed, the sound erupting from me like a dam

breaking. Tears streamed down my face as the weight of everything crashed down. The pain in my body, the relentless noise around me, the utter devastation of what we had endured—it was all too much. My screams turned to sobs, guttural and broken, as the realization hit me with unrelenting force.

This was real. Everything we had experienced—all the terror, the pain—it was reality. And it all started with him. My uncle, the man I loved so dearly, whose kindness had been the cornerstone of my world. I screamed again, louder this time, my cries filled with grief not just for the pain I was in, but for him. For the man whose loss had set everything into motion.

I wept for my uncle, for the innocence stolen from us, and for the nightmare that had become our lives.

Moments later, I felt the rough tug of a stretcher beneath me. My body jolted as they lifted me, and as I was carried through the yard, I caught a glimpse of Luke and Justin, both on stretchers. My arm shot out toward Luke, desperate to reach him.

"LUKE!" I sobbed, my fingers outstretched. An EMT gently but firmly pushed my hand back, strapping it down as they secured me with belts. "No, no, no! LUKE!" My cries were ragged, my voice raw, but the EMTs didn't stop.

"Hold still! Please, hold still!" the female EMT urged, her voice calm but strained.

"ETHAN!" I screamed again, thrashing against the restraints. "MY BROTHER—I NEED MY BROTHER!" Blood poured from the gunshot wounds in my shoulder and arm, soaking through the stretcher beneath me. The pain was unbearable, but I didn't care. All I could think of was Ethan, Luke, and the others.

The female EMT looked to her team, her expression grim. "She's losing too much blood. We need to sedate her!"

Three EMTs worked together, pinning me down as I struggled against them. "No! I need them! Please!" I wailed, my vision fading.

The sharp sting of a needle pierced my arm, and the sedative began to take hold. My body felt heavy, my head spinning. The adrenaline that had kept me conscious drained away, leaving only exhaustion. Through the haze, I caught a fleeting glimpse of the yard outside. Flashing lights illuminated the chaos—officers running, EMTs working frantically, and the distant sound of more sirens approaching.

The world blurred as my eyes fluttered closed, exhaustion and pain pulling me under. The last image I saw before the ambulance pulled away from the metal gates of the manor was my uncle. He stood at the foot of my stretcher, his familiar figure bathed in the flickering red and blue lights. His hand lifted to his lips, and he blew me a kiss—a gesture so simple yet filled with everything I needed in that moment.

And then, as suddenly as he had appeared, he vanished, leaving me with only the memory of his face. My vision faded, and the dark, spinning sky above was all that remained. The rhythmic thud of my own heartbeat pounded in my ears, drowning out the chaos around me as I slipped into the quiet embrace of unconsciousness.

"Well, I'll be damned," Michaels muttered as he rounded the corner of the house and approached Eric's body. Eric was still moving—barely—his blood pooling beneath him. Just a few feet away, Ethan lay on the ground, his breaths short and ragged. His trembling hand remained wrapped around his gun as a few bikers knelt beside him.

"Get an ambulance here! Around the house, NOW! The boy is down!" Michaels barked, his voice sharp and commanding. Officers relayed the message, and EMTs rushed to action.

Overhead, the thumping blades of the helicopter echoed in the chaos. Luke had already been loaded into one and was airborne, while another helicopter landed farther into the wooded area. The bikers revved their engines, clearing a path for the EMTs as they sprinted toward Ethan with a stretcher.

Amidst the commotion, Eric's hand twitched, fingers crawling toward the rifle near his side. His breathing was shallow, his eyes wild with desperation. Michaels froze for a second, then raised his gun.

Eric's hand gripped the rifle, but before he could lift it, Michaels fired. The shot rang out, loud and final. Eric's body jerked, then went still. Silence fell momentarily, the chaos of the night punctuated by the dull thud of the rifle slipping from Eric's grasp.

Ethan, his head turning weakly toward the sound, locked eyes with Michaels as he crouched over Eric's lifeless body. "Maeve…" Ethan stammered, his voice hoarse and broken. His chest rose and fell unevenly, his strength fading fast.

Two EMTs reached Ethan, their hands moving with urgency as they prepared him for transport. Blood stained the ground around him, a grim testament to his injuries and the night's horrors.

"I WANT THIS ENTIRE PLACE RIPPED APART!" Michaels shouted, his voice raw with frustration and anger. "The graveyard, the house, every damn inch of it! Don't leave a single stone unturned. I want answers—I want to know everything that happened here!"

Two officers emerged from the bunker, their faces pale, their hands trembling as they covered their mouths. One of them approached Michaels cautiously, his voice strained with the weight of what he'd seen. "Sir…both females…they're gone. And one of them…" He hesitated, his words faltering. "One of them isn't… all together."

Michaels's jaw tightened, his eyes dark with grief and fury as he turned toward the cellar. He stared at the wooden doors for a long moment, then slammed his fist against the wall. "We came too late," he said, his voice breaking. "We came too damn late!"

His shout echoed through the property, carried by the night wind, as the weight of the carnage pressed heavily on everyone still standing.

• • •

I didn't remember much. The ambulance pulled into the backside of the hospital, where a swarm of doctors and nurses waited, their faces tense with urgency. Overhead, the rhythmic thrum of helicopters filled the air, landing on the nearby pad. Were these the same helicopters that came to save us? Something inside me whispered that they were.

My vision blurred as I was rushed through a set of large double doors. Voices surrounded me—doctors barking orders, nurses shouting instructions—but their words were muffled, distant. I couldn't respond, couldn't even lift my head. My body felt like it was on fire, yet I was numb, detached from the pain.

Through the haze, I thought I saw familiar faces—my parents, their worried expressions flashing in and out of focus. Were they there? Was it real? I couldn't be sure. I didn't even realize that Luke's, Gwen's, and Tara's parents were there too, all following closely as I was wheeled down the hallway toward an ER room.

The white doors swung shut behind me, cutting off the scene. Just before they closed, I caught a glimpse of my mother collapsing into my father's arms, her cries muffled by the chaos.

Everything after that became noise. The sharp cadence of voices, the rapid shuffle of feet, the clatter of medical equipment—it all blended into an overwhelming cacophony. I couldn't make sense of anything. A white mask descended over my mouth and nose, and a calm voice broke through the chaos.

"Breathe deep, sweetheart," they said gently.

It was the last thing I heard before everything faded into darkness.

• • •

Beep. Beep. Beep.

The rhythmic sound echoed around me, breaking through the otherwise suffocating silence. It was all I could hear. My head felt too heavy, and no matter how hard I tried, my eyes refused to open. The silence pressed down on me, drowning everything else.

"I'm so sorry," a doctor's voice carried faintly through the walls. "But Luke… we couldn't save him."

The words shattered the quiet, followed by the heart-wrenching wail of Luke's mother. Her screams filled the waiting room, raw and unrelenting. My mother held her tightly, her own tears streaming down as she tried to comfort the inconsolable woman. Tara's parents, Gwen's parents—they were all there, their grief palpable, their sobs and cries blending into one anguished symphony in the private waiting area.

I knew none of this at the time. I was trapped in a haze, memories and fears twisting together. All I could remember was Eric's face, looming over me like a shadow. His voice rang in my head, cruel and haunting. *"I'm going to cut up that brother of yours and make you watch if you don't keep your mouth shut,"* he repeated, over and over.

My body shook uncontrollably, trembling as his words looped in my mind. My chest tightened, and a sudden jolt coursed through me. I was dimly aware of a voice shouting, but everything felt distant, blurred.

"I NEED NURSES, NOW! SHE'S HAVING A SEIZURE!" My father's panicked voice broke through the fog, sharp and desperate.

And then, nothing. Silence swallowed me again.

AFTERMATH

I DIDN'T REMEMBER MUCH. I didn't know what day it was or even where I was. When I opened my eyes, the room was dim and quiet. Rain tapped against the window to my left, streaking across the glass in heavy, uneven drops. The storm outside mirrored the weight pressing down on me, as though the sky itself was mourning—crying for us, for everything that had happened.

I tilted my head to the right, catching sight of my mother. She was curled up in a chair beside me, wrapped in a thick blanket, her head resting against the armrest as she slept. My father, James, was slumped over the edge of my bed. His hand was clasped tightly around mine, his head bowed as he dozed in the chair next to me.

I squeezed his hand weakly.

His head shot up instantly, his eyes filled with exhaustion but softening as they met mine. "Maeve, sweetheart," he said, his voice cracking with relief. He stood up quickly, leaning over me.

Tears welled in my eyes, but as I tried to speak, I realized I couldn't. Something was in my throat, a hard, foreign object that made it impossible to form words. Panic bubbled up inside me, and I let out a faint, muffled sound.

"Shh, hey… don't try to speak," James whispered, his hand brushing gently over my hair. "You have a tube in your throat to help you breathe."

My gaze darted downward, and I noticed my arms. They were restrained to the bed, thick fabric bands holding them in place. I tugged lightly, my silent question clear: *Why am I tied down?*

James' expression faltered. "I'm so sorry, Maeve," he said quietly, kneeling beside the bed so our faces were level. "You were thrashing… the seizures caused you to rip your stitches open. The restraints are only temporary, I promise." His voice cracked, and tears shone in his eyes.

I started crying harder, my chest heaving with muffled sobs. James pressed his forehead gently against mine, his voice low and desperate. "Please, Maeve. Calm down. Please don't cry. I don't want to have to sedate you again."

But I couldn't stop. The memories came flooding back—Eric, Luke, Ethan, everything—and the panic clawed its way to the surface. My heart raced, the monitor beside me beeping frantically as my blood pressure skyrocketed. My body began to tremble uncontrollably.

James stood, his face pale as he glanced at the machine. He let out a heavy sigh and turned toward a small cart in the corner of the room. He punched a code into the drawer, pulled out a syringe, and filled it with fluid.

"No, please…" I tried to beg him with my eyes, my tears streaming faster.

"I have to, sweetheart," James said softly, his voice breaking as he returned to my side. He removed the cap from the needle, his hand trembling slightly. "You're having an anxiety attack. You'll hurt yourself if I don't."

I felt my body convulse again, my chest heaving as my vision blurred. James leaned closer, his voice barely above a whisper. "I love you, Maeve. This is to help you, I promise." He pushed the syringe into the port of my IV, his eyes filled with anguish.

Within seconds, a warm calm spread through my body, the tension easing like a heavy fog lifting. My eyelids grew heavy, the sound of the beeping monitor fading into a distant hum. My father's face was the last thing I saw before the darkness pulled me under again.

It had been three days since I last woke, and this time, there was no tube in my throat. My voice was coarse and raw as I instinctively reached a trembling hand to my neck, the absence of the restraints both a relief and a mystery. Tilting my head to the right, I noticed the room was different—larger, quieter. My eyes settled on Ethan.

He was here.

He was in my room.

I tried to say his name, but no sound came out. My voice caught in my throat as my gaze focused on him. A tube was taped to his mouth, helping him breathe. His body was strapped to the bed, encased in thick white casts that swallowed both his legs and most of his torso. His chest was bare, stark against the bandages wrapping his arms.

Tears began to spill down my face, hot and relentless. I looked down at myself, my breath hitching as I took in the damage. My right arm was encased in a cast, hanging uselessly at my side. I could barely move it, only my fingers responding weakly. Pain rippled through me, dulled but ever-present, a reminder of how broken I truly was. The medication must have been wearing off; every ache and wound felt sharper by the second.

The door creaked open, and a voice pulled me from my despair. "You're awake!" My mother's voice was soft yet urgent, and in an instant, she was at my bedside. Her hands cupped my face, brushing the damp strands of hair from my forehead.

The sight of her brought a fresh wave of tears. I cried silently, my body too weak for sobs.

"Shh, it's okay, sweetheart. You're alright," she soothed, her hands trembling as they smoothed over my hair. Her presence was grounding, but I could only think of one thing. "Ethan," I rasped, my voice barely a whisper.

Her face tightened, and she leaned closer, her voice trembling. "He's in a coma, Maeve. He has been for days. Your father had to put him under."

The words didn't make sense at first, like they were in a language I couldn't process. "Why?" I whispered, my voice cracking under the weight of my fear.

Her expression broke, a mix of pain and guilt as she whispered back, "He was in so much pain, Maeve. He couldn't handle it. He was thrashing, and he tore out all his stitches. They had to take him into surgery again, and this time, they put him under so he wouldn't hurt himself."

I pressed my trembling hand to my face, trying to stifle the sob that ripped through me. Tears flowed freely, my heart shattering anew. "Ethan," I whispered again, his name a plea, a desperate prayer.

"Shh, shh, my precious," my mother whispered, panic creeping into her voice as she tried to comfort me. Her hands hovered over me, unsure whether to hold or let me be. "Please sleep. Please don't panic. You need to rest."

Her worry was palpable, but I couldn't stop crying. Ethan. My brother. My protector. How could this have happened to him? My tears blurred the room, but one thing was clear—I couldn't lose him.

My body burned with waves of heat and pain, the pressure mounting as anxiety clawed its way through me again. My eyes were locked on Ethan, lying helplessly beside me, his entire body broken and bound in white gauze and heavy casts. He looked so fragile, so unlike the strong, protective brother I had always known.

The sight of him shattered me. Fresh tears streamed down my face, uncontrollable sobs wracking my already weakened body. The sharp ache in my chest matched the raw pain in my heart. I couldn't stop crying, and with every tear, I felt like I was drowning.

"Please, sweetheart, please stop crying!" My mother's voice was desperate, trembling with worry as she hovered near me. Her hands moved uselessly, trying to comfort me but finding no way to reach through the storm of my grief.

"JAMES!" she screamed, panic overtaking her as she called for my father.

He burst into the room moments later, his face pale, his expression shifting from calm to alarm. The surgeon who had been treating us followed closely behind, his presence commanding as nurses swarmed the room like a tide. My father's voice was tight with concern as he asked, "What's happening?"

"She's been having seizures for the past three days," the surgeon explained urgently as he reached my bedside. My body began to shake violently, each tremor pulling me further from the room, from the faces around me. I felt my mother's hand being pulled away from mine as the nurses gently but firmly guided her out of the way.

"Maeve, stay with us," someone said, but the voice felt far away, lost in the haze.

The chaos around me blurred—the sharp scent of antiseptic, the hurried voices of nurses and doctors, the beeping of monitors all blending into a single overwhelming cacophony. My body convulsed again, and I heard my mother crying as my father barked orders, his voice steady but filled with fear.

And then, the darkness took me again. It wrapped around me

like a heavy blanket, quiet and suffocating. Everything disappeared—the pain, the voices, the world—until there was nothing but silence.

...

"Lieutenant Michaels," an officer stationed by the door of Justin's hospital room called out as Michaels approached. Justin's room was heavily guarded, flanked by officers waiting for him to regain consciousness.

"Has the boy woken up yet?" Michaels asked, his voice sharp, eyes scanning the guarded doorway.

"No, sir. According to Dr. Adams, his wounds are critical and severe. It'll be a while before he's stable enough for us to interrogate him," one of the officers replied.

"Good. Because I'll be damned if that boy dies before I get a single ounce of truth out of him," Michaels said, his tone grim. "You boys keep it tight. No one gets near him without clearance, and the moment the hospital says he's awake and ready to talk, you call me. Immediately."

The officers nodded, their postures rigid, as Michaels turned and walked briskly down the hallway, flanked by two other officers. His expression was hard, his eyes betraying the weight of everything he'd witnessed and the lives lost.

Earlier, Michaels had been with the families of Gwen, Luke, and Tara, offering his condolences. He'd stood in front of grieving parents, his hat clutched tightly in his hands, apologizing for not reaching them in time. Despite his heartfelt words, none of them blamed him or the police. How could they? No one had known the horror lurking on that property. What had started as a harmless Halloween outing had turned into a nightmare—a massacre that claimed three lives, and one more: April, the unborn child, a life stolen before it had even begun.

Michaels pressed forward, making his rounds to check on the

wounded bikers before arriving at our room. He stopped outside, took a deep breath, and removed his hat, knocking gently. Inside, my mother sat motionless at my bedside, her fingers twitching against the blanket draped over her lap. My father, seated beside her, stood as Michaels entered.

"Lieutenant Michaels," my father said, offering a firm handshake and gesturing for him to step inside.

"How are they?" Michaels asked, his voice uncertain, his hand nervously smoothing over the brim of his hat.

My father, noticing the tension, nodded slowly. "Both critical," he admitted. "But they're alive. Thank God."

Michaels let out a heavy sigh, his shoulders sagging slightly. "I didn't get the chance to come by when I was here three days ago," he began, his voice low and rough. "But I want to offer my condolences. I know those kids—" His words caught in his throat, and he cleared it, steadying himself. "I know they were family to yours."

"We loved them dearly," my father replied, his voice heavy with emotion. "But this wasn't anyone's fault except Eric's. No one could have known he was on the property."

Michaels nodded solemnly, his jaw tightening. "I appreciate that. I just… I wish we'd gotten there sooner."

"You did everything you could," my father reassured him. "Your team tracked him down to the manor and stopped him. If we hadn't learned the truth about Eric being Maeve's biological father—and a killer—we would've kept thinking he was just a harmless groundskeeper. He almost had us fooled."

Michaels exhaled, his grip tightening on his hat. "I understand. Please tell those kids I'm glad they're safe. We're still investigating the property," he said, his voice quiet but resolute.

My father placed a firm hand on Michaels' shoulder, his glance flickering to my mother, still sitting silently by my side. He didn't want her to hear the details. "Let's step outside," he said, guiding the lieutenant toward the door. Once outside, my father closed the door gently behind them.

"Sorry about that," Michaels said, his voice apologetic but firm. "I didn't want your wife to overhear."

James nodded, his face grim. "I understand. But I need to know everything," he said, his tone steady as he gestured for them to take a walk down the quiet hospital corridor.

...

It had been a week since Ethan and I were admitted to the hospital. Ethan still hadn't woken, and now our father and Dr. Jordan had decided it was time to bring him out of the coma. My mother, however, stood by Ethan's bed, her hands trembling, pleading with them not to proceed.

"No, please! He's too fragile," my mother said, her voice cracking as tears streamed down her face. She reached out, almost as if to shield Ethan from the inevitable.

"Amy, we have to," my father said gently, placing his hands on her shoulders. His voice was steady, but his eyes betrayed his own turmoil. "If he stays in a coma any longer, there's a risk of permanent brain damage. You know this."

"James," my mother whispered, her words soaked in grief. "You don't understand. This will destroy him. He doesn't know about Luke… he doesn't know Tara is gone—or that she was carrying a precious little girl, our grandchild! How can we wake him to that kind of pain? How can you expect him to survive this?" She sobbed, her hands covering her face as her knees buckled slightly under the weight of it all.

"Do you need a moment with your wife?" Dr. Jordan asked softly, his voice a delicate thread in the heavy air.

James shook his head, though his grip on her shoulders tightened briefly. "No. We will wake him," he said with a quiet resolve before turning back to her. "Amy, listen to me. I know Ethan won't handle this news—not yet. We won't tell him anything until his body heals more. But we *have* to wake him, Amy. He needs to heal fully, and we can't risk waiting any longer."

Amy's tear-streaked face hardened momentarily as she looked up at my father. It was the look of a mother torn between protecting her child's heart and trusting in the science that might save his life. With a sharp inhale, she pulled herself away from his grasp, stepping back. "I won't be here when you wake him. I can't… I can't hear him suffer like this. I just can't." Her voice broke as she pressed a trembling hand to her mouth and fled the room, leaving an aching silence in her wake.

I turned my head towards my father, my voice rising with emotion. "No!" I croaked, my throat raw and hoarse. "Mom's right! Ethan can't handle this!"

My father's gaze softened as he approached my bed, sitting down carefully beside me. He took my non-broken hand in his, his touch warm yet firm. "We have to wake him, May," he said quietly, his tone both pleading and resolute.

I shook my head, blinking back tears. "You don't understand," I whispered. "Mom's right. Ethan can't handle this—not now."

James sighed heavily, his fingers brushing against mine as if trying to transfer his calm to me. "Then we won't tell him anything yet," he promised. "Nothing about Luke, nothing about Tara. We'll let his body heal first. But, sweetheart, we need to wake him. He's been through so much already, and his body can't recover like this."

I let out a shaky breath, my eyes flicking away from him to the window. Raindrops streamed down the glass in heavy torrents, mirroring the weight pressing on my chest. "Fine," I whispered finally, my voice barely audible. "But I can't watch. I can't see it."

My father stood slowly, his hand lingering on mine for just a moment before he turned back to Dr. Jordan. Their quiet conversation filled the room as they prepared to wake Ethan. I stared out at the rain, my tears blurring the streaks on the glass.

I prayed silently. Not for myself, not even for Luke, but for Ethan—for his heart, his mind, his soul. I prayed that somehow, waking him wouldn't shatter what little strength he had left.

My father let out a heavy, deep breath as he carefully removed the tube from Ethan's mouth. Ethan's chest rose and fell steadily—he was breathing on his own. Dr. Jordan nodded, holding a syringe in his hand. "You're right about not telling him anything right away," Dr. Jordan said, his tone measured but concerned. My father ran a hand through his hair, his movements heavy with the weight of the moment, as Dr. Jordan injected the syringe into Ethan's IV.

"It'll take about five minutes for him to wake," Dr. Jordan said, his hand resting briefly on Ethan's shoulder. My father nodded silently, his jaw tight, and sat in the chair between our beds, his body rigid with tension. "I've increased his morphine, just in case," Dr. Jordan added, reviewing Ethan's vitals and jotting down notes on his clipboard. Before leaving, he paused at the door, turning back to my father. "When they recover... both of them. Therapy. They'll need it," he said firmly.

My father didn't respond right away, only nodded as Dr. Jordan left the room, leaving us in heavy silence.

"I won't go to therapy," I said abruptly, my voice hollow as my gaze remained fixed on the rain-streaked window. The downpour had eased into a faint drizzle, the sky outside as gray and heavy as my heart.

My father's eyes moved to me, his face lined with pain. Gently, he reached across the space between us, his fingers brushing against my broken hand, a tentative offering of comfort. "May, it's a good idea. You and Ethan need to work through this, especially Ethan. Therapy—"

"THERAPY?" I cut him off, my voice rising sharply, trembling with raw emotion. "Therapy is an *escape* from reality! No one understands what we went through... what we saw... what happened in that manor!" My voice cracked, tears spilling freely down my face. "I SAW MY BEST FRIEND'S BODY! *Gwen!*"

I broke down into sobs, my chest heaving with the weight of

it all. My father stood quickly, coming to sit beside me. He leaned over, cupping my tear-streaked face in his hands, forcing my eyes to meet his.

"Shh, shh, May. Look at me. Don't think about it. Don't go there," he whispered, his voice cracking with desperation.

But I couldn't stop. The dam had broken, and the horrors I'd buried surged out like a flood. "What he did to them, Dad! To Tara and Gwen—he hung them… on *hooks*. Their wrists cuffed in metal, dangling off the ground, bleeding out, dying…" My voice fractured into jagged sobs. "What he *did* to Gwen's body after! What he made Luke—what he made *us* see in that cellar!"

My father's face crumpled, his hands trembling as he held me closer, pressing his forehead against mine. "No, Maeve. Don't. Don't think about that, please," he pleaded, his voice breaking as he tried to absorb my pain. "Push those images out of your head. Please, baby girl."

"HE MUTILATED AND KILLED MY BEST FRIENDS!" I screamed, my voice hoarse, the agony in my chest too great to hold in.

"He took Luke's legs… and killed him. And Ethan… my brother… he tortured Ethan by trying to do the same thing he did to Tara. He made him *watch!*" Tears soaked through the thin hospital gown, pooling at the hollow of my throat. "What Ethan experienced, what he endured, Dad… he'll never be okay again. None of us will."

My father pulled me against his chest, his hand stroking my hair as he whispered broken reassurances. "Maeve, please… please stop crying. You have to push it away. Push it out, sweetheart. Don't let it consume you," he begged, though his own voice trembled with grief.

But I couldn't stop crying. I couldn't push it away. Those images, those screams, those moments of sheer horror—they were seared into my soul, and no amount of therapy would erase them. I knew it. I *felt* it.

Then, a groan. Faint, but distinct. My sobbing stilled as both my father and I turned toward the source of the sound. Ethan. He let out a slow, uneven breath, his chest rising in a labored rhythm, before his eyes fluttered open, unfocused and heavy.

"I'm here, son," my father said softly, rushing to his side. His voice cracked as he reached for Ethan's hand, gripping it tightly, as though holding on could anchor him back to us. I turned my face toward the window, biting my trembling lip to keep Ethan from seeing my tears. But inside, I was breaking all over again.

. . .

Ethan let out a heavy breath, his frustration evident as he remained immobilized in his half-body cast, propped upright in a sitting position. My mother had decided she would feed him his meal this time.

"Mother, you don't have to feed me like this," he muttered, his voice edged with embarrassment, as she sat by his bed holding out a fork of rice and chicken.

"Well, it doesn't look like you can feed yourself yet, young man," she replied matter-of-factly, waving the fork teasingly in front of his face. Her tone softened as she added, "Now, I made this with your favorite seasoning and ingredients, so no excuses."

Ethan groaned, shaking his head in resignation. He leaned forward slightly and took a bite, chewing with a mix of reluctance and appreciation.

From my own bed, I couldn't help but smile as I watched the scene unfold. Though my right arm was broken and, in a cast, I could still manage to eat on my own, one-handed. The table pushed close to me held a plate of mom's homemade food, which tasted as comforting as it always did.

"Yeah, Ethan, eat up!" I teased, flashing him a grin.

He turned his head toward me mid-chew, narrowing his eyes. "Shut it!" he said, his words muffled by the food in his mouth.

Mother chuckled, her patience unwavering, as she scooped up another forkful—this time with corn—and held it out to him. Ethan sighed and took the bite, his gaze lingering on her tired face. Letting out a deep breath, he asked, "Mother, you look like you haven't slept. Did you sleep?"

She waved the fork in front of him again, brushing off his concern. "I'll sleep when I know the both of you will walk out of here and back home," she said firmly.

This time, Ethan raised his left hand, the only part of his body not in a cast, and gently took the fork from her. "My left arm is fine, Mother. I can feed myself. Please, just leave the food here and go home to sleep," he said, his tone quiet but insistent, as he reached for the container.

But mother wasn't having it. She shook her head and quickly reclaimed the container and fork. "I said eat!" she declared with mock sternness, holding the fork out toward him again.

Ethan rolled his eyes, a groan escaping his lips, but he relented and took another bite. My mother's persistence was unyielding as she continued to feed him. Each time he sighed or muttered a complaint, she silenced him with a firm "Eat, and don't say another word. This is my job."

"Mother, I'm 24 years old. You really don't have to feed me like this," he protested between bites, though his voice had softened.

Amy's response was immediate and heartfelt, her tone light but filled with warmth. "Well, Ethan, one thing you don't seem to know about me is this: I might be your stepmother, but you are still my son, and I will feed you as if you were my own."

For a moment, Ethan's face froze, caught between surprise and amusement. Then, with a low chuckle, he pressed his left hand over his mouth and laughed—a genuine laugh, the first one I had heard from him since everything had happened.

Hearing him laugh sent a warmth through my chest that I hadn't felt in weeks. My mother's words, though spoken casually, carried a weight that even Ethan couldn't ignore. He hated it when she called herself his stepmother, a term he had long since dismissed. On every document, Amy and James had declared her as Ethan's mother, omitting the word "step" entirely.

The fact that she brought it up—even jokingly—broke through the heaviness surrounding him. That laugh wasn't just a laugh; it was a small glimmer of hope. It reminded us all, for a fleeting moment, of the strength we could still find in each other.

END GAME

POLICE HAD SCOURED THE MANOR relentlessly for weeks, as private investigators, crime scene technicians, and law enforcement flooded every inch of the property. FBI agents worked side by side with lieutenant Michaels, examining every crevice of the house and the surrounding grounds. The manor, once a grim and silent stage for Eric's atrocities, had become a hive of activity.

The kitchen bore the remnants of the chaos that had unfolded. Empty shell casings littered the floor near the overturned table, their dull glint a haunting reminder of the violence. The broken flare gun lay discarded near the pantry, its purpose spent. Blood stains painted the floor, smeared across the base of the pantry door and pooling near the first aid kit Ethan had used in his desperate attempt to save lives. Every surface was photographed, dusted for fingerprints, and meticulously analyzed for traces of evidence.

"LIEUTENANT!" a sharp voice called from down the hall. Michaels turned sharply, sprinting from the kitchen to the source of the call in what had once been my mother's room.

"What is it?" Michaels demanded as he entered the room. An officer knelt before the open wardrobe, a shoe box in his gloved hands. Its lid had fallen back, revealing a gruesome discovery: photographs—dozens of them—strewn across the floor like discarded memories.

"Look at this," the officer said, his voice low with shock. Michaels crouched beside him, carefully lifting a photograph. Each image was a snapshot of Eric's horrific acts. The box contained more than 50 photographs, far exceeding the 30 known missing persons cases tied to Eric.

"Fifty... no, there's more than fifty here," Michaels muttered, his voice trembling. "This bastard didn't just kill them. He... documented everything." His hands shook as he flipped through the images, each one depicting another layer of Eric's twisted, methodical violence. The realization hit like a sledgehammer: Eric wasn't just a serial killer—he was a meticulous, calculated predator who took pleasure in preserving his crimes.

"Michaels," another voice called. An FBI agent stood by the large patio doors, gesturing for him to follow. With heavy steps, Michaels rose and trailed the agent outside, his heart sinking further as the grim scene unfolded.

The graveyard behind the house had become a macabre excavation site. Shallow graves gave up their secrets as shovels unearthed bones and decaying bodies. Some remains were disturbingly fresh, others reduced to skeletal fragments, their presence a silent testimony to decades of horror.

"How the hell did he manage this?" Michaels asked, his voice hoarse as he surveyed the unmarked graves. "How did he bury all these bodies without anyone noticing? The family's been using this property for over ten years, haven't they?"

The FBI agent shook his head, holding up a tablet displaying property records. "No, sir. The family didn't use the property regularly after Joseph Emerson—Maeve's uncle—took ownership. After Joseph's death, Eric essentially claimed the land for himself. These bodies were brought here over time. This place became his private burial ground."

Michaels leaned in closer, the agent's words slamming into him like a freight train. Eric hadn't just killed; he had transformed the manor into a sanctuary for his sick fantasies. After murdering Joseph and disposing of his body in the Hobbs River, Eric had returned to the property, systematically transporting and burying every victim he had claimed over decades.

"This was all part of his plan," the agent continued, his voice tight with disgust. "Eric Stephenson wasn't just sadistic—he was psychopathic. His methods… the way he preserved bodies before burial… It's almost surgical, like Bundy-level meticulous. The man lived for this."

Michaels wiped a trembling hand over his face, his composure unraveling. Every detail was worse than the last, and the enormity of what had happened on this cursed property was almost too much to bear. The whir of helicopters overhead barely registered as he turned back to the agent.

"This is too much," he muttered, his voice thick with exhaustion and fury. "Keep working. Tear this place apart—every room, every damn grave. I want every piece of evidence cataloged."

He turned abruptly, slapping his hat against his thigh in frustration, and stormed toward the front of the house. The driveway was a desolate mess of broken glass, blood splatter, and tire tracks. The emptiness of it felt like a void, an echo of the lives lost here. As he reached his car, Michaels paused, his jaw tight with resolve.

"I'm going to the hospital. That boy," he growled, "he's not dying on me before I get answers."

With that, he climbed into his vehicle and slammed the door, the engine's roar drowning out the chaos of the scene behind him.

• • •

At the hospital, news of Justin's recovery spread quickly. Officers flanked his room, standing firm at the door to block the flood of reporters desperate to gain access.

"We want to find out what happened at that manor!" a woman holding a microphone barked at one of the officers standing guard. Her cameraman pushed the lens closer to capture every moment of the interaction.

"It doesn't matter. This room is off-limits. No one has access to that boy except authorized personnel," the officer growled, holding up a hand to carefully push the pair back.

"But the state of Nebraska has a *right* to know!" she shot back, her voice rising above the commotion. She shoved her microphone forward, undeterred by the officers' closing ranks in front of her.

Two more officers stepped in, blocking the reporters' view of Justin entirely. Inside the room, lieutenant Michaels stood beside an FBI agent and an interrogation officer, fully prepared to extract every ounce of information Justin had.

"I don't care who you think you are. Back off," the officer snapped, his voice dripping with irritation as he motioned for three others to remove the reporters physically.

"Hey! You can't touch us like this!" the reporter shrieked, twisting her body as the officers began escorting her down the hallway. She turned the struggle into a live segment, her voice loud and righteous as the cameraman scrambled to keep her in focus. "This is an assault on the press! The people *deserve* answers!" she declared dramatically, clearly playing up the tension for the camera.

As she stormed further down the hall, her eyes landed on our room. She adjusted her jacket and strode confidently toward it, her microphone raised as if preparing for her next act. "In light of the disturbing revelations about the fifty bodies uncovered on the Emerson property," she announced into the camera, "we aim to uncover what truly happened that night—"

"EXCUSE ME!" my father's booming voice cut through her monologue. James stepped out of our room and closed the door firmly behind him. His face was stern, his body taut with controlled anger as he blocked her approach.

The reporter turned her attention to him like a predator catching sight of fresh prey. "Mr. Adams, can you comment on the situation at the manor? What do you say to claims that the family might have known something about the killer's activities?"

James didn't flinch. "You're out of line," he barked, his voice firm. "My children are recovering from unimaginable trauma. Have you no shame?"

She leaned in closer, undeterred by his growing anger. "But the public *needs* answers. The media has the responsibility—"

"My *responsibility* is to protect my children," James snapped, cutting her off. "And you're not getting anywhere near them."

Two officers flanked James as the reporter persisted, cameras still rolling. "Why won't you address the fifty bodies? Why hasn't anyone explained how a killer operated on your property undetected for so long?" she pressed, her tone biting and relentless.

James took a step forward, his eyes narrowing. "Get this straight. You're not entitled to harass grieving families to sell your sensational headlines. Stay the hell away from my kids."

The officers stepped in, placing a firm hand on her shoulder. "That's enough," one said, guiding her back down the hallway.

Inside our room, Ethan ran a hand over his face, groaning as the muffled argument reached our ears. "I can't believe this shit," he said, his frustration boiling over. "Why can't they just leave us the hell alone? We're not talking to them. We're not giving interviews."

I sighed, mirroring his frustration. "I hate it too," I admitted, my voice heavy with exhaustion. "I just want it all to go away."

I leaned back against the pillows, staring at the window. For the first time since we arrived, the sun broke through, casting a golden glow across the room. It should've been comforting, but it wasn't. Ethan and I hadn't had a single moment to breathe since everything fell apart, and the relentless media circus made it feel like the nightmare would never end.

The tension in Justin's hospital room was palpable. He sat upright in his bed, the faintest smirk tugging at the corners of his mouth. His hands were cuffed securely, his hospital gown neatly fastened as though he were attending a formal meeting, not an interrogation. He remained unnervingly calm, his dark eyes flicking between the officers like a predator surveying prey.

Lieutenant Michaels leaned forward in his chair, his jaw tight as he placed a tape recorder on the edge of Justin's bed and clicked it on. The small device's mechanical whir was the only sound in the room as Michaels spoke.

"Listen up, boy," Michaels began, his tone cold and deliberate. "I want to know everything. Start talking, and don't you dare leave out a damn detail."

Officer Nathan McDonald, seated across from Justin, unfolded a notepad and adjusted his chair. "I'm Officer McDonald," he said firmly. "I'll be reading you your rights before we begin." He recited them methodically, his voice steady, though his hand trembled slightly as he held the pad.

Justin turned his head slightly toward McDonald, his smirk deepening as if the officer's professionalism amused him. When prompted, Justin responded to each right with a sarcastic drawl that set Michaels' teeth on edge.

"Alright," McDonald said, lowering the pad. "Since that's out of the way, let's start with the basics. Who are you, how did you meet Eric, and what exactly did you do with him?"

Justin's smirk turned into a grin. He didn't answer right away, letting the silence stretch uncomfortably long before finally speaking. "You already know the boring parts. Eric took me in as a kid. That's ancient history." His voice was mocking, his words laced with casual arrogance. "What matters is my hands are clean. I didn't kill anyone. Not a single one."

Michaels narrowed his eyes, his fists clenching. McDonald leaned forward, his voice sharp. "Your hands are clean?" he snapped. "You're telling me you didn't lift a finger while living with one of the most sadistic killers in history? You expect us to believe you've been a spectator to *fifty murders* and had no part in it?"

Justin leaned back, his grin unwavering. "I was Eric's computer," he said smugly. "I took photos, tracked his victims, dug up dirt. Social security numbers, bank accounts, family details. You name it, I found it. But Eric? He did the heavy lifting. The genius behind it all. My job was to watch and listen."

The room fell into a stunned silence. Every officer exchanged glances, their disbelief evident. McDonald stood abruptly, slamming his hand on the chair. The sharp crack echoed through the room, but Justin didn't flinch.

"Don't give me that bullshit," McDonald growled, leaning dangerously close to Justin. "Fifty bodies on that property. Fifty lives taken. And you're telling me you only *watched?* That you documented every single one without getting your hands dirty?"

Justin chuckled darkly, a sound that sent a chill through the room. "Did I forget to mention Eric's first kill?" he said mockingly, his tone dripping with feigned regret. "Where are my manners? Let me start there. She was a real beauty."

"Start talking," McDonald ordered, sitting back down, though his hands gripped the edge of his chair tightly. His knuckles were white with restrained anger.

Justin's voice dropped, becoming almost eerily casual. "Her name was Alyssa. College girl, sweet, shy, no family to notice she was gone. Eric found her on one of his late-night trips. He liked to call it 'fishing.'" He grinned at his own words, as though recalling a fond memory. "He lured her in, tied her up, and—"

"Enough of the theatrics!" Michaels interrupted, his voice cracking like a whip. "Stick to the facts."

"Oh, but the details are the fun part, aren't they?" Justin teased, tilting his head. "He kept her for two weeks. Starved her, tortured her. By the time he killed her, she was practically begging for it."

One of the younger officers standing in the corner turned pale. He swallowed hard, then quickly spun around, stepping toward the door to steady himself. His breath came in short gasps as he leaned against the wall, visibly fighting the urge to hurl.

"And you just stood by?" McDonald pressed, his voice low, his eyes blazing with anger. "You did nothing to stop him?"

Justin shrugged nonchalantly. "I took pictures. Eric liked to document his work. A little souvenir for every masterpiece. He had me build a whole catalog. You'd be amazed at how organized he was. Alphabetical, by date, sometimes even cross-referenced with—"

"Shut your damn mouth," Michaels snarled, slamming his hand on the tape recorder. "You're not some clerk filing papers. You're an accomplice to murder."

Justin's smirk faded, replaced by a blank, calculating stare. "You don't get it," he said quietly. "Eric was unstoppable. You could've raided that manor a hundred times, and you'd still be finding bones. I didn't help him kill anyone. I just made sure he had what he needed."

The room fell silent again, the weight of Justin's words pressing down on everyone present. Michaels leaned back in his chair, exhaling sharply. "We're not done here," he said coldly, standing and motioning to McDonald. "We'll get the rest of it out of you if it takes all night."

As the officers filed out, Justin's smirk returned, his voice trailing after them. "Take your time, gentlemen. I've got nothing but memories."

"How can that boy have his hands this clean?" Nathan muttered, his voice low but tense as he stood in the hallway. His eyes darted toward Justin, who sat upright in his hospital bed, his smirk unwavering. Officers stationed at the door kept watch, their expressions a mix of disgust and restraint as Justin's mocking gaze followed Nathan and Michaels' conversation.

"We still don't know how Maeve fits into all this," Michaels replied, his frustration leaking into his tone. "Why was Eric so obsessed with her? Why did he want her so badly—"

Justin's laugh cut through the hallway like a blade. "Oh, it wasn't just Maeve," he called out, his voice dripping with derision. "He wanted her to break her mother. Amy was the real target, and Maeve was the perfect tool."

Michaels and Nathan exchanged a sharp glance before storming back into Justin's room. This time, Michaels slammed the door shut behind them, the sound reverberating off the walls. Justin's grin widened, a predator cornered yet still in control.

"Let's cut the games," Michaels snapped, leaning forward, his fists clenched. "How does Maeve Adams fall into this mess?"

Justin chuckled, shaking his head. "You're asking the wrong questions, lieutenant," he said, his tone almost sing-song. "Why do you think her uncle bought that property from her mother ten years ago?"

McDonald frowned, his brows furrowed as he glanced at Michaels. "What does Joseph Emerson have to do with this?" Michaels asked, his voice sharp with disbelief.

Justin leaned forward, his cuffs clinking softly against eachother. "Joseph Emerson, your best damn investigator in Nebraska, was onto Eric long before any of you clueless idiots were. He was the only one smart enough to see the truth. That's why he bought the manor. He was getting too close to Eric— too close to ruining everything."

Michaels' jaw tightened as the pieces began to fall into place.

"You're saying Joseph knew?"

"That's why he bought the manor off Maeve's mother," Justin said, a mocking smirk playing on his lips. "Joseph's lead had him sniffing around that property way before Eric ever thought of using it as our… hunting grounds. Or should I say burial grounds." He chuckled darkly, shaking his head as if amused by the perceived incompetence of the officers before him.

"As soon as Joseph set foot on that property—setting up cameras, prepping the shed for whatever he thought was coming—Eric and I decided it was time to take the place and make it ours. Joseph was on us, always watching, always getting too close. He was ready to move in on Eric when—well, when Eric got to him first." Justin laughed again, the sound cold and unnerving.

"Yeah, Joseph almost ruined everything. He got too close, almost caused an endgame for Eric. But Eric, he's patient, you know? Kept that man alive for weeks. A really, really long time." Justin's voice dropped into a gleeful tone as he made obscene gestures with his cuffed hands, mimicking a knife being pulled from its sheath. He added a dramatic popping noise with his mouth, his face lighting up with twisted amusement.

"Kept him tied up and alive in that bunker… tortured him for information. But that man? He kept his mouth shut. Didn't say a word—not until Eric finally cut out his tongue." Justin's grin widened as he pantomimed cutting out a tongue, holding his hands up to his face like a camera and making exaggerated snapping motions. "I enjoyed that moment. Documented it, too. The photos were… *artistic.*"

The room fell silent for a moment as the officers stared at him, their faces a mixture of revulsion and disbelief.

"How do you think he knew Maeve was in Florida?" Justin added, his voice casual as if discussing a mundane topic. His smirk remained, daring the officers to challenge him.

"Boy, you are worse than that sadistic monster. This isn't over—not until I have your ass in jail for a long time," Michaels growled, his voice sharp with restrained anger.

Justin shook his head, a sly grin spreading across his face. "Hey, they won't find any evidence. Like I said, my hands are clean. Trust me, they can flip that place upside down, tear apart every inch of it, but they won't find my fingerprints on a single one of those victims." He held his cuffed hands up mockingly, as if to emphasize his point.

Michaels' jaw tightened, his fists clenching at his sides, but Justin wasn't finished.

"Speaking of which," Justin continued, a glint of satisfaction in his eyes as he leaned forward slightly. "I wasn't done with my story. See, after Eric got wind of Maeve, he killed her uncle— good old Joseph Emerson. Hung him in that cellar for days, like a trophy, while we took a little trip to Florida."

Justin mimed holding a camera, clicking his finger up and down in the air. "Snap. Snap. I documented every moment of Maeve's life for Eric. Every move she made, every place she went—it was all part of the plan."

Michaels' eyes narrowed, his face darkening as Justin laughed, the sound grating and cruel.

"Yeah, that's how I knew they were heading to the manor. I told Eric. Everything fell into place perfectly," Justin added, his voice thick with self-satisfaction. "Eric went back to the manor, dumped that old man's body in the Hobbs River, and set the stage—just as Ethan and Maeve were on their way." Justin let out another laugh, slapping his hand against his leg. "It was perfect. Timing, execution—it all worked out. You've got to admit, Eric was a genius."

Michaels slammed his fist onto the bedside table. "You sick little bastard," he hissed. "Why Maeve? Why target her?"

Justin's expression darkened slightly, though the smirk never fully left his face. "It was about Amy," he said, his voice quieter but no less twisted. "Eric wanted to break her. Torture her. Maeve was just the bait—a means to an end."

McDonald's voice trembled with anger. "Bait for what?"

Justin's grin returned, broader and more sinister. "Eric's *glorious endgame*. He was going to lure Amy to a secluded location. Promise her Maeve in exchange for... well, let's just say, some quality family time."

"Family time?" Michaels barked, his voice rising.

Justin leaned forward, his voice dropping to a conspiratorial whisper. "Amy would've watched as Eric butchered her in front of her daughter. Every. Single. Slice. And then he'd save Maeve for last. A slow, painful death, drawn out for days, just to show her how much he loved her. His *legacy,* he called it."

McDonald surged forward, his hand raised to strike Justin across the face, but Michaels caught him, holding him back. "Not here," Michaels growled, his voice tight with restraint.

Michaels' hands trembled at his sides, his voice barely contained. "Why are you even telling us this, you twisted son of a—"

"Because you can't touch me," Justin interrupted, his voice gleeful. "I never laid a hand on any of them. Eric did the dirty work. Me? I just kept things organized. No fingerprints, no evidence. My hands are clean. Like I said, what is it three times now?"

"You're lying," McDonald said through clenched teeth, leaning forward again. "You documented everything. You tracked those victims. You knew about every single one of them. That makes you just as guilty."

Justin leaned closer, his grin widening. "Prove it."

The two officers glared at him, their fists clenched, their breaths heavy. Behind them, the officers at the door shifted uncomfortably, their eyes flicking between their superiors and the smirking man in the bed.

"Get out of my face," Justin added mockingly. "You've got nothing on me."

Michaels stood abruptly, dragging McDonald toward the door. Before leaving, he turned back, his voice cold. "This isn't over."

Justin's laughter followed them into the hallway as the door slammed shut behind them. Both men stood there, shaken, their thoughts spinning as Justin's words replayed in their minds. Michaels let out a slow breath, his voice low but firm. "We'll nail him. One way or another."

...

Father had decided now was the time to tell Ethan about Luke and Tara, and he wanted me out of the room. A nurse wheeled me away, flanked by police since the hospital was crawling with news reporters. They took me to another room, but I didn't want to leave. My gut told me this moment would break Ethan.

"What is it, Dad?" Ethan said, his voice strained, his arm draped over his forehead. He let out a sharp, heavy breath. Father had raised Ethan's morphine dosage to its limit, knowing he would likely try to harm himself after hearing this news. Father paced the room for a moment before standing next to Ethan's bed.

"No one has answered me," Ethan said again, his tone growing harder. "No one has told me anything about Luke!"

Father froze for a moment, his shoulders sagging under the weight of what he was about to say. He took a long, steadying breath before speaking. "Ethan, I don't know how to tell you this, but... we couldn't save Luke. For ten hours, they tried everything..." Father's words came slowly, carefully, as if cushioning each syllable.

Ethan didn't react right away. His arm remained over his forehead, his expression unreadable. The silence in the room was deafening.

Finally, Ethan let out a low, hollow sound. "Hm."

Father glanced nervously at the heart monitor as Ethan's heart rate began to climb. From the pocket of his white hospital jacket, Father pulled out an ultrasound image and sat down beside Ethan's bed.

"Listen to me, Ethan. I am so… so sorry about Luke," Father said softly, his voice breaking. Ethan showed no visible reaction, his face stone-cold. Father gently placed the ultrasound image on Ethan's bare chest.

This time, Ethan moved. He picked up the sonogram, his trembling hand clutching the small, fragile image. His eyes scanned it, and when he saw Tara's name printed on the top corner, along with the words *Baby Girl, 2 months,* something inside him shattered.

"FUCK!" Ethan roared, the word tearing out of him like a feral scream. His chest heaved as he thrashed against the bed, his fist slamming into the mattress in blind fury. "No… God, no! Please!"

Tears streamed down his face as he held the image tightly against his chest. He clutched it as if it were Tara herself. "Ethan, I am so sorry—" Father began, but Ethan cut him off with another guttural scream.

"GET OUT! GET THE HELL OUT OF MY ROOM!" Ethan bellowed, his voice raw and shaking.

"I can't, Ethan," Father said, his voice firm but breaking with emotion. "Your blood pressure is spiking, and if it gets worse, you could go into cardiac arrest."

Ethan's response was a sound I will never forget. A scream so primal, so filled with anguish, that the walls of my room, which was next door, seemed to vibrate. My heart dropped as I heard the noise, the pain in my brother's voice almost too much to bear. I tilted my head toward the wall, straining to hear more.

"Take me back! Please take me back to my room!" I shouted at the nurse. The officers kneeling beside my wheelchair shook their heads apologetically. "We were told not to, Maeve. I'm so sorry," one of them said, his voice low.

I slammed my fists against the armrests of the wheelchair, my tears falling uncontrollably. "ETHAN NEEDS ME! TAKE ME BACK RIGHT NOW!" I screamed, my voice shaking with desperation.

The nurse placed her hand on my wrist, her face tense with worry. "We need help in here!" she shouted, calling for more staff. Three other nurses came rushing in, one holding a syringe.

"No! No!" I cried, thrashing in the chair. The officers stepped in to hold me down as I screamed Ethan's name over and over.

"Sedate her now," one of the nurses said, her voice sharp. I felt the sting of the needle in my arm, and my body began to slow. My screams faded into broken sobs as the world around me blurred. The last thing I heard before darkness consumed me was Ethan's raw, tortured cry echoing through the walls.

Ethan's entire body shook with rage and grief, his emotions spiraling completely out of control. The moment my father told him the truth, it was as if something inside Ethan snapped.

"Tara... why... why?" Ethan choked out, his voice cracking as he clutched the ultrasound image to his chest. His breathing grew ragged, tears streaming uncontrollably down his face. "This is all his fault. Eric... that sadistic, sociopathic monster. HE DID THIS!" Ethan's voice grew louder, filled with venom and anguish as his body writhed in the bed.

"I need nurses in here now!" Father shouted, panic overtaking his voice. Ethan's thrashing had torn through the stitches in his chest and side, causing fresh blood to seep through the bandages. The heart monitor screamed as Ethan's heart rate skyrocketed.

"OH GOD, PLEASE NO!" Ethan screamed, his voice reverberating through the room as if trying to purge the unbearable pain. Nurses flooded in, Dr. Jordan rushing to his side.

"We need to sedate him—he's going to have a heart attack!" Dr. Jordan barked, his voice sharp and commanding. "Get me a syringe!" One of the nurses darted to the cart, grabbing the necessary supplies as Ethan's convulsions worsened.

"Ethan, calm down, son. Please!" Father pleaded, his voice breaking as he tried to hold Ethan down. "You need to reduce the pressure on your body, please—"

"CALM DOWN? CALM DOWN?" Ethan shouted, his voice ragged and raw, each word like a dagger. "WHAT THE HELL IS WRONG WITH YOU? HOW CAN YOU TELL ME TO CALM DOWN?" His fist slammed against the nightstand with a sickening crack, leaving a visible dent in the metal surface. Blood dripped from his hand where the impact had split his knuckles.

Father grabbed Ethan's arm, pinning it against the bed as nurses scrambled to restrain him. "Ethan, stop—please!" Father begged, but Ethan's fury was beyond containment.

"GET THE HELL OUT OF MY ROOM!" Ethan screamed again, his chest heaving as his breaths came in rapid, shallow gasps. His body trembled violently, the heart monitor beeping erratically. Ethan's eyes widened in panic. "What's happening... what's... happening to me?" His voice faltered as he clutched his chest, struggling to catch his breath.

"His heart is racing! We're losing him!" a nurse shouted.

Dr. Jordan moved swiftly, injecting the sedative into Ethan's IV line just as his heart rate spiked dangerously close to arrest. "We need to stabilize him now!" he commanded. Ethan's body jerked once, twice, and then he slumped back into the bed as the sedative took hold.

The room fell into an eerie silence, save for the steady beeping of the heart monitor gradually returning to a normal rhythm. Nurses worked quickly to re-stitch Ethan's wounds and secure his arms and legs with restraints to prevent further damage.

Father stood frozen for a moment, his hand gripping the edge of Ethan's bed as he watched his son's unconscious form. "God, I didn't think telling him this would nearly kill him," he said, his voice barely above a whisper.

Dr. Jordan glanced at the heart monitor, documenting Ethan's vitals with a grim expression. "It had to be done, James," he said quietly, his tone firm but gentle. "You couldn't keep this from him forever. And at least he's in the hospital, where we could act quickly. Be grateful for that."

Father nodded, sinking into the chair beside Ethan's bed. He ran a trembling hand over his face, exhaling deeply as the adrenaline began to wear off. "Sometimes," he said, his voice breaking, "I hate my job."

In the room next door, I lay sedated, unaware of the chaos unfolding on the other side of the wall. My body was still, my mind caught in a fog of drugs and exhaustion, oblivious to the storm Ethan had unleashed. For now, I remained in my own cocoon of darkness, shielded from the truth I was desperate to face.

ONE YEAR LATER

IT HAD BEEN TWO DAYS since Ethan learned the fate of Luke and discovered he had a daughter. Today, we were given a one-day release from the hospital to attend the funeral of our beloved friends. Luke, Tara, and Gwen's parents had arranged for an extremely private ceremony outdoors, where they would be laid to rest together. An ambulance transported Ethan and me to the cemetery, where it waited for us to return afterward. Mom and Dad sat next to Luke's parents while Ethan and I were wheeled down the aisle to join them.

The sound of roaring motorbikes suddenly filled the streets surrounding the cemetery. Father stood, as did Luke's father. I tilted my head and saw a group of bikers arriving, their presence commanding attention. At the front of the group was Roger, the bartender. They had ridden twelve hours from Trenton to attend the funerals of our friends and my uncle. Tears streamed down my face when I saw them approach. Ethan, overwhelmed by his grief, could barely lift his eyes to meet Roger's gaze.

The bikers weren't there just to pay their respects—they had been invited as a shield. News reporters had swarmed the cemetery grounds, their flashes and shouts breaking the solemn atmosphere as they tried to capture images and spread information about the ceremony. Cameras perched on tripods lined the gates, and reporters strained to peer through the bikers' imposing presence, which formed a protective wall around us.

One reporter, standing at the edge of the grounds, gestured toward the gathering with a microphone in hand. "We are unable to give you any footage of the event here. It seems a group of bikers is blocking our view," she reported live, her frustration evident as she gestured toward Roger and his group, who stood firm, arms crossed, glaring back at the press.

"Thank you for inviting us," Roger said quietly, shaking the hands of Luke's father and my dad. Then, he turned to me, his expression heavy with sorrow. The bikers, who had been there the night everything happened, approached Tara, Gwen, and Luke's parents, offering their condolences and expressing regret for not acting sooner.

"I'm so sorry to the both of you," Roger said softly, bending down to meet my eyes. "And I'm grateful you're both still here, considering the circumstances... though I know my words mean little." He gently touched my hand, and I managed to nod before he leaned forward, giving me a delicate hug. Ethan remained motionless in his chair, unable or unwilling to speak. His lower body was still encased in casts, and he wore an open-backed hospital shirt because of the cast immobilizing his right arm. He didn't react to Roger's words or presence, lost in his own internal pain.

The ceremony began, and a priest stood at a pedestal, speaking solemnly about Tara, Gwen, and Luke. His words were meant to comfort, to remind us of their love, kindness, and the joy they had brought to everyone who knew them. But the weight of their absence felt unbearable, as if no words could ever fill the void they left behind. My mother held my hand tightly, her tears soaking the tissues she clutched, while my father and Roger remained close to Ethan, silently supporting him.

The service lasted an hour. When the time came to lower the caskets into the ground, we were allowed a moment to say our goodbyes. Father wheeled Ethan closer to the graves, positioning him between Tara's and Luke's caskets. Ethan placed his trembling hand on Tara's casket, his eyes fixed on Luke's. I watched him, my heart breaking as he silently cried, his shoulders shaking with grief he couldn't contain.

I lowered my head, whispering a prayer for Tara, Gwen, and Luke. The weight of the moment pressed down on all of us, the finality of their loss settling like a stone in my chest. The caskets began to descend, and Ethan's quiet sobs turned into loud, gut-wrenching cries that echoed through the cemetery.

Father and Mother gently pulled us back as the caskets disappeared from view, but Ethan couldn't contain himself. His cries grew louder, raw and unrelenting. It was as if every ounce of strength he had left crumbled, leaving him vulnerable and shattered. I wanted so desperately to wrap my arms around him, to comfort him in some way, but my broken arm and my own frailty left me powerless. All I could do was watch, my tears streaming as Tara, Gwen, and Luke's parents broke down as well, their grief spilling out in waves of anguish.

The funeral for Uncle Joe was scheduled for the following week. It would be a larger event, honoring his legacy as a private investigator and his contributions to the police department. A police escort would lead the procession through our neighborhood, and my aunt would receive an award for my uncle's dedication and sacrifice.

"Please... take me out of here," Ethan said suddenly, his voice trembling as he turned his tear-streaked face toward our father.

"All right, son. Let's go back to the hospital," Father said gently, wheeling Ethan away from the gravesite. An EMT arrived to assist, taking over Ethan's wheelchair while another EMT moved mine. Mother stayed behind with Tara, Gwen, and Luke's parents to offer her support as they continued to grieve.

Inside the ambulance, Ethan was transferred onto a stretcher, and so was I. As soon as the doors closed, Ethan broke down completely, his emotions crashing over him like a tidal wave. His sobs filled the confined space, raw and unrelenting. "Why... why did it have to be them? Why couldn't it have been me?" he cried, his voice cracking under the weight of his sorrow.

I lay on my own stretcher, helpless to do anything. I wanted to comfort him, to tell him something, anything, that could ease his pain. But I knew there were no words that could reach him in that moment. All I could do was watch and cry silently alongside him, knowing that our lives would never be the same.

. . .

Justin was released from the hospital two days later, walking out in handcuffs, flanked by officers and Michaels. As they passed our room, Justin turned his head, peering in briefly. His eyes locked with mine for a fleeting moment, and then he smirked, tapping his hand against his head as if to say, *See you around.* I refused to give him the satisfaction of a reaction, diverting my gaze instead to Ethan, who lay sedated for his own safety. My stomach churned with rage and helplessness, but I buried it, knowing Ethan needed me steady.

The following week, we were granted release to attend our beloved uncle's funeral. My aunt Mary and parents were transported by police in a black car, while Uncle Joe's casket followed in a hearse draped with the flag of honor. Ethan and I were taken in a separate ambulance, each of us still fragile but determined to be there. This funeral felt different from the ceremony we had attended for Luke, Tara, and Gwen.

We waited at the cemetery, joined by Luke, Tara, and Gwen's grieving parents. Thirteen bikers, led by Roger, formed a protective perimeter around the grounds, shielding us from the relentless news reporters who had invaded every corner of our lives. Cameras flashed incessantly at the gates as reporters clamored for a glimpse of the procession. Roger's men stood like sentinels, their sheer presence blocking the reporters' view. One reporter, defiant, spoke into her microphone: "We're unable to capture any footage of the ceremony due to the presence of these bikers. They've effectively shut down any access to the grounds."

The sound of motorbikes echoed in the distance, followed by the wail of police sirens. The air grew heavy with reverence as the procession arrived. The police escort and motorbikes flanked the hearse, signaling a moment of honor for the man who had devoted his life to justice—and lost it pursuing a sadistic monster.

As the ceremony began, everything around me felt surreal, like a movie playing out in slow motion. My memories of that hour blurred into fragments: the priest's words, the folding of the flag, the haunting crack of gunfire as the officers saluted our uncle, and the mournful sound of a lone trumpet playing *Taps*. My mother and aunt wept uncontrollably, their sobs mingling with the solemn tones of the ceremony.

Ethan and I couldn't contain our emotions either. The weight of grief was too much to bear. By the time Uncle Joe's casket was lowered into the family plot, Ethan's silent tears turned into gut-wrenching sobs. "Tara... why... why her?" he whispered, his voice trembling with anguish. His words pierced the air, raw and unfiltered.

"Take me out of here," Ethan said to our father, his voice barely audible through his tears. "All right, Ethan," Father replied, his voice heavy with understanding. He wheeled Ethan toward the waiting ambulance. An EMT came to assist me, gently guiding my wheelchair. I glanced back at the casket, the final resting place of a man who had sacrificed so much, and tears streamed down my face as I was loaded into the ambulance alongside Ethan.

Once inside, Ethan was placed on a stretcher. The moment the doors closed, he broke down completely. His grief came in waves, crashing over him with an intensity that left me speechless. "It should've been me… it should've been me instead of them," he sobbed, clutching the photo of April, his unborn daughter, taped to the heart monitor. "I failed them all. I couldn't save any of them."

I wanted to comfort him, to find the words that might ease his pain, but I knew nothing I could say would reach him in that moment. His sorrow was too vast, too consuming, and all I could do was sit beside him, crying silently as his anguish filled the small space.

• • •

Meanwhile, back at the station, Justin was undergoing a tense and relentless interrogation. Officers investigating the manor had uncovered a box containing a meticulously organized album. Each page was handwritten by Justin—a grotesque catalog of horrors. It detailed names, ages, birthdates, photographs, IDs, and personal effects from every victim Eric had claimed. Every abduction, every murder, every location, and every moment of torture had been logged with precision.

When lieutenant Michaels saw the album, his frustration boiled over. Storming into the interrogation room, he threw it down in front of Justin, the pages scattering slightly on impact. "Explain this!" he demanded, his voice shaking with anger.

Justin smirked, leaning back with an air of infuriating arrogance. "Told you I documented everything as Eric requested," he said, crossing his arms as if he were proud of his work. "My hands are clean."

Michaels' jaw tightened, his eyes narrowing as he leaned in

closer. "You think this clears you? You think writing down the details of fifty murders makes you innocent?"

Justin shrugged, unfazed. "I told you before: I was just his assistant. I tracked victims, gathered their info, logged everything he wanted. But I never laid a finger on any of them." His tone was dripping with mockery, his smirk unrelenting.

The officers in the room exchanged uneasy glances, their disbelief palpable. Michaels pressed harder, his voice rising with controlled fury. "You expect us to believe that you had no part in this? You cataloged their lives and their deaths like trophies. You're just as guilty as Eric."

Justin tilted his head, his smirk deepening. "Think whatever you want, lieutenant. But my hands are clean."

The interrogation stretched on for thirteen grueling hours. Nathan McDonald, the lead interrogator, pushed Justin repeatedly, his voice growing sharper with each question. Justin, however, remained defiant. Finally, he leaned forward, his tone sharp and mocking. "I'm done talking. Clearly, you all think I had something to do with this somehow, but like I said—my hands are clean. Now get me my fucking lawyer." He leaned back, crossing his arms with a smug grin, refusing to say another word.

Michaels slammed his fist against the table in frustration, his knuckles turning white. The room fell silent, the weight of Justin's unrepentant demeanor suffocating.

Outside the room, the officers who had been reviewing the album exchanged grim looks. One muttered under his breath, "How can someone document all that and think they're innocent?"

Michaels stormed out of the room, shaking his head. "We're not done with him," he growled. "He thinks his 'clean hands' are going to save him. But we'll bury him with the evidence he so proudly kept."

...

About a week later, the case against Justin progressed, and his trial began. To everyone's astonishment, he had secured one of the country's most powerful lawyers—someone who had ties to both Justin and Eric. I remember turning on the hospital TV one afternoon to see full media coverage of the courtroom proceedings. Reporters were dissecting every detail of the case, the courtroom filled with spectators eager to see justice served.

"Turn that shit off," Ethan said sharply from his bed, his voice heavy with frustration. I clicked the remote, silencing the coverage, though I couldn't shake the hope that Justin would be convicted for his involvement and not allowed to walk free.

The prosecution hoped to convict Justin based on the album and the overwhelming evidence presented in court. Michaels worked tirelessly to convince the jury that Justin was not just an accomplice or an accessory after the fact but that he had played an active role in the murders.

The goal was to secure a ten-year prison sentence. However, after two trials resulted in hung juries, the final verdict came in: accessory after the fact. The jury ultimately believed Justin's involvement was limited to being an accomplice.

The judge handed him a five-year sentence—the maximum allowed for the conviction. Justin, ever defiant, smirked and laughed as he was led out of the courtroom on verdict day, his arrogance filling the air like a bitter reminder of the justice that had slipped through the cracks.

I turned to Ethan, studying him carefully. He looked so different now—his once bright demeanor replaced by a heavy weight of hate, rage, and grief. His eyes held a hollow darkness that I feared would never leave.

I slowly shifted myself out of my bed, my legs still unsteady but strong enough to carry me across the room. Carefully, I sat down next to Ethan on his bed. He turned his head slightly toward me, his jaw tight, his chest rising and falling with measured breaths.

"When we get out of here…" he began, his voice trailing off as he stared at the photo of April taped to the heart rate monitor beside him. I reached out and placed my hand over his. He squeezed it tightly, his grip filled with pain and determination.

I didn't know what he was thinking in that moment, but I could feel the storm inside him. And as I looked into his eyes, I realized that neither of us would ever be the same. The scars of what we endured ran deeper than the physical wounds, and no trial, no justice, would ever erase them. The silence between us spoke volumes. The weight of everything we had endured hung in the air, unspoken but deeply felt. And for the first time, I realized that survival wasn't the end of the battle—it was only the beginning.

Three weeks later, I was released from the hospital. My cast was still on, and the stitches were set to come out in a few weeks. Ethan, however, remained hospitalized, bedridden for what felt like an eternity. His casts would stay for another month before they could be removed, and even then, his road to recovery was far from over. Mother and I took turns staying with him, ensuring he was never alone, but he was different now—cold, distant, and locked in his own grief.

When we were with him, he wouldn't speak. No jokes, no sarcastic comments, nothing that hinted at the Ethan we knew. Instead, he would stare blankly out the window or sleep, his silence louder than any scream. Mother tried to coax him out of it, sitting beside him and reading to him, but Ethan's only response was a heavy sigh or the occasional turn of his head away from her.

"Ethan, sweetheart," she said gently one evening, brushing his hair away from his forehead, "we're here for you. Please, talk to us. Let us help."

But Ethan didn't respond. He closed his eyes, shutting her out as tears welled up in her eyes. I stood by the door, helpless, watching the heartbreaking exchange.

When his casts were finally removed, it marked the beginning of the grueling process of physical therapy—a new kind of torture. Eric's brutal attack had left Ethan paralyzed from the waist down, and the therapists warned us it would take months of intense work before he could regain any semblance of mobility.

I remember sitting in the therapy room, my heart breaking as I watched him struggle. Ethan groaned and screamed in pain as therapists moved his legs, adjusted his back, and trained his body to work again. His frustration boiled over more than once.

"Damn it! Stop! Just stop!" he shouted one afternoon, gripping the rails so hard his knuckles turned white. "It's not working! None of this is working!"

The therapists tried to calm him, but Ethan's fury was a force of its own. I sat on a bench, my hands pressed over my ears, tears running down my face because I couldn't bear to see him like this. He was my brother, my protector, and now he was the one who needed saving.

Months passed. Slowly, the pain began to subside, and Ethan started making progress. The day he took his first steps was nothing short of miraculous. The room was filled with tension as he grasped the parallel bars, his jaw clenched in determination. Two therapists stood on either side of him, another behind him holding a support belt. I stood at the end of the rails, my hand extended toward him.

"You've got this, Ethan," I said, my voice steady despite the lump in my throat. "Come on. One step at a time."

He let out a deep breath, his grip tightening on the bars. Slowly, he moved his left foot forward, the muscles in his leg trembling with effort. His right leg followed, dragging slightly because of the metal bar holding his shattered femur together. He winced but didn't stop.

"Yes! That's it! Keep going, Ethan. You're doing it!" I encouraged, my voice rising with excitement.

He pushed forward, step by agonizing step, his face a mask of determination. By the time he reached the end of the rails, sweat dripped from his brow, but there was a flicker of something in his eyes—pride.

Ethan let out a shaky breath, his body sagging against the support belt. "I... I did it," he whispered, almost as if he didn't believe it himself.

I rushed to him, my broken arm forgotten for a moment as I touched his shoulder. "You did it, Ethan. You're walking. You're really walking," I said, tears streaming down my face.

The therapists clapped, congratulating him, but Ethan barely noticed. He turned his head toward me, his lips twitching in what could have been the beginnings of a smile. It was the first glimmer of hope we had seen in him since that horrific day, and for the first time, I allowed myself to believe that we might just find our way back.

Within five months, Ethan was finally released from the hospital. The day had arrived, and I couldn't help but feel a surge of emotion as I parked my car and walked toward the main doors. Dad stood next to him for support as Ethan emerged, walking carefully with a single crutch under his arm. The moment the fresh air hit his face, Ethan tilted his head back, letting out a deep, relieved breath. His eyes fixed on the clear blue sky, and for the first time in months, I saw something in him I thought I'd never see again—peace. He was back. My brother had clawed his way out of his own dark nightmare, walking again, the color in his face restored.

"Careful driving home, Maeve," Dad said, his voice calm but firm as he helped Ethan ease into the passenger seat.

I nodded and gave him a small smile. "I will, Dad."

We were living with our parents again, a temporary arrangement so Ethan could recover properly. Though he could walk now, he still relied on a wheelchair for long distances. The metal bar in his leg, holding his shattered femur together, caused bouts of excruciating pain that left him immobilized at times. He remained on painkillers, his recovery still a long road ahead.

Sliding into the driver's seat, I adjusted my seatbelt and glanced over at Ethan. He sat quietly, holding the sonogram of April, staring at it as though it were the most fragile and precious thing in the world.

"Hey," I said softly, reaching out to touch his hand. "You're okay, Ethan."

He turned to look at me, his tired eyes filled with a deep sadness, but also with strength. He clasped his hand over mine, squeezing it gently but firmly.

"We're okay," I added, my voice steady despite the lump in my throat. "I know this is going to be hard, but Dad thinks… maybe we should take therapy classes."

Ethan let out another heavy breath, his fingers brushing the edges of the sonogram before tucking it carefully into his shirt pocket. For a moment, I thought he might argue, but instead, he shook his head slightly.

"Not right now, Maeve," he said, his voice low and rough. "I just can't. Not yet." He squeezed my hand again, holding on for a moment longer before releasing it.

I nodded, respecting his decision. "Okay," I whispered, turning my attention back to the road as I started the car.

Dad stood outside the hospital, watching us with a protective gaze until we pulled out of the lot. The drive home was quiet, the silence heavy but not unbearable. I glanced at Ethan now and then, thankful that he was still here, still fighting, still my brother. For now, that was enough.

When we arrived home, I helped Ethan walk into the house, his arm slung over my shoulder as he held the crutch against his right side. Mother and Aunt Mary were waiting at the door, their faces lighting up the moment they saw us. I was surprised to see Aunt Mary—she hadn't been around much since the funerals, save for a few brief visits to the hospital. She, too, was staying with Mother and Father for a while. She wasn't ready to return to her empty home just yet and was having a hard time parting with Uncle Joseph's belongings. Despite living just three houses down from us, she wanted the comfort of family close by, and we loved her dearly for it.

"Welcome home," Aunt Mary said softly, her voice warm as she kissed each of us on the cheek.

Mother followed suit, smiling through the tears welling in her eyes. Together, we helped Ethan into the living room, easing him onto the couch. As he settled down, my eyes caught sight of two metal, military-style boxes sitting on the coffee table. Curious, I glanced at Ethan, who noticed them too.

"What's in the boxes?" Ethan asked, his voice low and tired but laced with curiosity.

Mother closed the door behind us while Aunt Mary took a seat across from the table. She gently rubbed her hands over the lids of the boxes, a faint smile breaking through her sadness.

"Your Uncle Joseph left these for you," Aunt Mary began, her voice steady but tinged with emotion. "He loved you both so much. He made me promise that if anything ever happened to him, these boxes would go directly to you." Her hand trembled slightly as she turned the keys in the locks and lifted the lids.

Inside each box were legal documents and two large yellow envelopes. Mother sat down beside me as Ethan, and I carefully pulled out our envelopes. I opened mine slowly, unsure of what I would find, and gasped softly when I saw what was inside. Ethan did the same, his expression unreadable at first.

"He left us…" Ethan started, his voice trailing off as he stared at the contents.

Inside was a significant portion of Uncle Joseph's pension, enough for each of us to buy our own homes or start businesses if we wanted. There was a letter accompanying it, explaining why he had left this to us, his words filled with love and pride. Ethan held his tightly, rereading the letter several times.

Aunt Mary's envelope contained a substantial amount as well, enough to support her for the rest of her life. It was a combination of his time in the military, his career as a private investigator, and his savings. Tears filled her eyes as she silently traced the edge of the letter he had written to her.

In our envelopes, there was also a framed badge from his military service—one for Ethan and one for me. But what caught my breath was a document that seemed out of place: the land title deed to the manor. I stared at it, my heart pounding in my chest, before looking up at Mother.

"Mom, what's this?" I asked, holding up the deed as Ethan examined his own.

Mother's face softened, and she reached over to touch my hand gently. "Your uncle wanted to make sure Eric could never get his hands on that property. He put the land under both your names as a safeguard," she explained. "He was a very smart man and knew exactly what he was doing."

She went on to explain how investigators at the manor had found a box of instructions from Uncle Joseph. In it, he detailed why he had bought the property from my mother years ago and how, unbeknownst to her, the deed she had signed over was in Ethan's and my names, not his. When the investigators handed the box to Aunt Mary, they assumed its contents were meant for her, but they were, in fact, for us.

Ethan's eyes widened with surprise and shock. He looked at the deed, then at me. "Why would he trust us with something this big?" he murmured, his voice barely audible.

"Because he believed in both of you," Mother said firmly, her eyes glistening with tears. "And he knew you would honor his legacy."

Aunt Mary reached into her pocket and pulled out a small key, holding it out to Ethan. His hands trembled slightly as he took it, the weight of its significance hitting him hard. He stared at it for a moment before nodding silently.

"You both deserve this," Aunt Mary said softly, her voice breaking slightly. "You deserve everything he left you. He loved you so much."

At that moment, as if on cue, the timer in the kitchen chirped loudly. "Cake's done!" Mother said, her voice a mix of cheerfulness and emotion.

Aunt Mary stood and followed her to the kitchen, leaving Ethan and me alone in the living room. We both stared at the boxes in front of us, the weight of what they represented settling heavily on our shoulders.

Ethan turned the key over in his hand, his expression unreadable, before finally placing it on the coffee table. "What are we supposed to do with all of this?" he asked quietly, his voice thick with emotion.

I didn't have an answer. I just sat beside him, my hand resting lightly on his arm, as we both tried to process the enormity of what our uncle had entrusted to us.

"We're supposed to live, Ethan. We're supposed to live!" I said after a few moments, my voice firm yet trembling with emotion. He looked at me, his gaze heavy with unspoken thoughts, then turned to the box in front of us. Letting out a deep breath, he finally nodded, the weight of it all settling over him.

• • •

It had been a year since the events at Aberdeen Manor left Ethan and me broken, claiming the lives of our beloved friends. This was the first time since then that Ethan and I returned to the manor—our family home. As I carefully pulled through the broken metal gates that once proudly bore our family name, I glanced at Ethan. Our breaths hitched simultaneously as the manor came into view.

The property was unrecognizable. The once eerie graveyard in the back was now nothing but churned soil, sealed and cleared by authorities. The far gate in the brick wall had been welded shut, and the shed was reduced to rubble. Nothing of it remained. As I drove into the circular driveway, the only structure still standing was the statue of our great-great-grandmother, watching over the house like a somber sentinel.

I parked the car at the base of the crumbling stairs leading to the wraparound porch. Ethan opened his door cautiously, his movements deliberate as he leaned heavily on his cane. I walked around to his side to help him out of the car, slipping my arm around his waist to steady him.

"I don't even know why we came back here," Ethan muttered, his voice laced with a mix of anger and sorrow. His eyes scanned the manor, cold and vacant as the memories of that night flooded his mind.

I tightened my grip on him, pulling him into a side hug. "Uncle wanted us to seal this place, rebuild it, and make sure no one could ever set foot here again," I reminded him softly. Ethan nodded, his jaw tightening as he let out a shaky breath.

Ever since the news broke about Eric's killings and the bodies found on our manor, we've had countless unwelcome guests attempting to enter the property—whether for pictures or the thrill of what happened here. Because of this, Ethan and I decided to completely rebuild the property, starting with a stronger, sturdier gate, and restore the once-beautiful home we shared. We wanted to ensure no one dared to enter—not for a joyride, not for thrills, and certainly not for pictures.

Our goal was simple: to let our home rest and allow it the peace it deserved.

We took the steps slowly, making our way onto the wraparound porch. The air felt heavy, as if the house itself still carried the weight of everything it had witnessed. That's when I saw him—our uncle.

"Uncle!" I called out, my voice trembling with shock and disbelief.

Ethan froze, his hand tightening around his cane as he turned toward me. "He's here?" Ethan asked cautiously, his eyes darting around the empty porch, searching for a figure only I could see.

Leaning casually against the porch railing, Uncle Joseph

smiled, a look of relief washing over his face. "My beautiful May, my Ethan," he said warmly, straightening himself. His presence felt so real, yet I knew this was his final goodbye.

"He's right here," I whispered to Ethan, gesturing toward Uncle. Ethan's gaze followed my hand, though his eyes held nothing but confusion. "He's smiling at us," I added, trying to convey the peace Uncle seemed to radiate.

Ethan's lips parted slightly as if he wanted to say something, but he stayed silent, waiting for me to relay Uncle's words. Uncle chuckled softly, his laugh as familiar and comforting as ever.

"Ethan," he began, his voice filled with pride, "you are still the same—curious, questioning, always wanting to understand. Stay that way."

Tears welled in my eyes as I repeated Uncle's words to Ethan. "He says you're still the same and to never lose that part of your-self," I said, my voice trembling.

Uncle turned his gaze to me, his eyes full of love. "And you, my beautiful May. You are the most amazing, strong girl I've ever known. Stay exactly as you are. Don't change," he said, his voice thick with emotion.

I relayed his words, forcing a small, tearful smile. "He says I'm amazing," I joked lightly, trying to ease the heaviness in the air. Ethan let out a soft laugh through his tears, but his expression grew serious again. "Uncle…" he started, his voice cracking. "Do you know… Tara, Luke, Gwen… are they at peace?"

Uncle's face softened further, and he nodded. "They are at peace, Ethan. I saw them off myself. And Ethan…" Uncle paused, his voice steady yet heavy with meaning. "You have the most precious little girl. She is at peace too. Let your heart rest."

I repeated his words to Ethan, who let out a ragged breath and leaned against the porch railing for support. "Thank you," Ethan said quietly, his voice barely above a whisper. "Thank you for watching over them."

Uncle smiled, his gaze turning to me. "Now, May, my time has come. My work here is finished, and I must cross over."

Tears streamed down my face as I nodded, unable to speak. Ethan noticed my tears and stepped closer, wrapping his arm around my shoulder.

"He's crossing over now," I whispered to Ethan, my voice breaking.

Uncle placed his hand over his heart, his final gesture of love. "I love you both dearly," he said, his voice growing faint. "Tell Mary… in my old blue military uniform, there's a key. She'll know what it's for. In the safety deposit box, everything inside is now hers."

Uncle began to fade, his presence growing lighter. His last words hung in the air. "This house is now yours. Protect it. Keep it alive if you choose. But never let it fall into the hands of others."

And then he was gone.

I covered my face with my hands, sobbing uncontrollably. Ethan pulled me close, holding me tightly as he whispered, "It's okay, May. He's at peace now. He's finally at peace."

We stood there in silence, the weight of the moment pressing down on us. The house seemed quieter now, almost as if Uncle's departure had lifted some of the darkness that lingered here. As we turned back toward the car, leaving the horrors and scars of Aberdeen Manor behind, I felt the faintest glimmer of hope.

And now, we are left to close the chapter on Aberdeen Manor and the horrors that my biological father, Eric Stephenson—a sadistic, psychopathic serial killer—left behind. The echoes of his evil, the lives he stole, and the scars he inflicted will forever remain etched in this place. But today, we take the first step in ensuring that those horrors will never touch another soul.

By sealing the property, rebuilding its broken pieces, and locking it away for good, we make a promise—not just to ourselves but to everyone we lost—that no one, not now or ever, will step foot on this cursed ground again.

Ethan and I stood on the porch, our eyes scanning the desolate remains of what once was. The memories swirled like ghosts in the wind, tugging at our hearts and weighing on our souls. The pain lingered, but there was also relief—a sense that, finally, we could leave this place behind.

With a final deep breath, we turned, leaving the manor behind us. It would remain here, frozen in time, while we walked toward a future filled with healing and hope. The horrors, the memories, and even the scars were ours to carry—but they would no longer define us.

As we reached the car, the sun broke through the clouds, casting a warm light on the ruins of Aberdeen Manor. And for the first time in what felt like forever, I believed we could find peace.

This is neither the beginning nor the end of our beloved family home—Aberdeen Manor.

RETURN TO ABERDEEN MANOR

(CHAPTERS FROM THE UPCOMING SECOND BOOK)

JUSTIN SHAWN SMITH

MAEVE & ETHAN

VICTOR STEELE

CELESTE EVANGELINE HART

Readers, Welcome to *Return to Aberdeen Manor: The Return of Justin Shawn Smith*

What follows is a sneak peek into the next chilling installment of the Aberdeen Manor series. These four chapters are <u>not the final, complete versions</u>, but they offer a glimpse into the darkness that lies ahead.

Yes, there is a second book, and it promises to be bloodier, darker, and more twisted than ever. If you thought Eric Stephenson was a sadistic serial killer with a chilling repertoire of horrors, wait until you see what Justin Shawn Smith has in store. His reign of terror is just beginning.

But that's not all. A mysterious new character enters the story—someone deeply connected to Eric Stephenson's sinister past. Their presence will unravel secrets that Ethan and Maeve never imagined.

The second book will also introduce a dramatic shift in the Adams family dynamic with the arrival of someone unexpected—someone who will play a pivotal role in the story. This new addition will test the unbreakable bond between Ethan and Maeve, pushing their sibling relationship to the brink.

These chapters will leave you breathless, filled with suspense and curiosity. And because I love to keep things interesting, you might just find a fresh kill or two to whet your appetite for what's to come.

So, buckle up and enjoy the ride. This is just the beginning.

– C.K. Smith

JUSTIN SHAWN SMITH

T HE PAST HAS A WAY OF coming back into your life when you least expect it, like a predator waiting to strike. For three years, Justin Shawn Smith—accomplice to the notorious Eric Stephenson—had been locked away in the Omaha Correctional Center. His five-year sentence had seemed like a laughable slap on the wrist compared to the horrors he helped orchestrate. But now, that slap on the wrist was about to sting.

Meanwhile, Eric Stephenson, the sadistic mastermind behind the murders that scarred my family forever, was nothing more than a faceless memory, gunned down by my brother Ethan in an act of sheer desperation.

"Inmate 132571!" The guard's voice rang out, sharp and commanding, as his keys jangled with every step. He strolled down the long corridor, whistling a tune that grated against the cacophony of the prison. Inmates shouted from their cells, pounding against the metal doors, their voices a chaotic backdrop.

Justin Shawn Smith sat quietly, unmoved. His smirk stretched across his face, smug and calculated. He knew what this was about. Parole.

Finally, his shot at freedom.

Three years ago, the trial had been a media circus, stretching on for weeks with reporters dissecting every detail. Twice the jury had failed to reach a verdict. They couldn't tie him directly to the murders—no fingerprints, no smoking gun, no direct evidence. Justin had been a ghost, an accessory to Eric Stephenson's atrocities, feeding him information, cleaning up the loose ends. The court had labeled him an accomplice after the fact. Not a killer. That technicality had saved him. Five years, with the possibility of parole. And now, good behavior had bought him an early ticket out.

The sound of the guard's keys rattling grew louder, closer, the clinking echoing off the walls. Justin tilted his head slightly, his smirk deepening. He had waited for this moment, prepared for it, played his role perfectly.

The guard finally stopped in front of his cell, face impassive. "Smith. Prisoner 132571. It's time."

Justin rose slowly, deliberately, as if savoring the moment. His smirk stayed firmly in place as he stepped forward, shoulders squared, exuding an air of defiance. The metal door groaned as it swung open, and the voices of the inmates swelled—taunts, curses, laughter.

"Dead man walking!" someone shouted.

"Don't come back, Smith!" yelled another.

Justin ignored them all, his eyes fixed straight ahead. They didn't matter. Not today.

The guard gestured for him to follow, and they began the long walk down the corridor, past the sneering faces and grasping hands of the other prisoners. Justin's stride was steady, purposeful. The smirk never wavered.

"Big day, huh?" the guard muttered as they neared the administrative wing.

Justin didn't respond, offering only the faintest nod. Words weren't necessary. His expression said it all—confidence wrapped in defiance, with just a hint of triumph.

The guard eyed him warily, as if he could sense the quiet calculation beneath the surface, but there was nothing to pin down. Justin had been the model inmate: compliant, unassuming, and just contrite enough to satisfy the parole board. It was an art, really—giving just enough to earn their trust while keeping the true Justin Shawn Smith buried deep, untouchable.

Inside, though, Justin hadn't changed. He was still the same man who had worked in Eric Stephenson's shadow, the architect behind the scenes. His brilliance had always been in his invisibility—pulling strings without ever leaving fingerprints. Eric had been the blade, but Justin was the hand that wielded it, always one step removed from the blood.

The guard led him to a meeting room, the metallic echo of their footsteps bouncing off the cold concrete walls. A knock on the door, and it creaked open. Justin stepped inside, where the parole board waited like judges at a tribunal. A single chair under a harsh light awaited him at the center of the room.

Justin approached it with measured confidence, his posture composed, his smirk carefully subdued into something resembling humility. He sat, his hands resting lightly on his knees, the picture of a man eager to prove himself.

"Mr. Smith," one of the board members began, peering at him over a thick stack of papers. His voice was level, professional, but lacked warmth. "Your record indicates you've complied with all requirements during your incarceration. You've attended rehabilitation programs, maintained good behavior, and adhered to all protocols."

Justin inclined his head slightly. "Yes, sir. I've used my time here to reflect on my past and make the changes I needed to."

The man nodded, though his expression didn't soften. Another board member, a woman with steely eyes and a demeanor to match, leaned forward. "You were an accomplice to one of the most infamous criminals in recent history. Eric Stephenson left a trail of devastation, and you were a part of that. Tell us, Mr. Smith, what have you truly learned from this?"

Justin paused for effect, lowering his gaze briefly before meeting her eyes again. His voice, when he spoke, was calm but laced with just enough contrition to be convincing. "I've learned that my actions—or even my inaction—have consequences. I supported someone who caused unimaginable harm, and I'll carry that regret for the rest of my life. This time in prison has forced me to confront that, to grow, and to ensure I'll never make those mistakes again."

He let his words hang in the air, watching their reactions with the precision of a predator sizing up its prey. Every answer was a performance, rehearsed down to the smallest inflection, and it landed exactly as he intended. Regret. Growth. Redemption. He offered them the redemption arc they wanted, and they seemed willing to take it.

The questioning continued, but Justin handled it with ease. He gave them humility, accountability, and the promise of a reformed man eager to reintegrate into society. By the end, the tension in the room had eased, the board members exchanging subtle nods.

"We'll deliberate and inform you of our decision shortly," the parole officer announced, gesturing for the guard to take Justin back.

Justin stood with the same calm composure he'd worn throughout the session. As he walked back through the prison corridors, his smirk began to creep back, slow and deliberate. He had won. The world outside was within reach, and it was his for the taking.

Back in his cell, he stretched out on the thin mattress, hands folded behind his head. The hours ticked by with agonizing slowness, but Justin was patient. He had always been patient. Victory was sweeter when savored.

Finally, the sound of footsteps echoed down the corridor. The guard returned, his face unreadable as he stopped in front of Justin's cell.

"Smith. Parole granted. You're free to go."

Justin's grin widened, sharp and self-assured. He rose with deliberate ease, as if the moment was his to control, not theirs. He glanced back at the cell, a ghost of a chuckle escaping his lips. He wouldn't be returning—not to this prison, not to this life.

The heavy doors groaned open, and he stepped through, the weight of their closure behind him almost poetic. The world outside stretched before him, vast and waiting.

Justin Shawn Smith was no longer content to be the silent hand behind the chaos. No. This time, he would play the game on his terms, and he intended to win.

...

As Justin waited to change and receive his release papers, his parole officer approached, clipboard in hand. The man's tone was clipped, bordering on disinterest, but his words carried the weight of authority.

"They're keeping an ankle monitor on you for six months," the officer stated flatly. "You'll report your location daily. If you leave the state, you call me. Get a job? Call me. Change your address? You guessed it—call me. I want to know your every move. Don't screw this up, Smith."

Justin sat near the parole board members, who were busy finalizing his release forms. He leaned back in his chair, his signature smirk in place. This wasn't a warning to him—it was a formality. He waited patiently, not just for the bag of his belongings, but for the moment that piece of paper would slide across the table. The paper that would make his freedom official.

The guard beside him bent down and unlocked the cuffs from his wrists. Justin rubbed his hands together, savoring the sensation. Another officer knelt to fasten the ankle monitor in place, the device cold against his skin.

"Understand, Smith? Every movement," the parole officer repeated, sliding the paper across the table with a sharp tap.

Justin's smirk deepened. "Crystal clear," he replied, signing his name with deliberate flourish. The officer snatched the form back, giving him one last glare before moving on to other tasks. Moments later, Justin was escorted to change out of his prison uniform.

When he emerged, dressed in the clothes he'd worn on the day of his arrest—dark jeans, a plain shirt, and a scuffed leather jacket—the transformation was striking. No longer just inmate 132571, he looked every bit the man he'd been before: confident, untouchable, dangerous. He let out a slow breath, not quite relief, but satisfaction.

The final step came as they walked him down the long, familiar corridors. The sound of his boots against the concrete floor echoed with a sense of finality. At the end of the passage, a large steel door loomed. It groaned as it opened, and sunlight spilled over him, harsh and bright.

For the first time in three years, Justin Shawn Smith stepped into the open air. He paused for a moment, squinting against the sun, before a guard nudged him forward. Parked at the curb was a taxi, its engine idling, the driver watching from the rearview mirror.

"Don't mess this up," the officer said, his tone sharp but tired. "We'll be watching."

Justin gave a single nod, his smirk playing at the corners of his mouth but never fully forming. Without a word, he opened the cab door and slid into the back seat. The driver, a wiry older man with deep lines etched into his face, turned slightly to glance at him.

"Where to?" the man asked.

Justin pulled a baseball cap from his bag and tugged it low, shadowing his features. "South Dakota," he said casually.

The driver nodded, adjusting his mirrors. "Bus station first?"

"Yeah," Justin replied, leaning back into the seat as the car pulled away. The plan was simple: the cab would drop him off at the Omaha bus station, where he'd catch a ride across state lines.

He reached into the bag of belongings returned to him—a time capsule of his old life. His wallet came first. Flipping it open, he found everything intact: IDs, credit cards, and just enough cash to get started. Each item was more than a tool; they were keys to the next chapter of his life. And there it was—the money, folded neatly in a side pocket, a reminder of the life he'd left behind but never truly abandoned.

Eric had ensured Justin's survival long before the trial, transferring a significant sum into an offshore account. The police had scoured every lead, but the money had remained hidden, untouched, waiting for this moment.

Justin's smirk deepened as he thumbed through the items in his wallet. That money was his ticket—not just to freedom but to control. With it, he could rent an apartment, secure a job if he had to, and discreetly access the funds that would guarantee his next move. This wasn't the start of a new chapter. No, this was the calculated continuation of a story he had been crafting for years.

He glanced out the window as the cab sped toward the bus station, the horizon stretching endlessly ahead. Prison had been nothing more than an interlude, a brief pause. The real story was just beginning.

This time, Justin Shawn Smith wouldn't linger in the shadows. This time, he would write the rules.

At the bus station, he approached the ticket booth. The man behind the counter barely glanced up. "Ticket to where, sir?"

"South Dakota," Justin said, sliding a few bills across the counter.

The clerk's fingers danced over the keyboard, and within moments, a ticket emerged from the printer. "Bus arrives in an hour," he said, handing it to Justin.

Justin nodded, took the ticket, and strolled toward the waiting area. He found an empty seat and settled in, casually swapping his weathered leather jacket for a dark gray hoodie. Tugging the cap lower over his face, he flipped the hood up, ensuring his features were well-hidden. A quick adjustment of his pant leg concealed the ankle monitor. Satisfied, he leaned back in his chair, letting his eyes wander across the station.

The scene was a hive of activity: travelers chatting on phones, families juggling luggage, vending machines humming in the background. Justin's gaze flitted from one person to the next, analyzing their movements, their conversations, their tells. It was an old habit—one he hadn't lost.

Then, a particular figure caught his attention. A tall, slender woman with long brown hair stood by the vending machines. Brunettes. Always brunettes. A flicker of nostalgia surfaced— Maeve. She'd been his for five years before things unraveled.

The woman muttered in frustration, hitting the glass of the vending machine. Her candy bar dangled just out of reach, trapped by the metal coil.

Justin smirked and stood, moving toward her with casual confidence. "The trick is to tilt it slightly," he said, sliding his foot beneath the machine. With a calculated nudge, the candy bar dropped.

"Oh, thank you! I hate these things," she said, flashing a bright smile as she retrieved the chocolate. Relief softened her features as she unwrapped it and took a bite.

Justin smiled back, his charm deliberate but effortless. "Name's Alec," he said, extending his hand.

She hesitated only for a moment before shaking it. "Sam. Well, Samantha, but everyone calls me Sam," she said, her cheeks tinged with a shy blush.

"Nice to meet you, Sam," Justin said, touching the brim of his cap in a casual gesture. He turned as if to leave, but her voice stopped him.

"So, you uh... going somewhere?" she asked, curiosity laced in her tone.

He paused, looking back with a warm smile. "South Dakota."

Her face lit up. "Oh, I live there! Heading back home now,"

she said, her excitement evident.

An idea began to form in Justin's mind, subtle and sharp. Befriend her. Play the role. Gather information. If the opportunity arose, extort her, then vanish. The plan was second nature, as natural to him as breathing.

"Care to join me?" he asked, gesturing to the seat he'd just vacated.

Sam hesitated for only a second before tucking a strand of hair behind her ear and nodding. "Sure," she said, following him.

As she settled beside him, Justin's smirk returned, slow and deliberate. The pieces were falling into place, just as they always did. Old habits, after all, weren't easy to break.

• • •

As Sam and Justin boarded the bus, they settled into their seats. The hum of the engine and the low murmur of passengers created a steady, lulling background. The long trip to South Dakota stretched ahead, and the pair passed the time chatting. Justin nodded and listened politely, though his interest began to wane the moment Sam mentioned her two-year-old daughter.

A kid. Great.

Justin masked his annoyance behind a faint smile. Fatherhood wasn't in his repertoire. He didn't like kids, didn't have the patience for them, and certainly didn't plan to get involved with someone who had one. Still, he kept the conversation alive. For now, Sam was a stepping stone, and he could tolerate her enthusiasm until he got what he needed.

"So, what about you? Any kids?" Sam asked, her tone light and curious.

Justin shook his head, a faint smile tugging at his lips. "Nope. Not really my thing."

"Oh, I see," Sam replied, a slight blush creeping onto her cheeks. She shifted in her seat, clearly uncertain how to keep the conversation going.

As she rambled on about her daughter and plans for her return home, Justin's attention drifted. He only half-listened, nodding at intervals, until something she said snapped him back to focus.

"Wait, you're not going to Rapid City?" he asked, his brows knitting in a frown.

Sam blinked, surprised. "No, I'm stopping in Sioux Falls. Why? Are you heading to Rapid City?"

Justin exhaled slowly, feigning disappointment. "Yeah, I am. Guess that's a shame for both of us, huh? I was starting to enjoy the company."

Sam's expression fell, her face clouded with disappointment. "Really? What do you have in Rapid City? That's too bad… I mean, I was just starting to get to know you."

Justin leaned back in his seat, smirking slightly. "Honestly? Nothing. I just picked it because it sounded nice. Rapid City—has a ring to it, don't you think?"

Sam giggled, relaxing a little. "That's kind of random."

He shrugged, his smirk growing thoughtful. "Maybe I should change my plans. Stop at your stop instead."

Sam's eyes widened, her excitement barely contained. She clapped her hands together, her smile radiant. "Really? Oh, that would be amazing! I mean—uh—are you sure? Do you need a place to stay or something? I don't want to assume, but—"

Her words tumbled out in an awkward rush, and Justin chuckled, lifting a hand to calm her. "Don't worry about it. I'll grab a hotel for now and figure things out later. No big deal."

Sam exhaled a small sigh of relief, leaning back in her seat as she fiddled with the wrapper of a granola bar. "Well, Sioux Falls is a nice place. I think you'll like it."

Justin nodded, though his mind was already working through the logistics. Sioux Falls did sound like a better idea. It cut his travel time significantly, kept him within South Dakota, and offered plenty of opportunities to regroup and plan his next move.

For now, keeping Sam on his side was a small price to pay for convenience. If playing the part made things smoother—and it seemed it would—then why not?

He leaned back in his seat, his smirk lingering as he stared out the window at the vast stretch of highway. This wasn't just a detour. It was an opportunity.

• • •

It had been three days since Justin arrived in Sioux Falls. He was staying at a modest hotel just a few blocks from Sam's place—conveniently close. Despite having no genuine interest in her, Justin had played his part well. Years of practice had honed his ability to charm, and by the end of those three days, Sam was officially his girlfriend—a pawn in the larger plan he was methodically piecing together.

Her two-year-old daughter remained an abstract concept, one he had no intention of engaging with. Tonight, however, was their first real date, and Justin intended to use it as a chance to extract useful information—particularly about her job. Money wasn't a problem, thanks to Eric's foresight, but an extra income stream never hurt. If there was a way to siphon something off Sam without leaving a trace, he'd find it.

Adjusting his shirt and straightening his collar, Justin glanced at his reflection in the hotel mirror. The knock at the door came just as he smoothed his hair into place.

"Let's get this over with," he muttered, not bothering to hide his disinterest. Sam had insisted on paying for dinner, which at least made the evening tolerable. A free meal was better than none.

When he opened the door, Sam stood there, beaming and eager. She wore a short, figure-hugging dress that stopped well above her knees, its plunging neckline leaving little to the imagination. Her makeup was subtle but effective, and soft waves framed her face. She looked… presentable, he supposed.

But as he assessed her, a thought crept in. Maeve would have been mortified to wear something so blatant. Maeve, with her effortless style, had always struck the perfect balance—elegant but understated. She was sharp, clever, magnetic in ways Sam could never be. The memory of Maeve stirred something in him, an ache he quickly pushed aside. That had been another life, and Maeve had been more than a girlfriend; she'd been a partner in every sense. But that was gone now.

"Uh… nice dress," Justin said finally, forcing himself back into the moment. His gaze swept over Sam once more before landing back on her bright, expectant smile. She didn't seem to notice—or care about—the lack of enthusiasm in his voice.

"I figured since you're new here, I'd take you out—my treat, not the other way around," she said, laughing as though the idea was revolutionary.

Justin returned her smile, though it barely reached his eyes. "Well, shall we?" he asked, stepping aside and motioning for her to lead.

Sam giggled, linking her arm through his as they headed for her car parked out front.

"There's this great bar on Tenth Street that I absolutely love," she said, unlocking the door. Then, almost as an afterthought, she added, "I actually kind of… work there."

Sliding into the passenger seat, Justin adjusted his seatbelt and raised an eyebrow. "You dance at the bar, don't you?" he asked, his tone casual but calculated.

Sam's face flushed as she laughed nervously, starting the car. "How'd you even guess that?"

Justin leaned back, letting his gaze linger on her briefly. His smirk curved slowly. "Just a hunch."

Her blush deepened, and she focused on the road, clearly flustered. Justin, meanwhile, felt a flicker of satisfaction. She was so easy to read, her body language and demeanor giving him all the answers without him having to pry.

As they drove, Justin's thoughts wandered. Maeve wouldn't

have been caught dead in this situation. She would've had questions, demands, expectations. Maeve wouldn't have fumbled nervously at a confession; she would've owned it outright. Maeve had been strategic and polished—a chess player, not a pawn.

Sam, by contrast, was a tool, a means to an end. Her naivety was useful, but it grated on him. The comparison felt almost insulting, yet he couldn't ignore how easily Sam's role fit into his current plans. They turned onto a dimly lit street, the hum of the car's engine filling the silence. Justin's mind churned, already plotting his next steps. If her job provided access to cash—tips, payouts, anything—he could leverage that. Sam didn't know it yet, but tonight's date was merely a stepping stone in a far larger scheme.

"Here we are," Sam chirped as she pulled into a parking spot. She glanced at Justin, her excitement evident. "Ready?"

Justin returned her smile, a faint glint of mischief in his eyes. "Absolutely," he said.

As Justin stepped out of the car, he adjusted his jacket, his smirk firmly in place. Sam was eager, willing, and blissfully oblivious—exactly the kind of pawn he needed.

Their date at the bar had lasted three long hours. Justin had met her co-workers, shared drinks, and extracted every ounce of useful information he could manage, one calculated question at a time. By the time they arrived back at his hotel, Sam's mind was spinning with anticipation. She'd built the moment up in her head—a perfect goodnight kiss, maybe even something more. It was the kind of scene women imagined at the end of a promising date.

Justin, however, was focused on logistics. "So, how long have you worked at the bar?" he asked casually, leaning back in his seat. "Is it just a stepping stone, or something long-term?"

Sam blushed, signaling as she pulled into the parking lot. "It's going to be permanent, at least for now," she admitted. "I've got my little girl to think about, and the tips are good enough that I might be able to open my own business or even buy a house in a year or so."

Justin nodded, turning up the charm as he responded. "That's impressive, Sam. Good for you."

The words rolled off his tongue effortlessly, as easy as breathing. For Sam, though, they were transformative. She had fallen hard for Justin—his looks, his demeanor, the practiced way he made her feel seen. The small matter of his indifference to kids? She was confident she could work on that.

When she parked in front of the hotel, she unlocked the doors. Justin stepped out first, walking around to open her door.

"Oh, thank you!" she said, her cheeks flushing again.

"My pleasure," he replied smoothly, stepping aside to let her out.

They walked together to his room, Sam hovering nervously as he unlocked the door. "Thanks, Sam. Tonight was… interesting," Justin said, flashing a polite smile that barely reached his eyes.

Sam hesitated, her fingers fidgeting. "I was wondering…" She shifted on her feet. "How about dinner at my place tomorrow?"

Justin paused, studying her. She was practically glowing with eagerness, so desperate to make the next move. He figured he'd keep the game going, string her along a little further. "Sounds absolutely great," he said warmly. "Just give me your address, and I'll be there."

Practically bursting with excitement, Sam handed him a business card from her purse. Justin tucked it neatly into his shirt pocket, offering her a practiced smile.

"Uh, so… yeah…" Sam stammered, clearly unsure how to end the moment.

Before she could overthink it, Justin stepped closer. He tilted her chin gently, brushed his lips against hers, and stepped back just as quickly. She blushed furiously, her hand flying to her cheek.

"Thanks again," Justin said, his voice low and smooth. "I'll see you tomorrow. Around 6 p.m.?"

Sam nodded, still pink-faced and dazed as he slipped into his room. She lingered for a moment, replaying the kiss in her mind, before heading back to her car.

Inside, Justin shut the door and locked it, letting out an exasperated sigh. "Unbelievable," he muttered, shaking his head. He hated kissing her, hated pretending this much, but it was part of the game. And he'd keep it up for as long as it took to get what he needed.

Throwing his jacket onto the bed, he sat heavily on the edge. "Dinner with a toddler? What the hell was I thinking agreeing to that? Stupid," he muttered, tapping his temple in frustration.

The faint hum of the air conditioner filled the room as Justin rubbed his temples, his mind already racing. "I seriously need to get out of this hellhole. Sioux Falls? Who even lives here?" he grumbled, shaking his head.

Then the realization hit him. He hadn't checked in with his parole officer that day.

"Shit," he hissed, grabbing the cheap flip phone he'd bought at the bus station. Flipping it open with a snap, he dialed quickly, his jaw tightening as the line rang. Each passing second added to his irritation, the weight of his parole conditions pressing on his already fraying patience.

• • •

That night, after a tedious conversation with his parole officer, Justin collapsed into the creaky chair in his dingy hotel room and flicked on the TV. Aimlessly flipping through channels, he muttered under his breath, "What the hell am I doing in this dump? Sioux Falls? Talking to Sam? Agreeing to this crap? Stupid, stupid," he grumbled, tapping his forehead in frustration.

A sharp knock at the door jolted him from his thoughts. He

froze, glancing toward it. His fingers tensed against the armrest. "What in fresh hell is this? Who even knows I'm here?" he muttered, tossing the remote onto the bed. Rising to his feet, he trudged to the door, peering through the peephole.

Standing on the other side was a tall man in his early 30s, impeccably dressed with an air of confidence that bordered on arrogance. A thick yellow envelope was tucked under his arm, his smile calm and composed.

Justin opened the door and immediately relaxed, his demeanor shifting. "Well, I'll be damned if it isn't Alexander. What's up, man?"

The two clasped hands in a firm grip, the kind born from old familiarity. Justin stepped aside, motioning him in.

"Heard you were out. Figured I'd swing by and check in," Alex said smoothly, striding into the room with the self-assurance of someone who belonged wherever he went.

Justin shut the door and leaned against it, his arms crossed as he smirked. "How'd you even know I was here?"

Alex laughed, shaking his head. "Come on, Justin. I've been keeping tabs on you since you went in. Let's just say I've got my ways."

Justin chuckled, gesturing toward the small table in the corner. They both sat down, and Alex set the envelope on the table, his expression turning serious.

"I'm not here just to catch up," Alex said, tapping the envelope with a finger. "This is business."

Justin raised an eyebrow, intrigued. He picked up the envelope and opened it. A cascade of meticulously prepared documents spilled onto the table—IDs, a passport, a fake birth certificate—along with three tightly wrapped bundles of cash and a small safety deposit box key attached to a folded note.

"Everything you need to get out of this dump," Alex said, his tone matter-of-fact. "Your exit strategy, courtesy of Eric."

Justin's fingers moved instinctively to the money, thumbing through the bills. His eyes narrowed. "Eric left me all this?" he asked, his voice quieter, more guarded.

Alex leaned back, his arms crossed. "Yeah. Eric planned for this. He knew you'd do time, so he wanted you set the moment you got out. That's why he made sure you kept your hands clean—relatively speaking."

Justin nodded slowly, a faint grin tugging at his lips. "Thanks, man. This couldn't have come at a better time. You have no idea what hell I've been through."

"Oh, I've got some idea," Alex said with a smirk, then leaned forward, his tone sharpening. "But seriously, who the hell is Sam? And what possessed you to hit her up at a bus station? You're screwed now, man."

Justin groaned, raking a hand through his hair. "Don't remind me. God, I've got a dinner date with her tomorrow, and she's got a toddler—a two-year-old. I fucking hate kids!" He spat the words like venom, sliding the ID and passport into the pocket of his jacket draped over the chair.

Alex burst out laughing, shaking his head. "A toddler? You've got to be kidding me. Man, you're in deep. Totally screwed!" His laughter echoed through the room as Justin stared at the safety deposit box key, his mind already spinning with plans.

As Alex's laughter subsided, he gestured toward the envelope. "Just don't lose focus. You've got everything you need right there to make moves. Don't let some random mom and her kid derail you."

Justin smirked, sliding the cash back into the envelope. "Relax. I know exactly what I'm doing."

But as he leaned back in the chair, the weight of the key in his hand, his expression darkened. Plans were forming—complex, layered, and inevitable. Sam might have been a complication, but she was also a means to an end. And Justin Shawn Smith always made the ends justify the means

MAEVE & ETHAN

IT HAD BEEN THREE YEARS—three long, painful years. After everything that happened and our return to Aberdeen, Ethan and I struggled emotionally, mentally, and physically. The scars ran deep, but we were determined to heal. Ethan committed himself to grueling physical therapy to regain his ability to walk. He never missed a single session, pushing himself with a determination that bordered on obsession. Now, he walks without a limp or any outward signs of his injuries, though the pain still haunts him on bad days. Painkillers are a thing of the past; instead, he manages the discomfort his way— by hitting the gym with the same intensity he brought to his recovery.

I joined him at the gym not long after, not just to strengthen my body but to rebuild my fractured mind. The sessions became a shared ritual for us, a way to keep moving forward. Therapy, too, remained a constant. Our father insisted we continue, even after we'd made significant progress. Early on, we attended nearly three times a week, but now, once on weekends is enough to keep us grounded.

Other parts of our lives began to stabilize, though never quite the same as before. Ethan bought a modest house in Nebraska, close to our parents. The proximity gave us a sense of security, a lifeline we clung to as we rebuilt our lives. The house, a cozy three-bedroom with a spacious kitchen and a welcoming living room, became our shared haven. I moved in after the hospital released us, staying to care for Ethan while he navigated life in a wheelchair. Even after he recovered, I stayed. We needed each other more than ever.

Work brought new purpose. I followed in our great-uncle Joe's footsteps, becoming a private investigator. It felt right—turning my pain and experience into something meaningful. Ethan, on the other hand, stayed in his field as a nurse practitioner, splitting his time between the hospital and helping at Dad's clinic when needed.

On the surface, it looked like we were moving on. But the truth is, we were coping, not forgetting. The memories of Luke, Gwen, Tara, and April lingered like ghosts in the corners of our minds. Their absence was a constant ache, creeping up when we least expected it.

Today, though, felt different.

I'd been called to the police station, a request I hadn't expected. As I pulled into the lot, I spotted a familiar figure waiting by the door. My heart lifted for a moment.

"Lieutenant Michaels," I greeted him with a smile as he extended his hand.

"Maeve Adams," he said warmly, his hand brushing my arm. "It's good to see you."

He ushered me inside, his presence steadying me despite the sterile surroundings of the station. As we entered, I noticed a gathering of officers in the meeting room, the atmosphere charged with purpose. The new chief stood at the head of the room, flanked by a cluster of officers.

"Have you returned to work?" I asked Michaels as he gestured toward the room.

He chuckled. "Not quite. I was asked to come in today, though."

We stepped into the meeting room, where the tone shifted instantly. "Good, Miss Adams and Michaels are here," someone announced. A few officers stood to greet Michaels, welcoming him back with handshakes and laughter. He fit in seamlessly, slipping into their camaraderie as though no time had passed. I followed him, taking a seat nearby.

"So, what's this meeting about? Why was I asked to come in on my day off?" I asked, reaching into my bag for a notebook. I clicked my pen, ready to take notes.

The chief clicked a remote, and a screen descended at the front of the room. The room stilled as he began. "Justin Shawn Smith was released three days ago for good behavior from Omaha Correctional Center."

The name struck like a thunderclap. My pen slipped from my hand, clattering onto the table. My chest tightened, and for a moment, I felt like the air had been stolen from my lungs.

"Wait—what? Woah, hold on," I stammered, my hands raised in disbelief. "He was supposed to serve five years."

The chief's gaze was calm but edged with sympathy. "That's why I called you and Michaels. His parole officer informed us of his release. We've taken over his case."

He paused, letting the gravity of his words settle over the room. "Every movement he makes will be monitored. He's required to call in daily to the station. One of our officers is supervising his parole, and he's wearing an ankle monitor for the next six months."

The words hung heavy in the air. My pulse thundered as I tried to process the sudden return of a name, I had tried so hard to forget. Justin Shawn Smith was out. Free. And the shadows he cast threatened to reach us once more.

I let out a deep breath, frustration bubbling beneath the surface. "Where's he living?" I demanded. "We have a restraining order against him…"

Before I could finish, the chief slid a file across the table toward me, passing another to Michaels. My fingers trembled slightly as I flipped it open.

"He called in today," the chief continued. "He's staying in Sioux Falls, South Dakota—three hours away."

I rolled my eyes, trying to suppress the wave of anger rising in my chest. Of all places. Sioux Falls wasn't far enough for my liking. Justin was a chapter of my life I never wanted to revisit. If he'd died in prison, I wouldn't have cared. Released early for good behavior? I didn't buy it for a second.

The chief's voice cut through my spiraling thoughts. "Maeve, you and Ethan know Justin personally. We know him as an accomplice to a serial killer."

I exhaled sharply, crossing my arms. "Yeah, well, that bastard isn't anywhere near here. Why is everyone so worried?"

Michaels leaned back in his chair, nudging the file toward the center of the table. "Exactly. He's three hours away. What's the big deal?"

The chief's jaw tightened, his eyes sharp. "I'm guessing you didn't read page ten of the file, lieutenant."

That caught Michaels' attention. His expression darkened as he pulled the file back. My stomach knotted as I flipped through my own copy, landing on page ten. There, tucked neatly inside, was a handwritten letter.

A letter from Justin.

It had been intercepted by the prison and rerouted to the police station instead of me. My stomach twisted as I stared at the familiar scrawl.

Maeve,

Yeah, I know it's been a year since the court trial, blah blah blah, all the crap that happened. Yeah, I get it. Anyway, thought I'd send you this letter.

Guess I'm doing five, huh? Well, when I'm out, don't worry—I don't plan on seeing you. I got the restraining order. But that doesn't mean I can't, you know… have a bit of fun tormenting you.

Your brother killed Eric—a man I admired and respected. Send this warning to him: he's a little fucking ass bitch, and I'm not done with him yet.

Anyway, Maeve, take care of yourself. Don't do anything stupid. And stay away from the drug stuff (haha). Yeah, I know you're smart. How smart are you really?

Justin aka: Mike

My heart stopped as I read the last line. My hands clenched the edges of the file, my knuckles white. The paper trembled in my grasp as rage, fear, and nausea threatened to overwhelm me.

"Son of a bitch," Michaels muttered under his breath, slamming the file shut.

The room erupted into chaos. Officers stood abruptly, some pacing, others huddled with the chief in hurried conversation. Their voices blurred into a background hum as my mind fixated on the letter's venomous words. Every officer in that room had been at the manor three years ago. Every single one of them knew what we'd endured—what Justin had orchestrated. They'd seen the carnage, the pain, the aftermath.

But now, Justin wasn't just a ghost from my past. He wasn't a distant threat locked behind bars. He was out. He was moving freely, and his words made it clear he wasn't done. I tried to steady my breathing, but the fear was already coiled deep inside me. Justin wasn't just a memory anymore.

He was a threat. And I wasn't sure I could ever feel safe again.

I'd spent three hours at the police station, listening to reassurances that everything was fine and that they'd keep Justin on their radar. But I wasn't convinced. I knew Justin—or Mike—far too well. Before his true nature was revealed, we knew him as a friend, someone we thought we could trust. Then we met him again, as Justin: the accomplice to a monster.

Eric Stephenson had murdered over fifty women, with more victims still unidentified, making him one of the most prolific serial killers in history. And Justin? He wasn't just a bystander.

He'd been Eric's enabler, feeding him the tools, information, and resources he needed to kill.

Now Justin was out, living just three hours away from Nebraska. The thought of it made my blood boil. The fear, the nightmares—of Eric, of Justin—still haunted me. I couldn't erase the memory of that night in the graveyard, when Justin pinned me down, trying to take what wasn't his. His eyes had been cold, his smile cruel. In that moment, he hadn't just resembled Eric—he'd mirrored him, a chilling reflection of the same sadistic nature.

I couldn't shake the feeling that Justin had a plan. He wasn't out because of "good behavior." He was out for a reason. I could only hope—pray, even—that his time in prison had changed him, taught him something. Anything. But hope felt like a fool's game.

As I pulled into the driveway of our small home, I noticed Ethan's truck parked in its usual spot. I parked and climbed out, slamming the car door harder than I needed to. My frustration bubbled over as I unlocked the front door and stormed inside, letting it slam shut behind me.

I cursed under my breath, muttering angrily as I shrugged off my jacket, letting it fall carelessly to the floor. My bag followed, tossed near the shoe rack without a second thought. I stormed into the living room, my steps heavy with irritation.

"Okay!" Ethan called out, his voice laced with amusement. He was sprawled by the fireplace, arms crossed, a grin plastered on his face. "Welcome home!" he added, dripping with mock sweetness. "Kinda missed you. Well, no, not really."

I shot him a glare, pacing near the fireplace as he watched me with exaggerated curiosity.

"So, yeah," he continued, pretending to hold a conversation with himself. "Hi, Ethan. How's your day, bro? Oh, it's fine, Maeve. Thanks for asking."

I stopped pacing and fixed him with a look sharp enough to

cut steel. He rolled his eyes and pushed himself off the couch, stepping forward to place his hands gently on my shoulders. Startled by the sudden gesture, I froze and looked up at him.

"What's wrong?" he asked softly, his grin replaced by genuine concern.

For a moment, my anger faltered, but it didn't vanish. "Justin," I said flatly.

Ethan's grin disappeared entirely. "What about him?" he asked, his voice lower, his tone cautious.

I stepped back, crossing my arms tightly over my chest. "He's out. Released early for good behavior. He's living in Sioux Falls."

Ethan let out a low whistle, leaning back against the mantle. "Well, that's... unfortunate." He rubbed his chin thoughtfully before smirking, his humor creeping back. "Did they at least put a GPS tracker on him? Or maybe a neon sign that says, 'I'm a sociopath shithead'?"

"Ethan!" I snapped, throwing my hands in the air. "This isn't a joke!"

"I know, I know," he said, raising his hands in mock surrender. "But come on, you can't just storm in here like a tornado and not expect me to at least try to lighten the mood."

I shook my head, exasperated. "You don't get it. He wrote me a letter, Ethan. A letter."

That wiped the smirk off his face. "What kind of letter?" he asked, his humor gone, replaced by a serious edge.

"The kind that promises torment and takes cheap jabs at you for killing Eric," I said, pacing the room again. "The police intercepted it before it could get to me."

Ethan straightened, his arms crossing tightly over his chest. The lightheartedness he'd shown earlier evaporated, replaced by a grim determination. "So, what's the plan? Because I'm not about to sit around waiting for that asshole to make his move."

"I don't know," I admitted, my voice tinged with frustration. "The police say they're monitoring him, but I don't trust it. I don't trust him."

Ethan nodded, his jaw tightening. "We'll figure something out," he said, his voice steady and resolute. "But let me make one thing clear: if that scumbag even thinks about pulling something, I'll make sure he regrets stepping foot out of that prison."

I stopped pacing, glancing at him. His face was set, the playful grin from earlier long gone, replaced by a fierce protectiveness. But true to Ethan's nature, a flicker of sarcasm slipped in.

"Honestly," he added, shaking his head, "what kind of idiot gets out early on good behavior and immediately starts threatening people? Justin must've missed the part of rehab where they teach you not to be a moron."

Despite myself, I let out a small, shaky laugh. "You're impossible," I muttered, but a hint of a smile crept onto my face.

Ethan shrugged, his lips quirking upward. "Gotta keep it real, Maeve. And seriously, if he wants to mess with us again, I say we remind him what happened the last time he underestimated this family."

I sighed, my frustration giving way to a simmering unease. The thought of Justin out there, free and likely plotting, was enough to keep me up at night. But having Ethan in my corner—sarcasm and all—gave me a shred of comfort.

I spent the afternoon explaining every detail to Ethan, laying out the station's plan for keeping Justin on their radar. We stood in the kitchen side by side, preparing dinner. This wasn't just any dinner, though. I realized I'd forgotten to mention one of the most significant changes in our family over the past three years.

"ETHANNN! MAAAAAYYY!" a sweet, angelic voice boomed from the front door.

Our little sister. Alice.

After years of miscarriages—something we believed was caused by the relentless torment and threats from Eric, which had put our mother under unimaginable stress—she'd finally given birth. Alice was now four years old, and today, we were celebrating her birthday.

Mom had given birth to Alice the same week I was released from the hospital. Ethan, still recovering from his injuries, had remained in his hospital bed, wrapped in a half-body cast. I remember that moment in the delivery room so vividly—it was chaotic, emotional, and unforgettable.

Dad had insisted I record it.

"Oh my God!" I squealed, bouncing on my toes as the camera jostled wildly in my hands.

"Maeve, honey, stop jumping around. I want this," Mother said between deep, steadying breaths, her face flushed but determined. "Record this, May." She exhaled again, gripping the bed-rails tightly as she tried to focus through another contraction.

Father sat beside her, calm but encouraging, his hand on hers as he coached her through the process. "You're doing great, Amy. Just a little more. Breathe with me."

The room bustled with activity. Nurses moved swiftly, adjusting monitors and prepping equipment, while the doctor stood poised at the foot of the bed. "Here we go, Amy. One big push," the doctor instructed, his voice steady but firm.

I couldn't contain my excitement, squealing again as I watched the scene unfold.

"Maeve, seriously! Stop squealing! You're on camera duty!" Father called over his shoulder, his voice a mix of exasperation and amusement.

"I'm trying!" I shouted back, taking a deep breath and steadying the camera as best as I could.

And then we heard it. Her first cries.

The room seemed to freeze for a moment, the sound filling every corner. Mother's eyes welled with tears as she sobbed with relief and joy. Father laughed, practically beaming as he kissed her forehead before turning to cut the umbilical cord with trembling hands.

As for me? I squealed so loudly I was sure the camera captured nothing but blurry chaos and muffled noise.

"Maeve!" Father scolded, laughing despite himself.

"Not my fault!" I protested, clutching the camera tightly. "I'm just too excited!"

The nurses cleaned and swaddled Alice, placing her gently into Mother's waiting arms. She was tiny, pink, and perfect, her little fists flailing as she let out another wail.

Ethan chuckled, shaking his head as he chopped vegetables with exaggerated calm.

"Maybe we should pretend we're not home," he teased, his voice dripping with faux seriousness. Before I could respond, a loud, unmistakable knock rattled the door, followed by the enthusiastic declaration that only Alice could deliver.

"EEEETHAAAAN! MAAAAAYYYY! I'M HEEEEEERE!"

Her voice rang through the house like a tiny hurricane.

"If we're quiet, she might go away," I said, crossing my arms and pretending to be serious, as though she were a persistent salesperson.

Ethan snorted, wiping his hands on a towel. "Yeah, right." He strolled to the door, pausing dramatically as he leaned against it, his ear pressed to the wood.

"Oh, come on, just open it," I said, rolling my eyes at his theatrics.

"Shhh, give me a minute," he whispered with a mischievous grin, still listening intently.

I stepped closer, ready to shove him aside and open the door myself. But we both froze as Alice's next line rang out loud and clear: "DAD SAID OPEN THE DOOR OR YOU'RE BOTH

GROUNDED!" Her words were followed by a cascade of giggles that only she could manage.

"There it is," Ethan said, breaking into laughter. Shaking his head in mock defeat, he turned the knob and opened the door.

Standing there, as radiant as ever, was Alice. She wore a sparkly pink party dress, her favorite teddy bear clutched tightly in her arms. Her long, curly hair framed her excited face as she bounced on the porch, her shoes clicking with every jump. Before either of us could say a word, she barreled inside, pushing past us like she owned the place.

"Uh huh," Ethan said, watching her with mock disapproval. "Runs in like she pays rent."

I laughed, shaking my head as Alice made her way into the living room, already claiming her territory. Behind her, our father stepped through the doorway, carrying a large container with her birthday cake inside. Our mother followed close behind, her smile lighting up the room like sunshine.

"Mom, Dad, come on in," Ethan said, stepping aside to greet them. His voice, though casual, carried the warmth of a son genuinely happy to see his parents.

"Hi, sweetie," Mom said as she walked in, planting kisses on both of our cheeks. Her warmth was infectious, and I couldn't help but smile.

Dad followed, setting the cake on the counter with practiced ease. His movements were steady, a picture of calm amidst the bubbling energy Alice had brought into the house.

As Mom and Dad settled in, Ethan and I lingered in the kitchen, watching Alice make a beeline for the couch. She immediately got to work arranging her teddy bear as if she were preparing for the grandest tea party imaginable.

"You know," Ethan said, leaning against the counter as he casually sliced a carrot, "I wasn't sure we'd ever get a little sister. She's basically a miracle."

"Yeah," I agreed softly, my gaze fixed on Alice, who was now pretending her teddy bear was having a very serious conversation. "A loud miracle."

Ethan chuckled. "True, but look at her. She's got Dad's persistence, Mom's charm, and... your attitude."

I raised an eyebrow. "My attitude?"

"Yeah, the whole storming-into-places-like-you-own-them thing. It's classic Maeve," he teased, a playful smirk spreading across his face.

I rolled my eyes. "You're insufferable."

His grin widened. "She's got you wrapped around her finger, admit it."

"Maybe," I muttered, watching as Alice paused her tea party to wave at us from the couch, her grin so wide it could light up the entire room. "She really is something."

"Something, all right. Like a walking hurricane," Ethan joked, though his voice carried a warmth that betrayed his words.

Despite his teasing, I caught the pride in his eyes, the kind that spoke volumes without needing to be said. Alice had brought something into our family that we hadn't had in years—hope and joy. For a brief moment, the weight of the past three years didn't feel so crushing.

It was a reminder, however small, that even after the darkest storms, there could still be light.

Mom rolled up her sleeves, expertly preparing the pot roast with quick, efficient movements. The kitchen was alive with activity as we all bustled around, finalizing dinner before the birthday cake and celebrations. Amid the clatter and chatter, a burst of giggling broke through, unmistakable and infectious.

"Yes?" Ethan said, barely glancing over his shoulder as Alice's tiny shoes tapped eagerly against the linoleum.

I pressed my lips together, suppressing a laugh, and slid the completed salad bowl to the side, pretending to focus on my task.

The giggles grew louder, more insistent. "ETHAN, guess

what?" Alice said, practically vibrating with excitement as she bounced on her toes.

Ethan rolled his eyes dramatically, leaning slightly toward me. "Give it a second," he muttered with a knowing smirk before straightening, still pretending to fluff the rice.

"Tell me, Alice," he said at last, his tone flat, his attention stubbornly fixed on the food in front of him. He didn't even turn to look at her.

"I'M TURNING FOUR!" she shouted, her little voice echoing through the kitchen like a bell. She proudly held up three fingers, her smile faltering as she realized her mistake. Quickly, she adjusted to four fingers, her determination as strong as ever.

Ethan spun around dramatically, placing a hand over his chest as if struck by lightning. "Wait, FOUR? Oh no! I thought you were turning TWENTY!" He gasped and shook his head, groaning. "Jeez, now I have to return the gift I got you. It's completely useless now!" With a heavy sigh, he leaned against the counter, looking as though the weight of the world had just fallen on his shoulders.

Alice blinked up at him, her face a perfect picture of confusion. "Mom," she said, turning to our mother for clarification, "am I turning four or twenty?"

Mom froze mid-table-setting, letting out an exasperated sigh before shaking her head. "ETHAN ADAMS," she said sharply, pointing a fork in his direction, "stop telling her things like this! My God, you're impossible."

Ethan clamped a hand over his mouth, his laughter spilling out despite his best efforts. Tears of amusement welled in his eyes as he held up his free hand in mock surrender. "Okay, okay," he said, his grin unrepentant.

He crouched down, scooping Alice into his arms and holding her close. "I *totally* know you're four today," he said, his voice mock-serious, his expression softening.

Alice's face lit up, her earlier confusion forgotten. "I'm a big girl! Daddy said I can go to school soon!" she declared, her excitement bubbling over.

"You sure can," Ethan replied, tapping her nose lightly with his finger. "One more year, and I bet you'll be running the place."

From the living room, Dad chuckled as he organized the mountain of gifts Alice had accumulated. It was clear she had been spoiled thoroughly—the undisputed queen of the day. As the first child born to our parents after 23 years of marriage, Alice was the sun around which we all orbited.

Ethan shot me a mischievous glance as Alice wiggled out of his arms and darted toward the living room, her giggles trailing behind her. "Mom really needs to loosen up," he whispered, his grin wide and unapologetic.

"Don't push your luck," I replied, shaking my head with a small smile. But deep down, I couldn't help but love how Ethan always managed to keep things light, even in the chaos.

As we all gathered around the table, Dad began scooping food onto our plates, his movements practiced and precise. Ethan leaned over to Alice's plate, piling a generous spoonful of corn and rice in front of her. Alice, practically buzzing with excitement, immediately reached for her spoon, aiming for a massive scoop of corn.

Before she could shovel it into her mouth, Mom's voice rang out. "Alice, what do we do before we eat?" she asked, clasping her hands together and fixing Alice with a gentle but firm look.

Alice froze, her spoon suspended mid-air. "Aww, but I'm hungry!" she whined, her exaggerated pout drawing chuckles from the table.

"Hands together," Mom reminded her patiently.

Reluctantly, Alice set her spoon down and clasped her tiny hands together, sighing dramatically as if this was the greatest injustice she'd ever faced.

We all followed suit, bowing our heads slightly as Mom led

the prayer. It was short and heartfelt, and the moment the "Amen" left her lips, Alice sprang into action. She grabbed her spoon, scooped an enormous mound of corn, and stuffed it into her mouth with an enthusiasm that left us all laughing.

Corn scattered haphazardly across her plate and onto the table as her feet swung under the chair in pure, unrestrained joy. Alice sat between Ethan and Dad, basking in the center of attention. She and Ethan shared a bond so strong it was almost comical. Alice had Ethan wrapped so tightly around her finger that if she announced plans to blow up the mall, Ethan would not only take the blame but probably help her set the charges while she walked away scot-free.

"Ethan!" Alice said, her mouth full of corn, bits of rice sticking to her cheeks. Ethan glanced at her and chuckled, reaching for a napkin. "Yes, Alice?"

"Can you tell Mommy and Daddy that I want a cat?" she asked sweetly, as if Ethan were her personal mediator. To her, Ethan wasn't just her older brother—he was the ultimate negotiator, capable of convincing anyone to give her whatever she wanted.

Ethan smirked, dabbing her cheek with the napkin. "You want a cat, huh? Really?"

Alice nodded vigorously, her curls bouncing as she turned her big, hopeful eyes on him. "Mommy said I can't have one because I'm not big enough. But I'm four now! I'm big enough!" She held up three fingers, then quickly corrected to four, her face alight with determination.

Ethan turned to Mom, raising an eyebrow. "She's got a point, you know. Four is pretty grown-up."

Mom gave Ethan a pointed look that clearly said: *Don't you dare encourage her.*

"Alice, cats are a big responsibility," Dad chimed in, sharing a quick, amused glance with me. The smirk tugging at the corners of his mouth gave him away. It was obvious he and Mom had already bought her a cat.

Alice's face fell slightly, but she wasn't giving up. "Aww, but I can *responabily* a cat," she insisted, stumbling over the word "responsibility."

For a moment, the table went silent. Then, as if on cue, we all burst out laughing. Alice, oblivious to her mispronunciation, looked around, confused but undeterred.

"I *can!*" she exclaimed, her voice rising as she pointed her spoon at us for emphasis, bits of corn flying onto the table.

"Of course you can, Alice," Ethan said, still laughing as he wiped a stray bit of rice from her face. "You're super *responabily*. But you know, cats take a lot of work. You have to feed them, clean up after them, play with them…"

"I can do that!" Alice shouted, her excitement building with every word.

"You also have to scoop their poop," I added, smirking as I leaned back in my chair.

"Every day," Dad said, nodding solemnly.

Alice's expression shifted instantly to one of pure disgust. Her nose scrunched up, and her lips twisted into a frown as if she were grappling with the weight of this terrible revelation. For a moment, I thought we'd finally talked her out of it.

But then, as if rallying her resolve, she lifted her chin defiantly. "Fine. I'll scoop their poop," she declared, though her voice wavered slightly. She hesitated, her eyes darting to Ethan. "But Ethan has to help me."

Ethan threw his head back, laughing. "Of course I do. That's what big brothers are for, right?"

"Right!" Alice said triumphantly, her curls bouncing as she puffed out her chest, her earlier hesitation forgotten.

But then, as the table quieted, she leaned closer to her plate, whispering to no one in particular. "What if the poop is stinky? Or… really big?" Her tiny voice was filled with a mix of horror and genuine curiosity.

The entire table erupted into laughter, even Dad, who nearly spilled his drink as he doubled over. Ethan wiped tears from his eyes, shaking his head. "Alice, I think you'll survive. Maybe."

Alice looked around, blinking at our laughter, but then grinned, clearly enjoying being the center of attention.

I shook my head, grinning as I glanced at Dad. The surprise would come soon enough. For now, though, the negotiations at the table were entertainment enough.

After dinner, Mom brought out the big, beautiful birthday cake she'd made for Alice. Four brightly colored candles flickered on top, their soft glow reflected in Alice's sparkling eyes. Unable to contain her excitement, Alice stood on her chair, practically vibrating with energy as the cake was placed in front of her.

Just as we were about to sing "Happy Birthday," Alice let out a giggle and blew out the candles in one big, dramatic breath.

"Aww, but that's not how it works, Alice!" I said, grinning at her. "We have to sing first!"

Alice giggled mischievously, her sticky fingers already pulling the candles out of the cake. "No! Cake first! I LOVE CAKE!" she squealed, bouncing in her chair like a spring-loaded toy.

"Well, that saves us the trouble of singing," Mom said with a laugh, grabbing a knife to start cutting slices. She began passing plates around as Alice clutched hers tightly, holding it out like she was begging for treasure.

"Me first, please! Me first!" she exclaimed, her voice high-pitched and urgent.

Mom, ever the tease, cut an enormous slice and held it teasingly above Alice's plate. "But birthday girls always feed their guests first. It's a rule," she said, feigning a stern tone.

Alice's face fell instantly. Her bottom lip jutted out in an exaggerated pout, her wide eyes staring at the cake as though the universe had betrayed her. "But... why?" she asked, her voice small and uncertain.

Mom laughed and slid the slice onto her plate. "Of course

you get the first piece," she said, leaning down to plant a kiss on Alice's head.

Alice's grin returned in full force. Without wasting a second, she grabbed her fork and dove in, her joy infectious. Dad chuckled as Mom continued serving slices, and soon the room was filled with laughter and the happy hum of forks against plates.

As we ate, Alice suddenly turned to Ethan, her brow furrowed in deep curiosity. She paused mid-bite, cake crumbs dotting her cheeks. "Ethan," she began, her voice muffled by cake.

"Yes, Alice?" Ethan replied, cutting into his slice.

She swallowed quickly, pointing her fork at him like it was an official inquiry. "Why do you have so many... mus-uls?" she asked, stumbling adorably over the word.

Ethan paused, raising an eyebrow as a grin tugged at the corner of his mouth. "Muscles?" he clarified, emphasizing the word.

Alice nodded enthusiastically, her curls bobbing. "Yeah! You have soooo many mus-uls! Like, do they just... grow on you?"

We all burst out laughing as Ethan set his fork down, pretending to consider her question with great seriousness. "Well, Alice," he began, leaning closer, "I water them every day, just like plants."

Alice gasped, her eyes wide with wonder. "You water them? With what?!"

"Milk," Ethan replied with a completely straight face. "That's why I drink so much of it. Muscles need milk to grow."

Alice's mouth dropped open as she processed this groundbreaking revelation. "Can I grow mus-uls too?!" she asked, her voice rising with excitement.

"Absolutely," Ethan said, flexing his arm dramatically. "But only if you drink all your milk and do a *million* push-ups."

"A *million* of push-ups?" Alice's fork clattered onto her plate. "I can't count that high!"

"Good thing I can," Ethan replied, winking. "We'll start tomorrow."

Alice giggled so hard she nearly toppled out of her chair, her laughter bubbling over and spreading to the rest of us. Mom shook her head, smiling as she handed Alice a glass of milk. "Here's your muscle juice, birthday girl."

Alice grabbed the glass with both hands, her determination radiating from her tiny frame. "I'm gonna be so strong! Just like Ethan!" she declared before taking a big gulp.

Ethan leaned back in his chair, smirking at me. "You know, I think I just created a monster."

After the laughter and fun at the dinner table, we all moved to the living room. Alice, the undisputed princess of the family, plopped herself down on the large round area rug in the center, claiming it as her royal throne. Ethan and I sat cross-legged on the floor while Mom and Dad disappeared to the car to retrieve their big surprise.

"WOOOOOOW!" Alice's voice boomed as she tore into my gift first, the paper flying in all directions. Her eyes went wide as she revealed her very own dollhouse. But this wasn't just any dollhouse—this one was special.

Growing up, I'd had a dollhouse passed down from Mom, who had received hers from Grandma. It was a tradition, and I wanted Alice to have something equally meaningful. She'd been asking for this particular dollhouse for years, but every Christmas and birthday, it was always sold out. I'd gone out of state just to track it down.

"THANK YOU, MAEVE! A DOLLHOUSE!" Alice squealed, bouncing up and down like a spring, her excitement infectious.

The dollhouse was nearly her size, with intricate little rooms and delicate accessories. Ethan leaned over to help her open the wide, heavy doors, his fingers carefully pulling at the tiny hinges.

"Man, I can't top that," Ethan muttered under his breath, leaning toward me.

"You knew I bought this," I whispered back. "How small did

you think it was going to be?"

He gestured with his hands, indicating something the size of a shoebox. I rolled my eyes.

"Your move, genius," I said, smirking.

Ethan gave me a sly grin and cleared his throat dramatically. He reached over to the table and picked up his gift, a massive box wrapped in colorful paper. Alice turned to him, her eyes lighting up like fireworks as he held it out.

"My turn, pipsqueak," he said, setting the enormous box in front of her.

Alice squealed again and launched herself at the box, ripping the paper to shreds like a whirlwind. Inside was an entire set of accessories for the dollhouse: a car, bathroom fixtures, kitchen furniture, and tiny living room pieces—all scaled perfectly to match.

"You got her the car, the bathroom, and *all* the furniture for the house?" I asked, crossing my arms as Alice screamed with delight, pulling out each piece one by one. Her laughter echoed through the house.

"THANK YOU, ETHAN! THIS IS THE BEST!" she shouted, her voice full of unfiltered joy.

"Beat that," Ethan said smugly, leaning back with his arms crossed, his grin practically glowing with satisfaction.

I glared at him, my fingers itching to punch his shoulder, but before I could act, Mom and Dad reappeared, stepping into the living room with a lightly wrapped box. The anticipation in the room grew instantly as all eyes, especially Alice's, turned toward their hands.

Their eyes went straight to the dollhouse. "You just *had* to go there, didn't you?" Dad said, shaking his head with mock disapproval.

Mom groaned, folding her arms as she surveyed the oversized gift. "Maeve, Ethan, how are we supposed to take this home?"

Ethan grinned innocently. "I have a truck."

"Good, because it's going with you," Dad replied, coming

around to inspect the dollhouse while Alice giggled and squealed with excitement.

"What's in the box?" Alice asked, her curiosity instantly shifting as she spotted the lightly wrapped package in Mom's hands.

Mom knelt down near Alice, placing the box gently in her lap. "Now, Alice," she began, her voice soft and teasing, "your father and I got you something very special."

Alice's eyes widened as the box wiggled slightly. "What is it, Momma?" she asked, inching closer, her excitement barely contained.

Mom raised a finger. "But you have to promise to be responsible and take care of it."

"I am responsibly, Momma!" Alice declared earnestly, stumbling over the word and making us all laugh.

With a warm smile, Mom opened the flaps of the box and gently lifted out a tiny gray kitten adorned with a red bow around its neck. The kitten let out a soft meow, its big eyes blinking curiously at the room.

"A KITTY!" Alice screamed, her giggles bubbling over as Mom placed the kitten in her lap. The tiny furball immediately snuggled into Alice, purring contentedly.

"I LOVE MY NEW KITTY!" Alice exclaimed, stroking the kitten gently, her joy lighting up the entire room.

"What will you name it, pipsqueak?" Ethan asked, leaning toward her with a grin.

Alice tilted her head, her face scrunched in deep thought. After a dramatic pause, she giggled. "I like… Honey."

I raised an eyebrow, stifling a laugh. "Honey?"

"Yup! That's her name!" Alice said confidently, beaming with pride.

Dad chuckled, his deep laugh filling the room. "Honey it is, then."

For the rest of the evening, Alice entertained us by trying to teach Honey tricks and excitedly explaining all the ways she'd care for her new kitten. As the night wore on, she sprawled out on the rug, Honey curled up in her arms, both of them fast asleep.

"I'll take the dollhouse over tomorrow," Ethan said, carefully scooping Alice and Honey into his arms without disturbing them.

"You both just *had* to go there, huh?" Dad muttered again, shaking his head as Ethan laughed and carried Alice to the car.

Mom gave me her usual goodbye hug, her protective instincts shining through. "You and Ethan take care of yourselves, okay?"

"Mom, we're fine," I reassured her, handing over Alice's teddy bear. "You and Dad have a good night. We'll stop by tomorrow."

She smiled, kissing both me and Ethan on the cheek before climbing into the car. Dad hugged us quickly, then started the engine. Ethan and I stood on the porch, watching as the car disappeared down the driveway, the house feeling just a bit quieter.

"Well, that was entertaining," Ethan said, stretching as we stepped back inside.

"Yeah. Now explain," I demanded, turning to him. "How did you find all those dollhouse accessories? I've been searching for *months*."

Ethan smirked as he locked the door. "I know people who know people, who bumped them off a dealer, who I then bumped off—"

Before he could finish, I jumped on his back, tackling him to the floor. He laughed, easily lifting me off and setting me down like I weighed nothing.

"Told you," he said, grinning. "You can't win."

I huffed, brushing myself off. "Fine, you clean up this mess."

He grabbed a trash bag, still laughing. "You love cleaning, admit it."

"Not tonight," I shot back, turning my attention to organizing the dollhouse accessories.

We spent the rest of the evening cleaning and laughing, the

warmth of family lingering in the house long after the noise of the celebration faded.

.

...

VICTOR STEELE

THE NEXT MORNING, I RECEIVED a phone call from the police station. The officer on the line sounded tense, his words clipped. "It's extremely urgent. You need to come down immediately."

Throwing on my jacket, I rushed out the door, my mind racing with possibilities.

Ethan had already left earlier that morning for an emergency at the hospital. A massive car accident had occurred, and all available nurses and doctors were called in at 7 a.m. The house felt strangely quiet in his absence, the kind of quiet that lets unease creep in.

I jumped into my car, started the engine, and reversed out of the driveway, fumbling with my seatbelt as I went. As I sped down the block, I caught sight of Mom in her yard, watering her flowers with her usual morning dedication. She waved enthusiastically, but I didn't have a second to spare. I gave her a quick honk and kept going.

The police station was quieter than usual when I arrived. The parking lot was half-empty, no doubt because of the accident that had the city scrambling.

Inside, Chief Rosenberg was waiting for me in the meeting room. As soon as I walked through the doors, he motioned for me to join him. His expression was unreadable, but the tension in his shoulders spoke volumes.

Lieutenant Michaels was already there, seated next to three men in suits. Their sharp attire and no-nonsense demeanor screamed FBI. Among them, a younger man stood out—his suit perfectly tailored, his brown eyes sharp yet unreadable, and his features strikingly handsome. He was unfamiliar, and my curiosity sparked immediately.

As I pushed open the glass doors, one of the agents rose from his seat.

"Maeve, this is FBI Agent Cliff Henry," Chief Rosenberg said, gesturing toward the man.

Agent Henry extended his hand, his grip firm but not overpowering. "Maeve Adams. A pleasure to meet you," he said, his voice calm but serious.

I shook his hand and offered a polite nod before taking a seat next to Michaels. The unease that had been simmering since the phone call was now a full-blown ache in my chest. "What's so urgent?" I asked, my eyes darting between the gathered faces.

Another man stood up but didn't offer his hand. He was younger, but there was something unshakably confident about his posture.

The chief introduced him, gesturing in his direction. "This is Victor Steele, a private investigator from Delaware. We called him in today to assist on this matter."

I nodded toward Steele, who offered a small smile and a nod in return. His dark eyes lingered on me just long enough to suggest he already knew more about me than I was comfortable with.

Rosenberg stood and walked over to a long metal table in the center of the room, its surface crowded with screens, cables, and various surveillance tools. My stomach tightened as I followed, my thoughts racing ahead of whatever he was about to show me.

Three years ago, after returning to Aberdeen, Ethan and I had taken ownership of the manor's land title deed. It was our way of reclaiming control, of ensuring no one else would dare step foot on that cursed property again. But ownership hadn't erased the horrors of what had happened there—it only made them feel more personal.

To protect the site, we'd requested full police surveillance of the area. Within weeks, the FBI and local police had installed cameras across every inch of the property—inside and out. Brick walls now lined the perimeter, bristling with cameras. The old, rusting gate was replaced with a reinforced one, accessible only by a code. Even the house itself had been gutted and renovated. The graveyard, with its haunting memories, was torn up and re-done.

But even with all these precautions, the past never felt far away.

As Rosenberg powered on the screen in front of us, my heart sank. Grainy footage began to play, the timestamp showing it was recorded two days ago. A shadow flickered across the monitor, and I leaned in instinctively.

"Is this… the outside perimeter?" I asked, my voice tight.

Rosenberg nodded grimly. "Yes. At first, we thought it might be wildlife. But after reviewing the footage…"

He clicked a few buttons, zooming in on the video. My breath caught as a shadowy figure darted between the trees just beyond the brick wall.

"This wasn't an animal," Agent Henry said, stepping closer and crossing his arms. His tone was sharp, professional. "We believe someone was scouting the property."

My chest tightened as I stared at the screen. My mind raced through the possibilities—Justin? One of Eric's old associates? Or could it be something else entirely?

"Did anyone breach the property?" I managed to ask, trying to steady my voice.

"Not yet," Rosenberg replied, his tone weighted with unease. "But whoever it was, they knew how to stay out of the main camera angles. They were deliberate. Careful."

A chill ran down my spine. Whoever this was, they were testing boundaries. And I couldn't shake the sinking feeling that this was only the beginning.

I turned my gaze away from the footage and toward the room. Victor Steele sat casually at the edge of the table, a faint smirk tugging at the corners of his mouth. His relaxed demeanor contrasted sharply with the tension filling the air.

Why was he here? The question itched at the back of my mind, but I held it back for now. Instead, I focused my attention back on the screens, my unease growing by the second.

"Seriously? Did anyone catch an image of who that was?" I asked, leaning forward to scrutinize the screen. My frustration simmered as I tried to make sense of the grainy footage. Michaels leaned in as well, his jaw tight and fists clenched. He let out a groan that carried years of pent-up frustration.

"Forgive me, Chief Rosenberg," Michaels said, his voice strained. "I retired for a reason. That place killed me. I'd like to be removed from this case."

Both the chief and I turned to him, caught off guard by his sudden declaration.

"Michaels isn't involved in this anymore," I said firmly, directing my words to Rosenberg.

The chief sighed, straightening his posture. "Unfortunately, it does involve him," he said, gesturing for us all to sit back down.

Michaels hesitated, his frustration now mixed with apprehension. Finally, he sank into his seat. "How so?" he asked, his tone sharp.

Rosenberg ran a hand over his face, letting out a heavy breath. "Since the events at Aberdeen three years ago, everyone directly involved—especially you, lieutenant—has been under FBI surveillance. This wasn't just for you. It was also to protect your families. The impact of the incident, combined with what was recovered, caused significant psychological trauma for everyone, including many of the officers. We know you retired because of this. That's why your family has been under protection ever since. We've kept a particularly close eye on your niece and her circle."

Michaels' eyes narrowed, suspicion and worry flickering across his face. "Okay, and?"

Rosenberg leaned forward, his gaze steady. "Your niece is planning a joyride with six of her friends this Halloween. They're talking about going to Aberdeen Manor."

Michaels shot up from his chair, his face darkening. "Shit. Don't tell me Kelly wants to go to the manor. That place is off-limits—she knows that! No one can get in or out." He grabbed his jacket, ready to storm out, but Rosenberg held up a hand to stop him.

"Yes, but she's a teenager," Rosenberg said, his tone calm but firm. "And her friends? Also teenagers. You know how they are. You have to make it absolutely clear to her not to enter Trenton or go anywhere near that manor."

Michaels cursed under his breath, pacing the room before pulling his phone from his pocket. "I'll call my sister right now," he muttered through gritted teeth, leaving the room as he dialed.

I shook my head, frustration boiling over. "What the hell? I have signs everywhere saying the property is off-limits. No one is allowed on the grounds!" I said, directing my anger toward the agents.

"This is why we're heading to Trenton," FBI Agent Cliff Henry interjected, gesturing toward his partner. "The chief, my partner, and I will block off the two main roads leading to the manor with barricades. No cars will get through."

I exhaled deeply, my worry mounting as I tried to process this. "Rosenberg, I want information on Kelly and her friends—all six of them. I want to know where they live and who they are," I demanded, my thoughts racing as I glanced at the surveillance footage again.

"Yes, I'll have that for you within a few days," Rosenberg

assured me, standing to match my posture.

As the agents stood, I couldn't help but feel my attention drift to Victor Steele. He remained seated, his calm demeanor and faint smirk unsettling me. Why was he here? His presence felt calculated, almost too convenient, but I pushed the thought aside for now.

Drawing in another steadying breath, I turned back to Rosenberg. "Ethan will know about this too," I said resolutely. "We monitor the manor from our place as well. He'll be looped in."

"Do as you wish," Rosenberg replied, nodding. "I'll get you what you need—quickly."

I let out an exasperated groan, frustration bubbling over. Before I could storm out of the office, Rosenberg's firm yet apologetic voice stopped me.

"Maeve, wait a second, please…"

Reluctantly, I turned back and dropped into the chair opposite his desk, my arms crossed.

"Sorry to have to do this," he began, sliding a folder across the desk toward me, "but Victor just moved to town and has been hired by our department. He's assigned to another case we've got going on, one that I want you involved in."

He leaned back, rubbing his temples. "You cracked the last three cases in record time—two weeks each. But this one… this one's different. It's too sensitive for anyone else."

From a cabinet behind him, he pulled two additional files. He slid one to Victor, seated beside me, and the other back toward himself. "I'm trusting you two to get this done."

Victor opened his file first, and I followed. The rustle of paper seemed unnaturally loud in the tense silence. As my eyes scanned the first page, my heart dropped.

"What the hell is this?" I muttered, my voice almost breaking. Memories of Aberdeen Manor flashed vividly in my mind, tightening my stomach.

"This," Rosenberg said, lacing his fingers together as he

leaned forward, "is the real reason I called you in today. I know the Kelly case won't be a challenge for you, but this…" His tone darkened. "This is something else entirely. And I need the best on it."

Victor read in silence, his expression calm and unreadable, while I struggled to process the contents of the file.

"A little over a year after Justin Shawn Smith was locked away, we started seeing a disturbing pattern," Rosenberg explained, his voice low. "Ten women disappeared within six months—no witnesses, no crime scenes, no bodies. Just… gone. Then, one year to the day after the first woman disappeared, this arrived."

He pulled out a copy of the letter, placing it on the desk. Even in print, the chilling words felt like a slap.

They're all dead.
The bodies will never be found.
Signed, Unknown.

I felt the blood drain from my face. My hands trembled as I closed the file, my mind racing.

"Could it be a copycat?" Victor finally broke the silence, his calm voice cutting through the tension like a blade.

"We've considered that," Rosenberg said, leaning back in his chair. "The precision of the letter, the timing, and the complete lack of evidence—it's eerily familiar. But Justin has an alibi: three years in prison, with a GPS tracker on him every second. Still, there's something… off."

Rosenberg's eyes narrowed. "The style, the taunting—it feels personal. And that's why I'm putting you two together. Whoever this is, they're calculated. They've stopped for now, but I don't think we've seen their full terror yet. I believe this person may have a connection to Eric Stephenson."

I inhaled sharply, the weight of Rosenberg's words pressing down on me. "Sir, I've been doing this on my own for two years.

I don't need a partner," I said, my voice steady but laced with irritation. "I've handled complex cases before. I can handle this."

Rosenberg nodded slowly, acknowledging my point, but his resolve didn't waver. "I know, Maeve, and you've done incredible work. But this isn't just another case. If this is a copycat, and if they're connected to Eric Stephenson, then you do need a partner. Someone who can work alongside you to get ahead of this guy before any more women end up dead."

My jaw tightened, and my eyes darted to Victor, who sat there flipping through the file with infuriating ease. Could he even keep up? What if he slowed me down—or worse, botched something critical? The thought of juggling two cases and a partner who might not be equipped for this gnawed at me. I'd cracked cases solo for years; why fix what wasn't broken?

Victor smirked slightly, his steady gaze meeting mine. I glared back, my frustration bubbling over.

"You think this is funny?" I snapped.

"Not at all," Victor replied coolly. "I'm just trying to figure out what's more intimidating—the case or working with you."

Rosenberg suppressed a chuckle, clearing his throat to refocus the room. "Maeve, I wouldn't pair you with just anyone. Victor's one of the best in his field. I need you two to trust each other if we're going to crack this case."

I exhaled sharply, glancing at Victor again. He was still flipping through the file, completely unfazed by the tension in the room. My chest tightened. This case was personal, even if no one else fully understood why.

With a reluctant nod, I leaned back in my chair and crossed my arms. "Fine. But don't slow me down."

Victor grinned, his confidence as irritating as it was unshakable. "Wouldn't dream of it."

Rosenberg leaned forward, his tone final. "Good. Because time isn't on our side, and neither are the odds. Find this guy before he makes his next move."

...

As I left the station, Victor trailed behind me, his presence as casual as the smirk plastered on his face. I let out a deep breath, rolling my eyes as I approached my car.

"Here's the deal," I said, my tone clipped as I opened the driver's door. "I'm heading over to investigate Kelly. We're doing a stakeout."

Victor leaned against the passenger side door, his smirk growing wider. "Are you always this bossy?" he asked, his voice laced with curiosity and amusement.

I shot him a look and exhaled sharply. "I just don't really need a partner, and I have no idea why the chief decided to stick me with you," I muttered, my frustration bubbling to the surface.

Victor chuckled, undeterred by my irritation, and casually opened the passenger door. "Would you prefer I was a woman?" he teased, sliding into the seat. "I could probably pull that off, you know. I'd make a very attractive woman."

I turned to him, deadpan, refusing to take the bait. "Kelly lives on Benson. Michaels mentioned it once. She's probably about to leave for school, so we're going to watch her every move today," I said, my voice steady and matter-of-fact. I turned back to start the car, determined to ignore his antics.

Victor shook his head, chuckling as he buckled his seatbelt. "Yes, ma'am. Whatever you say—you're the boss." His tone was mock-serious, and the grin never left his face.

I groaned audibly as I pulled out of the police station parking lot, his light chuckle echoing in the background.

I parked three houses down from Kelly's home, keeping the engine idling as I settled in. Victor sat beside me, his window slightly cracked, camera in hand, ready to document. Through my binoculars, I watched as Kelly stepped out of her front door, her long brunette hair swaying as she made her way toward the street.

A Camaro pulled up to the curb, filled with three boys and two girls, their laughter and chatter faintly audible even from where we sat. I could feel the pulse of anticipation in the air—this had to be the group planning the so-called joyride to Aberdeen Manor.

"That's the kid, huh?" Victor asked, snapping photos methodically, the rapid click of his camera cutting through the tense silence.

"Yeah," I replied, not lowering my binoculars. "The brunette. That's Kelly. And I'd bet good money those kids in the car are the ones she plans to take with her."

The Camaro did a sudden U-turn, the engine revving loudly as it sped past us.

"Our move, boss," Victor said, his tone calm but his eyes sharp.

I started the car, carefully pulling out behind them, keeping a steady distance. The Camaro led us to the local high school, pulling into the crowded parking lot filled with teenagers bustling about, their voices and laughter carrying across the open space. I parked discreetly near the curb, away from the chaos.

Victor lowered his camera, watching the group of kids as they exited the car and gathered near a cluster of students. "So, what's your move? I mean, our move?" he asked, his tone laced with mild amusement.

"For now, nothing," I said, my focus unwavering. "We know where she goes to school. I'll wait for the file on her friends to come through, and then we'll figure out our next steps."

I opened the laptop mounted in the undercover police car—a vehicle equipped with everything I needed to do my job effectively. Victor leaned closer, watching as I typed in my password and accessed the system.

"What do you think those kids are planning?" Victor asked, his voice curious but steady.

Before I could respond, movement caught my eye. Kelly and

her friends weren't heading toward the school. Instead, they circled back to the Camaro, climbing inside once more.

"What the hell? Is she playing hooky?" I muttered, my eyes narrowing as the group waited for the parking lot to clear.

"Yeah… where do they think they're going?" Victor echoed, his gaze fixed on the car as it pulled out of the school lot.

Slamming the laptop shut, I started the car, the tension building. "Let's find out."

I eased out onto the road, keeping a careful distance as we tailed the Camaro. My mind raced with questions—was this just a group of kids being reckless, or was something more sinister at play? Either way, I wasn't about to let them out of my sight.

As we followed the Camaro, the kids pulled into the mall parking lot. Victor and I exchanged a glance, and I signaled to pull in behind them.

"They're playing hooky. Classic move," Victor said, snapping a picture of their license plate.

I smirked, watching as they parked far from the main entrance. I chose a spot farther away and killed the engine, keeping an eye on them as they got out of the car, laughing loudly and shoving each other playfully. They disappeared into the mall's entrance, completely oblivious.

"Well, now I think it's time to have a little chat with these sweet little geniuses," I muttered, opening my car door.

Victor chuckled and followed me. "Sweet? That's generous."

We trailed the group into the mall, keeping a reasonable distance as they weaved through the crowd. They made a beeline for the food court, chatting loudly and throwing jabs at each other like only teenagers could.

"Wow," Victor said, raising an eyebrow. "Such colorful vocabulary. They're poets, really."

I ignored his sarcasm, observing the group as they ordered from McDonald's. Once they grabbed their trays, they slid into a booth, laughing and jostling each other.

"This is it. Time for a warning," I said, stepping forward.

Victor stopped me, his hand on my arm. "Hold up. If you walk over there guns blazing, they'll laugh it off and turn it into a joke. Trust me, kids like these need a different approach."

I folded my arms, irritated. "And what exactly do you suggest?"

Victor smirked, patting my shoulder. "Watch and learn."

We approached their table together. Kelly was the first to notice, her expression souring immediately.

"Yes?" she asked, her voice dripping with annoyance.

Her friends turned to look at us, their amusement dimming just slightly.

"Kelly Jessica Jamison?" I said, using her full name deliberately.

She rolled her eyes and groaned, crossing her arms. "Great. Did my mom send you to spy on me? God, that woman is so annoying."

I leaned slightly over the table, my tone flat. "Actually, no. Your uncle Michaels sent me."

Kelly's expression didn't change much, though I caught a flicker of irritation. "Ugh, I bet he already called my mom," she muttered, brushing off the seriousness of the situation.

One of the boys chuckled, leaning back in his seat. "What are you, cops or something?"

Victor stepped forward, his voice calm but firm. "No, we're not cops. We're private investigators. And," he gestured to me, "she owns Aberdeen Manor."

That caught their attention. The group exchanged glances before one of the boys burst out laughing. "That creepy old murder house? Seriously?"

Another boy chimed in, grinning. "Fifty bodies were found there, right? That's sick!"

Victor didn't flinch, his voice dropping an octave. "Listen carefully. Step foot on that property, and we'll have you arrested for trespassing. We're not joking."

I leaned closer, adding to the weight of his words. "You might think it's just a scare tactic, but let me be clear. I don't care if you're minors. I will press charges, and it'll go on your juvenile records."

Kelly scoffed, folding her arms. "Minors don't get arrested for trespassing. My uncle said we'd just get a slap on the wrist."

I smirked. "Your uncle's wrong. I own that property. Trespassing isn't just a slap-on-the-wrist offense when it's private land, and trust me, your parents will love dealing with that fallout."

Victor glanced at my phone as I opened the police database. "Let's make this clear for everyone. Steven Whitehead, 17, basketball player. Jessica Alexander Jones, 16. Clay and Roy Jones, both 18—congratulations, boys, you're not minors. And Whitney Grey, 15," he said smoothly, his tone almost mocking as he rattled off their information.

The kids stared, wide-eyed. One of the boys threw a fry onto his tray in frustration.

"You're bluffing," Kelly muttered, but her voice lacked confidence.

I straightened up, my gaze steady. "Try me. I have all your names, addresses, and every reason to make your lives miserable if you step out of line."

Victor crossed his arms, his expression icy. "So here's the deal: finish your food, get back to school, and stay away from Aberdeen. This is your first and only warning."

The group stayed quiet, exchanging uneasy glances.

"Fine. Whatever. Just leave us alone," Kelly finally said, her tone dripping with defiance.

As we turned to leave, I added over my shoulder, "And if I catch you skipping school again, I'll call every one of your parents personally. Trust me, they'll love hearing about this."

One of the boys mumbled something under his breath, but no one dared argue further.

Outside the mall, Victor shook his head, smirking. "Smooth,

boss. Very smooth."

As we approached my car, Victor struck up a topic I had zero interest in discussing. "So, you're the daughter of the infamous Eric Stephenson, huh?" he asked casually, though his tone carried a hint of curiosity.

I rolled my eyes as I opened the car door. "He's not my father. I only consider him a sperm donor," I said bluntly, sliding into the driver's seat.

Victor followed and settled into the passenger side, his face suddenly serious. "A serial killer responsible for the deaths of fifty women," he said, his voice cold and devoid of emotion.

I started the car, gripping the wheel tighter than necessary. "Yeah, not to mention what he did to my friends… and my uncle," I said carefully, debating how much I should share. Trusting Victor wasn't something I was ready for—not yet, anyway.

"Sorry about your friends and your uncle," he said softly, his tone surprisingly genuine.

There was a beat of silence before he spoke again. "But weren't you ever curious? About who he was as a man?"

His question hit a nerve. I shot him a look while stopped at a red light. "Why the hell would I want to know anything about Eric Stephenson? He's nothing to me," I said coldly.

Victor smirked, leaning back in his seat. "Fair enough. But it's hard to deny he'll go down in history. People will study him, write about him. Fifty victims—that kind of horror leaves a legacy, whether you like it or not."

"Legacy?" I scoffed, my voice sharp. "The only legacy he left was pain and destruction. He's not some fascinating historical figure, Victor. He's a monster."

Victor raised his hands in mock surrender. "Didn't mean to upset you. Just making an observation."

The light turned green, and Victor pointed at it. "It's green." His tone was casual, distracting me from my building anger.

I gritted my teeth and started driving again, trying to shake off the unease his words stirred.

"So, where am I dropping you off?" I asked, eager to change the subject. "I've got other things to do today. Rosenberg's working on gathering information about those missing women, but that'll take time before we have anything concrete."

Victor chuckled lightly. "Back to the station. My car's there."

"Station it is," I replied quickly.

My phone pinged, and I tilted it in the mount. "Great. It's my mother," I muttered, exhaling heavily.

Victor laughed. "Don't leave your mom hanging."

I read the message aloud. "'Maeve, honey, on your way back from work, could you grab your baby sister some ice cream? Rocky road, she said, and she also added a big kiss.'"

Victor grinned. "Rocky road, huh? Must be nice to have a little sister."

I glanced at him briefly. "Yeah, Alice is great. Keeps life interesting. Though, I'm not thrilled about being her errand runner," I said with a smirk.

Victor's expression softened for a moment. "I've got a step-sister. Never met her, though. Wish I had."

His words caught me off guard. "Oh… sorry to hear that," I said sincerely. "Ethan's my stepbrother, but I don't think of him that way. He's my real brother, through and through. We've been through too much together to call him anything else."

Victor nodded, a faint smile on his lips. "You're lucky to have him."

As I pulled into the station parking lot and stopped near the main entrance, Victor opened the door. "Well, lucky you to have such a great brother. Anyway, let's pick this up tomorrow—or whenever the file on those disappearances comes in," he said, stepping out.

I nodded. "You've got my number."

"Yup. Chief already made sure of that," he said with a chuckle. "See you later, boss lady!" He gave me a playful salute before shutting the door.

I stared after him, shaking my head as I pulled back onto the road. "Boss lady? Jeez, what's that guy's problem?" I muttered to myself.

CELESTE EVANGELINE HART

I HUFFED AS I PULLED INTO our family home, shaking my head at myself. Ice cream for my little sister Alice—what was I thinking? All I wanted was to go home, take a shower, eat something halfway decent, and maybe see what Ethan had planned for the evening. But instead, here I was, at my mother's home with a bag of rocky road.

Grabbing the bag of ice cream from the passenger seat, I gently closed the car door behind me. As I approached the house, I could already hear the high-pitched giggles of Alice near the door. It was like she had an internal radar for my arrival—or for sugar.

Knocking once, I barely had time to step back before the door swung open, revealing a beaming Alice, her bare feet sticking to the floor as she bounced in place.

"MAEVE!" she shouted, her excitement bursting through every syllable.

I grinned and pretended to study the receipt in my hand. "Ahem, I have a special delivery for a Miss… Alice Adams," I said, holding the bag out with exaggerated formality.

Alice giggled, her eyes lighting up as she extended her little hands for the bag. Behind her, my mother stood in the hallway, laughing softly.

"That'll be $8.45 for the ice cream," I teased, watching as Alice grabbed the bag and bolted into the house like a sugar-fueled tornado. "Hey, get back here! You have to pay for your delivery!" I called after her, laughing as her giggles echoed down the hall.

Mother stepped closer to the door, her warm smile reaching her eyes as she touched a hand to my cheek. "Maeve, honey, thank you so much. I hope it wasn't out of your way."

I chuckled, shrugging off her concern. "No, Mother, it was fine. My day was done anyway."

"Come in, sweetheart. Do you have time?" she asked, extending her hand to invite me inside.

I hesitated, guilt flickering in my chest. "Sorry, Mom. I'll drop by with Ethan when we can. I've got some work to catch up on tonight," I said, softening my voice.

Her face fell slightly, and I could see the faint trace of disappointment. It wasn't the first time she'd hinted at missing us being around more often.

"Mom, I'm sorry. Really," I said gently.

She let out a deep sigh but smiled nonetheless. "I understand, sweetheart. I just miss having you and Ethan around the house."

"I promise we'll come by soon, okay?" I said, reaching out to squeeze her hands.

She nodded, pulling me into a quick hug and planting a kiss on my cheek. "Okay. Drive safely, darling."

"THANK YOU, MAEVE!" Alice's voice rang out from the kitchen.

I leaned slightly to peek inside, catching a glimpse of Alice kneeling on the kitchen floor, a spoon in her hand, feeding ice cream to the kitten, who was lapping it up eagerly.

"Uh, Mom… she's feeding the kitten ice cream," I said, unable to suppress my grin.

My mother's face instantly shifted to that familiar blend of exasperation and amusement as she folded her arms and turned toward the kitchen. "Alice Adams!"

I laughed, stepping back onto the porch as Mom's stern yet loving voice echoed through the house. "Ice cream is for people, not kittens!"

As I closed the door behind me and walked back to my car, I couldn't help but smile. Knowing Alice, she'd probably charm her way out of trouble, but I couldn't help but wonder what 'creative punishment' Mom would come up with this time.

As I pulled into the parking lot of the house Ethan and I shared, I noticed his truck wasn't in the driveway. Strange. He wasn't scheduled to work today, just on call at Dad's clinic since the hospital was fully staffed.

I stepped out of my car, locking it behind me, and headed inside. "Ethan?" I called out, but the house was quiet. Dropping my bag near the door—a habit I couldn't seem to break—I spotted a note taped to the fridge.

Maeve,

Gone to Watson's Gym. Come join me!

– Ethan

I smiled despite myself. It was gym day, and truth be told, I'd started enjoying our sessions together. Running upstairs, I changed into my workout clothes, grabbed my gym bag, and was back out the door in ten minutes flat. The fax machine buzzed behind me as I locked the house, but I ignored it. "I'll look at it later," I muttered.

The gym was bustling with energy, the hum of machines mixing with faint music. As I scanned my badge at the door, I spotted Ethan at the squat rack, his form perfect as always. I waved at him in the mirror, and he grinned, finishing his set before grabbing his towel.

"Hey, Maeve," he greeted, his voice cheerful.

"Hey," I replied, dropping my bag near the bench. He was already setting up weights for me before I could argue, motioning toward the leg press.

"Warm up first," he said, pointing sternly.

"Yes, boss," I teased, rolling my eyes. I found a mat nearby and started my stretches, trying to ignore two women near the dumbbells, their conversation drifting my way.

"That guy over there—look at those arms," one said, not bothering to lower her voice.

The other giggled. "I know, right? Wonder if he's single."

I smirked to myself, finishing my stretches before walking back to Ethan. "Looks like you've got an audience," I teased.

Ethan chuckled, adding another plate to his barbell. "Not interested, Maeve," he said flatly, his focus unwavering.

I rolled my eyes and started my circuit, moving through the weights Ethan had set up. By the time I hit the deadlifts, my hamstrings were already burning, but I wasn't about to quit.

Bending down to grip the barbell, I exhaled deeply, lifting it in one smooth motion. My form was solid, and I set the weight down with a satisfying thud. That's when I heard it—a sharp whistle from across the gym.

"Check her out," a man's voice carried, loud and grating, making my stomach churn. "Look at those glutes. Bet she's been working on those for years."

Ethan's jaw tightened as his gaze shifted toward the source of the voice. His movements stilled, his muscles visibly tensed. I tried to shake it off, focusing on my breathing as I grabbed my towel. My water bottle sat a few feet away, and as I bent to pick it up, I felt it—a sharp slap on my butt.

The sound echoed in my ears, sharp and intrusive. Straightening, I turned quickly, anger tightening in my chest.

There he was—the same guy from earlier, his arrogant smirk twisting my stomach. "Nice form, sweetheart. Mmm, very nice," he drawled, his tone oozing smugness. His gaze lingered, bold and invasive, like I was some kind of spectacle.

I narrowed my eyes, frustration bubbling over as I clenched my hands together, resisting the urge to hit him.

"What the hell do you think you're doing?" I snapped, my voice cold and steady. Taking a step toward him, I stared him down.

He raised his hands in mock innocence, the smirk never leaving his face. "Relax, sweetheart," he said with a shrug. "Just a compliment. Thought you'd like to know you've got such a nice… ass." His gaze trailed over me again, making my skin crawl.

Before I could respond, Ethan was suddenly there, stepping between us like a protective wall. "Back off, man! You think that's how you treat women?" Ethan's voice was sharp, each word laced with anger. He pushed the man back slightly with an outstretched hand, his stance firm.

The man chuckled, holding up his hands in mock surrender. "Hey, calm down. It's not a big deal. Just giving this darling here a compliment," he said, puckering his lips and making an obnoxious kissing sound.

Ethan took another step closer, towering over him. "It *is* a big deal when you put your hands on someone without their permission. Do it again, and I'll make sure you can't walk for a week. Back. Off," Ethan growled, his voice low and menacing.

The guy's smirk faltered. Muttering something under his breath, he backed away, his swagger noticeably subdued. As he rejoined his group of friends, he glanced back one last time, his eyes flicking over me as he mimicked another exaggerated kissing sound.

I exhaled sharply, tension slowly leaving my chest as I unclenched my fists.

"You okay?" Ethan asked, his voice softer now as he turned

to face me.

"I'm fine," I said, forcing a small smile, though my hands trembled slightly. "God, I've never had that happen before. Some men are just jerks." My frustration boiled over as I threw my towel down onto the bench.

Ethan's hand touched my arm, his gentle grip steadying me. "You handled yourself just fine," he said, his tone softening. "But next time, I'll make sure he doesn't even get close."

I was about to respond when a voice behind us caught my attention.

"Some nerve," a woman said, her tone sharp but not directed at us. I turned to see her—dark hair tied in a sleek ponytail, her striking blue eyes locked on the man now slinking toward the free weights. "Some men are just like that here. Sorry it had to be you."

"Thanks," I said, still catching my breath.

She smiled warmly, but her eyes flicked toward Ethan for a fleeting second. There was something there—a quiet acknowledgment. Ethan noticed too, his gaze lingering on her for a moment before he turned back to me.

"You ready for your next set, Maeve?" Ethan asked, his voice steady, though his attention seemed split.

"Yeah," I said, glancing back at the woman.

She gave me a small nod before walking toward the treadmills, her presence lingering in my mind as I refocused on my workout.

Celeste was her name—I heard her friend call her that loudly, almost as if trying to announce her presence to the entire gym. The exaggerated tone caught Ethan's attention, and he turned his head slightly toward them. Celeste had just finished her warm-up on the treadmill, hopping off after only a minute.

Her friend, a petite redhead with a sharp voice, rolled her eyes playfully. "That's it? Come on, Celeste, don't be lazy. Let's hit the bench press."

"Fine," Celeste replied with a laugh, grabbing her water bottle. The two of them made their way to the bench press, their conversation light and punctuated by giggles.

Meanwhile, Ethan was wrapping up his circuit training. I was midway through wiping down a machine, preparing for the cardio set he always insisted I include. "Let's get to it," he said, his tone both encouraging and bossy. Typical Ethan.

As I climbed onto the elliptical, I noticed Ethan's gaze drifting toward Celeste and her friend at the bench press. They were chatting animatedly, clearly not paying much attention to their form or setup. Celeste lay back on the bench, gripping the bar as her friend stood behind her, supposedly spotting.

But something was off. The weights on the bar weren't locked in properly, and with every small movement, they inched dangerously closer to sliding off.

"Do about ten, Maeve," Ethan said to me, his tone distracted, his eyes still fixed on Celeste and her friend. I tilted my head toward him, curious and slightly amused—he wasn't even looking in my direction.

Ethan's sharp eye caught the issue instantly. Before I could process what was happening, he was already moving toward them.

"Whoa, hold up!" Ethan said, his voice cutting through their conversation as he reached for the bar just before Celeste could lift it fully. His sudden presence startled them, and Celeste sat up quickly, her wide eyes meeting his.

"What's wrong?" she asked, blinking up at him, her dark hair cascading over her shoulder.

"The weights," Ethan replied, his tone firm but not accusatory. "They're about to come right off. Didn't either of you check to make sure they were locked?"

Celeste's friend looked sheepish, her face reddening. "Oops."

"Oops?" Ethan repeated, raising an eyebrow in disbelief. "You're lucky I caught it in time. This could've ended really badly."

Celeste bit her lip, her cheeks flushing. "Sorry about that. We'll double-check next time."

Ethan's expression softened at her sincere tone, and he gave her a small nod. "It's okay. Just make sure you're safe. These things aren't forgiving."

As he stepped back, Celeste tilted her head, her lips curling into a faint smile. "Hey," she said casually, though her voice carried a hint of curiosity and boldness, "are you doing anything later?"

Ethan paused, glancing toward me for a brief moment before answering. "Not really," he said. "Just planning on heading home after this with my sister."

Celeste's expression flickered with disappointment, but she quickly masked it with a polite smile. "Maybe some other time, then," she replied lightly before turning back to adjust the weights.

Ethan returned to me, his face neutral, but I could see the wheels turning in his head. I hopped off the elliptical, grabbing my towel. "She's into you," I said matter-of-factly, smirking at him.

He scoffed, shaking his head. "Maeve, come on."

"No, seriously," I pressed, folding my arms. "She's smart, gorgeous, and clearly interested. Why not talk to her?"

Ethan let out a small laugh, looking down at the ground for a moment. "It's not that simple."

"Yes, it is," I countered, stepping closer. "Ethan, you've been through hell. I get it. But it's okay to move forward. Tara would want you to be happy."

He looked at me, his expression softening. "It's not about Tara. I just… I don't know. What if it doesn't work out?"

"Then it doesn't," I said with a shrug. "But you'll never know unless you try. Besides," I added with a grin, "what's the worst that could happen? She turns out to be just as weird as you?"

I really wanted Ethan to try again, to open himself up to the possibility of a relationship. After Tara's death, he'd been a wreck—not just because of her, but because of Luke too. There were days when I'd hear him talking to himself, saying something out loud, only to stop mid-sentence and look around, realizing Luke wasn't there to respond. "Stupid," he'd mutter under his breath, shaking his head as the weight of that absence hit him all over again. It broke my heart every time.

I wanted him to move on—not for me, not for anyone else, but for himself. Ethan had been through hell, more than me, more than anyone. He'd lost his fiancée, his child, his best friend—he'd lost pieces of his soul. Watching him carry that weight every day, trying to keep it together for the sake of those around him, made me ache for him.

This wasn't about the past anymore. It was about his future. He deserved a shot at happiness, at finding something meaningful again, something that gave his life a sense of purpose. Ethan had always been my rock, the steady presence in a world that often felt like it was crumbling around me. But now, it was his turn. He deserved to lean on someone else for a change, to let someone in who could bring light back into his life.

As I glanced at him, standing there with that familiar guarded expression, I saw the weight he carried in his shoulders, the subtle pain in his eyes that he probably thought he'd hidden well. Ethan had always been strong—too strong for his own good sometimes. But even the strongest people needed to heal, to feel again.

"Ethan," I said softly, my teasing grin fading into a gentle smile. "You've got to let yourself live. It's okay to want more than just getting through the day."

He looked at me, his brow furrowing slightly, as though he wanted to argue but couldn't quite find the words. I could tell he was thinking, weighing the risks in his mind. He always did that—overthinking, overanalyzing, putting himself last.

But for once, I hoped he'd take the leap. For once, I wanted him to put himself first

C.K. SMITH

C.K. Smith is a Canadian writer and the celebrated author of *The Haunting of Aberdeen Manor* series, a chilling collection that promises to leave readers breathless with suspense and captivated by dark romance. Blending spine-tingling horror with irresistible spicy romance, C.K. Smith creates stories that haunt the mind and stir the soul.

Her latest work, *The Aberdeen Manor* trilogy, is a masterclass in atmospheric storytelling. Each book in the series is crafted to send shivers down your spine, perfect for horror enthusiasts who crave a touch of the forbidden in their reads. From eerie halls to forbidden desires, this series is an unmissable journey into the depths of fear and passion.

Drawing inspiration from literary legends like Stephen King, C.K. Smith has a unique gift for weaving intricate tales that explore the shadows of human emotion. Her work is a testament to her love for storytelling, delivering an experience that lingers long after the final page.

When she isn't crafting her next haunting narrative, C.K. Smith enjoys immersing herself in the beauty of Canadian landscapes and discovering the extraordinary in everyday life. With every story, she invites readers to step into her world of thrilling terror and sizzling romance—where the line between fear and desire blurs.

Discover the world of C.K. Smith, where every book is an unforgettable escape. Follow for updates on her latest releases and insights into her creative process. For fans of Stephen King, dark romance, and edge-of-your-seat suspense, this is an author you don't want to miss!

CONNECT WITH C.K. SMITH HERE

FB: CKSmithAuthor
IG: @author_cksmith
TikTok: cksmithauthor
E-mail: cksmith.author@gmail.com

www.ingramcontent.com/pod-product-compliance
Lightning Source LLC
Chambersburg PA
CBHW020638120726
47906CB00001B/31